The Man on the Ledge

by

Jack McKie

This is my first book. I doubt I would ever have sat down and written it without a belief that I *could* write a book. That belief was given to me in the late 1960's, by my English teacher, a lady I have never forgotten and will forever hold dear. I therefore take the greatest pleasure in dedicating this book to Mrs Mary Wilson, the best teacher in the world.

Contents

The Man on the Ledge

by

Jack McKie

A Dream within a Dream

TAKE this kiss upon the brow!

And, in parting from you now,

Thus much let me avow —

You are not wrong, who deem

That my days have been a dream;

Yet if hope has flown away

In a night, or in a day,

In a vision, or in none,

Is it therefore the less *gone?*

All that we see or seem

Is but a dream within a dream.

I stand amid the roar

Of a surf-tormented shore,

And I hold within my hand

Grains of the golden sand—

How few! yet how they creep

Through my fingers to the deep,

While I weep—while I weep!

O God! can I not grasp

Them with a tighter clasp?

O God! can I not save

One from the pitiless wave?

Is *all* that we see or seem

But a dream within a dream?

Edgar Allen Poe

Chapter 1 - The Beginning

Wednesday 17th October 2018, Southwest France

Hi, my name is Joseph, but most people call me Joe. I'm a 63-year-old retired firefighter from Liverpool, England. This is a story that may well bore the pants off you. Or it may not. I hope it doesn't. I tend to 'go on' a bit on account of my age. That's what both my daughters tell me anyway. You be the judge. My gorgeous daughters are from my first marriage to Lucy. Who is now with Gordon. Who is a better chess player than me. Apparently. I am married, to my second wife, Pam. She is nearly two years older than me, but you wouldn't think so. She looks a lot younger and is fit and strong by anyone's standard.

Like I said, I have two daughters, who have given me four grandkids, two each. My daughters are Katie, who is married to Gary, and their boys are Peter, 10 and Henry, 6. And then there's my daughter Keira, married to Brad and they have two kids, one of each, Olivia, 5 and William, who is 3. I love them all and would give my life for them today, this minute. If I had to.

I am quite a straight sort of fella. I can be outspoken if it serves a purpose. I'm quite down to earth, very honest and when I've had a few drinks, just about the funniest fucker in the northern hemisphere. Bar none.

Pamela, my wife, also has an ex, John, and two daughters, Susan, married to Arthur. And then there is Kaitlin, who isn't married yet. Pam also has 4 grandkids. Another Henry, 16, Pam, 14, Jonathan, 10 and Frances, 8.

We live in France, Pam and me. Have done since 2015. Our property is a house with a converted barn next to it. Converted into a gite. If you don't know what a gite is, it's anything from a shack with running water, a pit to shit in, sorry, poo in, tons of uncomfortable cast off furniture and a wealth of spiders complete with Halloween webs…to a luxurious holiday home with beautiful décor, stunning gardens and a semi-Olympic sized (there's no such thing I know but I ramble, remember?) swimming pool. Speaking of which, we've installed a pool behind the barn or gite and we run it as a holiday home, renting out through the three main summer months. We get a decent income from it but find the work quite hard, hence only letting for the three main months.

We generally holiday in England and always go in November when all of our work is done and, November is the month of Pam's birthday. We use our week to see our girls and their families and we shop for things we can't get in France, like decent cheese. Sorry to all those people, including the French, who think that France is the bee's knees when it comes to cheese. That's a bit of a rhyme there isn't it. I didn't mean to write poetry; it just came out like that. Obviously don't know my own talents. But it isn't anyway. The bee's knees of cheese. France.

Don't get me wrong, there are some really nice cheeses here. And there are literally hundreds of cheeses. Hundreds and hundreds. Maybe even thousands. Millions. I'm exaggerating. There are…quite a few. Let's leave it at that. But they're all the same…very slight variations on very few themes. And, sorry, but most of them, or a lot of them, maybe even millions of them, don't taste of anything except a slightly…dusty taste, sometimes mixed with a kind of diluted sweaty feet taste. Not that I've ever tasted diluted sweaty feet, or even neat sweaty feet, you can perish that thought right away. Perish it to fuck in fact. You can't perish anything more than that. That is the pinnacle of being perished. But you know what I mean about the taste of sweaty feet. Y'know, taste and smell, they're sort of the same thing aren't they? Aren't they? Now I'm thinking about it, I'll have to look that up. Anyway, goat's cheese is goat's cheese. Goat's cheese with nuts is…goat's cheese with nuts. That's what I would call it…but here, they give it a fancy-Dan French name that sounds fantastic but means something really bizarre, like Fromage de chèvre aux pieds moites. Which means goats cheese with sweaty feet. You can't actually get that particular cheese. I don't think so anyway. I put that in here for effect. No, give me a good British cheese any time. Red Leicester, Cheddar, Cheshire, and so on. Proper strong-tasting cheeses with some…substance. Maybe you're reading this and thinking '*This fella is a philistine*'. I don't think I am but maybe I am. At least when it comes to cheeses, in particular French ones. But, and here's a thought…what would the Philistines think of that? Eh? You calling me a Philistine just because I'm not that keen on most French cheeses? You probably need to think about that.

Anyway, back to the story…it was Wednesday 17th October 2018, about half one, something like that. We'd been working out near the pool, tidying the hedges up ready for the winter. We came in, had a little bit of dinner, or lunch if you're posh, which, for us, was toast and marmalade and a mug of tea. Some days we had jam instead of marmalade. Strawberry is my favourite. No, wait, raspberry. Raspberry is top dog in the jam stakes. Mmmm but hang on, our home-made fig jam is pretty damned good too. Picked fresh from our own fig tree, you can't beat it, big juicy fig, some prosciutto, a dollop of goat's cheese, French, but not *Fromage de chèvre aux pieds moites* (perish that thought) some fresh crusty bread and butter and a glass of red, just a small one, it is dinner time after all. I can hear you thinking…*why does he have jam on toast when he can go pick a fresh fig and get the prosciutto out…not to mention that wonderful French goat's cheese?* Well, that's easy to answer…because mostly, I can't be arsed with foodstuff, I just tend to go down the easy route and it doesn't get much easier than toast, butter and marmalade. Or jam. So why did I mention all the figs and shit? Probably because I'm trying to sell you the dream of warm balmy days, sitting by the pool, sipping a mellow red and, see! I'm doing it again, I told you, I 'go on' a bit. Or meander as I prefer to call it…like drifting down a lazy Charente river in a wooden rowing boat, the hum of a passing bee, the gentle gurgling of the water as the boat slides effortlessly through it. Shit! Will you stop reading this? How do you expect me to stop writing it when you sit there in the sun, a jug of freshly squeezed…fuck! Now STOP! Please!

Back to the toast. On really adventurous days I would have peanut butter and jam on toast. I love it but Pam, my wife of 10 years doesn't. Obviously, I have a more refined palette than her. Breeding y'see. She is from Prescot, a suburb of Liverpool, but back when she was born it was a Lancashire town. Mind you, so was Liverpool, where I'm from. See what

I mean about breeding? City slicker me…woolly-back Pam. Woolly-backs are what scousers call just about any other northerner, but especially people from immediately around Liverpool who aren't scousers. Mind you, the Welsh are woolly backs as well. Don't ask me why woolly backs because I don't know. Something to do with sheep you would think. I would. But it doesn't matter, this is, ancient lore, as handed down to me by my forefathers. And who am I to argue with them?

Anyway, we were in the house after tidying up the hedges around the pool, that's all you need to know for now. Sorry I gave you all that other stuff now to be honest. So, the toast and marmalade was made, butter oozing onto the plate, steaming mug of Yorkshire Tea on the table, Pam's like builder's tea, just the way she likes it, mine more the colour of a light, no, a medium oak to a light teak. I took a bite of my toast and a sip of the scalding tea. My phone dinged, which was, in fact still is, the sound I'd set for a WhatsApp or a Messenger alert. Probably one of my daughters checking in, I thought. I picked it up, took another bite of toast. It was a Messenger alert from one of my two remaining sisters, Lydia.

I say 'remaining' because I used to have three sisters. The eldest of the three, but still younger than me, died in 2017, just a few days after her 60th birthday. Her name was Carla. She was divorced, lived alone and had no children. Carla and I were not on speaking terms and hadn't been for probably 20 years or so. Carla and me — what can I say — we just didn't get on. There've been times when we have, but, generally, for most of our lives, we just haven't. What is it they say? You can pick your friends, but you can't pick your relatives? Something like that. Never was a truer word spoken. Right out of the blue, Carla could make the most horrible remarks about virtually anyone and everyone. You could try to ignore it and let it go, try to laugh it off, try to turn an insult into a joke, but with people like Carla, doing anything other than enter the fray was like a red rag to a bull. Trying to defend yourself against her was, somehow, both an insult and a direct challenge for her to up the ante. She never let go and would hold a grudge for all time. And usually, any grudge was based on something she'd made up. She was a vindictive woman and would take offence where there was none. She could hear a word said in a way that it hadn't been said and interpret an innocent look as one of malice and then take action based on what she'd imagined. She could and would twist everything to suit her own, usually corrupt agenda. Apart from all that, she was a lovely woman.

'*Joe?*'

Both the Messenger and WhatsApp message were identical. This was a Messenger alert. It was a strange approach I thought. Normally Lydia would start with a *Hi Joe, hows things with you*? But this was odd. Unusual. I just knew there was something wrong. Intuition kicking in. Or whatever you call it. Premonition maybe. I'm not a hundred percent certain I believe in premonitions and such but then, I believe in ghosts and all sorts of other spiritual type stuff but not god. Or God, just in case he, she, it actually *does* exist.

My first thought was that it might be to do with Emily, Lydia's twin sister. My sister as well of course. Emily hadn't been very communicative with either me or Lydia. Hadn't been for months, since Carla died. I'm not really sure why, but, I think she took her sister's death quite hard and is maybe struggling a bit to come to terms with it.

During a little messenger conversation I'd had with Lydia, not that long ago, I was told that Emily had been...*quite bad*...I think, was the phrase that Lydia had used. I got the impression that Lydia hadn't *wanted* to tell me any more than that, I had to draw and cajole the rest out of her. I can be very persuasive. My mum always said that about me. 'You can be very persuasive Joseph.' she'd say, always with a raised eyebrow and a drawn out *persuasive*. It would have sounded really good in a Scottish accent but my mum was half Sheffield, half Liverpool, so it sort of sounded like someone trying to do both accents at the same time and failing.

Apparently my sister Emily had been smoking weed. A lot of people do. But not only had she been smoking weed, she'd also been giving some to my mum, who had chronic back pain. So, this had been a long time ago because my mum had been dead for, I dunno, quite a while, getting on for 20 years nearly. I'd managed to put Lydia's mind at rest regarding Em's criminality and just got her to accept that people grieve in their own way and in their own time.

So, my first thought was that it was to do with Emily, this premonition, intuition thing I was getting. It could also, of course, have been about Dan, my older brother, who had been estranged from me for a long time, probably decades, and other members of his family on and off over the years. I thought it had to be about Emily, or even Lydia herself. She wasn't the healthiest of people. Mind you, neither of my twin sisters were particularly healthy. They both seemed to have physical health issues from an early age, but rarely anything straightforward, always...complex, *layered* problems, one thing at odds with another, quite mixed up stuff. And they both had mental issues as well, in fact, we all did. All five of us. All five siblings. I don't think I've introduced you to my family, so, here we are.

My dad was Charlie. He was born in 1929, in North Liverpool, the son of a ship's painter. My mum was Roberta, born in 1928 in Sheffield. Her parents had brought her to Liverpool, in search of work between the wars and had settled in Bootle, North Liverpool. In December 1951, my parents had their first child, a boy, Daniel. And in 1955, September, they had another boy, me, Joseph. In 1957, on Christmas day, they had a daughter, Carla, and then in September 1966 they had twin daughters, Emily and Lydia, aged zero. Don't know why I said that, it just sort of came out. As daft things tend to do with me at times. We all do it don't we, think something daft and suddenly it's not a thought any more, it's words, let loose on the world. Anyway, that's all of us.

My phone dinged again. It was a WhatsApp alert from Lydia. The same message, *'Joe?'*

I took another bite of toast and a swig of tea. A blob of marmalade dropped onto my chin and before I could deal with it, dropped onto my shirt. A big blob as well. I didn't really want to look at the phone but knew that I had to. I decided to finish my dinner first. No point in trying to do two things at once, not really an efficient work practice. Imagine if that large blob of marmalade had splodged onto the button of the phone. I've just had a look at the phone and, really, unless it had landed right on or in the ear-piece slot, whatever you call it, it wouldn't have done any damage…easily wiped off y'see. So, discount that point I made. I still decided to finish my dinner first.

Then, as is my wont, I changed my mind. The oddness of her approach just said to me that Lydia was worried about something and I didn't have the heart to keep her hanging there in the ether waiting for me to respond. Lydia couldn't really pick the phone up and call me you see, as she was deaf. Had been since birth.

'*Wassamatter?*' I thumbed, using Messenger. I prefer Messenger because I usually use my laptop and it's just so much easier for me to type using an actual keyboard rather than those tiny little smart phone keyboards. They are not for people with agricultural thumbs and fingers like mine.

No reply. So, I finished my toast and tea. Or tea and toast. Nicer ring to it, I think. Toast and tea sounds a bit awkward. Don't really know why I said it to be honest. That's another little strange thing we say isn't it…'to be honest'? I said it, to you, a few minutes ago or so. It's almost like, if you don't say *to be honest* then someone might think you were being dishonest. Actually, speaking for myself, when someone says it to me, I always assume that they *are* being dishonest. Which, I suppose, presupposes that I assume that everyone is usually being honest with me unless they qualify what they're saying by adding *to be honest*, thereby telling me that they are being dishonest. Which is not true. To be honest. Fuck. I live in a complex little world as you can see. Well, we all do but I sometimes think I make my world a little bit more complex than the norm. I always like to go the extra mile, as they say. Whoever *they* are. My mum, Roberta, used to say that I over-thought things. But she also used to say that I didn't put enough thought into my schoolwork, my carrying out of daily chores, the shininess of my shoes, the grubbiness of my knees and the combing of my hair. Amongst other things. So, large pinch of salt there, I think.

Where was I…oh yeah, the honesty thing. Regarding the honesty thing, and to put it to bed, so to speak, I tend to not trust anything anyone says at any time and do this by default. That's my base line…and I start to come up from there based on about half a million things. I'm exaggerating. Slightly. I start from the bottom and work up to the 'line of trust' shall we call it, by taking into account all sorts of stuff. Eyes, mouth, things about the face generally. How people use their arms and legs, how they position their bodies, what they do with their hair and their fingers and it goes on. I also take into account the speed of speech and the words they use. Pauses are another indicator I use. I take into account the words used and I automatically look for anomalies of any kind in them. Anomalies. This is a word I use a lot. I mean a LOT. Anything that doesn't sit right with me is considered to be an anomaly and what I do with anomalies is store them. Don't even dream of asking me where I store them because I don't know. To be honest (true or false statement coming up?) I'm not even sure it's me who stores them. It just gets done automatically. And some things that get stored are stored in the form of a 'concept' rather than a proper thought…which sounds really weird and I'm not sure I'm explaining this very well, so I'll try a little harder. In the next paragraph.

This 'concept' thing is really hard to explain. I'm not certain that I'm even using the best words. Someone with a bigger vocabulary than mine, which is really not that big, could put me right here. Actually, when I think about it, I haven't really had much reason to try to explain this, so this is a first. First time in writing anyway. I think I've tried to explain it to Pam, usually when I've had a gin and tonic or two, but I'm not sure I've been very successful. So here goes…prepare to be bored. You might want to scoot forward a page or two.

Ok so, the sense of smell…incredible how evocative it is, right? You're in the shopping centre or mall or whatever, strolling past the shops minding your own business when WHAM! You get a smell that reminds you of something way back in your childhood, a warm, comfortable smell that instantly takes you to that day you baked a cake with your mum for the first time…you can see the furniture in the room from your height when you were six or whatever age you were, you can see the dust motes floating in the sunlight through the kitchen window. You can hear your mum's voice and can see her clapping her hands creating a flour cloud. All of these pictures and sounds from just walking through the shopping mall, which, incidentally, those sneaky bleeders from the advertising and marketing agencies harness in order to sell you stuff, riding on the feel-good factor that nice smells evoke. All of these pictures and sound are played out inside your mind as you walk along…you've been there, you know what I'm talking about. Right?

Here's another trick your mind performs. Or mine does, and I doubt that I am in any way unique, so there's a good chance you know exactly what I'm talking about here.

So, you're talking to someone or they're talking to you, or they are with you and you are talking to someone else or someone else is talking to you. I think I've covered most bases there. You say something or something is said that provokes a 'movement' in the face of the other person. The 'something said' may well have been said by them. But something happens in the other person's face, some kind of movement, some kind of *difference*, that is so fast or so small that you can't see, or rather, you *don't* see it, but you *know* it was there. You can't say to someone, *did you see that?* Because *you* haven't seen it, although you *have* seen it. I call such an event, an anomaly. Just that. An anomaly.

Such an anomaly might be accompanied by a movement of a part of the body, a hand, the head, the eyes. It might be accompanied by an unusual word for the circumstances or for that particular person, and it might be accompanied by a sudden change of subject. And then, it might not be accompanied by anything at all. But the interesting thing here is that what your mind does, what my mind does, is it takes what I call a snapshot of that moment when the anomaly occurred. The snapshot is not what you would think of as a snapshot, it's not a candid little photo that people take with their phones, it's not any kind of a picture at all, unless you think of a picture as a 'map' of the moment, a very detailed map, tucked away somewhere in your memory. This, to me anyway, is very interesting, but *the most* interesting part of all this is the recall of that anomaly, snapshot or memory map.

When I recall the anomaly, the map of the anomaly, I get what I call the 'flavour' of that moment. I don't get a picture of that person's face as they spoke or anything like that, more like an overall impression of what has happened, taking into account everything, expression, intonation, body shape, topic, peripheral things happening around me, personal history pertinent to me, the person or the event, and possible future history. The anomaly, the map, can change, as all maps do, but essentially, the lie of the land remains the same, so an 'anomaly' can be stored away as a version, then added to, layered up as and when the need arises, sometimes becoming a bit blurred but sooner or later, *eventually*, the picture clears and sharpens, and you can see that all those tiny pieces of information, all those ingredients, just like a recipe for a memorable meal, amalgamate into a flavour, a definitive picture of what has occurred, is occurring, or is about to occur. This picture is so clear that it can be challenged and tested, and this testing can produce other versions of the picture that can be laid on file, ready for more information to be added or taken away. The bottom line is that you end up with a number of versions of the same basic picture, all there, all preserved, all ready to be examined and compared and all that is needed then is to do that examination in as cold and dispassionate a way as you can manage. Simple as that. What I remember, what I recall, is that flavour. Not the ingredients, or the method of obtaining them, but the flavour. The details behind the flavour are there, if needed, but it's the flavour that is the important thing.

In a nutshell, my mind takes a snapshot, calls it an anomaly. An anomaly is made up of different ingredients, which gives me a flavour. Other ingredients can be added at a later date, changing the flavour and all versions of the flavour can be compared. I should've said that in the first place, could've saved myself a shitload of typing.

Here you go, here's an example of it working. Probably not a great one, but…

Years ago, I was having a normal conversation with my girlfriend and she used a word that I can't remember, but it was a word or way of using the word that was unusual for her. It was a word unusual for me to use as well. My girlfriend wasn't really one for using new or unusual words. I'm not trying to be unkind to her there, just stating a fact. So, it was automatically picked up as an anomaly — I don't get a say in this — and a snapshot was taken and stored. Some months later, during a coffee and cake conversation with her, something in her demeanour, I don't remember what, caused another anomaly. An interesting thing that happens, quite automatically, is that new anomalies are compared with previous ones and, presumably if a connection is made or suspected, the new anomaly is added as an ingredient, changing the flavour. The re-assessment of the anomalies caused me to latch onto that word that was the cause of the first anomaly and sometime later, in another everyday conversation, I slipped this word, in context, into the conversation and my mind snapshotted the moment. My use of that word had an effect on her and caused another 'anomaly'. Another re-assessment was made and the rather startling conclusion I was forced to make was that my girlfriend was two-timing me. Once that 'base' was reached, I started to look for other things that could be connected. I've probably bored the pants off you here, so I'll now cut to the chase. After just a few weeks I confronted her and it transpired that she *was* seeing someone on the side and had been for some time. I'm guessing, by the way, just in case you're still there, that the 'unusual word' that sparked off the whole thing, was habitually used by the other half of the affair.

We all do this, I think. This 'snapshotting' and re-assessing of situations. Maybe I'm wrong, I'm sure you'll tell me if I am. But anyway, my phone dinged again, and I picked it up. It was Lydia. She'd replied in WhatsApp.

'Emily has had a visit from our Daniel's solicitor today. To tell us that Daniel has passed away 3 days ago. I'm so sorry to break the news to you xx'

I put the phone down on the table. Face down. I didn't want to see it light up again. What had I been doing three days ago? I needed to just…assess this message. Not that there was much to assess, I mean, it's all pretty final isn't it when those words are on the table? Maybe that was what I needed to assess, the finality. I don't think I was ready for my brother to die. I had more life to live with him, even if he didn't want to live any part of life with me. I had hoped that life would deliver something to me. To us. That hope had just disappeared for ever. I got up and put the kettle on.

'Another cuppa, love?' I said to Pam. She nodded a little raised eyebrow nod, mouth full of toast and marmalade, handing me her mug. My mind was going 10 to the dozen. I'd love to know what that means. I mean, I know how and where to use it but, like a lot of our everyday sayings, what does it actually mean? I promised myself that I'd look it up later. Like I'd promised a hundred times before. No, a thousand times before.

I busied myself at the sink, filling the water filter jug before I could fill the kettle. The water here in France is bloody hard water. I've never seen anything like it. It'll ruin your kettle in no time at all. Literally weeks. Vinegar is one of the biggest selling products here because everyone uses gallons of it in their kettles. It cleans the kettle of the calcium build up, no bother but let me tell you, it makes a shit cup of tea. I know. I've tried it. My grandad on my mum's side, Albert, though his real name was Frederick…don't know why. I mean, I know why his real name was Frederick, because his mum and dad decided it was…I mean I don't know why he was called Albert. Albert was his middle name and I suppose he preferred it. Not Bert mind…no, the full bifters, Albert. I loved him to bits even though he hacked my head to pieces every month under the guise of barbering. He was supposed to be a barber, but I would've been very upset if I'd had to pay for his haircut. Mind you, I was only six so I was hardly at the age to pay for my own haircuts. Anyway, I digress, my grandad on my mum's side, Albert, real name Frederick, used to make us (me and my brother Dan) beer when we were kids. We thought it was great. He made it from brown vinegar and sugar.

Lots of sugar. Think about that. He would get this great chunky pint beer glass and fill it with brown vinegar and just keep spooning sugar into it until it didn't taste of beer but didn't taste of vinegar either. Not that I would've known what beer tasted like as I was only six, like I said. I put the kettle on and tea bags in the mugs. Got the milk from the fridge.

As I waited for the kettle to boil, I looked out of the window. There was a huge bird of prey sitting on a fencepost at the bottom of the garden, about a hundred feet away. Or 30 metres if you want it in metric. It was beautiful. Absolutely beautiful. The bright yellow of its legs and feet was so vivid it was hard to imagine how it maintained that colour. I don't recall any of the David Attenborough programmes showing me an eagle washing its legs. My brother would have loved it. He loved the countryside, especially the wildlife. I remembered him at 9 or 10 years of age, nursing and nurturing a young sparrow he'd found in the yard. My grandad's yard. We lived with my grandma and grandad when I was younger…as families did back in the 50's. Down by the North Liverpool docks. So close we could see Goliath or Samson, the gigantic floating cranes, drifting along over the rooftops, dwarfing the three storey houses on St Bridget's Road and Brassworks Road.

Chapter 2 - The Sparrow

North Liverpool, June 1959

It was sunny. Warm. A balmy breeze was ruffling the sheets hanging on the washing line that ran the length of the back yard. Me and my big brother, Dan, Daniel if he'd been naughty, were playing cowboys and Indians, as we often did. He was the cowboy. As he often was. And I was the Indian. I preferred being the Indian to be honest and the reason was this. You could make great Indian noises, like in the films, and, the main reason, I had a *real* weapon that could cause serious injury, possibly even death with a lucky shot, whilst my big brother had weapons that only *sounded* as though they could cause serious injury, maybe even death but couldn't actually fire any kind of missile. He had a pair of cap guns. Silver. Not real silver. In a dual holster set-up. They were actually mine, courtesy of Wild Bill Hickok, but he'd commandeered them, as big brothers often do with the best toys. But my weapon was a custom made, genuine bamboo, authentic Red Indian bow and arrow…made by my grandad. The string was proper string from the chandler's on Stanley Road, a shop that smelled of string for your bow, wood, paraffin and an indefinable smell that, in later life, became known to me as underarm smell…and the arrow, the one and only arrow, also made by my grandad, had a red sucker on the end that could batten itself to the centre of my brother's forehead, if only he'd stay still for long enough. Which he wouldn't. Hey, it's yet another thing that big brothers do. Or don't do. I did actually perfect the technique of aiming where I expected him to appear from behind the flapping sheets on the washing line but by the time my arrow winged its deadly way to that spot, usually end over end because it didn't have…tail feathers or whatever you call them, he'd gone, wheeling his steed around behind me and shooting me in the back. The dirty rat.

I'd just fired my arrow at Dan, missing him by barely a foot. It hit the window with a clatter and my grandma shouted at me to be careful and then shouted at grandad for being so bloody stupid as to make me an arrow in the first place. Grandad responded by saying that a bow is no good without an arrow and grandma said that he could have just made me a machine gun like anyone with a bit of common sense would have done. I liked that idea. A lot. If I had a machine gun, Dan could keep my silver Hickok pistols because it just wouldn't matter. A machine gun trumped a pistol, 50 times over. Everyone knew this. You've got to remember, this was 1959, wartime rationing had only been over for five years or so. Kids of that era were still machine-gunning Germans left, right and centre with their wooden guns made by grandads with nothing better to do, my grandad being no exception. He did eventually make me a machine gun out of a piece of fence paling and would have done right there and then, at that very minute, I'm sure of it. He'd have gone to the shelter (the brick and concrete bomb shelter we had in the yard) and ferreted about in there for the makings, but my big brother intervened.

'Grandad! Grandma!' he shouted at the top of his voice, 'come and see what I've found!'

It was a baby bird. It was lying on the floor, sort of shuffling about. I retrieved my arrow, loaded it onto the string and started to draw. 'Shall I shoot it?' I shouted. *'Can* I shoot it?'

'No y'bloody can't!' shouted Dan, pushing me away.

Grandma came bustling out of the kitchen door, wiping her hands on her pinny. 'You mind your bloody language my lad or I'll wash your mouth out with soap and water!' she said in her broad Yorkshire accent. 'What is it?'

'It's a baby bird grandma.' said Dan.

'Can I shoot it please grandma?' I asked. I was a polite little soul. Crafty as well. You always got what you asked for if you said please. That's what my mum used to say anyway. Grandad came out, his newspaper folded up in his hand, like you would if you were going to whack a spider. Or a cockroach. Born killers we were in our house. We had lots of cockroaches, in the lav at the bottom of the yard, under the lino, in the angle of the stairs under the tatty rug runner, even under the wallpaper. My mum said it was because we lived near the docks.

'What is it?' asked grandad.

'It's a baby bird grandad!' I shouted. 'Grandma said I could shoot it; can I shoot it grandad?'

Grandma wagged her finger in my face. 'I never said no such thing you little fibber.' she said. And then to grandad, she said 'Neck it Albert and put the poor bugger in the bin.'

The bird shuffled a bit faster. Heading in the direction of the back gate. I think it knew what grandma meant. I know I did. My arm was shaking from holding my bow string taut, ready to fire. Melvin, my best mate from next door had heard the commotion and had climbed up on the wall between the yards. The walls were about six and a half foot high, but all the kids were like mountain goats. We spent virtually the whole summer on the wall tops, walking around, looking in people's back windows, jumping back and forth across the back entries; the walkway that ran between back-to-back terraced housing, just wide enough for the bin man to get down. 'What are you gonna shoot Joe?' He sounded excited.

'He's not shooting anything,' said grandma, 'and get down from that bloody wall!'

I was intent on seeing blood. 'I'm gonna shoot this bird, me grandad said I could.' I said in the direction of Melvin, not taking my eyes off the quarry. Just then, while I was trying to look good, like Robin Hood, with the bow drawn taut, grandad cuffed my head with his paper, my thumb twitched and let go of the string but kept hold of the arrow. The string twanged onto my bow hand, stinging me and causing me to drop the bow and arrow with a bambooey clatter and shove my hand up into the fantastic healing properties of my armpit. 'OWWW!' I shouted, hopping about for a few…hops, before I realised that, overall, it wasn't a good look and Melvin was watching. Melvin was younger than me by at least a month, maybe even six weeks or so. That was a lot when you're a 5 year old alpha male. 'Grandma, Melvin's still on the wall.' I said. Melvin gave me a look which said *Clat tale!* and slid out of sight.

Grandad bent to pick the little bird up and groaned with his back. Very poor use of the English language there. I mean, of course, that he groaned because of his back, not with it. Tut, tut. The pain in his back stopped him from picking the bird up, wringing its neck and putting it in the bin with the potato peelings. Dan picked it up instead. He cradled it gently in his hand and the little bird tweeted, and opened its mouth wide.

'I'm gonna feed it and help it to grow up.' he said. 'Can we get a box to keep him in grandma?'

'You'll not be able to help it Daniel,' said grandad, 'poor little bugger's best put out of its misery, give it 'ere now.'

'No grandad, no. I need to see if I can do it. It needs me to try.' Dan said, covering it with his free hand. 'Please let me try.'

My twanged hand had recovered by now and I picked up my bow and arrow, fitting the arrow expertly, as only a five-year-old alpha male could do. I thought I'd have one last try. 'Can I shoot it please grandad?' I asked.

Over the next few weeks or so, can't really remember how long because it was such a long time ago, my big brother nurtured that little bird, the little bird that turned out to be a sparrow. He got a crisp box from Mabel's, the corner shop where the one-armed man worked, smart in his blazer with his school badge, or what I took to be his school badge, sewn on the top pocket, and his sleeve neatly pinned up. His tie was maroon with a little gold aeroplane pin on it and I wanted it. I was always staring at it. He asked me once if I liked it and I cacked meself because the one-armed man had spoken to me. Now, of course, I'm proud to have spoken to a paratrooper from the war. Maybe he fought at

Arnhem, maybe not. Either way, he lost his arm and worked in a corner shop. Maybe he owned it. Maybe he was the husband or brother of Mabel. It didn't really matter who he was. He wore his tie and blazer with his 'school' badge and pinned up sleeve with pride and because of him and thousands like him, my brother was able to go to that shop and cadge an empty crisp box to make a home for a sparrow in need. The Nazis would have probably trampled the little bird, crushing it under their jackboots. My grandma was always going on about the Nazis doing stuff with their jackboots so, to my 5 year old mind, it was a reasonable assumption to make that they would have jackbooted the sparrow. But then, I think if they'd tried, my brother would have stopped them. Having said that, I did try to obtain permission to shoot it.

The crisp box was kept in the bedroom that me and Dan shared. He put pages of the Echo on the 'floor' of the box and changed it every day. He made a nest out of newspaper that he tore and shredded into little strips and moulded it with his hands. He used an eyedropper to feed the little bird with whatever sparrows eat. He found out what to feed it from the RSPCA. Me and Dan were members of the RSPCA, we had certificates and badges. I can't really remember how we came to be members, but I can remember the man who came to our Sunday school to 'recruit' us. Tall, with grey hair, a limp, and a smart uniform. I thought he was a policeman, so was automatically scared of him, but Dan spoke to him a lot and the result of that seemed to be that we got certificates off the postman in a big envelope. Really nice they were, though I can't properly remember exactly what they looked like, but they had the RSPCA emblem in an arc across the top and my name, my full name, Joseph Croft, was under it. I was very proud of being a member of the RSPCA. I'm not sure what they would have thought of me wanting to shoot the baby bird, but it didn't really matter because we rescued it instead of shooting it. Or Dan did anyway. The badges were really nice as well, more like a brooch I think, but the colour was mostly blue and gold and it reminded me of medals, like grandad's.

After a while, the baby bird had feathers and looked dead fat and fluffy. And it became really noisy. Tweeting all the time but much louder than I would ever have imagined. It used to wake us up really early, tweeting like mad and it crossed my mind a few times that maybe I should have 'taken it out' when I had the chance.

Once it had feathers, Dan started saying that he was going to teach it to fly. I was amazed at what my big brother could do…and I couldn't wait to be as old as him so that I could fly too. I told grandma and grandad that Dan could fly, and he was going to teach the bird to do it. They laughed at me. I thought it was good that they laughed at me and I liked it. I must have told a good joke or something. One day, while I was sitting on grandad's knee, watching him cut his baccy up with his little pen-knife, which I wanted, I said to him that I couldn't wait to be as big as Dan so that I could fly and he laughed again and explained that Dan couldn't fly, that no people could fly. Dan had used a 'figure of speech' he said and explained what that meant. I couldn't work out what he was talking about and asked if I could cut his baccy up for him. He let me and showed me how to do it but told me not to tell grandma, which I never did.

Dan did teach the little bird to fly, sort of. He told me that little birds already know how to fly because they are 'programmed' to do it the same as little boys are programmed to run and wrestle and stuff. He told me that it just needed to be shown when to do it and where from.

I remember thinking, early one morning as the little bird woke us up when it was barely light, tweeting like a madman…that the 'time has arrived Dan! Teach him to fly…now!'

Dan used to slide our window open and put the little bird outside on the windowsill. It would get very excited and sort of…strut about a bit, ruffling its feathers and flapping its wings rapidly. It seemed to do this for ages and then, suddenly it just plunged off the windowsill and crash-landed in the yard, bouncing on the stone flags. Grandma's cat, Ginger, was basking in the sun on top of the wall, licking its arse when the bird fluttered past it. Ginger was so startled that he fell backwards and landed on top of next door's bin with a clatter and a strangled meow. Dan sprinted down the stairs and out into the yard. The bird was just sat on the floor with a 'wtf?' face. Or that's the way I would interpret it now. I didn't then of course, but it makes for better reading now. In my opinion.

After a few days or so of the bird launching itself off the windowsill, it actually flew off. Just like that. Just disappeared from our lives. The crisp box sat there for days. Empty. It had been a nest, a home, shelter for a little creature from all that is bad in the world and now it was just an empty cardboard box, with a strange smell. It was as if the bird had never existed. As if the few weeks of tweeting and shitting had never happened. There was a void and even though I'd wanted to shoot it, I felt a loss. Dan did too. I could tell. He was very quiet. I mean, he was a quiet boy anyway, much more so than me, I wasn't quiet at all, far from it. But he was just…different. Introspective I think is the word. It was almost like he wanted to have flown away with the bird, like he would have given anything to be able to do that.

The crisp box sat there for a few more days. I think Dan thought the bird would come back to see him. To thank him maybe. I thought it would as well, come back that is, but sincerely hoped it wouldn't. I was enjoying sleeping until it was the right time for a human to think about getting out of bed. But then my dad, Dan's dad, our dad, made sure it wouldn't. One Saturday morning, the sun shining through our open bedroom window, dust motes floating in the still, warm air, our grunts and groans punctuating the stillness as we had our habitual Saturday morning wrestling match, the bedroom door burst open, crashing against the wall and our dad was suddenly there, filling the hole where the door had been a split second earlier. Before we even had time to disengage our wrestling holds, he'd hit us a number of times with his thick leather belt. Hard. Neither of us cried out from the attack. Both of us knew better than to make a sound. He stopped after a while and threw his belt out onto the landing. My eyes followed the trajectory. My mum was standing there in the gloom. Our dad picked up the crisp box and upended it out of the window, emptying Dan's nest and bird-raising paraphernalia into the yard. I heard the glass eyedropper smash on the flags with a crisp tinkle. He then wrenched our RSPCA certificates off the bedroom wall. Dan's certificate tore as the drawing pin wouldn't let go of it. The drawing pin holding mine fast, popped out and ricocheted off the other wall, heading for the floor. I saw it, in slow motion almost, strike the lino and scoot under the bed, where it pinged against our tin potty. Funny how you remember the little sounds so well. He ripped our certificates to pieces, threw them out of the window and stormed out, slamming the door. He hadn't said one word.

Me and Dan looked at each other, tears welling in our eyes. I could feel the welts rising on my back and buttocks where I'd been hit with the belt. We must have decided, telepathically, to not cry because our tears dried up. 'Did you hear my drawing pin hit the po?' I whispered.

Chapter 3 – Conversations

Wednesday 17th October 2018 – France

Pam and I sat there drinking our second mug of tea. I re-read the message from Lydia.

'Emily has had a visit from our Daniel's solicitor today. To tell us that our Daniel has passed away 3 days ago. I'm so sorry to break the news to you xx'

It was a bit surreal. My brother was dead, and I was drinking tea in France. I should have been doing something else. I don't know what but, y'know, I just should have been doing something else. I hadn't said anything to Pam yet. I don't know why. I've never thought about why I sometimes think that I should carry on as though nothing extraordinary is happening. I just do what I do, I am who I am. Like the rest of us. Right? Yeah. So, I carried on drinking my tea and acting normal. I Messengered Lydia. Using my phone keyboard which I hate. Thumbs like bananas.

'How?'

Man of few words. Sometimes.

I wondered briefly why my brother would have a solicitor. And why that solicitor would be traipsing around to my sister's house. I suppose he could have had a will, my brother that is, but, if he only died three days ago, well, I thought, it's a bit soon for a solicitor to be calling at people's houses, y'know, getting in his car and driving across the city. To my knowledge, solicitors just don't do that. I'm not sure they *ever* work that quickly, or that *personally*. Not for people like us anyway. Maybe for a rich client, yeah. Maybe. But then, I thought, what do I know? Who am I to try to talk authoritatively about anything? Apart from firefighting and the argument for raspberries over strawberries in the jam-making stakes.

My phone dinged. It was Lydia. On Messenger.

'I really don't know Joe xx'

It flitted through my mind that, apparently, Lydia had made up with Emily and I wondered when this might have happened. If they had made up, I was glad that it had happened because family should be close. I know they're often not but in my ideal world, in the World of Joe, family would come first and family would be close and look out for each other. Always.

I set my thumbs to work, gave up and used the tip of my forefinger. The predictive text on the iPhone was pretty good but I always forgot to use it. I remembered now.

'Are you friends on fb with her?'

I knew that some time ago, I discovered that Emily had unfriended me on Facebook and had asked Lydia about it. Emily had unfriended Lydia as well. This unfriending was just part of the grieving, I told

Lydia, that she just wanted to be left alone and the best thing was to do just that.

'No x' she typed.

Emphatic. Softened with a kiss. Always makes me laugh the way people, especially women, put a kiss or two at the end of every message, no matter what the content or intent of the message. I mean, what's the purpose of it? A kiss after *every* message? Or most messages. Is it simply a thing that people do? I used to think it was but then I noticed that sometimes, kisses are missed off. And when they *are* missed off, it's virtually always significant in some way. Maybe not always obvious what that significance is right at that moment, but there is nearly always some kind of significance to a missed off kiss. That gives me, in my opinion anyway, the wherewithal to attach some kind of significance when there *is* a kiss. I mean, I know that there will be lots of times when there is a kiss that will have NO significance but…you *know* what I'm saying right? No? Hmmm maybe I don't really know what I'm saying either. This is one of those things that I *know,* or *think* I know, but have never had to explain it. It's always better to try to explain such a thing with examples. Or maybe it would be better to not even try to explain at all and just get on with being me and reading into things the things that I read into them, if that makes any sense.

I messaged her that I wasn't fb friends with Emily at the moment but that it was down to her, not me. Almost at the same second that I sent the message to Lydia I got a friend request from Emily. I sent another quick message to Lydia.

'Have you had a fb friend request from Em?'

As I was waiting for a reply from Lydia, I wondered how she'd come by the information that Dan had died because her message simply said that Em had had a visit from Daniel's solicitor. I asked her.

'How did she get in touch with you?'

One second later, I got a reply from Lydia. *'She spoke to Angela and Angela came round and broke the news to me x.'* Angela was Lydia's daughter.

'So, did you get a friend request from her?' I asked again.

'I don't know, I haven't checked x' she said. Then said, *'Have you? X'*

Something jarred with me. I don't know what exactly, I just know that, for some reason, something didn't seem right. There was nothing to see, nothing to hear, nothing at all. Just a gut feeling. A hunch, as they say in those US detective shows. *Maybe*, I thought, *maybe I'm just what you might call a suspicious bastard.* I don't know what but something didn't sit right. I answered her.

'Yes.' Just that. Like I said earlier, a man of few words at times.

'You accepted? X' she asked.

It was a perfectly normal question but for some reason it irked me. I don't like getting irked, especially when I shouldn't even be thinking of getting irked. Not that I ever think to myself *'I could do with getting irked.'* because I don't. *Y'know*, I thought, *Here you are Joseph, my man, your brother has died, your sister, one of your remaining two, is 'chatting' to you, asking you an, on the surface, innocent question and all you can do is get irked.* And then *that* irked me. I was obviously in an irksome mood.

'I haven't accepted it at the moment.' I replied. Her reply irked me further.

'Ah right ok x' she typed, thumbed, *said*.

I decided to put my irksomeness to bed because if I didn't, I could easily end up getting irked to fuck and you can't get any more irked than that. I'd never been irked to fuck and, to be honest, I didn't want to go there. *'I* will *accept but I've got to say I'm a bit put out.'* I forefingered. Quicker than my thumb. Right hand only. *'I know she was grieving, I get that, but I'm not a toy that she can pick up and drop whenever it suits.'*

Lydia answered very quickly. Fast thumbing. Probably two of them at the same time. Smart arse. Much faster than a single forefinger. *'I'm the same here Joe but I know I've got to. I could understand if you didn't accept xx'*

Again, I was instantly irked but couldn't put my finger on why. Then something popped into my mind. It was almost subliminal. Had *been* almost subliminal. It occurred to me that I was maybe being manipulated, that I was being ever so gently steered into a place where I wouldn't friend my sister Em but, instead, would rely on Lydia to liaise with Em on my behalf. I was instantly almost ashamed of myself and thought, *no, why would someone, least of all my sister, need to manipulate me here? Now? At this time?* But then, as soon as I felt shame, I also felt a flash of anger, based on there being two kisses as well. The previous five or six comments by her, I counted, as I scrolled through the convo, had only had one. What was the significance of two? *Was* there a significance? I decided that maybe I was over-thinking things, that there was *nothing* to think about here, nothing to take note of, nothing to analyse, just…nothing. *Get a grip*, I thought. But then, almost immediately after that thought, I thought, was my reply supposed to be *'Tell you what Lydia, you deal with Emily and let me know what transpires.'* or something like that? Like I said, I am a suspicious bastard. I see shadows everywhere. I think they call it paranoia. I resolved to do one of those Paranoia Tests online. Proper scientific one. You get them on social media all the time. I thought about my reply.

'I will as well.' I said, then added, *'This is a time when we have to stick together isn't it.'*

There was a pause. I decided I needed a drink. Not a 'drink' drink. Just water with some juice. Peach. My mind wouldn't let go of the manipulation angle. I knew I was a bit odd like this, a little bit intense at times. It was, I thought, why I didn't have many friends or even many people who liked me. I'd always been, *analytical* for want of a better word, always been someone who looks for the reasons people say and do what they say and do. A learned behaviour, if you like, of formative years spent at the mercy of a coercive bully, listening for every little nuance of every word, always without appearing to be listening with any intent...which was a punishable 'crime'. A learned behaviour of those same years spent watching, *scrutinising*, with the appearance of not doing so, for the tell-tale signs of a forthcoming beating, kicking...or worse. A glance. A lick of the lips. A sigh. A sideways glance at the clock on the mantelpiece. All sure signs of something bad in the offing. Signs that told you to move, to go out to play, to be somewhere, anywhere, other than where you were. And all had to be done with no outward signs of *knowing*. *Knowing*, y'know, having *inside information*, was not allowed. Sometimes, in order to facilitate the idea that *knowing* wasn't present, wasn't even *possible*, you would, *I* would, pretend that

I'd been taken by surprise and 'accept' my 'punishment.' It was worth it, sometimes anyway, to keep secret the fact that, at times, you knew what was coming. I suppose I'd make a good poker player. Actually, scratch that thought, I've played poker with some mates and was glad we were only playing for matchsticks.

So, all that aside, I made myself a drink of peach juice. Very refreshing. Peach cordial, or syrup, as the French call it, with water. Filtered of course, because of this calcium-ridden French water, that would grow you an extra skeleton where you didn't need one, i.e., inside the one you've already got. I'd half-finished the peach drink when my phone dinged. It was Lydia.

'I know what you mean. I agree, we're all in this together and should forget our differences. X'

A little alarm went off. I don't know why but I filed it away and told Lydia that I would friend Emily now, on Facebook and did what was required. I got an immediate reply from Lydia…

'xxx'

Three kisses, I thought…*what does that mean? Something? Nothing?* I was back on the manipulation trail, just minutes after telling myself to get off it. I Messengered my sister Emily.

'What's goin on Em?'

No preamble, no greetings, let's just get on with the business. Told you, we were not a 'normal' friendly family. Not to each other anyway. Her reply came straight back.

'Heir hunters knocked on my door today, said Daniel had died three days ago Joe'

Heir hunters? I thought, *like off the telly?* You've probably seen that programme on the TV, where people make a living, a good living apparently, by searching out people who may have something to be gained from someone's death, y'know, the *estate* and claiming that estate on behalf of the person or persons involved and getting paid, presumably, a percentage, a cut, commission, whatever. It was a profession, in my opinion, sort of like ambulance chasers, except they were chasing hearses. As far as I could make out, they filled a few forms in, which is basically all that filing for probate is. I mean, I'm sure that some of you reading this will say *'Hang on for just one minute there matey! When my uncle's estate went into probate it took two bloody years to get sorted out!'* Which, of course, I would not dream of disputing…having said which, the process is still all about filling in the right forms with the right information at the right time and then giving it to the right person at the right place at the, er, right time. Isn't it? I rest my case m'lud. Thank you.

So, where was I? Yeah, so, as far as I could make out these hearse chasers fill a few forms in…like your secretary would if you had one…which I haven't, and nor would I want one to be honest, which possibly means that I might be being dishonest, which, believe me, I'm not. I mean, I don't have anything against secretaries, but, I dunno, I don't think I'd ever want *anyone* working for me. I don't like…I dunno, I don't really like the idea of someone being, now this might be totally the wrong word here but, I don't like the idea of someone being *subservient* to me. I don't mind telling people what to do, I quite often do that, and not always politely, so…maybe I'm more inclined to discuss things and work in a team rather than as a boss with a gaggle of underlings. Quite garbled that isn't it. Mixed up, not thought out. Not like me at all. I mean, I don't even like being waited on in a restaurant, part of the reason I rarely go to restaurants to be honest and I am being honest so don't think I'm not just because I said I was. When I'm in a restaurant I often feel like saying to the people serving me, '*Hang on, look, sit down here and I'll get* you *a glass of wine.*' I mean, it's not an easy job serving people in a restaurant…long hours, shit wages, demanding chefs and those maître dee people, and probably quite a few customers who treat you as though you don't exist and talk to you like you're a servant or something if they decide you *do* exist after all. Sorry, but I don't like that. So no, I don't have a secretary and I don't want one. So don't even bother applying. Well, I'm glad we've sorted that out.

Fucking hell Joe, I thought, *is this how your mind really works? Do you constantly meander about the place, going off on tangents? Flickering between subjects?*

Yes, I answered, *yes, it is. Doesn't yours?* Bizarre conversation, I know, me talking to me about me and comparing me to me. *This is how my mind works, if you don't like it then, er…do one!*

I can't believe I just told myself to do one. Where am I even going to do one to? Didn't think of that did I? Did you?

Anyway, now that I've just said all that, I think I might need a secretary after all. We. *We* might need a secretary.

I replied to Emily in our private Messenger conversation.

'*Heir hunters? Wtf? How did he die, do you know?*'

I wondered how an heir hunter company had even got involved. How did they know about my brother? I wondered if the police inform them or something. But then, how do the police get involved in this kind of thing, I wondered. Surely, they would only get involved if there was some kind of *strangeness* about the death? Y'know, something other than a straightforward hospital death. I was a little baffled. I realised that I didn't know enough about all this stuff. I mean, as a firefighter, I'd dealt with dead people on many levels but, my involvement only ever went as far as finding, rescuing and recovering a body, delivering it to a place of safety whereupon my job was done and we then left it to others to carry on after us, so how had these hearse chasers got involved? What was the process here? How did the body of our brother find itself being used as a commodity of some kind? A thing to be used as a bargaining tool or a lever to extract money from someone living via someone dead? As you can see, I am not very forgiving towards these kinds of people and tend to always see them in a negative way. They *feed* off the dead. I know I am making them sound terrible and I know that, at the end of the day it's just a job and there would appear, in some cases anyway, that there is a need for such businesses. But I wouldn't want to do that job. I couldn't do that job. Anyway, I came to the conclusion that I didn't have enough information and decided to just deal with basics until I did.

Emily messaged me back. *'He didn't know how Dan died or where he died.'* and then, *'He wants me to go to his flat with him to get documents but wants to go in for 5 mins first alone just in case I get scared of something or upset'* and then another message, obviously another fast thumber. *'They have left details to get in touch with them tomorrow to see if we want them to sort the funeral or they do it for 10* percent of what Daniel has left if he has anything. *I don't trust them at all.'*

So, they *were* on the hunt for money. *Heir hunters my arse* I thought. Alarms went off. My hackles were up. Croft hackles…quick to rise sometimes. Lots of times. And this, for me, was one of those times. *'I don't trust them either Em.'* I messaged, immediately followed by *'How the fuck did they get involved?'*

'I don't know.' she answered, *'I think the coroner gets them involved. I asked how he knew all our names. He had my number…where from he wouldn't tell me.'*

I was suddenly angry. These people had been delving into us, the Crofts, finding out stuff about us, searching their databases, getting addresses and phone numbers and who knows what else and all because my brother, our brother had died and WE didn't even know about his death. They were beavering away behind the scenes, compiling a file…*a fucking file*…on us…with our brother lying in a morgue somewhere, because they *sniffed* the possibility of some money coming their way. *They were fucking vultures* I thought, *carrion eaters, maggots.* I decided, there and then, that I hated these people. I now didn't care who they were and that they had a job to do and that *someone* had to do it. I decided they were skanks and I didn't want anything to do with them. They were after his money, assuming he actually had any but didn't even know how he had died or did know but weren't prepared to be the ones to break such news…no, leave that to a public sector worker while we get on with chasing the pound. Pricks. Yeah, I hated them. With a passion. How dare they. How dare they try to get in first, because that is what was going on here. *They were trying to get in before someone else* I thought. Before that someone else got a signature…which suggested an urgency to me. They were *desperate* — probably the wrong word but choose a similar one yourself — to get to us because they *knew* there would be other sharks circling and probably very soon. Yeah, my passion was growing. I was doing a number on myself, thoughts racing around in my head, racing to conclusions, all of them not good for the hearse chasers. There would or might be others, so they wanted to get a signature and quick. So, I thought, does that mean that somehow, the death of my brother was in the public domain somewhere? Somehow? If these heir hunters were on the *desperate sniff of money trail,* then they were seeking expediency for fear of someone getting there before them. So, I thought, if it is in the public domain, where would it be?

I typed my brother's name into a search engine. It came up straight away. I was a bit taken aback at how, suddenly, here was my brother, famous, sort of. Noticed. Or a Notice about him, not quite the same as being noticed I know. It was a Police Notice to the effect that a male aged 66 had been found dead at his home and that there were no suspicious circumstances. And they wanted any relatives to get in touch. There was an email address. It took me no more than 45 seconds to get this information, and that was in spite of the dreadfully slow internet service provided by our French phone people…and I mean dreadfully with a capital D. In fact, I mean dreadfully with every letter in capitals. Do you know what, why didn't I just write it in capitals and then again, *why* did I even bother just asking *that* question? DREADFULLY. There you go. Job done.

There was no way of me telling how long this Notice had been in the local press, but let's say that it's been there since he was found dead, so, three days. People have known about my brother's death for three days; some people have opened a file regarding his death. Some people were already attempting to make some money on the back of his death. Death Notice browsers…and there are some…had been able to read all about it and speculate over a cup of tea and a chocolate biscuit. But his remaining family had just been going about their business, oblivious. The business of obliviousness. I was angry. Angry at all those people going about their business and angry at me for going about my oblivious business. And I was angry at the brother I have always thought of as my hero, for setting himself against the world, especially the world that contained his family. I was angry at all those wasted years. Now there could be no restoration of our brotherhood, something I had yearned for, for more than 30 years, more than half of my life. Now, it was never going to be. Whatever had happened in his mind to turn him against me was never going to be discovered, was never going to be resolved or understood. I was angry. And sad. But more angry than sad. Yet more damage, irreparable damage caused by Charlie, our father. Would it never end?

Something occurred to me and I scrolled back through the conversation. What was it that had been said? Yeah, here it was, Emily said, *'he wants me to go to his flat with him to get documents but wants to go in for 5 mins first alone just in case I get scared of something or upset.'*

The implication was that this fella, whoever he was, knew or suspected that there would be a document or documents that would be significant. What kind of documents? I thought. And is it right that this fella should make a sort of demand that he be allowed unrestricted and unsupervised access to the property, albeit under the guise of making sure it was not too upsetting to my sister? I told you earlier, I am suspicious of virtually everyone I come across and this situation was setting off alarm after alarm. My mind was racing. The documents…the only documents of any significance to an heir hunter would be a will, bank documents, an insurance policy and papers to do with ownership of the property. I couldn't think of anything else. But then, what if my brother was someone who stashed banknotes under his mattress? Was it right that this heir hunter bastard should be demanding or at the very least *suggesting* five minutes of unsupervised access to the home?

This fella, this heir hunter, this situation, stunk and I could smell the stench of a carrion eater. This was someone, a person, a company, who have got the tiniest whiff of money and were going to pursue it as only a carrion eater will pursue a meal. Ruthlessly mercenary. Heartless. Totally uncaring of anything except the end product, the bottom line. This fella, this company, this type of business… makes me sick when it is populated by unscrupulous people and where there is money, more or less free money to be had, well, unscrupulous ruthless people are there in abundance. Like maggots on a corpse. I know there is a need, of sorts, for these businesses. Without them, the government would absorb all unclaimed estates, acting like the apex predator. The rest, all these heir hunter companies, were no more than scavengers and, in amongst the scavengers were what I would call apex scavengers. And this company had been the first out of the blocks, which made them, in my book, apex scavengers. I could appreciate the need but nevertheless I despised them. With a passion. As you can see.

The documents…I knew that my brother had always had a bank account and I knew that he had a works pension. Dan had worked for a giant pharmaceuticals company for many years. He'd retired quite early, something to do with a bad foot my mum had told me, though in what way a bad foot had interfered with him working in a lab I didn't know. So, there *would* be bank documents about the place. He would probably have insurance but, a will? I didn't expect my brother to have a will. I don't know why because it is an eminently sensible thing to do, but, I don't know, it just didn't seem to be something that people like us did. I didn't have a will though I was constantly thinking about making one because…it was just such a sensible thing to do. It saved such a lot of hassle. His property was owned by him and I imagine that his mortgage would have finished when he was 65, about a year ago. So, there was value to his property though, exactly how much was anyone's guess. But, I thought, if all these documents are there, waiting to be picked up, they could just as easily be picked up by me or one of my sisters and dealt with in exactly the same way that the apex scavengers would deal with them if allowed. Except the apex scavengers would put their hand out for, apparently, 10 percent.

And then there was the line about my sister being possibly 'scared' or 'upset.' Obviously, this apex scavenger knew something about the circumstances of the death of my brother that he was keeping to himself, or at the very least had an understanding of the consequences of a lonely person dying in their home. I also had such an understanding. I'd dealt with lots of people dying in their home, not to mention their cars and workplaces. I had been called to homes where access was required, where 'smells' had been detected, where the occupant hadn't been seen for a while. I knew what the likelihood was, what the property might well be like if a body had lain for a while undiscovered. So, assuming this apex scavenger was given his 5 minutes of unsupervised access to the property, what was he going to do? Tidy up? Clean away the body staining? Get rid of the smells? Or just spend that time looking for his next meal ticket? I despised them more and more with every second I spent thinking about those few simple words my sister said he used.

I realised I was probably doing a spot of over-thinking. I messaged Emily. *'Don't let him in the place Em. Give me the number and I'll ring them.'*

As I was waiting for the number, I decided that it was an email address I really wanted. Phoning someone never worked the way you wanted it to when it really mattered. Not in my world anyway. But putting things in writing was different and the immediacy of emails, especially contractually speaking, was what I thought was needed here. I remembered that I'd been having a conversation with Lydia. I messaged her.

'I'm speaking to Emily now. Heir hunters called at her place'

As I sent it my phone dinged again. It was Emily. *'He had my address and Lydia's. He's been to Lydia's, said to me, is Lydia deaf that would explain why she never answered the door.'*

Something in what she said struck me as an anomaly. Things were rapidly filling my head up. Overload. Too much stuff coming in way too fast. Brother. Death. Body. Police. Two sisters at loggerheads. And these anomalies, probably of my own making, just kept popping up. It was almost like I could hear a comic 'pop' sound every time a little anomaly alarm was set off. My brain started fizzing. That's what I feel like when I get bombarded with info and thoughts. I knew that I had to step back a little and start to trim and thin things out. I needed to get things working in a logical way, needed to have the incoming info slow down and be sorted and categorised as it occurred. I texted Emily.

'I'll come over Em. ASAP.'

This was something that had to be done but it was impossible for me to just up and go. I had a business to run and things had to be done before I could leave. These things had consequences, different consequences depending on the state you leave them in, some of those consequences having knock-on effects that were, undesirable. So, things had to be dealt with in a logical and sensible way, and for me to do that, I had to slow things down in my mind. My phone dinged. It was Lydia.

'And? xx'

A two-kiss question. I briefly wondered what she was talking about then realised it was her reply to me telling her that heir hunters had called at Emily's. That wasn't quite the response I expected from Lydia and my mind returned to a previous alarm. I scrolled up the conversation. Emily had told me that the heir hunter had asked her if Lydia was deaf. How would he know to ask that? Did he *know* that Lydia was inside the house when he called? Had he seen someone or heard someone inside the house? A thought occurred…Lydia was married to Edward, who was also deaf… I felt pretty certain that they had a doorbell fitted to the house that flashed a light when someone 'rang' it. But how would the heir hunter know that? Was there a sign fitted to their front door? I cast my mind back to the picture of their front door the last time I'd been there. There was no outward sign that the occupants were deaf. Not that I could recall. So, had he rung the bell, thereby flashing the light and had maybe caught sight of someone peeping out between the curtains? And if that was the case, why wouldn't Lydia open the door? Another thought occurred…did he ring the bell, flash the light, she peeped out, saw a well-dressed man, maybe with a briefcase or something and automatically thought that this could only represent trouble? I know that some people, especially people on benefits, like my sister Lydia, in fact, like both my sisters, are very wary of opening their front doors to people who look 'official' in any way. An understandable reaction. I didn't like opening my front door to suits either. Mind you, I didn't like opening my front door to anyone. I was now contributing to my information overload…adding a bit of fizz to my already fizzing brain. I told myself to stop it and try to slow everything down, put my slow-mo thinking cap on. Funny saying that isn't it…the old 'thinking cap' thing. My grandma used to say it all the time and so did my mum. I remember getting asked a question by my mum when I was probably about 4 or 5 years old. It was to do with her leg. She was sitting on the sofa, having a cup of tea with grandma and I'd been playing with my cars on the floor by her feet. Her legs were crossed, and I was intrigued by her calf and the way it wobbled when I poked it. I was a bugger for poking things to see what would happen. I poked grandad's ear once when he was sitting in his chair asleep with his mouth open. He'd growled and puffed his cheeks out, still asleep, and his teeth slid out of his mouth and clacked on the watch chain of his waistcoat then seemed to turn around as if they were looking at me. Which was a massive shock to me as I didn't know anything about false teeth. I thought me poking his earhole had somehow caused him to jettison all his teeth, all in one lump, and I had a quick look about for witnesses, before disappearing to the parlour to play with my cars. So, anyway, mum asked me what I was doing, and I said that I was wondering what was inside her calf that made it wobble. She asked me what I thought it might be and after a while pondering this question, during which grandma said 'Ey up…he's got his thinking cap on.' Which made me feel the top of my head for this cap, making them laugh. Anyway, I decided that my mum's wobbly calf must be full of blood and said so. They both laughed and then when grandad came in from 'down the yard,' which meant he'd been to the toilet, they told him, and he laughed as well. I liked making people laugh and so I was happy in spite of not being able to find the thinking cap. I noticed, later that day, that no-one told my dad about it, which was a pity because he might have laughed as well. I replied to Lydia's two-kiss question.

'They apparently called at yours today.'

I got back to thinking how this heir hunter came to the conclusion that maybe Lydia was deaf. Could it be that a neighbour had been passing, or just nosing, and had told him that the occupants were deaf? But then, wouldn't that neighbour also know that Lydia had a flashing bell? And possibly know whether or not they were actually in the house or had maybe gone out? Lydia and Edward did have a car and Lydia wasn't particularly mobile, so if the car was parked at the roadside, the chances were strong that Lydia was inside the house. My phone dinged. Lydia.

'Yes, neighbour told me xxx'

Three kisses. Was this significant or not? There were kisses, three of them, so therefore this statement was a non-threatening, meaningless chit-chatty type of statement, no meaning other than the obvious, no agenda, no reason for being written or said apart from informative. Nevertheless, I thought, would it have been a relevant thing to have already said in this conversation? Is this not something rather strangely significant?

Emily dinged me in our private Messenger convo.

'I'm not letting them do any funeral arrangements or anything else they can fuck off I don't know them from Adam. He said I'm an ex-copper I said I don't care what you are mate, it doesn't mean I gotta trust you.'

I laughed out loud. Pam looked at me with a raised eyebrow. 'Our Em being Em.' I explained. She laughed at that. She knew what I meant. I texted back.

'I'm gonna include Lydia in this convo ok Em? We need to work together on this.' She sent a thumbs up.

I was very conscious of wanting to deal with this whole situation as a team. I wanted everything to be decided by all three of us…the last three members of our generation of Crofts. I didn't want any strange goings on to occur, I didn't want anyone being able to point an accusing finger at anyone else. We'd had enough of that in this family, especially at the time of the deaths of my parents, just one month apart. There had been nothing that you would consider to be an 'estate' left by my parents. Nevertheless, certain of my sisters colluded to, I dunno if the word swindle is the best one to use here but if it isn't, then the correct word is of the same family. So yeah, certain of my sisters did a bit of swindling. I know that without doubt, my sister Carla played the largest part. Emily also played a part but not *as* large and I heard that Lydia played a part too, albeit a smaller part. The smallest part. Makes me think of the Three fuckin' Bears, Daddy Bear, Mummy Bear and Baby Bear. That analogy possibly makes me, or my brother Dan, Goldilocks. Well, I am definitely not Goldilocks as I am bald as a coot, whatever a coot is. A bird, I think.

So, Dan is Goldilocks. Not sure he'd like that but sorry Dan, you're stuck with it.

In some ways, and this is going to sound a little strange, I wouldn't have minded getting swindled if millions, or, sad to say, even thousands of pounds were at stake when they died, but, it was no more than hundreds. Unless my sisters know more than me, which is very possible. Mind you, I do recall my sister Carla buying a new car at the time. When I say 'new car' I mean one new to her, not properly new. It was small, quite a basic model. Dark brown in colour, quite faded if my memory serves me. It had beige seats but the front passenger seat had a very large, yellowy brownish stain on it. Like someone had spilled a runny curry on it. Or been sick on it. Which would mean the driver wouldn't it? I mean, if you're the front seat passenger you're not gonna jump up and vomit all over *your* seat, are you? And equally, if you're about to vomit, but you're sitting in the back, you're not gonna squeeze between the seats to vomit on the front passenger one, are you? I wouldn't. But if you're the driver, just ambling along, minding your own business, listening to some soothing music on the tape, when you suddenly get the urge to vomit, you might be tempted to just casually lean over and vomit on the front passenger seat. Stands to reason. Having said all that, probably the most likely cause of the stain is a spilled curry or something similar. Or maybe something worse. Just re-read that last little bit. From what I've just said above, I don't want you to think that I listen to tapes in my car because I don't. I have CD's or even iPods in my car. Can't quite get my phone to Bluetooth its music to the car but, wtf, who cares?

So, where was I?

Yeah, so, Goldilocks and the Three Bears. The swindling, as far as I know, was not worth more than hundreds of pounds. Rather sad. And I did not want anyone being able to accuse anyone of anything in this instance, so I wanted us to work together as a team.

I set up a 'group chat' thing in Messenger. It took me a while and as I was doing it, I told Pam that my brother had died. She was shocked, more at my business-like way of delivering the news, rather than the news itself. She'd never met Dan and was never going to now. She asked me if I was alright and I said yes.

I had a bit of a struggle with setting up the group chat. I'd done it before but couldn't really remember how to. I mean, apart from the basics, all this social media stuff is a tad boring and so I tend to leave it be. I just put photos on it for my kids and friends back in the UK to see what I'm up to in France. Plus, I have the odd rant against the government. And I'm anti-bullying, anti-racist, anti-everything that singles some people out in order to put them down in some way, so have an occasional rant on that subject. Once or twice a week maybe. I'm all for people all being the same, all bleeding red blood, all wanting the same things, good health, prosperity etc. and so I occasionally also have a rant about equality. Plus, I think there are some incredibly talented people on this planet and I love it when you get those little videos showcasing someone brilliant, so I share them and make comments. Plus, there are some very funny people out there who do the maddest daftest things and just make me laugh and I love having a laugh and love people being daft. I can be a bit daft myself. So, I share them and make appropriate comments. Plus, of course, my daughters and stepdaughters share photos of all our grandkids growing up and whilst they are a reminder of how far along your particular mortal coil you are, they are still wonderfully valuable and entertaining. Apart from all that, I don't really use social media.

The group was set up and I 'waved' to them. Emily showed up first. I texted the group.

'Hiya Em, this all sounds very suspicious. What do you think?'

'I think so too' she replied.

I spotted Lydia arrive in the group. We were all now in the same room so to speak. Progress. I greeted her.

'Hiya Lydia, what about you? What do you think?'

She took a few seconds to reply. I assumed she was reading what little had been said.

'Hiya' she replied.

I expected a little more than that. She knew, because I'd told her just minutes earlier, that the man who'd called at their homes was an heir hunter. But nothing, no surprised comment, no wtf…no woe (what on earth) no…woeigo (what on earth is going on), just a big fat nothing. I knew that there was *something* going on here. I just *felt* it. Something behind the scenes, some little secret thing. It could have been simply that she was a bit subdued, upset about what had happened and couldn't contribute much. I knew that, at times when stress plays a big part in people's lives, such as a family death, that my fireground brain clicks into gear and I become quite, *cold* I suppose. Quite dispassionate in some ways. As a firefighter, I learned very early on that as soon as the bells went down you had to switch on and get focused. All the banter and joking stopped when the bells went down and we got our fireground heads on. If you didn't, you could easily get injured and an injured firefighter is not much use to himself, herself, or others. So, I had a tendency to become very business-like very quickly when the need arose, and I knew that some people could easily have a problem with that. I tried to not do it at times but, I've got to say, I'm rubbish at switching my brain off when maybe I should. And, I thought, maybe my expectation of the type of reply I expected from Lydia was too high.

I noticed that Emily didn't greet Lydia and that Lydia's *'Hiya'* was a sort of general hiya rather than a targeted one. Listen to me. I told you, my brain just won't stop chattering. No wonder I've got no hair. Emily said something; *'Plus Jonah came home from work today said he got a call off the heir hunters yesterday…how would they know to contact Jonah?'*

I wondered briefly who Jonah was before it came to me. He was Millie's boyfriend. Millie was Emily's daughter. I was puzzled. How on earth did these heir hunters get the phone number of the boyfriend of my niece? Where would that be stored for this company to find? I mean, they found *Jonah's* number before they found Millie's number? Or Emily's or Lydia's? And it was all connected up with the fact that my brother had died? Wtf?

'How the fuck did Jonah get a call?' I asked.

Emily replied. *'I dunno…'* she said, *'Jonah isn't our family so wtf?'*

Lydia piped up; *'How come Jonah got the call?'*

Emily answered, *'I dunno. I've rung them and it went straight to voicemail but…'*

'What the hell!!!' It was Lydia and it seemed she was mad. Angry is what I mean.

I thought I should try to defuse what I thought was a developing situation.

'Listen,' I typed, *'we have to keep cool and calm here, try to deal with this logically.'*

There were a few minutes where no-one said anything. I got on the internet and typed the name of the company into the search box. A load of solicitors and accountants came up. I modified the search by adding *heir hunters* to it. That did the trick and I clicked on them. On the home page you could click on a *Meet the Team* box and I went to meet the team of grasping money grabbing twats. Sorry, got carried away a bit there. I went to meet the team. I would not have wanted to be waiting for a job interview with any of this lot. I'm sorry but they just all looked like the kind of people you expect to come across in a car showroom or a mobile phone sales place, estate agents, you know the type of places I mean. You know the type of people I mean. The type who will say anything and do anything to extract what it is they want from you, whatever that is and it's not always your money. Not the kind of people you would want backing you up in a sticky situation. I wondered which one of the jackals had called at my sister's homes. Which one was trying to extract something from what, if anything, had been left behind by my brother? I briefly wished that I hadn't moved to France, so that whoever had called at my sister's may have called at mine. I would have liked that. I returned to the conversation.

'Well look, re this fella who called at your places, don't do anything, don't give any permissions, don't agree to anything and above all, don't sign anything whatsoever'

Emily responded almost immediately, *'He's going to Dan's flat whether I go or not. He's invited me to go with him'*

I was incensed. Absolutely instantly furious, almost to the point of violence. This was some fella, some fucking mealy-mouthed, grasping, twat, sensing that these vulnerable women were all alone in the world, were dreadfully upset that their brother had died, which they were, and was going to 'take charge', was going to arrive like a knight in shining fucking armour and save the day, not to mention gather whatever he needed to start the probate proceedings or whatever their 'job' was. He's going to MY brothers flat? Whether one of us goes with him or not? And magnanimous fucker that he is, he's actually INVITED one of us to go with him? My heart was beating fast, adrenaline was coursing through me. Suddenly, deep in my mind, my dad, Charlie, was standing over me, dictating what was going to be. All I can say is that I was glad I was sitting in France and not in the same room as this fella, whoever he was.

'He's got no right to go to his flat' I typed.

My typing, and the words used were my fireground brain taking over. I was adrenalined up to fuck (the most you can ever be adrenalined up) and the circuit in my head that governs cool, calm, and logical, was doing the thinking. *If he is going to my brother's flat in England and I am sat here in France*, I thought, *then there is nothing I can do physically, to stop this. And if he is going there, whether or not one of us is going with him, then we need to gain some control over this situation.*

Plus, if he is going there, then he must have my brother's keys. And the only place he could have gotten them was from the police.

'OK then' I typed, 'both of you go with him.'

Emily responded. *'Ok we can both go. I'd rather do that anyway'*

'Do not let him go in the place on his own, no matter what he says and watch everything he does and do not let him take anything away.' I replied. *'And do not agree to anything or sign anything at all, nothing, not even a form that he tells you just gives him permission to enter the property. Don't trust anything he says and don't get friendly with him.'*

Lydia responded within a few seconds. **'No! I'm not having Jonah going to Dans flat Em No!'**

Obviously, Lydia wasn't keeping up with the conversation. Which, in my mind begged the question, what *was* she doing? Told you, I don't trust anyone. When you grow up being continually attacked and hurt by the ones that are supposed to protect and cherish you, your default position is one of distrust of everyone. And I mean everyone. Apart from my own two daughters and maybe my wife Pam. I am often *not* an easy person to live with. Probably. My wife Pam is *very* understanding.

'I meant you two Lydia.' I typed, *'I meant you and Emily go with him.'*

Lydia was quick to respond but it was obvious she wasn't responding to anything actually being said here. *'No! Jonah is not having anything to do with it Emily!'*

I noticed that nothing said by Lydia in this group conversation had ended with a kiss. There was definite hostility here. So, ending something *with* a kiss meant *something* or, to put it another way, ending something with a kiss didn't mean *nothing*. If you see what I mean. I know that they hadn't been talking for a while, I don't know why, but surely, such a situation as this, you would think, would count for different behaviour, burying of the hatchet even. It just seemed to me that any hatchets that were going to be buried, would be buried in someone's back. Or maybe I was misreading the situation. It had been known. Emily replied, and I could almost hear the quiet exasperation in her voice, had she spoken.

'I meant you Lydia.'

And then straight away, quick as a flash Lydia sent; *'No! I'm not having it!'*

I was a tiny bit stunned. It was possible that she'd typed her 'not having it' statement in the midst of Emily sending her 'I meant you' message. I decided to just sit back and say nothing, give the situation time to settle, give Lydia time to step back from what seemed a belligerent stance, a stance I was a tad surprised at. Even though Lydia was my sister, I didn't really know her particularly well, but what I felt I *did* know of her was that she was usually composed and sensible. I'd never seen this side to her but, like I said, I didn't really know her too well. So, I waited. A couple of minutes went by. No-one said anything. I could see that both my sisters were still in the conversation. Their green blobs were still lit up, so, as far as I'm aware that meant they were still here. I assumed that both would be re-reading what had gone before, as I was, both making certain that they were correct in what they'd said. A few more minutes went by and no-one said anything. I could almost feel the anger, could almost hear it bubbling and seething. From nowhere I was suddenly upset. Not like me at all. Suddenly I could feel my eyes filling with tears. I glanced up at Pam to make sure she wasn't looking my way. She was busy knitting. I never wanted anyone to see that I was upset and certainly never wanted anyone to see that I was close to tears. I wasn't supposed to show that I was anything other than in control. I wasn't supposed to show that I was upset or scared or…anything. I was supposed to just be…me.

When I was young, a kid, I could never show any emotion. To do so was to attract attention from my father…and that was something you didn't want to do. It's sad to say, and I'm now almost ashamed of this, that, as a kid, I was…happy, though happy is too strong a word for what I really mean… probably relieved is a better word…if one of my siblings broke and showed an unwanted emotion. Because his attention would be drawn to them and that usually meant that I was safe for the time being. Not always, but usually.

Actually, I've got that slightly wrong. I *was* allowed to show an emotion. I was allowed to show that I thought my father had made a good decision…I was allowed to show that my father had done something or said something funny, especially when that funny thing was disparaging to someone else, some other sibling or my mother. In fact, I had to *properly* laugh, even in the eyes, because he would check your eyes. If you were not showing the correct face, the correct expression, the correct *look*, then his eyes would narrow as they stared at you, his face would…change somehow…like the change you might expect a time-lapse film of drying concrete to show, subtle but there, only visible because you'd time-lapsed it. His face would take on a look that was terrifying to me as a child, well into my teens even. It wasn't a look that could be seen, as such, more a look that could be felt. It was a set of the face, a deepening of the blue of his eyes, a…set of the mouth that was indefinable, a tenseness about the shoulders, the hands, that just simply told you that you were in danger and that the danger was approaching, coming up behind you and coming up *fast*. Very, very occasionally, this *set* of my father, as if for battle, would be held for seconds, sometimes minutes, like there was an argument going on in his head, and then it would disappear, like water down a plug hole. But that didn't mean you were safe because, sometimes, in those first seconds of clemency, he could snap, almost like there was another person whispering in his ear, jeering at him because he'd 'let you off.' taunting him because he'd 'gone soft'. And when that happened, it was like he suddenly thought to himself *'aaah y'know what…fuck it! Let's just go for it!'* and you could get a beating that, given you were a child and he was an ex-army boxing champion, could only be described as savage. But anyway, I digress.

The silence between us all had gone on too long. I decided to break it. I laughed. By text. *'hahahaha'* I typed, immediately followed by *'Lydia, she meant you, not Jonah.'*

I put one of those emoji things at the end of it…a happy yellow face with a big toothy grin. It seemed to break the spell. Emily came back to the table, so to speak. *'I never mentioned Jonah Lydia and what is it you're not having?'*

I felt they were squaring up here and so I tried to establish some order. *'Listen both of you…I said at the start that we should all try to stay calm and cool.'*

Emily's reply was instantaneous with, I thought, a hint of anger, in spite of her words. I intuited the hint of anger. It's almost impossible to tell *how* something has been said in a text, which, of course, is why they can cause such a huge amount of trouble. But sometimes, I could be wrong but, sometimes, you *can* just tell. In my opinion. *'I'm calm.'* she said.

The implication, for me, being that someone else wasn't. She had a point. Lydia seemed intent on only seeing what she wanted to see and getting quite angry at nothing.

'I know Em.' I said, *'Lydia, Em never meant Jonah she meant you. You and her go with this fella.'*

Once again, there were a few minutes of silence. Five to be exact. And then Lydia piped up.

'We both go with what fella?'

I realised that Lydia had no knowledge of the short conversation I'd had with Emily, discussing the hearse chaser. I typed a request to Emily; *'Tell Lydia please Em.'*

'Tell me what?' Lydia replied.

Once again, I just got the impression of anger or, maybe something else, I don't really know what but, I felt uneasy. This whole conversation was something I didn't like and, apart from the obvious, that it was about the death of my brother, it was the hostility. It was palpable. I could almost touch it. Don't ask me how that happens because I don't know. How you get a *feeling* from a few words in a text. Of course, it could be that I was completely wrong anyway and simply reading things between the lines that weren't actually there. It could just be that my, admittedly overactive imagination was going into hyper-drive. Nevertheless, my mind was fidgeting. It does that when I can't quite get a grip of something. It's the best way of me describing it. I feel like I want to scratch my brain, my mind, like it's itchy, like I've got that restless leg syndrome but in my brain. The word I've already used works well for abbreviating my feelings. Uneasy. I felt uneasy. I sometimes use the word 'fizzing' to describe the same thing…my mind is fizzing. I know I'm a bit strange, a bit of a crank in Liverpudlian speak, but hey, I'm all you've got here, so get used to it.

There were about 10 minutes of silence from my sisters. I assumed that Emily was filling Lydia in about the hearse chaser fella in a private conversation. I took the time to have another look at something I'd almost forgotten…the Notice in the local Liverpool newspaper, from Merseyside Police. I was going to ring them in the morning but noticed an email address, so I rattled off an email. I always prefer to do everything in writing anyway. Phone calls are way too easily fobbed by someone with an agenda. And in my mind, rightly or wrongly, virtually everyone you have to deal with in any organisation, seems to have an agenda. Probably under the guise of 'policy' but that translates to 'agenda' for me.

The fella's name was Richard. He worked for Merseyside Police as the liaison officer for the coroner's office but I'm not sure whether he was an actual police officer or a civvy working for the police. Not that it matters. I asked him if the police or the coroner's office had handed the keys to my brother's flat to this heir hunter bloke. I sent the email, got back to the group conversation and told them what I'd just done.

'I've just emailed a fella called Richard, who works for Merseyside police and the coroner's office. He'd put a Notice out, looking for Dan's next of kin. I've cc'd you both into the email.'

Emily asked me what cc'd meant and I explained it to her, along with BCC and how that facility could be used. There was a minute or two were I presumed they were reading the email I'd sent them, then Emily got back to business.

'We don't have to go through these heir hunters at all, it's just a probate service thing. We can sort all this ourselves and I think we should tell them where to go. What do you two think?'

I agreed with Emily and said so. Lydia wasn't saying anything, unless she was saying it to Emily privately, which, if she was, begged a question or two. Then a little anomaly cropped up. From Emily.

'I don't know' she sent.

This didn't belong to the group conversation so it seemed obvious that there was a private conversation between my sisters in the background and, as can easily happen in such circumstances, she'd sent a text not intended for me. As I was pondering this, she sent another message.

'Yeah I understand that'

And this was followed, very quickly, by one from Lydia.

'Joe where did you get that information from? The police notice stuff?'

No kisses. This, to me, suspicious bastard that I am, was nothing more than deflecting me from Emily's last words. Em's '*I don't know*' and '*yeah I understand that*' were part of another conversation and she'd cocked up by sending it to where I could see it. And Lydia's deflection tactic was designed to get me on another track and away from the cock-up, which begged an obvious question...*Why would you want to deflect me from what could easily be passed off as a simple mistake?* So therefore, apparently, it wasn't a simple mistake, at least in Lydia's eyes. She, apparently, saw it as something else entirely. For me to become suspicious about this cock-up, I would have to know the other half of the conversation, which I didn't. It could easily have been laughed off but instead, she was trying to cover it up. I mean, it's there, I can see it and read it as often as I wanted. It was there for all time. It was too late to hide it. But she tried. Her question about the Police Notice spoke volumes to me.

I ignored the police notice question to see what would happen. If it was a deflection tactic, I expected something else to be said and pretty soon. And I expected that whatever it was would *not* refer to the obvious mistake made, but instead, try to deflect me further away. I was struggling to understand what was going on here, but I knew that *something* was. As far as I was concerned, right at that moment, my sisters, enemies up until just a few minutes ago, were colluding and if they *were* colluding then that is only required when they have an adversary, or is there something wrong with my logic there? And if, in their minds, an adversary existed here then that adversary was...me. They were colluding against me. *Wtf was going on,* I asked myself. A tiny voice in my mind gave a benefit of the doubt to my sisters but a much bigger one shouted it down. Strongly. Emily sent the group a message.

'I gave that hearse chaser fella your email address Joe, so check to see if you got it.' followed by, *'He told me he was an ex bizzie, worked on the murder squad.'* Immediately followed by, *'He said he wants to go in the flat for five minutes on his own, do you think our Dan was murdered?'*

A 'bizzie' is a Liverpool word for the police. The word may well be used elsewhere as well, I'm not sure, but I've only ever heard it in Liverpool. Mind you, I've only ever lived in Liverpool, apart from where I live now, which doesn't count, so, stupid thing to have said really. 'Scuffers' is another one… one that I used a lot when I was a kid. I think 'bizzies' is a more contemporary term. There were other words too, some of them utterly non-complimentary, which I won't use because I don't like them. 'Rozzers' is another one. Again, I have no idea where these words come from.

So, anyway, now, it seemed as though my sisters or sister Emily at least, wanted me to 'go off' and check my emails, go away from this group chat and do something else, go away and ponder the question of whether or not my brother had been *murdered*…I mean, murdered! WTF? WTF was that all about? Who on earth would want to murder my brother? For what? Why? What a leap that was by my sister! It was pretty blatant in my opinion. If that wasn't Emily assisting her twin sister to deflect me away from the conversation and their apparent mistake, then I was a monkey's uncle. Now, *that* is a saying I do know the foundation of…and an interesting foundation it is too. Go check it yourself… Scope trial, USA, nineteen something or other.

So, I *did* do what my sisters wanted me to do. I went away and checked my emails and there was nothing from the hearse chaser, and so I did what my lovely grandad used to do…I sat. And pondered.

I thought back to the deaths of my parents, and remembered that Carla and Emily, arch enemies for years, suddenly became like proper sisters. I thought at the time, that maybe the deaths of our parents had become one of those 'silver lining' moments, serving to unite a fragmented family. And I thought *that* until I knew to think differently. I thought *that* until I knew they had been *friends* because they were colluding…and their collusion had been because there was money involved…that root, as they say, of all evil. It took me a few minutes of grandad*esque* pondering to come to the conclusion that any collusion between my younger twin sisters must, or definitely *could* be, because of that same reason. Money. I could think of no other reason.

I was plunged into despair. Despair is a place in my mind, a place that has kept me safe since I was a little kid. Which, I know, probably sounds a bit strange…a despair that keeps you safe. So, let me explain…

When I was summoned to Despair as a child, as I often was, it was always because either I, my mum or one of my siblings was being attacked by my father. When an attack occurred, there was only ever one outcome and the only variance was to what level the physical hurt and mental anguish would reach. When it became apparent that an attack was imminent, and that 'warning' could be just a few blinks of an eye, you mentally hunkered down, mentally prepared yourself to show no fright, show no fear, show no impudence, show no defiance, in other words, act as though what was about to happen or what was already happening, was perfectly normal, perfectly everyday and humdrum.

And that thought, that 'getting ready.' would send me to my place of safety, my 'cupboard under the stairs', the place where I was taught to accept that this is what life is, that there was no escape, that what was about to happen or was happening, was inevitable. Normal. It was something that everyone had to put up with because this was it. I didn't like it but, I didn't like the spoonful of cod liver oil my mum used to give me every day either. I just accepted that the cod liver oil was part of being alive and so too were the attacks by my father.

I didn't like the cod liver oil, but it was nothing, not really. And at first, the attacks by my father were treated the same in my mind. I didn't like it but hey, let's get it over with. Those attacks though, they became such that, something, I didn't really know what, and I still don't really know but, something deep in my mind, that didn't ever surface as an actual thought, y'know, one that gets put into words and spoken by that voice inside you that no one ever hears, *that* something told me that this wasn't part of life, that your father is supposed to cherish and protect you, not attack you, put you down and disparage you constantly.

And so, when an attack was imminent, I went into a kind of sudden downward spiral to a secret place I called Despair. My brother went there too. To his own form of it, his own *type*. I could tell. His eyes were the same as mine and I could feel his hurt.

Once I went to this place, I was safe. Frightened, but safe. This was a place of sanctuary for me because, once I was there, as soon as I landed, I felt…comfortable. I was scared, terrified for what was about to happen, but I was comfortable. When I landed in Despair, it was where I lived until the trouble went away. I inhabited Despair.

When I landed in Despair, a person I thought of as Big Joe would put his arms around me and whisper to me, tell me not to worry, that everything would be OK. If I had to speak to the outside world, he would tell me what to say and how to say it. He would compose my face, make my body look smaller or bigger, depending on what he wanted me to do, he would paint my eyes with the right expression.

When I landed in Despair, my face wanted to be the face of an old man just shy of the grave but Big Joe would make it look like the face of a child.

When I was staying in Despair, someone I thought of as Little Joe, would soothe and sort my shattered hopes, would allow me to see the hurt of my brother and sisters and think of and say the right words at the right time. She, for that is how I thought of Little Joe, as a she, would liaise with Big Joe and make the transition back to my world a smooth one.

Without my comfortable nest called Despair, I may not have come through my childhood as well balanced as I have, though I'm sure one or two of my proper friends would laugh at my use of the words 'well balanced.'

I still land in Despair when I need to or when I'm forced to. I now understand my nest more fully. I now know the people that live there intimately and when I need to, I allow them to fully take over the running of me.

I now know that there are just the three people, Big Joe, Little Joe and me. I used to think there were more. If I am ever forced into Despair, Big Joe is like a security force. He takes charge of everything to do with my protection. He will make use of me in whatever way he deems fit to ensure my protection, and there is nothing he won't do to achieve that. It is him that has made me, on occasion, self-harm. It is him who knows that self-harming is a misnomer. It is him who knows that there are times when, in order to release dangerous pressure from inside me, I should do so by causing myself pain. I don't know how he knows that, but he does and even though such action sounds a bit... radical...it actually works and works very effectively.

I remember the first time he made me do it, remember it like it was just yesterday.

I was about 15 and I'd come home from school for my dinner. You might call it lunch but, in Liverpool, the mid-day meal is called dinner. No-one was home. There was a teacher at school who was making my life miserable. She didn't like me, and she picked on me all the time. She said things that made other kids laugh at me. I liked people laughing at me but only when it was me that made them laugh. Something deep inside told me that what she was doing was wrong but, there was nothing I could do about it. She was an adult, the head of my year and she had a certain amount of power over me, for want of a better way of putting it. There was no one I could turn to, there was no point telling my parents, it would only get me into deeper trouble because I felt that they would take the side of the teacher and would assume that she was picking on me because I was disruptive or something. Which I wasn't. I was in the top sets for all my lessons and was one of the best sportsmen in the school, captain of the football team, member of the rugby team, captain of my athletics year, captain of the school chess team.

And so, on this day, a day when she had been mercilessly baiting me, I went home, ate my dinner, a truly fantastic cheese and onion pie from the baker's on Wood Street, and then, quite suddenly, as the fingers of the clock inched towards *going back to school time*, and my thoughts became more and more agitated, so that I couldn't see anything ahead of me, there was just...*noise*...and when this happens I feel like a little animal must feel when it's trapped by a predator and all I can focus on is escape. I went into the back garden, held my right cheekbone hard up to the rough brickwork of the house and scraped the skin from just under my eye down to just above my mouth. Not recommended as a way of sloughing off your dead skin but it worked for me.

It bled quite a lot. I was surprised at the amount of blood, as I always am. The effect on me was instantaneous. Like a switch being thrown. In an instant, the teacher in school, waiting to get at me again, as I'm sure she was, turned into nothing more than a stupid adult woman with a grudge against a teenage boy and my agitation disappeared, substituted with a detached calm and, in just a few seconds I was back to being me. Big Joe had seen my agitation growing to a dangerous level and stepped in. He told me what to do and helped me do it and brought me back from some brink that I'd been heading for.

Of course, people asked me what had happened, and I simply said I'd fallen over while I was running back to school. And of course, I got questioned about where I'd done it and who'd seen me, and Big Joe answered all the questions for me. And after that day, whenever the teacher tried to bait me, Big Joe took over and controlled me.

So, I know you're interested…you want to know about my self-harming. You want to know how often and what damage I've done to myself. So here goes.

I've probably self-harmed no more than a dozen times since I was 15. All of the injuries have been caused to my face. Though you wouldn't know because there's nothing to see. All of the injuries bar three or four were caused by a razor blade I took out of my fathers' razor, to places around my eyes. When I'd finished, I'd wipe the blade and put it back in his razor. I always derived a certain pleasure from knowing that he was shaving with a blade that had cut my face. Weird that isn't it…yeah, I thought so.

Anyway, none of the razor blade wounds have left scars but maybe if you look hard enough you might see thin lines were the blade sliced me. I don't know if there is anything visible because I tend not to look at myself very often. Not in detail anyway. The three or four injuries not caused by the razor? Three of them were caused by brickwork and one was caused by me shattering a heavy glass tumbler over the right side of my head. Now, *that* caused a lot of blood…in fact, a shitload. It also caused me to have over 30 stitches, half of them inside the deep wounds. That *did* leave scars, quite deep ones, plus some lasting nerve damage to my scalp. You can't see the scars, mind, because, amazingly, they absolutely coincide with the furrows on my forehead. The hospital wanted to know how I'd come by the injury and I told them I'd fallen off my push-bike. They didn't believe me, I could tell. But I didn't care what they believed.

Any despair I've ever felt has never been more than fleeting, my comfortable place called Despair has always seen to that. Any conflict

I've ever been involved in, my security guard takes over and looks after me, gets me ready to act in whatever way he sees fit. He takes over and allows me to think clearly whilst he stands ready to repel all boarders.

When I land in Despair, for a few moments, while I'm still very agitated, my eyes truly become the windows to my soul. Those are the windows that you may peer through at me from the outside but very quickly the veil, the security screen, is pulled and when that happens it's no longer me peering out at you, I am safely tucked up in my comfortable place, coming down from my plateau of agitation, getting my thoughts in order, putting my thinking cap on as my grandma would say, and, at that point, it is you that, dependent on what you do next, will be sent to your *own* despair, *your type* of despair, whatever that is.

When danger has passed and it's safe for me to come out, Big Joe will go back to his watchtower and either me or Little Joe, depending on what needs to be done, will appear and ordinary life will resume.

So, there you go. We all do this kind of thing don't we? Not necessarily the self-harming but, we all have our big people who look after…*tricky* things when needed? Our little people who look after the nicer things when required? We all have our retreats. Our places of safety. Don't we?

An interesting little addition to this, interesting to me at least, is this, I self-harmed before I joined the fire brigade and I did so, or have done so, just the once, since leaving. But I never even thought about it during my service. It never once crossed my mind. Maybe I had more of a sense of *belonging* with the fire brigade, more of a feeling of being *wanted*. Or something like that. Probably talking through my arse, again, but anyway, life is what it is, isn't it?

I have to say, Big Joe and Little Joe? I love them. I owe them everything. So, where was I? Oh yeah, my sisters. Colluding.

I wanted to just say to my sisters, 'Do you know what girls, I know you're up to something and I know what that something is…and I don't care. Knock yourselves out. Enjoy your lives.' But I couldn't. I couldn't just abandon my brother as he had abandoned me. He was dead and even though he would have nothing to do with me, I was going to do the right thing, for me, if not for him. I was going to clear up his affairs, whatever they might be. I was going to allow him to leave this world in a clean, and proper manner. And if he wanted to look down on me from his lofty perch, assuming he would occupy such a perch, and *still* treat me with contempt, then that would be his problem for all eternity. Not mine. I decided that I would get to the bottom of what was going on with my sisters if it killed me. Little did I know that it would come close.

An alert popped up on my laptop screen. I had new mail. It was from the hearse chasers. There was the usual stuff you would expect, sorry for your loss and all that shite, and the name of the person dealing with this matter, cheeky fuckers, and four attachments, that was it. Now I had a name, I went back to their Meet the Team pages and had a good look at him. He looked like a bit of a slimy fucker. End of. The attachments explained what their 'service' comprised and gave me a consent form to fill in, sign and send back to them, at which point I would be contracted to them. Their service, in essence, was filling in paperwork, sending it to the correct places, and, if you wanted it, organising the funeral. And their 'charge' was 10 percent of everything recovered. I messaged my sisters in the group conversation.

'I just got an email from the hearse chasers. It includes a form to be filled in which allows them to act on our behalf.'

Lydia replied very quickly. *'Give them my email address please Joe'*

I wasn't going to give them Lydia's email address. If I did that then I'd have to also give them Emily's email address and I thought that things would be much simpler, for all concerned, if there was just one point of contact. Me. I thought again about the deaths of my parents a while ago, and how all my sisters colluded and hid things from me and Dan. I still don't know exactly what went on but I know that something did. And then the three sisters seemed to become two, with Lydia being left out. And then it went on from there, Lydia starting an argument, making accusations, and suddenly I somehow became the fall guy. It was all very embroiled and, in the end, got quite vicious. And I had spent a good part of the last 15 years or so attempting to fix things. To fix the Croft family. I may as well have tried to fix the Arab Israeli situation. I maybe would have gotten further with that one. So, to be honest (this is a proper truth), I didn't have a lot of trust in my sisters, but this wasn't the time or the place to open that can of worms. I evaded the 'instruction' from Lydia, to give them her email address.

I messaged the group. *'OK, this is what I'll do...I'm gonna email the police and the coroner again, find the keys. I'll reply to the hearse chasers as well and tell them that all correspondence should be sent to me but cc'd to both of you as well. OK?'*

'Yeah as long as we're all getting the same emails that's fine' said Lydia.

Emily wasn't on the same page as us. She was obviously going over what the hearse chaser had said to her. *'So he blatantly lied to me.'* she said.

I wasn't really interested in anything said by anyone from the hearse chasers. Like I said earlier, they were no more than leeches and so anything said by them was, to my mind, worthless. I was NOT going to deal with them in any shape or form. Currently, they were involved only superficially and, if I had anything to do with it, they would get the heave fucking ho. Nevertheless, it seemed that Emily was a little upset by him, them, so I replied to her.

'Why what did he say?'

'He said he was contacted by the coroner.' she said.

I let that reply sink in. 'Contacted by the coroner.' I supposed that the coroner's office had better ways to use their resources, than to try to discover whether a corpse in their office, so to speak, had a relative or two plus the possible whereabouts of such relative. So, it seemed as though they gave the work to hearse chasers. I could see that such an arrangement was a necessity. I wondered how the coroner's office made their choice, how did they arrive at their preferred hearse chaser? Did some of any recovered commission find its way back to the coroner's office? As I said, I could see the necessity of this partnership, but maybe I'm just too cynical, I couldn't help but see that there was a possible 'seediness' to it. Maybe it was necessary seediness. If such a thing exists.

Lydia piped up. *'They probably were, Bagshot and Booth are a company contracted to find the next of kin when an estate is left.'*

It was almost like a sound bite. That wasn't how my sister spoke, that wasn't her phraseology at all, and I idly pondered who she had with her. A few minutes went by with no new messages flashing up. My mind was becoming agitated, like it does when there are lots of things going on inside it. Inside it. Like it's a container. A tin or a box. I felt like mine was a box, a little shoe box, mostly beige, y'know, cardboard coloured, and stuff was hanging out over the sides. It needed a sort out and a tidy up. Just the death of my brother was enough to think about and contend with. I didn't need all the negative stuff that came with my sisters. I didn't need the looking backwards at the deaths of my parents. Our parents. I didn't need, or should I say, *want*, to revisit the knowledge I had of the shenanigans of that time. I didn't *want* to but probably did *need* to revisit the knowledge, because I had a horrible feeling that, for some reason, this death of my brother, our brother, was going to be truly defining with regard to this family of mine. It had been less than 12 months since the death of my sister Carla, which had filled my head with thoughts, not all of them good. Not any of them good. And just before the death of Carla, literally just a few weeks before, was the death of Lydia's first husband, Robert, who was found at the foot of a ladder...probably doing some DIY on his place. He was a really handy fella and a good father. I can't say I missed him, because I didn't really know him, but he was a good bloke.

A message flashed up. From Emily. *'So we need to take this off them and sort this ourselves don't you guys think?'*

I replied straight away, *'yes Em I agree'*

Another message from Emily flashed up, *'need to find out where Dan is too'*

I told the group that I would try to get all relevant information and told them to keep an eye on their inbox. Emily acknowledged and said she would. Lydia didn't respond. I asked them if they'd actually seen the Death Notice in the newspaper. Emily said she hadn't, and Lydia just didn't respond. Probably busy doing something or other.

I messaged the group. *'All the death notice says is that he died at his home and that it's not being treated as suspicious and I'm guessing he's at the coroner's office, or wherever they keep bodies, awaiting a post mortem.'*

Emily replied ok and again, there was no response from Lydia. I sent another message. *'Fuckin hell y'know what I just knew something bad would happen this year with Dan, I just knew it.'*

'I did too. I spoke to him not long ago.' typed Emily.

I wondered how long ago she'd spoken to him and what was said but just as I was about to type that into the conversation, Lydia came back to it. *'Okay Joe, Angela is going to be calling a few places in the morning as well to get any information so we will all share what we have x'*

I realised that's what Lydia had been doing, chatting to her daughter. I was relieved. I'm not sure why I was relieved, but I sort of *felt* that I should be. I wondered why Angela would be making calls on our behalf and felt a little put out by this. Dan was our brother and the uncle to Angela, Angela was family but, I don't really know why, I felt that it should be one of *us*, his siblings, that ought to be making calls about his death and the whereabouts of his body and such and if Lydia, understandably, felt as though she couldn't make these calls on account of her deafness, then she should be keeping this stuff amongst us and asking one of *us*, me or Emily to make the call. I mean, I'm probably sounding a little or even a lot, sort of, I dunno, *territorial* about it but, I couldn't shake the feeling. It just didn't feel right. Not to me.

I typed a message. *'Ok ladies...shall we leave it like that for tonight then?'*

Emily replied, *'Yeah. Shit day, shit year. Night'*

I felt sorry for Emily. She seemed down, which, in the last few years seemed to be the norm for her. She had had ongoing health problems for many years. So too had Lydia and the fact that both twins seemed to always be in need of medical care made me think that maybe, when they were still in my mum's womb, which was one of the worst times to be a child in my childhood home, the high levels of adrenaline followed by cortisol in my mum's body had something to do with that...you know, similar to that foetal alcohol syndrome. I wondered if maybe there's such a thing as foetal cortisol syndrome. It would make sense that high levels of any chemical in the mother's blood would be passed through the baby's blood. It just seems logical to me but then, what do I know? I'd have to look it up sometime.

Lydia typed in, *'Yes ok let's leave it for tonight x'*

Of course, I couldn't relax now that I had things that had to be done. I was terrible for this. I was the world's worst taker of one's own advice. The number of times I would say to someone, W*ell, you know, the problem won't be solved by you working yourself into the ground. tomorrow is another day so pour yourself a beer, put your feet up and watch a bit of TV.'*

I would say such things to people and, let's face it, it's pretty sound advice. But would I do it? Yeah, I could pour myself a beer alright but would I put my feet up and watch TV? Not a chance! If I ever did try to take my own advice then the words being spoken on the TV would just be a drone in the background. All the meaningful noise would be inside my head, thoughts swirling around like flakes in a snowstorm. For me to take my own advice during such a storm was impossible…impossible until I created a mind blizzard that would align all those randomly swirling flakes and get them all going in the same direction. And once they were all going in the same direction they would begin to stack up in corners and along edges and so a plan of action would become defined. And then, only then, could I put my feet up and watch TV. Only when my mind was ordered could I relax. Which didn't mean that if my mind was ordered I could relax, if you see what I mean.

I emailed the hearse chasers and thanked them for their interest and concern but told them we would be handling matters ourselves and I told them to ensure that any belongings of my brother that they may have had, should be returned to either of my sisters, enclosing their addresses

I read all the PDF's that the hearse chasers had sent me, forwarded that email to my sisters and then messaged my sisters with my thoughts on the PDF's, *'Lydia, Em, I've read all the PDF's from the hearse chasers…the upshot is that there was a form to fill in…which…as soon as you have done so and returned it, you have given them a contract to act for us. Needless to say, I have NOT done this. I've told them we do not need them to act for us and that we will handle the matter ourselves. I've also told them to deliver to one of you EVERYTHING that they might have that belongs to Dan.'*

I wondered if my sisters had gone to bed or were they just sat there contemplating like me. I had a chat with Pam and we both thought it would be a good idea to get over to the UK as soon as we could. We started to list what we had to do with our own affairs before we could contemplate leaving.

I thought I should let my sisters know my plans ASAP, it might give them a little boost to flagging morale, so to speak, to know that they were not on their own. So, I sent another message to the group, *'We'll be over there ASAP but not sure when that will be. We've got some things to wrap up here before we can travel. I'll let you know our plans as soon as we know them. In the meantime, we all keep everyone informed of what's goin on, OK?'*

Seconds later, Lydia dropped a little bombshell. *'Joe I've not agreed to do this ourselves.'*

I was a bit flummoxed because the whole premise of using an heir hunter company in these circumstances, was, surely, dependant on there being something that would make their efforts worthwhile…or was I missing something.

My brother, *our* brother, to my knowledge, hadn't worked for a long time, maybe more than 20 years and so, whatever pension he had from his employment was almost certainly going to be small. He'd been getting his state pension for around about a year and so I felt that his mortgage would almost certainly be finished, making the property completely his. That was assuming he'd not taken out any loans or anything secured on the property or done anything daft financially that meant the property now belonged to someone else or some other organisation.

The top and bottom of it was, that I had had no meaningful contact with Dan for over half of my life and I was 63 years of age. Lydia was, apparently, keen to hand the matter of his death and the outcome of that death, whatever that proved to be, to a company that dealt in *searching* for stuff. For relatives and…papers and shit.

Well, the relatives we had. It was us three. There were no wives, no children, no-one in the world but us. One brother and two sisters. So, the only thing missing here, was papers…documents. What possible documents would Lydia expect…or maybe hope…that this company would find if they were allowed to search? A will? To will what? Like I said, I was flummoxed. This was a complication.

I texted a reply, *'Why?'*

There was no reply. I could see she was still online because her green dot was lit. I assumed she was thinking or, more than likely, chatting with her daughter Angela. I sat and watched my laptop screen for a full five minutes. My mind was fogged with questions. I asked her a question, *'So, Lydia, do you want these people to do it all?'*

Another five minutes went by. I got it into my head that she was staring at me. Don't ask me how that works because I don't know. I could almost feel the hostility, could almost feel heat radiating from my screen. Her green dot was still live, she was still there. But there was no response. I thought to myself, *Joe, it's been a long day, you're letting your imagination run riot, leave it, go to bed.* But another part of me thought that going to bed and leaving it would be tantamount to running away. And I never ran away from anything. Something wasn't right here. I had no idea what but I just felt that something was not right.

I let another five minutes tick by. It seemed like five hours. I was sat in my living room in France, looking at my laptop screen and she was sat in her house in Merseyside, looking at her screen. I could see her green dot and she could see mine. My eyes strayed to the little camera lens fitted into the top edge of the screen. I knew I had it turned off, I always did, and yet I now felt as though the lens was looking at me. I felt as though I was being stared at by my father, his jaw muscles rippling his face as he pondered whether to assault me or not…punishment or mercy…mercy or punishment. As the fifth minute passed, I messaged the group again. And covered the lens with a yellow *Post-it* note. *'Lydia? what is it you want?'*

No sooner had I sent it than there was a reply… *'Leave it till tmrw Joe x'*

It felt like an order, like an instruction. Yeah, it was softened with a little 'x', a little kiss, the equivalent, in my mind anyway, of a pat on the head…but it was an instruction. I replied straight away. By return of post, my grandma would have said. *'No Lydia. I need to know what it is you want? Are you aware that they will charge a huge amount of money — just for filling forms in? Why would you do that?'*

Lydia's smiling profile face looked out at me, eyes looking straight into the lens, straight into my eyes. Her green dot glared at me and I glared back at it. Minutes sank away into the past and suddenly her green dot disappeared too. She'd gone.

There was something wrong and she seemed reluctant to say anything in this group chat. I got the impression she was hiding something but she could have been wary of saying something in front of Emily for some reason. I messaged her on our private WhatsApp. *'Lydia are you scared of something? do you know something I don't? What's the matter?'*

There was an immediate response. It was like she'd been waiting for me. *'No Joe it's just that I know what Emily is like. She will take over and I'm not having it. I want to be the one with the keys to Daniel's flat this time. X'*

Again, my mind went into overdrive. I sort of knew what she was getting at with regards to Emily 'taking over.' She was referring to when our parents died, but I would've said that it was Carla who took over at that time and, I dunno, maybe Em wasn't fully aware of what Carla was doing. But then, this wasn't about what went on years ago, this was about now. Her message only mentioned Dan's flat, but was mixing up two things. The manipulation alarm was humming again. Not that it had stopped at all. I decided to act as though I was completely sucked in by her concerns. I wanted her to show me her hand.

'I understand perfectly Lydia, so please don't worry, Emily will NOT be having any control over this. This will be handled by all of us, no one is in charge here. He was brother to all of us and all of us will sort this out. Try not to worry.'

I thought that last message was pretty comprehensive in a relatively few words. For me, in the situation we were in, there would be leaders at different times and in different aspects and there was no need for any one person to be 'in charge' so to speak. We would all have our role, and some would be more suited to certain tasks than others. The message showed that all I was interested in was doing the right things at the right times, which, in essence, summed me up as a person. But I sensed that Lydia, maybe even both my sisters were…different than that. I always felt that they would do what suited them best in any given situation. And so I felt I had to tread carefully, had to appear to be the person they saw, which was rarely me in any case.

Lydia replied to me, *'Thank you Joe. So please let me have the keys to Dans property this time. With you being in France it's easier. XX'*

Another pat on the head. That's how it felt. Maybe I was wrong, maybe I was being too sensitive, maybe I was seeing what I wanted to see. Was I being bad minded? I'd ponder that later but, at the moment I decided to go with my gut instinct. A pat on the head it was. It was like, 'Thank you Joe, *pat, pat*, good boy, mission accomplished, now, the keys…'

Please let me have the keys? I didn't have the keys, which she knew, so, what she was doing was attempting to use me to ensure that Lydia, and not Emily, would have the keys to our brother's flat. I was to somehow obtain them and get them to Lydia. It was *easier*…because I was in France. In other words, I would be out of the way and Emily would be barred from entering the flat of our brother at will. Cynical bastard aren't I?

For me, logistically speaking, it would make sense that, if only one key was available, then out of Lydia and Emily, it should be Lydia that had it simply because she had a car at her disposal and could therefore go to the flat at any time she chose. Having said that, it also made sense that everyone, all of us, including me in France, should have access to the flat at any time. Yet Lydia had made no mention of any other key being made or found or anything. She wanted exclusive access to the flat. And she wanted me to obtain it for her. She wanted me to 'take charge' of

Emily and safeguard Lydia's exclusivity. It crossed my mind that Angela was at university studying psychology.

I could almost imagine Angela discussing what Lydia should say to me, how she should say it, even typing it out, pretending to be Lydia with Lydia sat next to her, nodding and agreeing before the send button was pressed. *Thank you Joe…*act like the 'big man' has the power to grant you your wishes, use his name, put a full stop after it to emphasise the sentence, the impact of those three little words… *Thank you Joe.* You are so kind to me, your worried little sister, fretting about the big bad-mouthed, straight talking, weed-smoking twin sister.

Then the *So please…*imploring, beseeching, then, *let me have…*allow me, grant me, I know you have the power to grant me this wish so please, please do so…and then, it would be so much *easier…*with you being in France.

It all reminded me of something that I couldn't put my finger on. It was there, on the periphery of my vision, like seeing that dark shape in your bedroom when you wake from a nightmare that shifts and threatens when you're not looking at it but disappears when you try to pin it down. Whatever it was, was on the edge of my mind and I couldn't grab it, couldn't *get* to it.

I messaged her, *'When you say, 'this time', does that mean there's been another time when someone other than Dan has had control of a key to his flat?'*

There was a lull. Lydia was there but she went quiet. My question was apparently unplanned for, a little bit out of left field maybe. I say the question was maybe unplanned for but, y'know, this was the second time she'd used the phrase in the last few minutes. I waited for her to reply. I wanted to type out another message, saying that she had used the term twice in a few minutes but thought that it would be better to leave the gap and wait to see what, if anything, came into it.

Six and a half minutes went by and then she stepped into the gap, *'My dad's. She n Carla had control over dads. I had no part of it and I was pissed off.'*

That, in my mind at least, didn't fit with the statements she'd made. She'd said, written, on two separate occasions that she wanted to be the one with the keys to *Daniel's flat*...on *this occasion*, at *this time*. Reading those statements, over and over, you *could* put it down to bad use of the language, poor sentence construction, whatever, but...I dunno, for me, it was a bit of a stretch to do that in this case. For me, the two statements she'd made *told* me that there had been at least one other time when, for whatever reason, Dan had relinquished sole control over who accessed his flat, and, given the keys to someone other than Lydia.

I asked myself if it mattered. Was it relevant, to *me*, that he may have done this at some time in the past? A past that, for whatever reason, my brother had decided I was not a part of? Did it *really* matter? *Now*? I came to the conclusion that, in *itself*, the possibility of this key tenure thing wasn't important. It would or *could* only become important if it was part of the overall feelings of wrongness. I decided that a stance of innocent neutrality at this point would be more beneficial to me. I made my reply quickly, *'Ok I'll send another email to the hearse chasers (not cc'd to Emily) asking them to get the keys to you asap.'*

Lydia was apparently intent on having more to say about the deaths of our parents, but all I could see was someone who was mixing two different eras in the murky Croft family history and trying to muddy the present day waters. Another message arrived from her. '*I know about dads*' she typed, '*but not the details. I still have lots of questions about both deaths. I was left out in mum's as well. I wanted to have a part of it but had nothing xx*'

I didn't want to get side-tracked and let the deaths of years ago interfere with this present one and the questions surrounding it so I tried to shelve it. '*Yeah well, I know how you feel about it Lydia. There were some discrepancies back then. I wrote it all down at the time but shall we save that for another day?*'

A few minutes went by and then she pinged back into the conversation, '*Good I'm glad you did bro x Thanks xx*'

So she was glad I'd written things down all those years ago. I'm not sure she'd be so glad if she was to read the things I'd written down all those years ago because, she wasn't as 'left out' as she liked to claim. The thing was, it all happened years ago, nothing was going to be owned up to, admitted, reconciled, so, what was the point of dredging it all up. It was water well and truly disappeared under the bridge and we had more pressing matters to be concerned about.

I had a beer and watched some telly.

Chapter 4 - The Red Kettle

Thursday 18ᵗʰ October 2018

I woke up about seven thirty, which was a little late for me. Normally I'd wake about six to six thirty and acclimatise myself to the day, think through what I was going to do, where I needed to go, and so on. I lay looking at the ceiling, a typical French country house ceiling of pine tongue and groove painted white. Sorry France but, it's not a good look. I don't care why you do it, how cheap it is etcetera…it looks shit. As a lot of French 'décor' does. They haven't got the foggiest idea when it comes to this stuff but constantly drone on about how 'chic' they are. Anyway, for the hundredth time I examined the ceiling, the sound of a crowing cock drifting in through the open window.

It was still quite hot where we live, and the sun was making its way around to the back of our property. We're south facing and once the sun gets on the back, it can become quite stifling. Nice but not always so. October back home in Liverpool could easily be sunny…but cold. Here, the cold didn't arrive until quite a way through November but once it did, it was just the same as Liverpool.

As I lay there, I remembered waking from a disturbing dream, one of those dreams that seem so real that when you wake up, it's hard to work out what's what, hard to shake off the grip it has on you.

It was about my brother. He was standing looking at me from some trees. I think they were fir trees but that isn't definite. I could make out the fir tree shape from their silhouette against a night sky, black on lighter black. I don't know where I was but I was outside. It was raining, quite hard and the rain was running in rivers down my face and dripping down onto my chest. It was warm. I shouted him but the words wouldn't come out. They were loud in my mind but I couldn't get them to come out of my mouth. I was looking at him and he was staring at me. I couldn't see his eyes, but I felt them. I tried to move towards him but couldn't because my feet wouldn't move. I tried to beckon him but I couldn't move my arms. He was about 30 feet away, standing at the edge of the trees, absolutely still, just looking over. The rain got heavier and heavier and the sound of it was roaring in my ears and drumming on the top of my head. He started to become obscured by it, slowly fading and receding into it and then, I just couldn't see him anymore. I felt like he was still there and so I stayed there, the rain battering down at me for what seemed like ages and all the time I was trying to call him back to where I could see him but, he was gone.

When I woke up, I could still hear the rain for a while. It wasn't raining in the real world but I could hear it pattering on my head. There was a hollow feeling inside me. That's the best way I can describe it. There was something missing from inside me and I was bothered by this feeling. I loved my brother, had never stopped loving him but, he had turned his back on me a long time ago. Over three decades. How could I feel as though a part of me was missing? I couldn't work it out. I lay there and looked at the ceiling. The join between the ceiling and the walls. The door. The dressing gown hanging on the back of the door. They were all exactly as I remembered them from the last time I lay here and did a recce of the room just, I don't know, hours ago? Days? I didn't know. I couldn't work it out. They were all the same and yet they were different. Very different. For the first time in my whole life, I was viewing a world that my brother didn't inhabit. And somehow it looked different. I realised, not for the first time in my life, what a big thing this was. This dying. It was big. Very big. I got up and got dressed.

As I was waiting for the kettle to boil, I checked to see if I'd had any messages during the night. I keep my phone under my pillow, so I can use the torch on it for when I need to pee in the night but the sound is always turned off. There had been a message to the Messenger group, from Emily at 01:32 UK time.

'I'm not signing anything with them. They are in charge then, as if we're thick and we can't sort it ourselves. We can.'

Obviously, she was referring to the hearse chasers and I was glad she was on the same page as me. Lydia was on her own with this and so would get voted down.

Pam and I had breakfast, muesli for Pam with a big mug of tea, coffee for me with a bowl of All Bran, Sugar Puffs and Corn Flakes. All in the same bowl. I often mixed two or three cereals together, I don't know why. Maybe the other people living inside me wanted different things for breakfast, who knows?

Once breakfast was out of the way, I sat down with my laptop on my lap, just where it should be, opened up Messenger and sent a message to the group. *'Yes Em I agree. We can do everything ourselves. The hearse chasers would just become a middle man then claim their commission for filling a few forms in and as far as I'm concerned that is not gonna happen. I've been ripped off one too many times in my life and I'm not gonna be ripped again'*

As I sent the message, an email arrived from the hearse chasers, telling me that they did not have anything belonging to my brother and understood I didn't want them to act for me but that they needed my sisters to fill in the same forms as well, so asked me for their email addresses. Again, I was incensed that they had just *injected* themselves into our lives via the death of our brother and I wanted to just tell them to fuck off. But I knew that these bastards would be persistent and that *fuck off* wouldn't work. I gave them the email addresses and told my sisters about the development.

Lydia pinged into the joint Messenger convo. *'Spoke to the coroners. Daniel might have died 5-6 weeks ago. They are doing a post-mortem today. The police were called after neighbour reported not seeing him for a while. They forced entry. Found him under a pile of rubbish. Had to get fire brigade in to get him out x'*

The first thing to spring into my mind was the time. It was nearly eight thirty in the morning in France, making it nearly seven thirty in the morning in Liverpool. And she had spoken to the coroner's office? *What time do they get to work?* I thought. And the next thing was those simple statements, written the way they were. A few little words but a nightmare scenario was unfolding in front of me.

A six-week-old corpse buried in rubbish. Firefighters digging him out. Bagging him up. Carrying him downstairs. Undertakers boxing him up and putting him in the van. Then driving him down his own street, past the places he knew well, to another place where they'd store him in a fridge. These were all words that belonged to me, not my brother. These were all words that were part of my job for over three decades, part of my life. Jobs involving people, bodies, corpses, injuries, car crashes, suicides, drownings, electrocutions this was *my life*, not my brother's. Or my sisters'. This was not the way things were supposed to be. Other people became part of a firefighter's list of casualties dealt with… not my family.

I knew, some time ago, that my brother was a bit of a hoarder but, what did they mean by 'rubbish'? Did they mean his fishing magazines? I knew he'd kept stacks and stacks of them. I also knew that he tended to collect flattened beer cans until the bin was full before putting them out for the bin man. In the 30 years or so that I hadn't had contact with him, had he taken to 'collecting' other stuff?

My mind was overloaded and slightly disorientated. I couldn't, at that moment, assimilate all the information. I'd 'work' on it as we went along, let it sink in as and when it sunk in.

'Shit that's terrible' I typed.

Lydia pinged again. *'I got the forms from them. Reading through them now. Speak later.'*

I acknowledged Lydia's message, typed that I had to go out for a little while and went for a ride on my bike. It was lovely weather, and I donned helmet, jacket and shorts, and went cycling. I put shoes and socks on too. Well, you have to don't you. I felt like I needed to get some air deep inside me and beast myself. As best I could for a 63-year-old. I still had something about me when it came to exercising, could still 'put a shift in' so to speak. I liked to think so anyway. Nothing like I could in my 40's or 20's…almost forgot my 30's there…but still pretty good for my age I'd guess. I only did about 15 miles or so, twice around a little circuit through the fields and lanes by the house, but it's the *way* you cycle that matters, not the distance. As hard as I could all the way. Hard until I needed to rest, rest until I recovered then hard again, over and over. It's got a name, that kind of exercise. Can't quite recall it but I know it's got a name. It's in there somewhere, filed away. Anyway, I worked quite a sweat up, went home and showered. That feeling, for me, is one of the best feelings. Hard work, sweat and hot shower, as hot as you can stand. Makes me feel like I exist, like I'm more *visible* than normal, less like Mr Nobody and more like, er…Mr Somebody whose name escapes me. I feel like I have a place in the world that is known, recognizable, y'know, a *real* place. I know I'm not explaining that very well but, at the moment, it's all I can come up with. It makes me feel 'cleansed' in some way, does for my mind what I imagine a dermabrasion treatment does for your skin, or a colonic irrigation might do for your innards. Not that I've ever tried either of those things.

I got dressed after my shower, as it was the polite thing to do, went to the kitchen and drank a pint of water mixed with my peach syrup. Then poured another to be drunk more leisurely, sat down and reached for my laptop. I opened Messenger and went to the group chat we'd been having.

There was nothing new. The thought of my brother being dug out of a mound of rubbish came to my mind and I pondered that for a while. It was hard enough to think of him as a corpse, let alone a corpse hidden under a pile of rubbish. How had he gotten there? Did it fall on him? Did he burrow into it? Lie down and scoop it onto himself? What? The fire brigade had to 'dig him out.' That conjured up some pictures for me. I'd dug corpses out of stuff before. One corpse, poor bastard, we had to get out of a grain silo. Let me tell you, you do not want to get yourself into a grain silo, not without proper equipment...because if you go in with no gear, you'll be getting dug out by firefighters. And you will be dead. No question. It's like quicksand. Standing on grain, you just sink and very quickly. And the more you try not to sink, the more you sink. We had to empty the silo from the bottom to get to him. It was not a quick job. I'm not sure if it was a quick death, but, I hope it was. He must have dropped something in from the top, possibly his glasses because we extracted him and a pair of glasses. I know he could have been wearing them when he went in and they came off but, y'know, he got in there for some reason and no-one could give us one and people, when confronted with other people who have died a needless death, will look for reasons for that death. That's just a fact. You need an *explanation* of some kind. If there isn't one, you'll weigh up the facts, then make one up.

So, I know what it means when the likes of the police stand aside and call for the fire brigade to extract a body by digging it out. I know that the police are capable of digging some rubbish away from a corpse and so, as my mind started to get into my old fireground groove, I started to assess the situation.

In a nutshell...the police will have broken the door in and entered the property. They would have been hit by a god-awful smell. Stench would be a better word. As police officers, they would have known they had a rotting corpse to deal with. They would have made a cursory examination of the property and come to the conclusion that there was a body under the rubbish. At that point, they would know they were not equipped to deal with the situation. It would require people with the correct personal protective equipment and the correct tools…which means firefighters. The brigade would have been called to a non-emergency situation 'assisting police.' so, normal road speed, no blue lights. The officer in charge of the fire engine would have assessed the situation and the firefighters would have donned appropriate PPE. They'd have gone in and carefully removed the rubbish from around the body, uncovering a possible crime scene, hence the care. When the body was uncovered, a CID officer would have assessed the situation and decided that it wasn't a crime scene and so recovery of the body would have been undertaken. The body would have been bagged up, taken out of the premises and become the property of the undertakers acting for the Coroner, who would put it in their van and take it to the appropriate morgue, where it would await a post-mortem. I'd done it all enough times to know what was what.

I decided that I'd try to speak to some fire brigade people…especially the station that would have got the job. I'd start with my mate Dennis and was just about to message him on Messenger, when Emily pinged into the group conversation.

'So has anyone been in touch with the hearse chasers and told them to hand stuff back to us immediately? B4 the sneaky fucker goes into our Dans flat on his own because he will. I'll ring them now if no one has.'

'Yes Em.' I replied. *'Scroll up.'*

Two minutes later, she was back. *'Ok, got the forms from them, sent it back, told them to fuck off. So where are the keys? How do we get into his flat?'*

I had to laugh. I loved these conversations with Emily. No messing about, no soft talking, no buttering up, just straight to the point. Very business-like. When it suited.

Lydia appeared. *'Right, Angela has spoken to the coroner's office and the heir hunter people. They have said that if they handle things, they will cover everything, arranging the funeral costs, registering, filling out any documentation, searching for the will if there is one etc. We can be as involved as we want in arranging the funeral they don't just take over. They've said if a will is recovered, they don't get any of the estate even if they have already paid for the funeral etc and that whoever is stated in the will gets everything. They don't have access to the flat and don't have any property belonging to Daniel. I would prefer the heir hunters to handle things as it means everything is covered, they know what they are doing and we won't be fighting over who does what. Their costs are 10 percent plus vat.'*

Once again, I was a little bit 'put out' that Angela was being given the wherewithal to act on my behalf. I was actually beginning to get a bit wound up about it. I read and re-read what Lydia had just sent to the group and I was…perturbed, shall we say. I couldn't believe that someone could be so naïve, but then, Angela was, in my opinion, someone who had little or no life experience, she was a young woman with all sorts of knowledge gleaned from books and lecturers but…y'know what I'm saying? If it was Angela doing all the talking, or, to be probably more precise, doing all the listening on the phone to the hearse chasers, then she was being spun a line and wasn't listening properly, because there were a few holes in what was being reported to me and Emily…from Lydia…via Angela…in this group. A few gaping holes.

For a start, I was…interested, for want of a better word…in the phrase '*searching for the will if there is one etc*'. If I'd been making this 'report' I'd have said 'a will' not 'the will.' It's just a word and a little one at that but, it was one of those *anomalies* as I call them. It was just something that didn't sit comfortably in the scheme of things as I saw them. Another phrase she'd used…'*arranging the funeral costs*'. Arranging the funeral costs isn't the same as paying them, that's obvious, yet Lydia or Angela seemed to believe that this company *were* going to pay for the funeral, or they wanted us to believe that this company were going to pay for the funeral, otherwise I could see no reason for her statement that '*if a will is recovered, they don't get any of the estate even if they have already paid for the funeral etc*'.

Another little anomaly was the statement about whoever is named in *the* will, gets everything. And this was all gleaned at first reading. I felt sure that the more I read and re-read her message to the group, the more strangenesses I would discern.

If I distanced myself from the whole thing and read what she'd said as a newcomer to the conversation or as an onlooker, I would probably think that she *knew* of the existence of a will but was trying to both put me and Emily, the onlookers if you like, the audience to this…communication from Lydia, off the scent and *warn* us of an impending *discovery*. Again, something didn't sit right with me and I questioned myself, asking if I was applying fairness to my assessments.

Asking if I was applying 'reasonable man tests' to things. My gut feeling was that I *was* being fair, but I decided to shelve my feelings, for now, and see what panned out. Talking of gut feelings, I felt that, even if my brother *had* left a will, he would be more likely to leave everything to the dogs' home or something like that.

I made a little statement of my own to the group…mostly for Emily's benefit. *'Listen girls, don't worry about the hearse chasers because they can't do anything at all without a signed contract by all three of us and I will certainly not be signing any contract with them.'* I then asked an obvious question. *'So, Lydia, are you saying that this company are willing to pay* up front *for a funeral for our brother?'*

There was no reply. No comment from either of them. I waited five minutes or so and then threw another comment in, *'Well, all I can say to you Lydia is No. I don't agree with using this company. If you're not confident of dealing with all this then leave it to me. I'll deal with the lot. It's not a problem'*

Lydia came back at me very quickly. *'So who's paying for the funeral then?'*

'It's the same as most other funerals Lydia,' I typed, *'the deceased pays for it. Dan has an estate, he owns his property, he maybe has money in the bank, he maybe has life insurance. We need to calm down and look at all these things first, don't you think? But the main thing to bear in mind here is that some random company of hearse chasers are NOT gonna just stump up £4k to pay for our brother's funeral with no guarantee of getting it back…and that's just common sense.'*

There were a few minutes of nothing. Both my sisters' green dots were lit so I knew they were there. I wondered if they were having a private conversation in the background. Not that it mattered. Lydia pinged up. *'No you won't do it all Joe.'* she said, which was a bit of a red rag to me. *'It's already happening we are arguing! His estate won't pay for the funeral as we won't have access to it for a while so we will have to pay'*

'No Lydia' I said, *'that is not the case at all. None of us can be* made *to pay for anything. Dan has an estate and that estate pays his debts, including* HIS *funeral expenses. There is a strict protocol as to who and what gets paid first from a decedent's estate and I feel pretty certain that a funeral will be at the top of that list based purely on the fact that no one wants a dead body just hanging about for ever. And we're not* arguing, *we're* discussing *things. Or at least,* I am.*'*

Lydia was intent on putting forward what she thought, which was fine, but, y'know, there comes a point when surely you can see that maybe what you're saying just doesn't have any substance? Doesn't it? I mean, our brother dies and *suddenly* a member of his family is *plunged* into debt because *someone somewhere* will insist on a funeral being arranged and paid for, like, *NOW*?

'They don't release everything immediately.' she said, *'it takes a while for everything to be put in place and the funeral would be arranged for next week or the following and we're not going to have access to anything before then'*

She seemed to be panicking and I couldn't work out why. This was only day two since we discovered his death. Day two. What on earth was the rush? *'Lydia, I really think you need to just walk away from this for a few minutes.'* I said. *'There is no rush to do anything.'*

For the first time in what seemed like ages, Emily entered the conversation. *'His funeral is covered by his estate, once his estate is sorted out through probate then the funeral people take the funeral costs. Lydia I'm not agreeing to the hearse chasers either. I'm willing to sort my brother's funeral out for him'*

I agreed with Em. I have to say that I thought Lydia was in a flap and needed to calm down before she did something stupid. *'Think about it Lydia,'* I typed, *'we can arrange a funeral, it's easy, we've all done it before. We can sell his home, I've bought and sold half a dozen houses, that's easy as well. I've never done a probate claim but how hard can it be? From what I understand, it's basically the government working out how much money they can steal from you in the form of a tax, which means that we fill in the right form at the right time and send it to the right department...it can't really be anything else can it?'*

'The hearse chasers are just people who are willing to do all the dirty work for a fee and I am not letting them do anything.' said Emily, reinforcing everything I'd said.

'Why on earth' I typed, *'would we pay someone else 10 percent of his estate to do what we can do? Just think, suppose his estate was worth £100k, which is not a huge sum of money these days, especially when he owns a property outright. If we let them do the work, they will take £12,000 off us including VAT. Why would you want to do that? Sorry Lydia, but it's ridiculous to even consider it.'*

'I agree,' said Emily. *'But we all do it together. Lydia, they are people who work for people who are thick, lazy or incapable of sorting things out and we are none of those things. Lydia it really is silly giving strangers anything when we are capable, we really are'*

There was a bit of chat between me and Emily, mostly underlining and repeating what had already been said and I again reiterated that all this to-ing and fro-ing didn't constitute an argument. We discussed what we thought we knew about the probate process and stuff like that. A good 10 to 15 minutes went by where Lydia was there but made no comment. She was digitally staring at us. I could almost feel it. I was beginning to notice a real…sinister trend. Maybe sinister was too strong a word but, if I could think of a word that meant the same but was a little less severe, I'd use it here. Just thought of one…disquieting. Yeah, I was beginning to find Lydia's way of dealing with this a little disquieting. As I was busy becoming disquieted, Lydia pinged up, *'If you don't want heir hunters to get involved then I'm handling it.'*

Now, call me a bit of a diva or a prima donna or whatever, but NOW, I was properly disquieted. I found that last comment to be sinister, never mind disquieting. I was becoming sinisterised.

Emily responded while I was in the throes of disengaging myself from being disquieted and converting to being sinisterised. Do you find that you use a new word as often as you can? I do. Sometimes.

'We are all handling it Lydia not just you not just Joe not just me, all of us'

Emily was spot on and I was just about to shrug off my sinisterisation, yet another new word, and back her up when Lydia replied. *'That's fine we will work together. But I'll handle things first.'*

There was a sort of stunned digital silence. I broke it; *'What do you mean by that Lydia?'*

Lydia didn't reply. Instead, the WhatsApp app made a noise on my phone and I looked at it. It was Emily. *'What the fuck is Lydia on about? I'm handling things first? WTFF?'*

'I don't know. Stay calm.' I said.

Emily was as fast as Lydia on the typing. *'Lydia really needs to chill out.'* It seemed that Emily was becoming disquieted as well.

'I know' I said, *'she's panicking for some reason'*

Emily dragged us back into the group Messenger chat. *'What gives you the right to demand and say I'm handling things first? Whats that all about? We are all his siblings Lydia'*

That was very diplomatic for Emily and I silently congratulated her. I knew or at least felt that she wanted to blow her top. I added to what she'd said, *'Can I just underline that we don't want this to break out into an argument. We should avoid any kind of inflammatory language and so Lydia, you cannot make demands.'*

What I said made no difference. Lydia had created a spark with her comment about handling it first, whatever the fuck that meant and now the spark found its way to the fuse and an argument exploded between my sisters. It went from nought to sixty in the blink of an eye and I was taken back to my childhood, back to the living room of our house in Halewood, where my father had come in from the pub one Saturday afternoon, full of joy and happiness, a rarity in that house.

Sometime in the late 1960's

He'd probably had a good win on the horses, Everton had won, and everything was good in the world. He told my mum that they were going out for their tea and to get herself ready. He boiled a kettle of water to take up for a shave and, for some reason known only to my mum, she took against this rushing about to get ready to go out and it showed. I, like my brother and sisters, was, excited I suppose the word is because, our parents would be out for ages and we could watch telly, eat crisps, and drink lemonade all night without a care in the world. It was a taste of freedom, though we never actually thought of it like that. And so, I was put out at my mum being put out. Don't get me wrong, I get where she was coming from, y'know, he comes in, full of the joys of spring, looking to get ready and go straight out, whereas she'd been shopping, cleaning, cooking and all the other things she would have done that day, and suddenly here he is, the big man, he comes in, clicks his fingers, and hey presto we're all supposed to be full of the joys of spring along with him. I get why she would not be jumping through hoops. I get it. But y'know, doesn't there come a time when, for the greater good, you just go with what makes life easy for everyone? Shouldn't that be a consideration? And when the person 'calling the shots' is, basically, a thug, and can and will cause murder for everyone if a stick is shoved through his spokes, shouldn't that be a consideration too? Maybe I'm right, maybe I'm wrong, but I know that on that day, in my mind, a voice was shouting out to my mum to just go with the flow. He was not, no matter what you wanted, no matter what would be the right thing, the kind of person you could reason with, so, y'know, why try? Not that trying to reason with him was what she did because she didn't. She went at things as if she was deliberately trying to cause trouble. Which is exactly what happened.

My mum had recently bought a new kettle. One that you put on the gas ring, not an electric one. Electric ones were only for posh people. Having said that, this new one was a bit special. It was metallic red and instead of having a whistle that came off, it had a hinged top spout thing, and instead of whistling it hummed like some kind of musical instrument. It was my mum's pride and joy. Her red kettle.

Anyway, on this day, it was used to carry up some boiling water for our father to have a shave. We could hear him singing in the bathroom. He was a good singer. My mum was too and they would sometimes duet while getting ready to go out. He was singing a Matt Monro song, Born Free. Me and Dan had been to see the film, which was great, we loved it. Our father must have had a really big win on the horses and the 'feel good factor' was beginning to infect us. The next thing, the door to the bathroom could be heard opening and then there was an almighty crash and smashing sound, as the kettle came hurtling down the stairs, bouncing on one of them, and smashing through the window at the side of the front door, going down the path like one of the Dam Busters bouncing bombs and hitting the front gate with a clatter. The funny thing was, the hummer hummed as it went past the living room door. I almost laughed.

There was a stunned silence in the house for about a minute and then we heard my mum go up the stairs and a row started that went from a few imperceptible words to anguished muffled screams within 30 seconds. There was the sound of a struggle on the landing and I thought my mum was going to get thrown down the stairs, then footsteps ran into my bedroom above us and the door was slammed shut then it was slammed open, crashing into the bedroom wall, then another scuffling, fast moving struggle that danced across the floor above us, muffled screams and shouts, noises like something hard hitting something solid but not like, say, a piece of wood hitting a stone, more of a solid meaty sound and then there was just silence.

A few minutes went by and then footsteps, soft and light, went quietly across my room and along the landing. Soft footsteps, like the kind I'd expect from my mum, not aggressive enough to be my father's. I looked at Dan and it was obvious, to me anyway, that he was thinking the same as me, that the footsteps belonged to our mum, which meant that she was walking away from him, that she was walking along the landing and our dad was still in my bedroom, not making a sound. That maybe she'd killed him. Maybe, I thought, maybe, she'd gone upstairs with a knife or something and maybe she'd stabbed him, and he was dead. Hope blossomed in my heart as I realised that those retreating footsteps had been my mum's, they must have been my mum's. I almost wanted to cheer as I realised that it was her who had emerged triumphant from my bedroom.

All of us were too scared to move. We didn't even speak. We just looked at each other and at the ceiling, like we were trying to see through it. Our eyes were wide. The faces of my siblings were pale, ashen. I assume mine was the same. Carla was shaking. I was desperate to know what had happened but daren't move. All we could do was wait.

A door closed quietly upstairs. It was the door to our parent's room. I could tell what all the sounds made in our house meant. Or nearly all. Footsteps came softly down the stairs and I was staring at the living room door, waiting for it to open, waiting for my mum to come in to tell us that it was all over, that we could breathe and live, when, instead, the front door opened and then quietly closed. And then I saw my dad walking down the path, dressed in his going out stuff, suit, white shirt and tie, shiny shoes. He opened and quietly closed the gate as he went through it, the kettle softly grating on the path. I jumped up and hid

behind the curtains to watch where he was going. He went to the bus
stop on the main road. Which meant he was going to the pubs in Hunts
Cross or Woolton. Maybe even Liverpool city centre. I waited a few
minutes until a bus came. It stopped and I could just see the back half of
it sticking out beyond the walls of the pub. If he got on it, he'd go
upstairs where you could smoke, and he'd go to the back if he could. I
saw him walking to the back of the upstairs. And he was lighting a
cigarette as the bus pulled away.

We went upstairs and found our mum lying on the floor of my
bedroom. She was conscious but covered in blood from her nose, which
was broken. Her lips were split, and her left eye was already massively
swollen, black, purple and closed. Her face looked strange and it
transpired that her left cheekbone was broken. A thought was running
through my head, over and over. I couldn't stop it. 'You should have just
got ready and gone out mum.' *Was all I could think.*

Dan was helping mum get herself together and I retrieved the kettle
from the path. It had a few dinges, and a few scratches but I needed it to
make my mum a cup of tea. I filled it and put it on the stove. It still
worked. The hummer still hummed but sounded a little bit weird. Funny.
As in humorous. But weird.

And so, returning to the here and now, my sisters, Emily and Lydia,
went at it for a little while, typing furiously to each other, no doubt
hitting the keys or their phone screens hard, as if raising their voices,
neither of them bothering to read what the other had written, both intent
on emitting as much bile as they possibly could in as short a time as
possible.

I let the double tirade slow down and when I felt that it had abated, I jumped in, *'Right, where was I? Oh yeah, Lydia, I don't think it's a good idea for you to make demands'*

My sisters had argued about who had done what when our parents died. They'd been divorced for 20 years and had never set eyes on each other in all of those 20 years. My mum wasn't ill or anything, y'know, she didn't have anything *terminal*, she just got sick enough to go into hospital suddenly and the next thing she was dead. Just like that. It was like he crooked his finger at her.

Anyway, Lydia was aggrieved that she hadn't had much of an input into either of those funerals, but I was pretty sure that at that time, Lydia hadn't even lived on Merseyside, I was almost certain that she was living in the midlands with Edward. They also argued about this upcoming funeral and who would do what and who would pay for what. Lydia was definitely panicking but I couldn't for the life of me think why. There was a definite edge to her demeanour. Listen to me, talking about demeanour when all I'm going on is written words in a computer chat thing, whatever they call it. Lobby. Room. But, I dunno, you get a flavour of mood don't you, and if you know the person, you get an idea of what body language would belong to a particular group of words and so maybe me talking about demeanour in a Messenger chat is not so strange. The thing was, our brother was our brother and family is family but, y'know, at the end of the day, our brother hadn't cared that much about any of us and had not had a whole lot of time for us or any of our kids. My daughter Katie was the oldest of all our kids at 32 and Dan had seen her twice I think, back when she was a toddler. He even bought her a Christmas present. A little ball. So, y'know, in a nutshell, I couldn't quite get my head around the panic that Lydia was displaying. It was another anomaly in a sea of anomalies. A sea of anomalies. Get me.

I typed another message into the conversation, *'One of the first things we have to do is secure his property.'*

No response was made to this and I was about to type it again when my sisters went in for round two. They went over all the stuff they'd argued about just minutes before and I found the whole thing depressing as fuck. I monitored the arguing, looking for significant things said, but there was nothing, just a lot of to and fro on how funerals get paid for and who did what back then and who should do what now. On and on.

It was getting on for dinner time so I made some tea and toast. With marmalade. A healthy dollop of it per slice. French marmalade…it's ok but I'd give it no more than a six out of ten. Not like your normal Chivers' or Rose's Lime Marmalade. Now *that* is a marmalade I love. When I was a kid, my mum would buy Rose's Lime Marmalade but we weren't allowed to have it. I'm not sure why, maybe it was too expensive to give to the kids. Actually, now that I've mentioned it, there were a number of foodstuffs in our house that were exclusive to the adults. I'll have a think on that and get back to you with an exhaustive list. So don't go away. Getting back to the jam and stuff, we, the kids, could only have the jam or the orange marmalade, the cheap ones. When mum wasn't looking though, by which I generally mean she was out of the house, I would nick the odd spoonful of her exclusive Rose's Lime Marmalade. Anyway, to return to my original point, the French haven't got a clue about marmalade. Not a clue. Marmalade half-wits. All the stuff they sell is like the cheap stuff I was allowed as a kid. Every time we go to England, usually in November, I will go through a jar, or two, of good

English marmalade. And bring a few jars back with me. And every time I dip into a jar of Rose's Lime Marmalade, every single time, I am transported to the kitchen of my childhood and the sneaking out of banned foodstuffs. Good old days…not. See, you've digressed me again.

I came back to the Messenger conversation. They were talking about *when* a funeral gets paid for.

Lydia was still in panic mode. *'Who's going to pay for the funeral? we're not going to get any help before, and you have to claim from his estate afterwards and I can't afford a funeral.'*

Is that what this was all about I wondered. Is Lydia thinking that she is going to have to somehow pay for a funeral?

'Listen everyone,' I typed, *'nobody is going to have to pay for a funeral. None of us have got money put aside to pay for our brother's funeral and no-one is going into debt to pay for the funeral of someone who has treated us all the way he has treated us, brother or no brother…so don't be panicking over a funeral. We have more pressing matters at the moment. Someone has to go and ensure that the property is secure and get a hold of his documents etc.'*

Another five minutes of arguing about funerals went on between my sisters and I was getting close to the end of my tether with them. No-one even acknowledged that I'd said anything. Like I said, I don't even think they were bothering to look at what their opponent was saying, they were just typing comments and arguments, regardless.

I typed it again, with a little addition from my Ouija board days, *'HELLO! ANYBODY THERE? KNOCK ONCE FOR YES, TWICE FOR NO! Someone has to secure the property and the documents!'*

They weren't listening so I started using all capitals. They were louder than lower case. *'DAN MIGHT HAVE LIFE INSURANCE! HE OWNS THE PROPERTY! HE HAS AN ESTATE! WILL YOU STOP WITH THE ARGUING FOR FUCKS SAKE!'*

They stopped with the arguing. No one said anything for about five minutes. I had a picture in my mind of all of us sitting staring at our screens. Emily broke the silence, *'Lydia I know it's not about money but at the end of the day, heir hunters are not entitled to have a penny are they? Be truthful now.'*

Lydia made no response. I started to ponder the turn to money rather than funerals and then thought better of it. I just wanted to ensure that the property was made safe. Y'know, if the police had broken in then the likelihood was that the door was in little pieces. They couldn't break in like firefighters. The police always went for the lock, whereas we always went for the hinges. Hinges are held on by screws, locks are often mortised into the frame. Simple really. A well-aimed blow at the hinge with a heavy sledgehammer often does the trick in one but smashing a mortice lock in often takes a lot of blows.

'You BOTH need to get into the flat ASAP and get all his documents into safe keeping.' I typed. Again.

There was a general discussion between me and Emily as to where the keys to the property would be. I doubted that there would be much need for keys. If I'd been there, I would have just gone round to the flat and taken it from there.

Emily asked a question, *'So what do we do? Shall I ring the police and ask them about the keys or what? I'm gonna ring them now.'* she said and disappeared.

I was pondering. Maybe, I thought, the keys were on my brother's person when his body was taken to the mortuary. If so, the mortuary staff would have packeted them up ready for collection by someone. I quickly compiled an email for the coroner's office but before I sent it Emily came back on.

'Coroner and police don't have any keys. The door had to be smashed open.'

'And Joe said that heir hunters don't have the keys' said Lydia.

Emily replied, *'I've just said that the door had to be smashed open, the place will be boarded up. We have to go there and secure documents and stuff.'*

I commented that I agreed with Emily and was about to say that someone should get there asap when Lydia sent us a curve ball. Whatever that is. American baseball term, I think. I'm gonna replace that with an English term. Lydia sent us a googly. Whatever that is. I know it's cricket and I know it's something to do with bowling but cricket was never my game. Boring. I'd rather watch paint dry. In fact, I'd rather drink the paint. Lydia commented from left field. Whatever that means. Ahh fuck it, you get the picture.

'Just queried with 2 funeral directors and they expect an upfront payment of over £1000.' she typed.

This took me by surprise. I think it took Emily by surprise too because she never typed a word. What was Lydia talking about? Why on earth was she going off and looking into funerals? Wasn't it a bit sudden? Why the rush? I just couldn't work it out. She was panicking, but why? Our brother had died. People die all the time. Why the urgency about the funeral? We hadn't even secured his property. Surely there should be some kind of structure to what we were doing. The feeling of unease grew the more I took part in this conversation.

'Lydia' I said. *'There's no rush to get a funeral organised. We'll get to that in good time. Right now, I think we should concentrate on securing the property, gathering documents etc.'*

Emily WhatsApped me privately. *'WTF?'*

'Dunno.' I replied.

Emily messaged the group conversation. *'Lydia I'm willing to meet you wherever you want. I'll get a cab and we go sort something out at Dan's place hey?'*

I think Emily was trying to swerve Lydia away from her headlong rush into the arms of a funeral director. Lydia didn't respond. A few minutes went by.

'So Lydia,' I typed, *'there's no need to be rushing into the arms of a funeral director yet. Shall we just concentrate on the property and documents for now?'*

Almost straight away a reply zapped onto my screen. *'I haven't got money and I can't afford to get a loan or anything to pay for a funeral, have you?'*

I felt the conversation sliding away. Not only from me but from reality. I know it's not easy to 'feel' from a text conversation but nevertheless I felt panic, hostility, a certain amount of bellicosity. Was she genuinely worried? Genuinely panicking? Or was there something else here? I felt as though I was being goaded. Don't ask me how that works and don't even think of telling me that I was imagining it...which obviously I was...but...I dunno...I get *feelings* sometimes and more often than not my feelings prove to have been justified. In some way at least. My mental whiskers were twitching as I typed my response.

'No Lydia, I haven't got money either. And I certainly don't intend to get a loan or anything in order to pay for the funeral of someone who has treated me like a leper for over 30 years and nor should any of us feel that way. But the main point here, is this… he might have life insurance… he might have money in the bank…Dan may well be able to pay for his own funeral…which is why we need to get to the property, secure it and secure all his documents. There is no need to panic or rush off to do things we don't need to do yet. Do things logically. Don't you think?'

There was no reply. I attempted to bring Emily into it. *'Waddya reckon Em? He was a smart fella, there's a good chance he had life insurance don't you think?'*

Emily didn't reply. Five minutes or so went by. And then it seemed as though she attempted to deflect Lydia. *'So Lydia what do you say? Do you fancy this? Shall we go round to his place and try to sort something out?'*

Lydia made no reply. None that was visible to me anyway. I got the impression that they were having a private chat. If they were, I hoped Emily was calming Lydia down, reasoning with her, getting her to see that things didn't have to be done all in a rush. I genuinely struggled to see what the panic was. Dan hadn't been close to any of us and had treated all of us quite badly. I understand brotherly and sisterly love and I get that people can get upset at times like this…but the insistence regarding the funeral and the apparent panic as to how it was to be paid for…puzzled me. I couldn't compute.

'Lydia,' I typed, *'maybe you should just take a step back from this and let your thoughts settle for a day or two?'*

Within the blink of an eye a response from Lydia flashed onto my screen. *'No. Edward is willing to pay for the funeral and we will pay him back once the'*

I waited for the sentence to be finished. Nothing happened. No one said anything. What was the missing word? Or the missing words? How do you even do that? Type something out but don't finish what you're typing but send anyway? And if you do happen to do that, or, should I say, if I happened to do that then I would fill in the blank almost immediately. Never mind almost, insert definitely. I would definitely fill in the blank. I waited another few minutes and still nothing happened. I typed out a response.

'Lydia it's very kind of Edward to offer that so please thank him from me. He's a good man, but, IMO, he needs to be careful what he offers here because, though it's possible our brother has the means to buy his own funeral, it's also possible that he doesn't. We just don't know what state his finances are in do we? Which is why I keep saying that this is surely our first job...to get to his place and secure all documents etc? Don't you think?'

Again, a reply from Lydia was instantaneous, fair splatting onto my screen. *'No. Edward is willing to pay for the funeral and we will pay him back once everything is sorted.'*

Exactly, word for word, the same sentence but different ending. *And we will pay him back once the... And we will pay him back once everything is sorted.* Once the...once everything is sorted.

I studied the two sentences. My mind, always suspicious, always alert, always drawn to anomalies, focused on the final words of the two sentences. Once *everything* is sorted. The implication being that there is *something* to become sorted. But at the moment, as far as I am aware, no one knows that there is *anything* to sort out. No one *can* know anything until the state of his finances are known. And no one knows what state the finances are in because no one has been to the house to gather documents. However, Edward, is willing to lend money to the cause and will get repaid *once everything is sorted.* Which implies that Edward knows or strongly suspects that there IS something to get sorted…which implies that Edward knows or has an inkling that the finances of my brother were…in order. Which further implies that Edward only knows *anything* because Lydia knows it. So, bottom line, Lydia knows or has an inkling about Dan's finances. Which is fine…nothing wrong with that…except…if she *does* have an inkling then why not share that inkling her brother and sister? I suspected just a few minutes earlier that my sisters were having a private chat and now that suspicion grew. Had Lydia shared her thoughts or knowledge with her twin sister but not with me? If so, why not me? And IF Lydia had shared her thoughts with her twin sister but not with me, then, at the same time, her twin sister was also not sharing her newly acquired thoughts with me.

And the other sentence…the first one…the one that ended but didn't end…*Edward is willing to pay for the funeral and we will pay him back once the*…once THE…The what? Once THE what? Once something called THE whatever it is, is sorted out, Mark will be able to recoup the money he has lent out. Which means there must be a will. Lydia must know that her husband was going to get his money back and so therefore she must know that there is money to be had and that she is 'guaranteed' getting it back. Or Edward is. Or, maybe, she knows there is money to be had and intends to make sure that no one else gets any of it. Let me tell you, when it comes to scheming, my family are second to none. My family have no familial honour. None. Maybe that is a consequence of growing up in a place, in a family where survival, day to day survival was top of the agenda. It never happened with me, not in my estimation. I mean, at various times as a child, I definitely, fleetingly thought only of escape and my own safety. But the familial bond, in my mind at least, has always been strong.

So, if there is a will, and Lydia knows about it, then why isn't she saying anything? If the situation was the other way around, I would just say it straight out. Were the two of them chatting behind the scenes? I didn't know. I couldn't tell. I thought they were. Or maybe were. Possibly.

The scent of collusion wafted into my mind, as putrid as the smell of burning refuse. I had to stop these thoughts, not entirely, just arrest them, stow them in the overhead locker for now. Or into cold storage. Maybe even…*on ice*…y'like that one? I do. Yeah, I had to stow these thoughts, put them on ice. It was pure conjecture on my part, and I had to be careful. My natural demeanour, unfortunately, is to think ill of people around me, especially members of my family. My original family, not the one that I made. Admittedly, it's a terrible way to think but, in my defence, when you grow up and learn to *not* trust before you can even speak properly, when you learn at a very early age, and continue to learn throughout your life, that when you *do* trust someone, when you *do* put your wellbeing into the care of another person, very often that wellbeing becomes damaged in some way. Once bitten and all that.

I was alert and had to stay that way, but I didn't want to show myself. I could be wrong about things. I didn't think I was wrong, but it was certainly very possible. I always want to be wrong when I have such thoughts but, sadly, often, I'm not. *'Ok then.'* I typed. *Good. Just say thanks and well done to Edward for me. So, OK then, when are you two gonna get round to our brother's?'*

Lydia responded. Fairly quickly. Maybe too quickly. She'd been sitting, watching, waiting for me to reply. For *me* to reply. *'All I'm saying is that I can see what is being said here and I agree with everything and that if we can't make any kind of claim, you know, insurance etc, and there's a deposit to pay then Edward is happy to help out'*

I sent a big blue thumbs up sign thing that Messenger has. You know the one.

There was a lull…maybe a minute, maybe two. I was staring at the screen, waiting for the 'pat on the head.' that, in my eyes would signify that my sisters were doing the WhatsApp equivalent of high-fiving…high-fiving the success of their gambit…a gambit designed to re-direct me, to 'jump' me off the track I was perceived as being on. They wanted to disarm me and shift my gaze away from… *something*…something to do with those two identical sentences with different endings. That and their newly formed team. If I was right about this collusion, then a move away, a sidestep would occur with the next thing said by one of them. And because Lydia was seemingly pulling the strings, I assumed, for the sake of some kind of cockamamie balance, that the next person to speak, type, comment, whatever, would be Emily.

It arrived. And it *was* Emily. *'So, shall we go to Dan's?'*

I couldn't prove anything, but I didn't need to prove anything to myself. I know how people work and I knew my sisters. I knew that if there was an edge to be had, they would look for it, even if that edge gave them superiority over me, their one remaining brother. For me, you shouldn't need to gain an edge over a member of your family. Everything should be open and above board. I know that's a very simple, even naïve way of looking at things but, that's me. Sometimes. Now that, in my mind at least, my sisters had played to gain an advantage, it was OK for me to look to protect myself. It was OK for me to start playing the game as well. It's sad. Very sad. It's a game I did not want to play, but there ya go. Such is life.

Depending on how I now responded, my sisters would either be congratulating themselves or preparing to scrap it out with me. I didn't even know if there was anything to scrap about, but it seemed apparent that they did. Amazing how, in the space of just a few minutes, they have moved away from slagging each other off to a frightful level, moved away from their bile and anger towards each other, and were now seemingly united in keeping me at arm's length. To my way of thinking, only one thing could do that when it comes to my sisters. Money. The same sentiment could easily be applied to an awful lot of people in this world.

'Yeah I think you should.' I said, accepting their edge, playing into their plot, plan, whatever you want to call it. *'ASAP.'*

The conversation then carried on for another 15 or 20 minutes, carried on the way it should have been carried out in the first place…friendly, business-like, the odd little personal thing thrown in…just three people, three siblings, getting to grips with the death of their older brother, getting to grips with the stuff that a dead person leaves behind them, the legal stuff, the funeral, the property, and the belongings. It all had to be sorted out and organised.

I was in France and until I got over to Liverpool there wasn't much I could do except chip in and advise where necessary and be someone who was remote from it and therefore, maybe, able to think a little more clearly. Mind you, it's sad to say that I didn't need distance in order to think clearly, I nearly always *was* able to think clearly. To be honest I think that a lot of the time I was a bit cold, emotionally cold, a bit distant. I didn't particularly *want* to be like that, but I just was. The me that was really me, was, unfortunately, buried so deeply inside me that he rarely saw the light of day. He was often looking out, watching what was going on, but rarely in charge of proceedings. The people inside me that looked after the real me were too strong, too dominant. I didn't know how to break that hold they had on me. Most of the time, like, maybe 99.9 percent of the time, I was more than happy for my dominant selves to be in charge. I don't really know why that was, but I just knew it to be. It was too hard for me to break out of me. I know…I sound mad don't I…I can assure you I'm not. But then…if I were, I would say that wouldn't I? Anyway, you can see the effect that dealing with people who are apparently trying to manipulate me, has on me.

I spotted a mate of mine appearing on Messenger, a serving firefighter, Dennis. I knew that he was in charge of the adjoining station to the one that served the area my brother had lived in. I sent an 'hello' and after the opening pleasantries, in true fire brigade fashion, I got down to business and told him about the job involving my brother. He knew about the job but, of course, not that the body involved had been my brother. He said he'd have a word with the officer in charge of the attending appliance and get back to me.

Thirty minutes later, Dennis got back to me. The station in question had sent one pump with four firefighters to Dan's address, to 'assist police.' He told me that the police had smashed the door to bits, as they do, always attacking the lock side of the door, and carried out a basic search. Based on the smell, the police strongly suspected that a body was inside but couldn't identify exactly where it was. The firefighters donned hazmat PPE, Personal Protective Equipment, just in case you don't know and, using breathing apparatus, searched for a body. They located it and were instructed by the police to clear a path to the site, nothing more. And that was where their job ended, the rest was done by the police.

In our group conversation, my sisters had arranged to meet at Dan's place as soon as they could. I assumed they were getting ready and asked them to keep me informed.

I decided I needed a cup of coffee and some biscuits and set about that little task. Pam asked me how I was getting on and I explained that I had misgivings about my sisters and didn't trust them. She simply replied that such a state was nothing new for me and to do what I always did and go with my gut instincts until matters became clearer. I said that we were going to have to go over there, maybe for a couple of weeks and asked if she would start looking for somewhere to stay.

I made my coffee and a cup of tea for Pam and got back to the conversation on Messenger.

While I'd been away Emily had rung the police and discovered that the place was indeed boarded up. I'd come across a fair bit of boarding up, both from the taking off and the putting on perspectives. I knew that getting boards off wasn't ever easy as the companies tended to use annular or ring nails to hammer the boards up. They're not easy to get off when you're experienced, let alone a novice and I said so.

'Ok then,' I typed, 'It's boarded up, we need to get there asap, secure whatever documents we can and re-secure the building. How are we gonna do this?' I badly wanted to be there because what they did next was critical to everything…this couldn't be messed up. Dan lived in an area that had, how would I describe it, a peppering of the loveliest, most down to earth, kind-hearted people, surrounded by a sea of scum, you know the kind of area I'm talking about. Or maybe you're lucky enough to not know what I'm talking about. If my sisters, with maybe the aid of one or two well-meaning but misguided helpers, didn't secure the place properly, then the feral rats posing as people would ransack the place and probably burn it to the ground when they'd finished. They both responded in exactly the way I knew they would but hoped they wouldn't.

Emily said, 'We can let ourselves in as long as we board it back up again.' And Lydia said, 'Yeah last time I was there the door wasn't very secure anyway.'

I changed my tack completely. I needed to dissuade them from opening the place up, then re-securing it themselves, 'Ok look,' I typed, 'forget whatever documents are there…as it stands, the police have had it boarded up so they'll have used a reputable company for this task, which means we can assume it is as secure as it was prior to the door being smashed in. I strongly suggest we leave it until we can get someone to assess the damage AND replace the door if needed, as soon as *possible…I know a joiner from my time in the job so I could ask him what the score is…and once we get this done THEN we can think about coming and going to the place and retrieving documents etc…waddya think?'*

Lydia simply never even noticed that I'd said anything and seconds later typed, *'Em me and you can go there today then, when do you want to go?'*

It seemed that Lydia was desperate to get to Dan's flat. Maybe I was being unkind but there just seemed to be an unnecessary haste in what she'd said. I waited to see what happened next, hoping that she had simply not seen what I'd written but once she *had* noticed, would acknowledge the sense of what I'd said.

That didn't happen. Instead, she typed, *'I can get there in about 20 mins, if you get a taxi we can have all afternoon to find whatever documents we need and then we can get on with things.'*

Emily didn't answer her. I hoped Emily was thinking something similar to me. She had at least read what I'd said. *'Yeah ok'* she said, *'we can meet whoever is goin to fix the door so I can get ready now Lydia and get a cab. I'll probably be about an hour.'*

I pointed out to my sisters that there was no point in going to the flat unless they could secure the place when they'd finished and that me getting in touch with someone to do this for them was not going to happen in twenty minutes. Lydia just ignored me and answered Emily, *'Yes ok Em. We can pull the board off ourselves and get in x'.*

I hurriedly typed a response to this; I could almost see Lydia putting her coat on and shooing Edward out of the door. *'No you can't pull the boards off...do not pull the board off. Listen to me, this is what I used to do for a living...do not pull the boards off.'*

Another message flashed onto my screen from Lydia, *'OK I'll be over in a bit so I'll meet you there Em x'.*

This was immediately followed by Emily, *'OK but listen, we have to put it back on properly cos its proper rough-arse around there, full of smackheads and gobshites'.*

So, my two sisters, two women who'd never done anything more 'workmanlike' than prune a rose bush or paint a wall in the bedroom, were going to go there with their toolboxes, probably consisting of no more than a pair of pliers and a cheap Chinese screwdriver set from a Christmas cracker with maybe an old shoe as a hammer, remove a closely and securely fitted plywood board or more likely an OSB board, fitted with a shitload of ring nails driven in with a nail gun, and then refit it perfectly and securely once they'd finished their search for god knows what in my brother's flat. I could feel a catastrophe looming…to add to the already existing catastrophe of the death of Dan. I let my fingers do the talking. ***'FOR FUCKS SAKE! IS ANYONE LISTENING? DO NOT PULL THE FUCKING BOARDS OFF!!!'***

There were about five minutes of radio silence. Don't know why I decided to call it radio silence, but you know what I mean. I was looking at my screen, my eyes almost frantically looking from one side of the screen to the other, like I expected to see something happening, like my two sisters rushing out of their homes, shoe hammer in hand, creating a dust cloud as they scooted over to Dan's place.

'That's what I'm saying Lydia, unless we can put the boards back there's no point, and I can't do it, can you?' It was Emily. Another comment that seemed to belong to a different conversation but at least it seemed she was having second thoughts about going there. *Good,* I thought.

A few minutes of normal conversation took place and I managed to get them both to properly understand the task at hand and the importance of doing things logically and correctly. My method of operating had always been the same…I always took the stance, both mentally and physically, of my time as a firefighter. It was just in me to be forthright when needed and cautious when needed. Now that they had been held back a bit, I asked my mate Dennis if Andy the joiner was still joining. He reckoned he was and said he'd make some enquiries and get back to me with a phone number.

As I was waiting for Dennis to get back to me, I tried to take stock of what was happening. I know that people act out of character when someone in the family dies, I know that grief causes strange things to happen in people's minds. But I couldn't help but feel as though something else was at work here. The feeling was uncharitable, maybe even unkind, but I knew my sisters and, loathe though I am to say it, I didn't trust them. My mate Dennis I trusted, all my mates in the job, most of them anyway, I trusted, with my life many a time, but…sadly, members of my own family…I hate to say it, hate to even think it but, no, I just didn't trust anyone in my family enough to not think uncharitable, unkind thoughts at times. Times like now.

Pam brought me a cup of tea and a ham and mustard sandwich. I love ham and mustard. We couldn't get English mustard here in our part of

France. Not very often anyway. Occasionally, very occasionally, our 'foreign' section in the local supermarket would have it but it would sell out very quickly. You had to be quick and, generally speaking, we weren't often quick enough. Which was why the mustard on my ham sandwich was Dijon mustard. Almost as good as pure-bred English mustard but not quite. As I was eating my sandwich, I watched the conversation happening on my screen.

Emily was talking about the area Dan had lived in and that she thought an empty house wasn't going to be safe for very long around there. I agreed with her. I'd worked in a rough area or two in my time and I knew that Dan's area was quite rough. The good thing was, his place was sort of 'tucked away', not somewhere that people actually had reason to go to unless they were specifically calling at the address for something.

'*Smackhead city around there.*' said Emily and Lydia replied, '*It's in a right state. The door is not safe. Cracked glass panels.*'

'*They'll be dossing in the livvy when we get there.*' said Emily, and I briefly wondered what the 'livvy' was. For a second or two I thought she'd misspelled 'lavvy' and wondered why they would be dossing in the toilet, when it occurred to me that 'livvy' was the living room. I'd never heard the living room reduced to another word; it'd always just been the living room to me. I wondered whether everyone called it the livvy or was it just Emily. And then, as I was thinking, *what the fuck does it matter Joe?* Lydia replied, '*Yes definitely. They'll have trouble getting in there Em, cos there's piles n piles n PILES of rubbish x*'.

Now this set a little alarm bell off in my head. Firstly, it was obvious that Lydia fully understood the term 'livvy' and secondly, she quite obviously had good knowledge of his flat. Why this should set off an alarm bell I didn't really know, I just know that it did. I stored that fact away somewhere in my head. Or one of my 'people', my head 'people', stored it away. I wondered if the man from the Beezer comic, the one who had the 'Numbskulls' living in his body, had a name, presumably so that I could refer to myself as that man. With who I should or would have this discussion I have no idea. Probably with myself. Which I've just done more or less so…Should that have been 'With whom' in that last sentence? Do you know what, sometimes I wonder why almost everything I think has to come out in some form or other. Probably stress or something.

Emily responded, *'I know, our Dan was like stig of the dump xx'.*

I didn't know who Stig of the dump was but apparently Lydia did as she laughed in the form of a Lol and added *'The stairs are full of rubbish too x'.*

There was a discussion between my sisters about hospital appointments. I couldn't believe how many appointments they had between them over the next week. Edward as well, he had a number of appointments. I thought how lucky I'd been in my life. I'd had injuries and things, y'know, the normal everyday injuries, part and parcel of being a firefighter, but proper illnesses and stuff…so far, touch wood, I've been relatively fit and healthy. Fairly robust, you might say. I thought, not for the first time, if or how my sisters had been affected in the womb, by the horrendous treatment of their mum by their father.

Summer 1966

It was a Saturday, sometime after England won the World Cup but before my sisters were born. In fact, they were still inside my mum but didn't have that long to wait before seeing the world in all its union-jacked glory. It was probably sometime between July 30th, World Cup Final day, England 4 West Germany 2, and September 26th, 1966, the birthday of my twin sisters. In fact, I tell a lie, no, let me call it an untruth rather than a lie. It was sometime between August 6th at the earliest and September 26th, 1966, because, the day England won the World Cup, I'd just arrived in Colomendy, North Wales, with my brother Dan and our old school, from when we used to live at grandma's. St. Paul's in Kirkdale, North Liverpool, not far from the north docks. St. Bridget's Road. St. Paul's school on St. Bridget's Road. There was a St. Barnaby's school on St. Bridget's Road as well.

I don't know why we were allowed to travel with our old school, but I think it was because my brother Dan was famous on account of having won a scholarship to a Grammar school on the outskirts of Liverpool. Mr Wentworth, the headmaster, liked our Dan because he was dead clever. Our Dan, not the headmaster, though I suppose he must have been dead clever too. My mum once told me that he liked me too, the headmaster, not our Dan, though I suppose our Dan must have liked me too...back then anyway. I say 'must' have liked me but you don't have to like someone just because you're related to them, do you? I never liked my father. In fact, I hated him. Still do. A fact that makes me sometimes envious of people who talk in glowing terms about their dads. I say 'sometimes' but I really mean all times. Yeah, let's be honest, I'm very envious of people, especially men, who quite obviously thought the world of their dads and miss them when they've died. Me? I couldn't wait for mine to die. I wished a sudden, violent death on him a million times. I day-dreamed about it. I even had a little spell of praying for it. My prayers usually went along the lines of 'Please God, can you make my father have an accident of some kind, doesn't matter what, as long as it kills just him. If you do this for me, I will go to your church every week and light candles, and brush the floor and stuff.' I was and still am an agnostic. Don't get me started on the god thing. Y'see, I would go to Sunday school, every Sunday at St Paul's, and learn all about God and how he loved little children and looked after them, and loved all mankind and looked after them as well, and then my dad would beat me with his big leather belt, break my things, kick our telly in and hit me with hair brushes, so, y'know, it was a bit hard to reconcile the teachings of Sunday school with what happened in real life. Nevertheless, not one to look a gift-horse in the mouth, I had a little spell of praying to the big man, woman, whatever God was or is, to grant me a little wish or two. Instead of granting me a little wish, and ridding the world of my father, which, let's face it, he could easily have done. I mean, he made the world and everything on it in just six days but made the seventh day a day of rest, which has since come in really handy for mill owners and the like, over the years, he apparently chose to ignore me. He saw me, heard me because, as we are taught, he sees and hears everything, so therefore he must have chosen to ignore me. Maybe he didn't like me asking for a fellow human being to be killed. But, as he didn't seem to mind men slaughtering other men in the name of god, I thought that he could do me a turn and get rid of my father. Instead, he or she just carried on letting my father do whatever he wanted to do to my mum and us kids, so I gave up on the praying after a little while. Told you not to get me started on the god thing.

So, where was I, yeah, the headmaster, Mr Wentworth. My mum told me that he liked me too, on account of the gruesome stories I wrote in Comprehension, usually involving fires in houses that killed little babies, or battles where lots of Germans were shot and bombed or Normans were slaughtered and thrown from the walls of their castles, smearing the walls with their blood as they plummeted into the moat. The stories were all accompanied by pictures crayoned in full colour. Looking back, maybe Mr Wentworth was a little...intrigued by the five-year-old with the blood-lust. But anyway, by the time we were invited on this week-long holiday to Colomendy, my brother Dan was 14 and I was nine...so, truth be told, I have no idea how we got to go on this trip, nor do I really care. Suffice to say, we were there.

Colomendy, in case you're wondering, was, maybe still is, a camp owned by the old Liverpool Education Committee I think, so that underprivileged kids from inner city Liverpool, could get to sample the colour green, see cows, sheep and acorns and stuff. I liked it at Colomendy. It was exciting. We got to swim, walk up hills and roll down them, look for wild animals, of which there were none, though one kid shouted that he could see a lion. A fucking lion! Everyone, by which I mean all the kids, believed him, and ran to the tuck shop. I waited to see this fake lion, which of course, wasn't there, and by the time I got to the tuck shop, all the crisps had gone. Not the first time in my life I'd been duped and not the last.

So anyway, we were in Colomendy for a week. I got to sleep in a bunk bed, swim in an outdoor pool, see England win the World Cup,

walk up my first 'mountain', Moel Fammau in Mold, eat Nut Brittle,
which I'd never seen before, and see the movie, Gulliver's Travels, which
I thought was fantastic and made me want to go to Lilliput where I could
lord it over the little people. I loved the scenes of Gulliver dragging the
navy of the little enders or the big enders, can't remember which, but I
think it was the big enders, and I wanted to be a hero just like Gulliver.

We got home from Colomendy the Saturday after England won the
World Cup, which was August 6th and it, the 'event' didn't happen that
day, so therefore, it happened on either Saturday 13th August, or any of
the Saturdays leading up to September 26th, which was a Monday. There
were seven Saturdays so, take your pick. I'm guessing it was a good few
weeks before the birth because maybe the hospital would have noticed
bruising on my mum and done something about it...or maybe I'm just
being naïve, maybe times were very different back in the mid-60's or
maybe god just didn't allow any kind of natural justice to occur whether
to do with mums being beaten by fathers or kids being abused by parents.
Either way, it doesn't matter. What happened, happened, and the best
way of dealing with it is to file it away as best you can and move on.

It was probably about teatime, which meant five or six o'clock in our
house. Us three Croft kids, me, aged 10, Dan, aged 14 and Carla, aged
8, were watching telly, so I assume we were waiting for our tea. There
was some kind of show on, can't remember what it was, one of those
variety type shows that they still show on a Saturday evening. It started
with voices in the kitchen. Not a row, as such but not a normal discussion
about stuff. You could tell because there was something about the voices
that didn't belong to an everyday mundane conversation. As normal, we
strained our ears to try to catch a word or two, to try to work out the

tone. It was hard to make out words but if you could catch an 'edge' or a 'hardness' to a voice or an 'abruptness', you could maybe be forewarned of trouble heading your way. The speed of speech was another little sign you could discern, words not required. The 'key' of a voice could be discerned. Human vocal chords become constricted when under stress and the voice changes. Sometimes such a change is almost impossible to hear but a practiced ear can pick it up, even through walls and doors. On another tack, controlling this stress effect on the vocal chords can be achieved when you need to make a person believe that you are not worried, not scared, even though you are. I was always told to not show fear to a snarling dog, even though you are afraid. Some people, just like some dogs, batten onto your fear if they can sense it, and it empowers them to 'go for the kill' so to speak. To be able to hide something that can give away your fear is a handy weapon to have in your locker...the human equivalent of stealth technology.

As well as voice sounds, other sounds can be used that might give you an idea of the seriousness of the event, the way something is put down or moved can be discerned and take on meaning, maybe give an indication of whether or not violence was on the horizon. I say 'horizon', which sort of implies distance, but the fact is that my father's 'horizon', was something that could approach very rapidly, sometimes literally in the blink of an eye. He could have genuine humour in his eyes and around his mouth, but by the time his eyes re-opened from a blink, the humour had been replaced with malevolence. The humour was sometimes still evident in the creases around his mouth but the malevolence in his cold eyes injected cruelty into the situation in huge doses, a cruelty that took pleasure from the terror it invoked. Once the violence began, the mouth lost its humour and took on a workmanlike expression, as if getting the job done in a satisfactory way was of paramount importance.

The sounds from the kitchen went quiet and we exchanged glances of relief. There was no row. It had just been a few short words, that was all. But then a low moan was heard, a low moan that rose in pitch, as if someone were in pain. In that moment I knew that my father was twisting my mum's arm up her back. I remembered uttering a similar, involuntary moan when he had taken me by surprise one day, twisting my right arm up behind my back, holding my right wrist in his huge vice of a hand and my left shoulder with his left hand so that I couldn't twist free. One second, I'd been making myself a jam butty and the next second, my right arm was being pushed and twisted up my back, the pain sudden and excruciating, like an electric shock. And just like an electric shock, some mechanism in your body or your brain, decides to let a sound come out of your mouth, to force a sound from your mouth, not a word but simply an expulsion of sound. On that occasion, I'd been guilty of helping myself to food, a crime in my home that I wasn't aware of until the punishment was meted out. I didn't know what my mum had been guilty of on this occasion, but my mind's eye could see her at the sink or the cooker and him holding her still with his left hand while he pushed her arm up between her shoulder blades.

The next second there was a sudden loud scream or shout and a flurry of angry words from my mum that came closer to us in the living room as she made her way from the kitchen. The door burst open, and she rushed in, going straight to the dining table. There was no sign of our father. No sound from him. No sound from the kitchen. I hoped she'd stabbed him. We didn't look at our mum because if he had come in and *saw any one of us acknowledging that something was amiss, you became part of what was about to happen. So, we kept our eyes on the telly, though Carla stole a glance at her but quickly looked away.*

I could tell from the sounds she was making that my mum was hurt and was crying. I could hear her putting her coat on, but struggling. I very briefly thought about helping her when my dad silently appeared, moving fast, like a panther.

He didn't glance at us as he moved through the room, his eyes fastened on his quarry. He reached my mum and punched her in the chin, an uppercut, a harsh sound that resulted in my mum dropping instantly to the floor, no screams, no utterances of any kind, just a silent collapse to the floor. I was watching what happened in a silver reflective plate at the side of the radiants of the gas fire. It was slightly distorted but still a good enough view to see what was happening.

He kicked her as she lay on the floor, three of four times, leaning on the back of the chair and the edge of the table for balance. She started to make sounds. Not like any sounds a person would ever make unless you were being kicked whilst semi-conscious. The sounds from my mum started to get louder, more coherent and so he stamped on her back, on her ribcage, again, holding the chair and table for balance. I saw her draw her knees up as high as she could, protecting herself and her unborn children, my twin sisters to be. Carla turned and stole a glance. Her eyes were huge, like saucers, and almost bulging from her head. Her little chest was convulsing in dry sobs, almost like she was choking. I saw my dad turn his head and Carla quickly turned back to the telly. Dan was stoically watching the screen, looking like he was completely absorbed in the programme, his eyes unblinking. I could see a slight tremor in his chin. I was terrified. My body was frozen. My mind was frozen. I couldn't think past the moment. I was careful to keep my head very deliberately turned away from what was happening, but my eyes never left the reflective plate on the gas fire. Herman's Hermits were on the TV, singing a song. I don't know what the song was called but it had a lyric that has never left me... 'I've got a feeling you won't be leaving tonight.'

My father finished what he was doing, finished the job, apparently to a satisfactory level, went upstairs and got in the bath. After five or ten minutes our mum got up and hobbled off into the kitchen. We could hear her carrying on making our tea. We didn't move. We didn't speak. We didn't look at each other. We looked at the telly like nothing untoward had happened. When our father came down, bathed, shaved, and dressed smartly, shirt and tie, trousers, jacket, he threw his shoes at me and told me to go and polish them. I was good at polishing shoes. My grandad had taught me to spit on them to get the shine, a trick he'd probably learned in the army. I liked polishing shoes; it gave me satisfaction. When I came back with the polished shoes, he put them on, and I caught Dan staring at them. Our father fastened his laces, got up and walked out of the house, closing the door quietly.

Carla stood up and went to the window to watch where he went. It was important for us to know how far from the house he was going. The further away he went, the harder it was for him to suddenly appear back at the house. He went to the bus stop and when the bus came, he went upstairs to the back and lit a ciggy. Carla went out to the kitchen to see mum, but mum told her to go away.

We ate our tea in silence, not even looking at each other, though I did 'feel' as though I was being watched at one time and when I looked up from my plate, Dan was staring at me while he chewed his food. Flat eyes. I wasn't even certain he was looking at me or was just facing in my direction, lost in his thoughts.

Our mum had a bruised chin and a cut lip from the punch. One of her legs was bruised and that is all we could see. Weeks or maybe days later, our twin sisters were born.

Chapter 5 - Enter Andy

I'd left a message on my mate's phone. Andy was a good joiner, time served but now serving as a firefighter. Of course, just like a lot of firefighters, he worked another job on his days off and Andy was always in demand, as any good tradesman is.

While I was waiting for him to get back to me, there was some discussion between us about funerals and things like that, y'know, all the stuff that has to be talked about but, I dunno, I thought it was something that could wait a day or two maybe. I felt that there was, like, an order to what we had to do and that securing his premises and his documents was at the top of the list, that we should concentrate on that before anything else. Lydia seemed very keen to get a funeral organised and started talking about a day before the end of next week. But then, as soon as I mentioned prioritising things, she switched conversations and tried, again, to get Emily to meet her at the flat now, within the next half hour and just rip the boards off and search the flat. Yet again I explained that unless she was capable of making the place properly secure, she should simply not even think of taking the boards off…unless she intended staying the night to guard the place. She laughed at that with a LMAO thing and simply answered, *'NO'*. Emily said that she was willing to stay the night if Lydia was and our conversation went quiet for about 10 minutes, during which, I assumed, they were having a private conversation about the question. I pondered what they could possibly be saying privately that they couldn't have said in our group conversation. I felt like I was being side-lined by my little sisters and, not for the first time, felt unwanted, which, I've got to say, is sort of a Croft family thing, something *bred* into us. Us kids I mean. It made me sad, not for me, strangely, but for them, for their apparent desire or need to exclude me from something that, ultimately, did actually include me. I couldn't work it out, but then, working any of us out, me included, had been a lifelong quest that, so far, had eluded me. As usual, I asked myself if it was me that was at fault and examined things. I was always willing to take the blame and look at myself sideways but decided that, on this occasion I was right to feel the way I did. They were having a private conversation about something that should have included me and that was all there was to it. *Having said that,* I suddenly thought, *I don't actually* know *that they* are *having a private conversation, they might* not *be.* Time would tell.

My phone rang, it was Andy. We spent a few minutes exchanging pleasantries and then got down to business. He already knew what was needed at the flat, as one of his mates had been on the job and had told him about it. Andy had been a bit shocked to hear from me that the body had been my brother but that was put to one side. 'You're gonna need a new frame and door mate.' he said, 'The police obliterated it, apparently. Clueless.'

He said he could get there the following day for 12, whip the boards off and measure up for everything so my sisters could get in for maybe half an hour before he'd have to get off. He said he'd be back early the following day with all the gear and would get the job boxed off for dinner time.

I got back to our group conversation, *'OK, I've got a mate of mine, Andy, a joiner, to meet you there tomorrow at 12. He'll take the boards off and measure up what's needed. You'll have about 30 mins to go in and do what you can before he'll have to put the boards back on and go.'*

There was no response.

I made a cup of tea for me and Pam, grabbed the biscuit barrel and went outside to sit in the sun. Even in October we got fantastic weather. Or rather, I should say that, if it was sunny, it was warm, if it was cloudy, it wasn't much different to Liverpool. We were usually in shorts and sandals well into November. You wouldn't set foot in the pool in these months but deffo stay in the shorts and sandals. Not that the locals did, oh no, as soon as 1st September arrived, they donned their jeans and jumpers and got their winter coats out of mothballs. Nesh they are. Good word that my Yorkshire relatives like to claim as their own but, nesh is a word used by scousers for as long as I can remember. It's Viking or Saxon or something. Celtic maybe. But me being a linguistics expert, I'd go for Norse of some description, know warramean der lar? We finished our tea and I went back in. Pam walked across to dead-head some flowers in one of the borders.

I checked the conversation. Still no response. *'Hello?'* I typed. Nothing. *'Hello?'* I typed again, *'Is anybody there?'* My world-famous

Ouija board routine. *Is anyone there? Knock once for yes, twice for no.'* I typed. Still no response.

I sat and stared at the screen. It had been about 25 minutes since either of them had said anything. I looked out of the window and down to the bottom of the garden. I could see Francis and Marie Therese busy with their crops. They worked hard and in all weathers and were no spring chickens. *'C'est ma passion!'* was something they would both say, with a shrug of the shoulders.

I watched our neighbours and thought *'What the fuck am I doing here, all the way down here, at this time?'* I decided to just get in the car and go, but then, within a second or two, as always, common sense kicked in and I knew, as I always did, that going off half-cocked rarely ended well. And then I thought of all the snatch-rescues I'd been involved in and thought *'Hmm it doesn't always end badly when you go off half-cocked now does it.'* and then I thought *'Yeah but a snatch-rescue is hardly going off half-cocked now is it? It's part of your training, it's calculated risk-taking, not half-cockedness.'* I think I just made that word up, but it fits…*cockedness*…yeah, it fits. I was just about to tell my other self to do one, when the group conversation came back to life. Just thinking, 'cockiness' might have been better but, if the situation arises where you can make a new word, well, why not take it?

'Well let's hope he can come today. I'm going round there anyway, just to make sure.' Lydia opened up, followed immediately by Emily. *'Well, I'll get ready and get a taxi there Lydia, what time are you going?'*

'Just to make sure of what?' I asked.

'On my way.' said Lydia, 'Just entering the tunnel.' Lydia lived on the Wirral, across the river from Liverpool. The 'Dark Side' we called it. Scousers that is. Anyone who went to live on the other side of the river were crossing over to the 'Dark Side'. So, she was entering the Mersey tunnel, which meant she must have left her house at least 15 minutes ago, during the 'silence'.

'Ok well I've just called a taxi, gonna get me clobber on.' typed Emily. I stared at the screen, my mind processing things as quickly as I could.

'The lad can't come until tomorrow,' I said, '12'. No one answered me. 'What's the rush?' I asked. There was no answer.

I felt like I was being railroaded, corralled, or by-passed for some reason. I was being, shall we say, *treated rather strangely*, or, to put it another way, being shit upon, for some reason. I mean, don't get me wrong, I could understand the reasoning behind going there just to make sure the place wasn't currently being stripped but, the thing was, the secrecy. It was obvious that during the silence my sisters had been having a private conversation, as I suspected, and they'd decided to, for want of a better way of putting it, 'place it on record' that the decision to go over there *NOW* had been taken during the group conversation, when it obviously hadn't. What was going on? Why the subterfuge? In my mind, there was no subterfuge without fire, so, what was on fire?

A few minutes went by. My phone pinged. It was Emily. 'On my way.' she typed. A big blue 'thumbs up' appeared in response from Lydia.

'Don't take the boards off' I typed. There was no answer.

Chapter 6 - First Photos

Two photographs from Lydia arrived on my phone, of the outside of Dan's place.

The board was still in place and looked secure. The ground was completely covered in stuff. What looked like a mixture of rubbish and household things. It looked like the aftermath of a gas explosion. I could see Dan's push-bike lying on the grass of his garden. A shoe hung from a tree branch. God knows how it got there. Kids probably. It was a woman's shoe. Not a stiletto, one of those…other ones…don't know what they're called, a low-heeled shoe, let's call it. The kind of shoe my mum would have worn. An old woman's shoe, hanging perfectly in the tree, as though it had been staged.

It instantly reminded me of a job I'd attended one morning at the end of a night shift, where the shoes of a young girl who'd been hit by a car on her way to school, had ended up in a tree. The car had been travelling way over the odds and the driver had completely failed to see the pelican crossing was on red and had hit the girl, probably about 11 years old or so, with such force that her broken little body had been shunted more than 30 feet from the crossing, scattering her school bag contents across the road, pencils and pens, an apple and a few books. A pink pencil sharpener. And her shoes…one of the saddest sights of my life, hanging in a tree at the side of the road like grotesque Christmas tree decorations. I wanted to get them down straight away, but the police wouldn't let us move anything…not until all the photographs and measurements had been taken. The poor kid, obviously dead, lay in the gutter with a coat over her for what seemed like ages before they allowed her to be moved. We erected salvage sheets on a frame made from small ladders to hide the youngster from onlookers.

I wondered what a woman's shoe was doing hanging from the sycamore tree in my brother's garden. A message arrived from Lydia… *'OMG it's terrible. It stinks. I'm not doing anything, just having a look.'*

Seconds later Emily, apparently not yet arrived, joined in, *'WTF is all this? WTF is it all doing out there?'*

'What a mess.' I typed. Lydia replied, or commented, can't make my mind up which, *'The neighbours came over and said they've spoken to the council about removing it all'.*

Everything went quiet on the Messenger front and I guessed that Emily had arrived. I messaged them to make sure they did a good search of the stuff lying around outside for any important docs…not that they needed telling but, maybe just for something to say. The comment from Lydia about the neighbours getting onto the council sort of 'spooked' me a bit and I didn't want them, the council, or the neighbours come to think of it, making off with personal documents. There was no reply and I hoped they were busy searching and that they weren't tempted to pull the boards off the entrance.

Later that evening, having not heard anything from my sisters, I sent a message saying that the joiner would get to Dan's about 12 noon, take the boards off, measure up and assess everything, put the boards back up and go get all the stuff. They didn't have to be there for him to do this but if they wanted to get in while he was there, they'd have to be there in plenty of time and just have a quick scout about the place. I didn't get any reply from them.

I was in bed reading at about 11.30 that night. Just before midnight, as I was drifting off, my phone vibrated. It was a message from Lydia saying that they would be there for 12. She was 'speaking' on behalf of them both. I have to say that I expected to have heard more from them during the rest of the day, y'know, a little commentary of what, if anything, they'd discovered in the stuff lying in the garden. It briefly occurred to me before I dropped off, that waiting until just before midnight, ensured that one of my sisters had responded to me 'on the same day'. Just a few minutes later and we would've been into the next day and I would've been able to point a finger, accuse them of keeping me in the dark. If this proved to be the case, and I don't think I could ever prove it, or would ever try to prove it, then it was, to me, quite contrived and controlling behaviour. Because of their silence, I could only assume that nothing of significance had been found.

How wrong that assumption turned out to be.

Chapter 7 - Getting Prepared

During the night, as was often the case with me, I slept well and my mind sorted the events of the day and looked for solutions to any problems I went to sleep on. I had a method to this process. I always read my current book, always a novel at night, textbooks and stuff during the day, novels at night. I find the reading of a good novel empties my mind by taking me into another world, into someone else's life. For me, a novel has to paint pictures, I have to be able to see the characters, not necessarily what they look like or what clothes they wear, but what kind of people they are. I have to be able to properly imagine the places that the story takes place in.

Once my mind is empty and sleep beckons, I close my book and slide it under my pillow…I use a Kindle so it's really slim and neat and easily fits without giving me a 'neck'. I then lie on my back and look at the ceiling and 'disappear' it, so that I'm looking up into a void, into nothing, just darkness. Sometimes I see very bright lights far away in the darkness, flashes and streaks of startling colour. I can't actually see the lights but, I've no idea how this works or even if I am explaining it right, y'see, I've never tried to explain it before, so, bear with me on this. I can't actually see the lights and coloured streaks because they appear and disappear very rapidly on my peripheral vision. It's like, when you're looking into total darkness and you can feel your eyes are like the size of saucers, trying to pull in all the available light, and even though it's completely dark, you get the impression that someone, a shape, is there, in front of you on the edge of your vision but, when you try to look at the shape it moves and stays on the periphery. Well, my colours are like that. Vivid streaks and flashes of colour that happen on the periphery of my sight but I can never actually look right at them because they just move. Or disappear.

Anyway, once I'm relaxed and settling into my disappeared ceiling, I calmly go through all the things I want to think about while I'm asleep and once I've catalogued stuff I turn to my side, always the right side first, and go to sleep. In the morning, almost invariably, there is some kind of resolve or solution to things, right there, at the front of my mind. It's a bit like a magic trick. I mean, don't get me wrong here, I can't go to sleep pondering the reasons for our existence and wake up with an answer, nor could I consider an em see squared type question and solve whatever it is that the em see squared thing solved. No, I'm talking about little, I dunno, *logic-train* things, where your information is jumbled up and a bit complex and…ahh you know what I mean. Also, because my mind takes so many 'pictures' of points in the day, takes 'flavourings' from the day, well, they get sifted through and re-presented to me in the morning as, I dunno, *clear* pictures. See what I'm saying? I wouldn't blame you if you couldn't. I'm not sure I can see what I'm saying myself sometimes, and I'm the one saying it. Suffice to say that I go to sleep pondering stuff and often wake up with most things resolved.

When I woke up, I felt relaxed and well rested but also a bit let down. I checked the texts from yesterday and noted that my sisters had gone to my brother's at about 2.30 p.m. They weren't gaining entry to the property and so could only be scouring the outside for anything of any importance that had been chucked out by the firefighters.

Now, Dan's garden was small. Very small. I would say about 18 feet by maybe 10 or 11 feet, let's round it up to 12, so, what's that…216 square feet, or 24 square yards. There were three of them, Lydia, Edward, and Emily. Split the 24 square yards between them and they each had eight square yards to search through.

I'd already seen the 'fireground' so to speak, in the photos Lydia had sent me. There wasn't a huge pile of stuff. It was a scattering. There was a pile immediately below the upstairs bedroom window, Dan's bedroom, that was about six feet wide and, at its deepest part, two feet high and it stretched into the garden by no more than three to four feet.

I would estimate it to take me about 30 to 40 minutes tops, to do a recce of this stuff and pick up any important documents. On my own. So, a proper estimate of the job for three people, would be about 10 to 15 minutes. Adding other factors in, like, for instance, Edward wasn't too good on his feet and used a walking stick, Lydia was quite overweight and not particularly fit, and Emily wasn't overly fit either but quite capable of physical work, I estimated that they would take double the amount of time that I would take, so, 60 to 80 minutes. I added another 20 minutes on for the horror factor, and so, at most, I could expect them to be finished for about 4 o'clock at the latest. I expected them to have something to report but, there had been nothing said.

I expected Lydia to give Emily a lift back home and for Emily to invite them in for a cuppa, maybe they would even go to the supermarket on the way home, get some food, have a little meal together, a soft bap and some sliced ham, maybe a doughnut for afters. That's what I'd do. A nice little tea together, discuss the day.

Maybe I'm being too…something…I'm not sure what, too organised? Too…fire service orientated, too…*regimented?* Maybe it was me at fault here and not them. Maybe I was expecting too much. Yeah, I was expecting too much.

But then a little voice inside my head told me that it wasn't too much to expect. That *my* brother had died too, that *my* brother's stuff was strewn about his garden and maybe contained important documents, important personal belongings. The task had been an important task to carry out and it was important to report to all and any interested parties that the task had been carried out and had uncovered something, or nothing. How long would such a message have taken to compose and send? Seconds? Minutes maybe. At most. But neither of them thought it was something they should do. Neither of them thought to put my mind at rest about the state of play at the place of my brother's death.

I got up and Pam had prepared breakfast out on the patio for us. It was a gorgeous sunny morning and we sat under the umbrella. Coffee, hot croissants, butter, and jam, raspberry. Goes without saying. Though I've just said it so, ignore that 'goes without saying'.

I loved the way sounds carried in warm air, and the birdsong was almost deafening, only going quiet momentarily when a huge bird of prey circled above, taking advantage of the early thermals. I poured another coffee into my mug, the sound rich and pleasant. I took a sip. It was slightly too cool but what the hell. I checked my phone. Nothing from my sisters. I sent them a text in Messenger.

'Did either of you know that I put our cousin Shirley in touch with Dan?' There was no answer, so I sent another. *'A long time ago, before you two were born they were really close. They're about the same age. Shirley wrote to him and he phoned her in June just gone. She sent this msg to me at the time...'.* I copied and pasted the message that Shirley had sent to me in April. She'd been responding to my query as to whether she'd managed to get in touch with him. I sent it to my sisters.

'He was great Joe, he said my letter was lovely and he was so pleased to hear from me, he said of course I remember you Shirl and that he used to enjoy my company. He said we used to get the train to the beach and what beach we went to, but I can't remember what beach it was now. We talked about Carla dying and him talking to Lydia ages ago. He sounded over the moon to hear from me, I was so pleased that he was pleased as I didn't think he would get in touch with me so it's made my day. He said how he has always thought of himself as ugly but I told him he definitely wasn't but told him that funnily enough I have always thought of myself as ugly too, my dad used to tell me off about it. He seemed fine Joe and sounded really happy to hear from me. He said he had to get a new phone as the one he phoned me from wouldn't charge up, but we had over half an hour's chat before his phone lost charge. Xxxx'

While we were washing the dishes after breakfast, I was thinking about the things we had to clear here in order to get over to the UK. I had a pretty big scaffolding tower up at the back of the main house, with about three or four square metres of pointing to be done before the proper winter arrived. I'd already machined all the old mortar out and disposed of it. All that remained was for the new stuff to be put in. That would have to be done before I could leave for the UK because, maybe by the time I got back, the weather may well have broken and be too cool for the lime mortar to set and blah blah blah. In other words, it made sense to get on with the job, get it finished and take the scaffold tower down before going home. To the UK. Much as I like France, it could never be my home. Home is where the heart is and my heart was in the UK, in Liverpool.

We'd have to book accommodation, Eurotunnel, overnight stay in Folkestone, and then there was the question of what tools I was going to take with me because, getting involved with Dan's place would need tools. I didn't know what the state of play was at his flat, so didn't know what tools were required so couldn't work anything out.

I decided to try to switch off and get on with the job I currently had in hand. The pointing. I checked my phone. Still no replies. Of course, they both had hospital appointments so might have their phones switched off, so, maybe there was nothing to be concerned about.

I got on with the work in hand.

Chapter 8 - They are Inside

I checked my watch. It was 12.30, 11.30 back home. My sisters needed to be en route to Dan's place, if they were going to meet up with Andy, which they said they were going to do. It wasn't necessary for them to be there but I hoped they would because I was keen to know what the state of the place was.

I messaged them. *'Morning ladies, how did your appointments go? Are you on schedule to meet up with Andy? Doesn't matter if you can't make it, but let me know or you can ring him yourselves, I'll text you his number''*

There was no answer from either of them, so I assumed they were still busy. Andy had said he would give me a call when he knew what was what, so I got on with my stuff. I was just about to start mixing some mortar when my phone rang. *At last!* I thought, assuming it was one of my sisters, but it wasn't, it was my mate, Dennis. I answered.

'Have you been in your brother's flat yet mate?' Was his opening, no hello's no introductions, nothing, just straight into it…just the way I liked things. It was obviously something important enough to warrant the directness.

'No Den,' I said, 'why? What's the problem?'

He took a deep breath. 'I've just spoken to the lad who was OIC of the job, it was a full hazmats job mate, you're gonna need decent PPE, something suitable for biohazard.'

'OK' I said. 'Obviously, we're not gonna have chemical suits or BA so, what risks are we talking about here?'

'His body had been there for a while mate; it was completely rotted down. The place is overrun with vermin, rats, mice, all sorts, Frank, the OIC, said they took no chances, used the full bifters, you know the score.'

I did know the score. Full bifters, in context, would mean full fire kit, full BA, breathing apparatus, a chemical suit, which is a one-piece suit with integral boots and gloves, that completely covers you and your breathing apparatus. Once inside the suit you are completely isolated from the planet. I always used to take my knife in with me because if you run out of air in there, you could die. Not that such a thing would happen as long as you had outside help on hand but, y'know, I always thought *worst case scenario* and prepared for it. Better to be injured and on a ventilator than dead, as they say. Just made that up. The bottom line was that any firefighter worth his or her salt, would and should do the same and take a knife in so you can cut your way out. Always secure your exit.

'Ok Den, listen thanks mate, I'll speak to you later cos I think my sisters might well be on their way into the flat as we speak.' I cut the call and opened my contacts list to call Emily, and as I did, a message arrived in the joint Messenger conversation. From Lydia.

'Fuck.'

'What?' I typed back.

'Fucking awful inside.' she said, *'Television is on'*

I was taken aback. *'What?!!! Actually on? Can you video what you're seeing Lydia?'*

A few seconds went by and then Lydia said, *'I'm trying but it's too dark up there x'*

Two or three minutes went by and then a video arrived in Messenger.

It was dark and jerky because Lydia was walking. The phone was about chest height, and straight away I recognised the staircase in my brother's flat. I'd not been there for a very long time, since probably the mid-80's, so we're talking three decades. But I still recognised it. It was the same as the day he'd moved in there all that time ago, painted white up the edges with bare wood down the middle. It must have had a carpet on it at one time because I could see the gripper rods nailed into the angles. It was also filthy with years of grime. I could make out the odd muddy boot print here and there…even dog prints, y'know, paw prints I mean. There was some refuse, as in rubbish, the stuff you'd put in your bin but not much as the stairs had been cleared by the fire team. I spotted a muddy footprint on the bottom few steps. A *foot* print, mind, not the print of a shoe or boot, the print of a foot, looked to be about my size, which meant it was probably Dan's.

I could hear voices but not either of my sisters. It was the TV, the sound quality a bit tinny, but the volume was quite loud. It sounded like the BBC News. Lydia reached the top of the stairs and aimed the phone into the living room, sweeping it slowly from side to side. It was very gloomy but I could make out that the room was full of rubbish, five, maybe even six feet deep, everywhere. The rubbish went halfway up the window, which was covered with something that made the light filtering in, browny-orange. The floor wasn't visible anywhere.

I heard Lydia say 'Jesus Christ!' Then Emily said, 'Let me see Lydia, let me get up.' The phone jiggled about a bit as Emily inched up beside Lydia and then I heard her sob and say, 'Oh my fucking god, what the fuck is this all about?'

The phone swung round, and I could see a TV, flat screen, probably about a 32 inch, perched skew-whiff atop the rubbish. A crisp picture of a BBC News presenter standing on Parliament Green in London was talking about Brexit and in the background someone with a big booming voice was shouting 'Stop Brexit!'

The video picture suddenly disappeared, and a couple of minutes later a series of photos started to ping and ding into the conversation, all from Lydia. They were very dark, but I could make out the doorway into his bedroom and the one into the kitchen. Rubbish was piled high everywhere you looked. It was impossible to see how anyone could have lived in there, easy to see how someone could have died in there.

'They're very dark Lydia.' I typed. *'Have you got flash on your phone?'* I was amazed that the TV was switched on and had been left on by the various agencies who'd been in the flat, but, having said that, it was a police incident, so the fire brigade would have only done exactly what they were asked to do and no more.

'I'm shocked that the TV has been left switched on' I typed.

'I am too,' said Lydia, 'I was scared because I thought someone was in the flat watching it. Emily did too.'

'It's disgusting,' I wrote, 'The police are disgraceful. I'm livid.'

'I am too.' said Lydia, 'Emily said it's disrespectful.'

I agreed with Emily. I couldn't envisage me, as a police officer, attending such an incident and going away having not attended to a TV blaring out atop a mound of rubbish, most of which was probably combustible. Granted, the police could probably claim that it was impossible to find where the TV was plugged in but, y'know, the fuse box was situated by the front door, so, let's engage a couple of brain cells and flip the main switch on the way out, sorted. To simply walk away from that flat, having removed a dead body, well, y'know, why leave the TV on? It beggared belief and I think Emily's words were spot on…it was plain disrespectful.

I opened my other laptop, the one I used only for photographs and transferred the photos Lydia had sent, opening the first one in Photoshop. A message arrived from Lydia, 'Dan probably set TV up for it to come on n off. Maybe to wake him up I don't know. X'

The thought that someone in the same position as my brother would set his TV to come on in order to wake him up seemed, I dunno, wrong somehow. Maybe I was doing my brother and others like him a disservice, but I just couldn't see it. 'Yeah possibly.' I replied.

I suddenly remembered the conversation I'd had with Dennis regarding the possible biohazard. I called Emily. She answered straight away. 'Where are you?' I asked.

'At Dan's.' She said, her voice teary.

'No,' I said, '*Exactly* where are you?' Before she could answer the question, I asked another one, 'Are you inside or outside?'

'Outside.' she said.

'Where's Lydia?' I asked.

'Standing next to me.' she said.

'OK good.' I said, 'stay out of the place now, it's very likely a biohazard and you need protective equipment to go in there so *do not go back in*. OK?'

I could hear her telling Lydia. I butted in, 'Em, is Andy there? Can you put him on?'

Andy came on the phone. 'Fuckin hell mate that's fuckin *baaad* up there lar...never smelt a smell like that in me fuckin life. Nearly vomited.'

I told him what I'd just told Emily and he told me not to worry cos he wasn't going up there again. 'I've measured up and gonna go get it all now and I'll fit it in the morning. I'll sort everything out with your sisters, mate. OK?'

He put Emily back on and I could hear Andy putting the boards back on the entrance.

'Joe, we're going back to mine for something to drink, it's shocking, can't believe what I've just seen y'know. I'm shaking all over, just can't believe it. What the fuck was he doing? I'm struggling with this Joe, we'll speak to you from mine later, OK?'

We goodbyed each other and I went into the house. Pam was hoovering the living room. I showed her the video that Lydia had sent me. She was stunned by it and just sat on the settee. I went to make a cuppa. Then I thought better of it and got a cold Leffe out of the fridge for Pam and a warm one from the cupboard for me. I don't know whether I've said, but I prefer it not chilled…better taste. Yeah, I think I have mentioned it. I'll probably mention it again.

We sat in the living room. A huge purple bee buzzed past the open French windows, and then turned back to investigate the dark opening. It came in, heavy and ponderous, sounding like a chopper in a Vietnam movie, did a sweep of the room, hovered for two seconds at the mouth of my beer bottle then gave me a glance, saw me giving it the one eyebrow look, *'Really mate?'*, buzzed off out and headed down the garden. South.

'So, what now?' asked Pam, taking a swig of beer and giving me a glance. Two glances in less than a minute…that must mean something…I'm joking.

'Dunno.' I said.

Neither Emily nor Lydia got back to me that night. They must have been busy.

Chapter 9 - It's Not Safe in There

Next morning at 8.30, I'd literally just finished the render repair I'd started the day before, when my phone dinged. I finished hosing down and washing all my stuff, buckets, mixer, trowels and such, washed my hands and put the kettle on. As I was waiting for the kettle to boil, I checked my phone. It was a message from Emily. Sent at 7.30 a.m. UK time. Very unusual for one of my sisters to be up and about at that time.

'Right Lydia found Dans bank statement outside brought it to mine so I rang the bank told them the situation all ingoings are still ongoing and outgoings have stopped as Daniel has no kids or parents his only family is us 3 you Joe are not his next of kin the bank said as he is on his own with just 3 siblings all 3 siblings are his next of kin and all 3 siblings need to bring photo ID into the bank to verify we are his family they said we need a fact of death temp death certificate letters of administration the bank statement was just on the floor by the way'

A number of little things flashed through my mind, one, no punctuation. And two, the word *Right*, as if we were in the middle of a conversation. Three, why didn't Lydia tell me this? Four, this must have occurred yesterday, why not tell me yesterday? And five, the phraseology *'You Joe are not his next of kin the bank said'*, I don't remember ever saying that I was his next of kin and I don't think I would ever have used that phrase, because I *know* that we are all his next of kin.

I replied, *'On the floor outside? Are you going to be there when Andy does the work? BTW, well done finding the statement, can't have been a pleasant task.'*

Lydia came on, *'Yes it was outside on the floor. Firemen threw stuff out the back window to get Dan out x'*

Don't ask me why or how or any other questions but, and this is a huge 'but', I somehow took Lydia's statement to be a bit...defensive, aggressive, something with an 'ive' on the end. Like I said, I've no idea how a statement on Messenger, with no intonation or inflection, no sideways glance or posturing, can possibly carry the meaning I attached to it. It was almost like my question 'On the floor outside?' was seen by Lydia, or by both of my sisters, as accusatory.

A voice in my mind said, *'Take a step back mate, you're reading things that aren't there, nothing is 'going on', just chill out'.* I resolved to follow the advice from inside my head. But then another voice said, *'Yeah but hang on now, every 'plot', every dastardly plan, every deceit, has a beginning, an opening phrase, an opening 'exchange', an opening gambit and recognising an opening gambit is a weapon that shouldn't be ignored, just because you don't want to think that people are plotting, so, by all means take a step back but do not, I repeat, do NOT chill too much. Stay vigilant and if there is no plot you've lost nothing, but if there is a plot, you're prepared.'* I resolved to follow the advice from my other head and act as though all the little signs that might not be signs had passed me by, and appear to be *chilled.* Until the time came to act if required. It's sometimes complicated being me. Too many people with a voice. I like the teamwork though.

I replied to the conversation, *'OK well I've spoken to someone about the actual job the fire brigade attended and you're gonna need to get some PPE gear to work in there…here's what I think you should know and do.'*

I told them what I thought they should know and do, and armed with this information, we got our heads together and worked out what gear we'd need, to be able to work in the environment created by our brother. We had to find all his documents, insurances, assuming he had any, bank paraphernalia, cheque books, cards, statements, letters, photographs, you know the stuff, the stuff that, essentially, makes a person into a real person, with a history, a life before the finality of death.

When I was talking about the quality of the masks that would be required, Emily said, *'Yeah I know, Ive been thinking of the gloves and mask I'd need. I've got some dust masks I used when I was moving stuff about in the loft, will they be ok?'*

She'd got them from the decorating section of a local DIY shop. Lydia chimed in that she had some of the same ones and also some paper suits from the same place. It was obvious that my sisters were out of their depth, way outside any comfort zone they'd ever lived in, let alone envisaged. It was one thing clearing out the flat of your hoarder brother but quite a different thing doing the same job when a human body had decomposed into it. That contaminated rubbish would be quite hazardous. I asked Pam to call the local council in Liverpool, to see whether they had a service to deal with such a task. They did, but the cost was exorbitant and they would do no more than a shovelling out exercise, they wouldn't be sifting stuff, a necessary part of what had to be done. To do a sifting job was going to cost thousands of pounds that we simply didn't have, and when Emily told us that she had to be careful because she was on two inhalers because she had breathing problems they hadn't fully diagnosed yet, I just thought to myself that this was hopeless. It just wasn't safe for either of my sisters to work in our brother's flat. Simple as that.

'Listen,' I typed, *'it's not safe for you to be in there working, or even moving stuff about, you're not geared up for this, physically or mentally, whereas I am. I'll finish off some stuff here and be over within the next few days. I'll do the job on my own, it'll take me a week or two. If you can sort out with a local firm for skips, and be on hand to take away everything of interest that I find, that'll be the best way of utilising our team. How's that sound?'*

Lydia responded almost instantaneously. *'And in what way are you geared up for it?'*

I was taken aback. Her question just seemed hostile to me. Yeah, I was in my 60's, I get that. But y'know, even though I say it myself, I was very fit for my age. Strong too. I worked out regularly, cycled, weight-trained, flexibility stuff, even a bit of Pilates with Pam. I ate properly, didn't drink too much, and didn't smoke, plus, y'know, I'd worked for over 30 years out of one of the busiest fire stations in the UK. I'd dealt with *stuff* in those 30 years. Lots of stuff. I reckoned, no, I *knew* that I was more than qualified to deal with this task our brother had left for us. Luckily for Lydia I let my fingers reply.

'I used to do this kind of stuff, remember?' I attached one of those smiling emojis on the end of the message, which was far from how I felt and wondered how many million false emojis were sent each day across the world.

Emily laughed with a 'hahaha' and Lydia made no reply.

A longish conversation then took place between me and Emily, as to exactly how the job would be done. She was quite intuitive with her questioning of me and, I have to say, I was impressed. But then, Emily had always been very hands on, always willing to get stuck in, a very practical woman. All the time me and Emily were chatting, Lydia was there, online, still joined into the convo because her green blob was lit, but she said nothing. There were a few lulls in the conversation, usually followed by a flurry of new questions and I couldn't help my extremely suspicious mind interpreting this as an indication that there was another conversation going on in the background, that I was being 'pumped' for information as to how to perform this distasteful task. I just knew that my sisters were going to agree to me doing the work but then do it themselves. If I was right, there would be certain 'pointers' to this. Me being paranoid again? Probably. But then, what was that saying…'Just because I'm paranoid doesn't mean they aren't out to do me in' or something along those lines?

If I was right, *if* it wasn't a case of paranoia, then the burning question was this, why would they want to do this task themselves when they had me, their remaining big brother, willing and able to do it? *If* this question was ever to be an operative one, then, to my way of thinking, the only feasible answer was that they thought there was something in my brother's flat that they did not want me to see or even know about.

And knowing the way my sisters had acted in the past, the thing they did not want me to see would be either money, the promise of money, or something that could easily be converted into money. It seemed that every time I had relations with my family, my life became one of guessing and second guessing, where the words IF and THEN were used a lot, where a sort of Boolean logic was the only way to work your way through to where *they* were at…because they always seemed to be at a place you weren't, and always seemed to be in the process of preventing you getting there.

For me, the most important thing, the most valuable thing, that would be secreted in my brother's flat was actually priceless…photographs. Family photographs. He was a prolific photographer and took lots, probably hundreds of photographs of the house we started our lives in, our grandparents house down by the North docks in Liverpool. To me, they would be a real genuine treasure, greater than the treasure of, that, erm, dragon…Smaug. Yeah, greater than the treasure of Smaug, the dragon from The Hobbit, a book which my brother introduced me to. Lord of the Rings as well, he introduced that to me and allowed me to read his paperback copy as long as I didn't fold the corner of the page to mark my place. He even bought me a leather bookmark from Crich Tramway Museum so that I didn't have an excuse. Where was I…yeah, Dan would have hundreds of photos of our early life and I would dearly love to set eyes on my lovely grandma and grandad again.

There was a lull in the conversation. A long one. I was just sat there, in my living room in France, my laptop on my lap, thinking about my brother. I hadn't seen him for such a long time. Hadn't spoken to him in decades but thought about him virtually every week. I often wondered what he was doing and often thought about how he would love it where I lived, the peace and quiet, the lanes, the weather, the insects and wildlife, he would have absolutely loved it and been totally in his element. I always wanted him to come over for a few weeks, or for as long as he wanted. He could have moved in permanently if he'd wanted, as long as he'd pulled his weight, which I'm sure he would have done. We could have gone cycling together, something we both loved, but of course now, that would never come to pass, I would never speak to him again and I would never get to know what drove him to his final destination.

I was just about to close my laptop when a message arrived from Emily, *'Broke my heart this.'*

Both of their little green lights disappeared. They'd gone. I closed Messenger and then closed my lappy.

And wondered what they were cooking up between them.

Chapter 10 - The Skara Brae Bed

I toyed with the idea of getting in touch with Andy and asking him to stop my sisters entering the flat unless they had proper PPE, but thought that this would be too onerous on him. He was just there as a joiner, doing a job that he'd get paid for. It wasn't his responsibility to police my sisters and I thought that involving him in my family politics would be wrong. If my sisters wanted to mooch about in the flat, there was nothing I, or anyone else was going to do about it, it was their business. They were aware of the pitfalls, it was their health at stake, it was up to them. Sounds a tad callous I know but, I couldn't sit outside the flat like a security guard and they were two women who only took notice of others when it suited them.

I got on with removing the scaffold from my house and stowing it away, then I started to gather the tools I needed to take home with me. My main toolbox with quite a range of stuff was first. A circular saw together with the masks Pam and I used plus the normal boots, gloves and stuff. We'd get one-piece disposable suits and hats once we got to the UK. I didn't intend for Pam to work in there with me but, you never know what's around the corner and she was very handy and well used to working on projects with me.

I gave the car a good hoovering out, washed it and did all the roadworthiness checks, you know the score. The car always had to be as right as it could be for me to make a long journey. The car being right put my mind in the right groove. A clean and shiny car makes me a clean and shiny driver. Or something like that. Don't ask me why this is the way it is and has to be because I don't know. I've never had to think about it, it's just the way it is.

Once the car was ready, we went to our local supermarket, in Sauzé-Vaussais, a good 20-minute drive through beautiful rolling countryside, to get essential journey supplies, by which I mean toffees. As many variations on the toffee as we can. Our favourites are the various Werther's, from Germany, the hard ones, and the ones with soft centres, which are particularly good but don't last long enough. They should be bigger but then, if they were, I'd probably choke on one of them. Walker's toffee in England is also right up there with the very best in the world but, of course, we can't get it in France.

We'd just got back in the car at the supermarket when my phone rang. It was Andy.

'Alright mate, listen, I've finished that job. Frame and door's solid as fuck and I put the exact locks on that you said. All the keys are with your sisters and they've got the bill too, but look, don't even think about paying the bill until you've got everything sorted.'

I thanked him, we had a little chat about stuff and then Andy got off, 'Get back to my ongoing job now mate,' he said, 'take care, see you when you're over if you get time.'

We drove back home and I had to sample a Werther's or two, just to make sure they hadn't 'gone off' or anything, y'know, sometimes toffees can be, errr, *temperamental*, so they need to be checked. You know what I mean.

Later that night, after I knew all the soaps would have been and gone on UK TV, something my sister Lydia could not and would not miss for anything, I texted into our joint conversation; *'How did the door look after Andy had finished?'*

Lydia answered, *'Everything was fine, he's done a great job, the door is excellent and needs a coat or two of paint, which Edward said he'd do. We've got loads of keys to share out. XX'*

We spoke briefly about the bill from Andy, which was mate's rates and very generous mate's rates at that, and decided that we'd speak about it more in person when I got over there.

'Ok, so,' I said, *'did you have a good look around? What's the state of play?'*

Lydia explained that it was a very small flat, like I had no idea what it was like, and that there was only about a square metre of floor on view, right by the door into the living room from the stairs, and a narrow path cleared to the place he'd died in, the rest being covered by mounds of rubbish. *'It's really bad in every room x'* she typed, *'really, really bad. Can't get rid of the smell, all our clothes are in the washer, we've showered but I just can't get rid of the smell. Edward's the same x'*

I knew the score with this. There were just some smells that somehow clung on inside your nose or your brain, or wherever it was that a bad smell, or, for that matter, a good smell, lingered and there was nothing you were going to do to get rid of it. For me, as a firefighter, the smell that lingered to fuck was that of a burned body. It was a sickly, sweet, meaty kind of smell that, even years after you last smelled it, you could somehow 'recall' it to your mind and smell it again. Some firefighters used to say it smelled like pork cooking, but I couldn't say that it smelled like any pork I'd eat. Interesting though, that cannibals, y'know, those tribes that regularly ate their enemies' bodies after a battle, or explorers that they just came across and took a dislike to, used to refer to a cooked man as 'long pig'. I read that somewhere. I wonder what they ate with their 'long pig', chips and peas? Mashed potato? Salad? They must have eaten it with something, surely. Probably yams or something like that. Yam salad. Long pig and yam salad. And garlic bread. Of course. I'm not sure I even know what a Yam is.

'It's very dark in there as well x' she typed.

I wondered about the electricity supply. *'So, the lights don't work?'* I asked.

'Yeah there's electricity,' she said, *'Andy tried screwing a light bulb in but it wouldn't go in. I think there's an old one in that needs taking out x We can see where Daniel died I've ringed round it x'*

A photograph arrived of a doorway, through which I could see Dan's bedroom, which meant it had been taken from his living room. The light was on in the bedroom, which raised a question about Lydia's previous statement that I didn't bother to ask. The filthy pink curtains were closed. Rubbish was piled high across the whole room and I could see that, for the most part, if I'd been standing there, at my regal height of five foot eight, I would have been looking across the top of the pile. The door was fully open, and I knew from memory that, hidden from view around the corner, assuming he still had it, was a lovely leather topped desk, the green leather with gold tooling around the edge beautifully inlaid into the top. I remembered him buying it from an antique furniture shop. He was dead proud of it and I immediately wanted one of my own. I loved it. Just thinking about the desk and the day I went around to see it; I recalled our excited and animated conversation about the chair that had to be bought to complement it. His ideal chair, a Chesterfield green leather Captain's chair, absolutely matched mine and we had a chuckle about that synchronicity. I said that a brass desk lamp with a green glass shade was the only lamp that belonged on it and he agreed. We'd had a coffee and sat, side by side on the desk, talking about studying, him chemistry and microbiology, me, the science of firefighting and what we wanted to do with our lives. I'd ended up getting too enamoured with actual firefighting and rescue rather than studying it, and he, apparently had become too enamoured with booze and collecting shite to store in his home. I hoped the desk was still there. If it was, I'd rescue it, restore it if needed and use it. Assuming my sisters agreed. I'd sit on it, have a coffee, and ponder what might have been.

In the doorway, in the space between the door, which was flat against the wall, and the assumed desk around the corner, was, I don't quite know how to describe it but here goes…have you ever been to Orkney? If you have, you'll almost certainly have been to Skara Brae and if you haven't been to Orkney, you may have seen TV programmes about Skara Brae, and if you haven't, then have a look on the internet. Now.

Skara Brae is the remains of a Neolithic village on the shore, over 5,000 years old, older than the Pyramids and Stonehenge. So says the blurb on the website and I have no reason to disbelieve it. Anyway, within the houses, there are beds built there by the inhabitants, built from the local rock. They either cut or gathered slabs of the rock and 'slotted' them into the ground to form a sort of shallow box that they would fill with mosses and grasses as a mattress and then cover themselves with, I dunno, sheepskins probably. The 'beds' were placed around the central fire pit and must have been very cosy.

The photograph of Dan's place showed something similar in the space between the open door and the desk around the corner. It looked like he'd used folded cardboard to form the edges, making a sort of box, and then filled the box with rubbish as a mattress. The box was almost coffin shaped, the narrow end in the bedroom, the wider end, the shoulder end, in the living room, close to the photographer.

Once in his bed, I assumed, he covered himself with rubbish as a duvet. Lydia had drawn a rough circle on the photograph, around the narrow end of the 'bed'. That area looked very black…black with a shitty green tinge to it. Like something biggish, maybe heavyish, had rotted there, had become, I dunno, paste, runny shitty paste and matter.

I studied the 'bed'. Zoomed in on different parts of it and sharpened it up as much as I dare then re-examined it. I decided that the black and green mess at the narrow end of the bed, was probably where his head rested, based purely on the fact that, I imagined, when a human head rots, the brain turns to some kind of porridge and seeps out. It probably became a skull-sized bowl of thick gooey soup. I imagined. I just couldn't see the feet, which, let's face it, seemed to be mostly bone, sinew and stringy muscle, causing that much discolouration. I'm no scientist but I just had my brother as lying in his coffin-shaped bed, with his head in the narrow end. The wrong way around as far as I was concerned.

I thought to myself that if I went to the trouble of making myself a box bed from stiff cardboard — sounds like a Blue Peter project — and rubbish, and shaping it like a coffin, that I would tend to lie in it the right way around, head and shoulders in the wide end, feet in the narrow end. It just made sense to me, not that making a bed of cardboard and rubbish in the shape of a coffin made any kind of sense but, you can see where I'm coming from. I hope. That, I'm afraid to say, was an anomaly for me. It was something that just didn't sit right. For me, the whole thing of making the bed in the first place, smacked of logic, even though it defied normal human logic and behaviour. For whatever reason, the place you would normally rest your head at the end of the day is, shall we say, barred from you, so, you need a place to lie down, to sleep. So, you make one and do so from the materials you have available. Simple. In this particular case, strangely complex, but, simple at the same time.

So, scenario one, you lay down to sleep after an exhausting day clambering across your in-house landfill site…and die as you dream. If it were me, I'd lie down with my head at the wide end and my feet in the narrow end.

Scenario two, you feel ill and want to lie down, you go to your bed and you lie down, as the manufacturer intended, with your head at the wide end and your feet in the narrow end. Why wouldn't you?

Scenario three, you're having a heart attack or something, and you simply collapse. But do you collapse straight into your Skara Brae bed, perfectly aligned with your head at the sharp end? To do so, you would've had to have been standing in the bed with your feet perfectly placed. It was possible but just didn't seem feasible to me.

And then, there's scenario three 'A'. I could have called it scenario four, but it sort of belongs with scenario three in a way because it's *medically* connected. So, scenario three 'A', you're not well, not well enough to be up and about, you need a duvet day, to coin a phrase, so you lie down in your Skara Brae bed in such a way that you can see your TV, you lie down the wrong way around, with your head in the sharp end. And, for whatever reason, you die whilst watching the TV. Probably of boredom as there is so much shite on TV these days.

Whichever scenario was the right one, something didn't sit right with me. I knew that everything was no more than conjecture mixed with a fertile imagination, so I just filed it away, for now, as an anomaly.

I wondered if he'd been lying on his back or his front, and where, or how, his arms had been positioned. And his legs, were they just straight out or bent or what? You don't just lie down to sleep in a perfectly straight position with arms straight down by your sides. I don't anyway. So, I wanted to know how he was positioned. I needed to know, because it would answer questions that I knew would just ferret away inside my brain for ever. Maybe the answers to these questions would simply pose other questions, both answer and pose. Or pose and answer? I settled on answer and pose. A & P. I needed an A & P session with the people involved with my brother's extraction from his cardboard Neolithic bed.

I didn't expect the police to help me in this respect, I dunno why, but I just thought they'd have some sort of party line they'd trot out so as to 'spare me'. I needed full, no-frills disclosure, and for me, the only place I knew I was gonna get that was from the firefighters involved. I needed to speak with the fire crew who'd dug him out, or uncovered him. I imagined that the police would just want the firefighters to properly ascertain his whereabouts and make the area safe for them to deliberate, or whatever they do. I thought they'd want to find out whether or not they were dealing with a crime scene before the body was actually moved.

I decided to get in touch with my mate Dennis and ask him if he could set up a meet between me and the OIC of the appliance. As I was considering how this meeting was going to take place, I decided that it would be best for me if it were an online kind of meet, say in Messenger or something, because I could be more precise with the questions, would maybe have more time to think before asking, could get my phraseology just right. And also, I'd have those answers to look at and think about without having to remember them. I realised I was over-thinking things again, a big problem of mine, though, it had served me well on occasion. My mind tends to run away with things at times though, and the speed of it could be, sort of, overwhelming. Yeah, that's a good word to describe it. A bit like an avalanche.

Often at such times, one of those fellas living inside me takes charge and shuts everything down for a few moments, and just leaves the emergency circuits running. I look as though I'm cool and relaxed, detached, calm as a mill pond. But I'm not. What's happening is my hard drive is running the fan, trying to cool everything down, just allowing me to concentrate on the most important things and in the right order. One by one, stage by stage, bit by bit. It's something I sort of 'developed' when I was a kid and came under the scrutiny of the man who was my father. My survival trick. Look unperturbed, i.e. not guilty of anything, whilst seeing through the clutter and formulating the best way through it.

'That all looks pretty bad.' I typed, *'I've seen worse but it's still bad.'* The truth was, that I don't think I had seen worse. I'm not even sure I'd seen anything as bad. It was, even on a photo, quite shocking. I think I wanted my sisters to not feel quite so bad as they would undoubtedly feel, being in there. Probably quite a clumsy attempt but, it was all I could come up with right there and then.

I studied the photograph of the 'bed' again and saw something I didn't like the look of. Not that I liked the look of anything whatsoever but, y'know. *'I recognise where we are in the photo Lydia, I can see what looks like a 7Up bottle with brown stuff in it, is that what I think it is?'* I asked.

'Yes I think so,' she said, *'we think it's piss.'*

I asked Lydia about the state of his bathroom and while I waited for her answer I felt the need to think out loud and started to type into the conversation.

'He started keeping rubbish in his house before he stopped talking to me and that was about 86, 87' I typed. *'Just before he stopped talking to me I criticised his boozing and told him that he smelled like our father, y'know, that blackcurrant smell? Remember? And I said that to him because I found out that he was cycling from home to his job in Hunts Cross and couldn't actually remember doing it cos he was still pissed in the mornings. I told him off, called him a stupid bastard because I'd recently had a job in the city centre when a cyclist got run over on a bend by an articulated lorry, the back wheels just catching him and*

drawing him in and up, grinding the cyclists body into a mush between the back wheels. Only buckled the front wheel of the bike though. We had to wait for a huge tow truck to lift the trailer unit up so we could take a wheel off to recover the body bits. Smelled like a butcher's. We swilled his blood and fat and shit down the drains. I got angry at him cos I didn't want me or any of my mates to have to do all that with him.'

'*The bathroom is full of rubbish*' she replied, '*It's about our height. X*'

'*Full of rubbish? So, not usable?*' I asked.

'*No.*' said Lydia, '*The door is open about six inches and the rubbish is up to my neck. You can't see the bathroom at all.*'

'*WTF?*' I typed and thought to myself, WTF? WTFF? And then, as the real significance of this information started to bloom in my head, I thought FHWTFF? I couldn't think of a way of getting any more fucks into the expression so I switched to thinking OMG and other versions of that.

'*I remember him coming to see mum from work drunk.*' Lydia said, '*But only the once.*'

'*Really?*' I typed, wondering why no one had said anything to me about this. '*So, he must've been drinking in work then?*'

'*Dunno x*' she replied. '*He was drinking vodka straight from bottle at Carla's funeral, I saw him x*' I briefly wondered, for about the millionth time, why some things typed by Lydia were followed by a kiss and some weren't. I'd get to the bottom of that little puzzle some time. Maybe.

Again, it occurred to me that this, drinking from a bottle at his sister's funeral, was, I dunno, *noteworthy*, and I wondered why no one had mentioned such a thing to me before now. Apparently, it was something that someone somewhere had decided I didn't need to know. I mean, this was October and that funeral had taken place in December, not far off a year before.

The conversation petered out. I was locked up inside my head, my thoughts a whirligig of the pictures of his home, the idea of a human being actually living in it, and memories of my first 20 years on this planet, sharing a room with this man who, to my regret, I just didn't know.

I needed to be there, in Liverpool, hands on, doing something. Sitting in my living room in France was just useless and I felt like a burst length, to use a fire brigade term…burst length of hose, useless. I wondered what Emily was thinking and where she'd gone, she'd said nothing for ages. *Probably in shock* I thought.

Later that night, I came back to the conversation, to see if anything else had been said. There was nothing. I typed in a thought that had occurred to me during the day, one to end the day on, maybe give people something to think about during the evening, I dunno. I just typed it anyway. I probably just felt the need to 'talk' to a member of my family. Not something I was used to or, to be honest, not the dishonest type of honest, very good at. *'Did you know he had mental problems with his eye bags so had surgery on them? And then he had mental probs with the scars from the surgery, which were micro scars I think he called them. He was convinced people could see them from miles away and if anyone in his vicinity was laughing, then in his mind they were laughing at him.*

And then he was regressed by a psychologist and apparently learned that our father (who art NOT in heaven) had tried to kill him in Germany. He was one fucked up lad.'

It was the early hours of the next morning before anyone replied, not that I was waiting for a reply or even needed one. At one o'clock in the morning, Emily came to life, 'E*xtremely sad.'* she typed, '*I knew nearly all of that, but didn't know about the regression. What a fab dad we had. Pat on the back Charlie you blurt'.* When I woke up, about 7 a.m. and checked my phone, Emily had added, at 0350, '*Yesterday proper traumatised me and it was in the dark so fuck me, whats it going to be like in the light. Its horrendous. It's like a movie set, I can't believe it.'*

I had a little think about what she'd said, lying in my bed looking at the white plank ceiling and I found it sad that it takes such statements to bring me down to earth and into a place where I can understand that, to me, as horrible as some things are, I at least had a part of my mind prepared for it, a receptacle waiting to have these new sights stored away, *sort of like partitioning a hard drive on a computer,* an unknown voice said to me in the background. *I was lucky*, I thought, *I have these devices whereas my sisters don't.* My mind flitted to the things witnessed and dealt with by murder detectives and I mentally winced at the pictures and smells they'd have filed away in their memories. I took my hat off to them. Not that I was lying there, in bed, staring at the ceiling with a hat on because I wasn't. Honestly.

I'd just finished my breakfast when I heard my phone ding on the kitchen table. Pam was making her second cup of tea. She couldn't get going in the morning until she'd had at least two cups of it. I couldn't stand it too strong, don't know how she drank it. 'Want one?' she asked. I no thanked her and picked my phone up. It was Emily.

'I know you've seen it worse Joe but I never have.' she typed, *'I can't sleep, keep seeing the spot where he died. He was our brother and that stain was his body. It's fucked my head up. I've Googled a body decomposing and what that black stain is. I know now. It's from him poor man. I feel so bad so sad. I'm broken at the moment, destroyed, no words can describe what is going on, it's mind blowing to me. I know where he died god love him. Poor man'*

I was in two minds. Literally. I had one mind, which found everything upsetting but my other mind, which, I think the best way of saying it is to say, just didn't. It just didn't. And that mind, the 'just didn't' mind, was in control of me. Emily's words upset me but my 'just didn't' mind switched that part of me off. Amazing thing, the human mind, absolutely amazing. I had to try to be less of a firefighter and more of a brother but, I wasn't sure I could pull it off.

'I understand Em.' I typed. *'It must have been hard for both of you. It's not an easy thing to deal with, especially when it's someone you know and love. Doing what you've just done, talking about how you feel, is the way to tackle it…it's how firefighters deal with things. Talking and talking about it, over and over again. Even making jokes out of some things, which sounds terrible but, sometimes you have to break the circle of horror otherwise you'd become ill.'* I stopped and had a little think about what to say next. Just be you, I thought, just say what you need to say. *'Over the years I've become too used to death and horror, so I'm probably a little bit emotionally cold at times, because I use a different mind for dealing with things. When stuff like this occurs y'know, Dan*

and Carla, I'm lucky, or unlucky, depending on your viewpoint, to be able to put my fireman's head on and deal with things dispassionately.' I wanted my sisters to maybe understand how I worked and, I dunno, maybe trust that I was a little bit different when dealing with trauma. Things like this family tragedy, made me properly realise how useful it was to have a fireground head, a head quite capable of taking over completely from the other.

Both of my sisters then had a conversation within our group conversation. Some of it was heart-breaking to 'listen' to. Emily explained how she couldn't cry but kept having intervals of uncontrollable sobbing, that came from nowhere and was always accompanied by the image of the place where he lay and decomposed.

I explained that Pam and I were changing our holiday booking so that we could come over earlier than planned and that I could get on with sorting the mess of his flat out.

Emily explained how she'd spoken to the council about clearing the flat. Apparently, the council were well aware of the state of the place, as the police had sent them photographs expressing concern over the potential biohazards involved with any clearance. This angered me because my sisters had been told by the police that it was safe for them to enter. I wanted to make waves over this but knew that it was pointless, that they would, like all such organisations, close ranks and more or less just slap you off. Complaining would give you no more than the short-lived satisfaction of making your voice heard and, for me, the energy expended in doing that would be better utilised in other ways.

Emily spoke about how our father had destroyed minds, her exact words being, in true Emily style I'm happy to say, *'What a fuckin cunt our fuckin dad was. He's done all this. He's destroyed peoples way of thinking, made them weak. Cunt'.*

That made me laugh, and I thought, *Nice one sis!* I couldn't have agreed more with her and not for the first time in my life, wondered what the point of my parents having children was. I mean, I was glad, *very* glad they had had children but, really, what was the point? Did he father his children in order to have a ready supply of sexual toys, a ready supply of human beings that he could belittle and beat, a ready supply of human beings that he could control and bully, to make himself feel better about himself? Or what? I just didn't get it. Couldn't understand it. Had no words to explain it. For me, being a father, something I desired from the age of about 12, was the, and I mean THE greatest privilege that a man could have. The bond I felt as soon as I set eyes on my daughters was the strongest, greatest emotion I have ever felt. Nothing could ever beat it. And to then have the great adventure of raising those little people, of teaching them and nurturing them, and seeing all your work come to fruition, well, that is why we are here. Everything else we do is just something to hang from that tree, that tree of life. I know that's a very simplistic way to explain the answer to the greatest human question, What's it all about? Hey? Alfie? What's it all about mate? I know it's simplistic but, I can only speak for me and being a father is, and always will be, my greatest and proudest achievement.

The conversation meandered on between the three of us, switching from emotional things to practical things and back again. We talked about his bathroom situation and how we just couldn't fathom it. Emily had a theory that maybe he had some sort of medical bag fitted and all his waste emptied into it, and Lydia thought that he just shit into his kecks and bought new ones all the time. I had to shelve the question, at least for now, because every one of such places I'd been to in my career had always had use of a toilet…they might have been no more than incredibly filthy porcelain holes encrusted with shit but, and this is a massive 'but', they were still usable as a toilet…so I put my thoughts on their thoughts to one side until I saw the place for myself.

I once again spoke to them about the pitfalls of working in his place, that there would be all sorts of stuff, especially moulds, that you really didn't want to breathe in. I spoke about the practical difficulties of, for instance, using a toilet or should I say, going to the toilet. The work was going to be heavy and disgusting. I asked them to think about the most distasteful and disgusting job or task that they'd ever done and multiply it by a thousand. And I asked them to reconsider doing the work themselves. I told them that it just wasn't a safe environment for working in, especially for two people, three including Edward, who had ongoing health issues and I told them, again, that I was more than capable and also willing to get the job done. I was more than happy for them to act as support staff, so to speak, organising skips and skip removal and obtaining the stock of consumable PPE items that would be required, but, let me do the work.

There was a long lull in the conversation, but an hour or so later, while I was watering our fruit trees, my phone dinged and vibrated in my pocket. They agreed with my work suggestions.

We had a Messenger chat later that afternoon and Pam and I changed our booking arrangements, such that we were due to arrive in the Liverpool area on Saturday 10th November. Today was Tuesday so we had a few days to make final preparations. We'd drive up through France on the Friday, catch the tunnel train in the late afternoon and stay where we always stayed on this trip, in Folkestone, then drive up north the following morning.

Chapter 11 - The Post Mortem Report

The email app on my phone trumpeted the arrival of an email just as I was finishing my breakfast. Kellogg's Corn Flakes. No-one makes Corn Flakes like Kellogg's. Other corn flakes are usually lacking in something, not quite as crisp, or a bit too chewy for a corn flake, or too many little bubbles in the surface of them, or whatever, they're just never quite as good as Kellogg's. And that's just a fact. Might even be a *food science* fact. I don't even know what *food science* is, so it might be best to discount that claim to a *food science* 'might-be'. I looked at my phone. It was the post-mortem report from the Liverpool Coroner's office. I sent it to my printer because I couldn't be arsed trying to read it on my phone and went upstairs to get the pages.

I knew that the post-mortem was going to be a bit 'tasty' for want of a better word. Once it was known that he'd lain dead in his flat for so long, it was a given that he'd be in a sorry state. What had it been? Five to six weeks since his friend or neighbour from across the road had last seen him? So, let's see, police break in on Sunday 14th October, go back six weeks and we're at about 2nd September, so let's just say he died during the first week of September.

The TV news has been banging on about this year being the hottest year on record in the UK, so, though it would be interesting to know the exact temperatures between the first week of September and the 14th October…and when I say interesting, I actually mean mildly so or even actually not interesting at all, plus, they'd mean nothing to me anyway, in terms of human bodies decomposing… suffice to say that I know if I left my corn-fed chicken from the butcher's on a plate in the living room in the first week of September, then, regardless of the ambient temperature, it is gonna be pretty ripe by the time mid-October arrives. I mean, that's not rocket science, is it? Was it food science or maybe just science? I think it's just science. I think food science is…something I probably don't think it is. Either way, my chicken would be rotted and that's a fact. Simple as that.

So anyway, I made a little pot of coffee in one of those whatchamacallits, I can never remember what they're called, a glass jar with a plunger on it. One of those. And I was right, the PM was tasty. Very tasty.

It started with some details of the deceased and gave his date and time of death as the date and time he was found. I suppose there wasn't really anything much that could be said about that. No one would ever know when he died. Only god. And he, or she, wasn't going to be giving any information out. That's another fact. Two nil.

The first section was entitled *'History'* and stated that he'd not been seen alive for five to six weeks, that the police had forced entry to the property and he'd been found, *'in an advanced state of decomposition'* on his bedroom floor. It was said that the property had rubbish piled high and, made a point of the fact that there were bottles of urine present.

Bizarrely, I found that interesting and wondered why there was special note made of this here. I mean, to most people it *is* an unusual thing, I get that, but, I dunno, for this Doctor of whatever it was, *forensic pathology*, to make a special point of it was, interesting, or, better still, *intriguing*. Anyway, to continue with the report.

A full body CT scan was performed to rule out stabbing, shooting and strangulation. There were no fractures to the long bones, his skull, vertebra, or hyoid, which I quite bizarrely remember, from reading a book by Professor Keith Simpson, a Home Office pathologist, is a little bone in the neck that snaps very easily when someone gets strangled. Funny the things that stick in your mind. The scan also showed that no organs were present.

The '*General Observations*' section showed that Dan was of slim build, 160 centimetres in height and weighed 28 kilogrammes, which was a bit shocking to say the least. Google told me that 28 kilogrammes was close to 62 pounds. Those pesky varmints had certainly feasted on my brother. I looked at his height, 160 centimetres. That seemed like it might be small and I know that me and Dan were the same height, same measurements exactly, leg, inside leg, chest, neck, everything. We could interchange clothes flawlessly if we'd wanted to, which we never did. I liked the way my brother dressed, he was always very smart, but I was, different. I didn't like to dress smartly, I preferred to look a bit, I dunno, *worn*. That was one thing he tried to do with his younger brother, that he utterly failed at, trying to get me to buy similar clothing to him, to use the same shops but, we were different in that way. But we *were* the same size.

I used the same Google converter to convert my height of five foot eight inches, to centimetres and it told me I was nearly 173 centimetres tall, what, 13 centimetres taller than my brother. That equated to over five inches in real money. That was a big difference. Had he shrunk? *Do you shrink? In life? In death?* I looked it up and yes you do shrink as you get older, but, without going right into it, which, to be perfectly honest I didn't want to, it seemed that to shrink more than, say, an inch, you probably had something other than age affecting your height, an illness or something. Maybe he had particularly thick soles on his feet, like a hobbit, or a thick scalp, I dunno, I was talking out of my arse, something I occasionally do. So, I left it at that. Dan had shrunk. Do Hobbits have thick soles? I'd have to check but I'm sure they do. Or did. Do they still exist? I'm joking, I know they don't.

But, do they…

The body was completely discoloured a brown/black combo and was covered with pupae cases, maggots, coffin flies and a number of beetles. There were multiple defects, or holes, in the body and some areas of the body were completely skeletonised. There were '*a few teeth*' present in the upper and lower jaws and I thought about Dan and his teeth, his perfect teeth and perfect smile, that is, until our father punched him in the face. A lifetime of boozing probably hadn't helped either.

I sighed and poured the last of the coffee. *Fuckin hell Dan* I thought, *I hope you enjoyed your life but, somehow, I don't think you did.*

There then followed a section headed '*Regional Examination*', starting with the '*Head and Neck*'. It made for stark reading. Complete tissue loss of the right side of the upper face and scalp. Skull and facial bones were exposed, eyes, ears, lips and nose severely decomposed, the trachea was exposed.

The '*Chest and Abdomen*' paragraph was the same, stark and brutal, two full thickness defects in the chest over the right side and the left side, which extended over the shoulder. The right side of the lower abdomen had two full thickness defects, and there was a large defect over the right side of the upper back and also around the anus and perineum. I didn't know what the perineum was. I do now.

Both hands had extensive tissue loss, exposing the bones, to the extent that it was possible to ascertain that no fractures were identified. Both upper arms had full thickness defects exposing both humeruses. Humeruses? Did I just make that word up? Is it a word? Doesn't sound right. Should it be Humeri? Or Humerii? Tell you what, let's do it like this; the right arm was eaten away such that the head of the humerus was exposed. And the left arm was the same. Both wrists were eaten through, exposing the bones.

Getting onto the feet and legs, both feet were skeletonised with no obvious fractures. The right femoral shaft and the tibia were exposed. On the left, the femoral head and left side of the pelvis were exposed.

Back to the '*Head and Neck*' area, the scalp was completely missing on the right and heavily decomposed on the left, the skull being intact but the brain and upper spinal cord completely missing.

The cervical spine, the neck part of your spine, was exposed and dislocated with the dislocation being put down to loss of tissue. The mouth, tongue, pharynx, which I think is your throat and the oesophagus were *not assessable*.

The soft tissue and strap muscles of the neck were missing and the trachea was *not assessable.*

In the chest area, the chest wall was partially exposed and all the bones, ribs, collar bones and thoracic spine were intact.

The air passages were *not assessable* and the pleural cavities contained brown powder-like material. I wondered what that was. I quickly checked the rest of the report to see if there was an explanation of this powdery stuff, found that there wasn't, but it was mentioned again as being present in the abdomen, so I fired a short and sweet email off to the coroner's office asking the question.

There were some scraps of lung still in his chest, the right one weighing 88 grammes and the left one weighing 57 grammes. Eighty-eight grammes seemed incredibly small and light to me and I had a quick look through the kitchen cupboard to get an idea of what this compared to. The right lung remnant was about the weight of 35 tea bags and the left one was about 23. I then checked on the internet and found that the normal weight for a man's lungs is about 1300 grammes, and there were just 145 grammes remaining.

Dan's heart and aorta were completely gone and the coronary and pulmonary arteries *not assessable.*

His abdomen contained, what I assumed was the same powder-like brown material as the pleural cavity and not much else. Everything that should've been in the abdominal area, was gone. No wonder he didn't weigh much.

The Cause of Death was, as expected, 'UNASCERTAINED'.

The report was dated and signed off by a specialist registrar in forensic pathology, Dr. E. M. Jones, who was supervised by a Home Office Registered Forensic Pathologist.

We'd asked for the full report and, I've got to say, we got it. Stark, we expected, stark we got. It must have made for shocking reading for my sisters who had probably never come across such stark and brutal reports as this. I didn't have much experience of such reports either but I at least had *some* experiences with forensic reports of people having been involved in fires, all of which were pretty brutal. So, the post-mortem report was maybe not as shocking to me as to them. Having said that, the thought that my brother had become a feast for insects and vermin, was not easy to deal with. It was expected, given the circumstances, but the thought of your brother being slowly consumed was…not nice. Yet again, I got angry at my brother for choosing to go down the road he went down. He had a family who wanted him in their lives. He had options available to him that were very different to the ones he'd taken. His life could have been so different but his mind wouldn't let him out.

I now knew the name of the person, his neighbour, that had alerted the police to the fact that Dan hadn't been seen for a while. His name was Walter Fitzgibbon, and the thing that struck me about his statement, was that, you're mates with your neighbour, to the extent that you 'often' have a drink with him, yet it takes five to six weeks before noticing that you haven't seen him for a while. Feasible I suppose but, you're not really 'mates' are you. Acquaintances maybe but certainly not mates. Mind you, this Walter Fitzgibbon had had more social interaction with my brother than I had, so maybe, I thought, maybe I shouldn't make judgments, y'know, do my normal thing, and instantly distrust people or their motives for doing and saying what they do and say. It was hard to not do that; I'd done it all my life and it had worked well for me. I had a little think about that and decided it was possible that there had maybe been times when it hadn't worked out so well for me as well. I couldn't think of any of those occasions off the top of my head but, y'know…maybe.

I went and emptied the coffee grounds on Pam's roses, and was contemplating the garden, thinking that the grass could do with cutting, another hour of my life wasted, but at least I had a large petrol mower, which trumped my mum's bacon scissors by a fair bit. Which took me to the place I go to every time I cut grass or contemplate cutting grass, the place where I ask myself the question as to why a father would make his young son cut the grass on the front garden with a pair of scissors, when there was a perfectly good rotary mower in the coal hole? Of course, there is no answer. Another thing was, regarding the mower, only he was allowed to use it but never did because he made us, me and Dan, cut the grass with hedge shears and a pair of scissors. I mean, WTF? Actually, there was one time, maybe two, when we *were* allowed to use the mower…when he 'loaned' us out to one of his mates, or one of his cronies, as my mum called them. He sent us around to his mate's house to cut his grass and we were allowed to use the mower. Didn't make any sense to me then, and still doesn't now. Hey fuckin Ho.

I was on my way back into the house when I heard the email trumpet sound on my phone. It was from the coroner's office.

It was from Richard, the liaison officer. He said that the powder mentioned was most likely the dried remnants of the lungs after complete tissue breakdown and that the majority of his decomposition was mummification, so, intense drying of the skin and organs.

So, my brother had become mummified. I reckoned he'd have liked that. Like Tutankhamun. He always had a fascination with rotting meat *and* Egyptian mummies, so, ending up, sort of like King Tut, would have pleased him, I think.

He studied rotting meat, really studied it. He was fascinated by it. He knew all about the different insects that came to feed and how the whole thing worked. He was an angler and we used to have to get two buses to the bait shop on Smithdown Road to buy our maggots. I say 'we' because my brother was determined to make me into an angler as well, a task he failed at. I liked roaming the lakes in the city parks and the various crater ponds dotted about the outskirts of Liverpool from the blitz, but I never took to fishing. Dan was always moaning about the cost of our bait, the bus fares plus the maggots themselves, plus the Caramac or Aztec Bar we had to buy from the shop by the bus stop. So, he decided to grow his own maggots.

I think he started with some chicken offal he kept from cleaning the chicken out one Sunday. He actually liked cleaning the chicken out and sometimes I'd stand and watch. I hated it, hated the smell and the overall messiness of it but he loved it.

He put the offal on a plate in the little greenhouse-cum-shed outside and waited. Sure enough, he was able to harvest maggots from it in no time. I can't remember the details but I think he used to harvest different maggots at different times. To me, a maggot is a maggot is a maggot but he reckoned fishermen like different maggots for different fishes, or something like that. I found it all a bit boring. One time, he actually caught a rabbit in Sefton Park, using our box, stick and string trick and brought it home as a pet, but it died soon after and he used that little corpse as a maggot factory. He'd be called an entrepreneur these days.

If I haven't already told you, the box, stick and string trick worked like this. We'd put bread out in the middle of our dockland street for the pigeons, but leading to an upside-down box that was held up by a stick that had string tied to it, which led across the pavement and into our letterbox. We'd watch through the letterbox and when a pigeon went under the box we'd pull the string, which pulled the stick and the box would fall and trap the pigeon. Usually, a few seconds later the box would start moving down the street in the same way a pigeon moves. It was dead funny. After a few minutes we'd let the pigeon out and it would walk off, and then, if it could be arsed, fly away. Our grandad taught us that little hunter-gatherer trick. He taught us lots of good stuff.

The email from Richard, the police liaison officer, raised more questions than it answered and I only wanted one answer to one question. As soon as I read it, a little, *something*, not quite an alarm but on that scale, was humming in the background. I couldn't quite bring whatever it was to the forefront of my mind, but I knew I'd get there eventually. The anomaly was logged and it would work its way out, I knew that.

I went and cut the grass. As I walked up and down the expanse of sheep food, I thought about Dan and his mummification. I remembered a conversation on the fire station years before, me, Dennis, Vic and Gerry, sitting around talking about a series on TV about the boy king, king Tut. There was this fella detached into our station from an adjoining station for the day because one of our lads had gone off injured after a falling roof tile hit his arm, breaking it. The arm not the tile. This detached lad,

Billy, had a really strong scouse accent and when he heard us talking about the TV series he said, '*warra yers talkin about, toot'n car moon?*' and we all fell about laughing. From that day on, whenever Tutankhamun was mentioned, the boy king was always referred to, in a strong scouse accent, as *Toot'n car moon* and, in true fire brigade fashion, the name was, first of all elongated to become *Root'n Toot'n car moon*, then shortened to become *Root'n Toot'n*, then shortened again to become simply *Root'n*. The boy king of Egypt, otherwise known as *Root'n*.

Chapter 12 - The PM Penny Drops

The morning after the post-mortem report, having slept on it, the anomaly was out in the open and I could see it. I wasn't completely certain of my thoughts, by which I mean, I could be talking out of my arse. Again. But…

My brother died under a pile of rubbish. He lay there and became a feast for insects and their offspring, rats and mice. And this is where I could be talking rubbish, but here goes…the things eating him would, to my mind, just keep eating until there's nothing left. From what I can make out, different creatures eat, apart from each other, different parts of the body at different stages of decomposition. All of his internal organs were gone, apart from some lung remnants, approximately, I'm not good at working out percentages, so let's say 10 percent of the average starting weight of a pair of male lungs remained. He started with about 1300 grammes and ended up with 145 grammes.

So, while the diners were eating his heart and liver for instance, did they eat his lungs as well, or not? I mean, why wouldn't they? They ate everything else, so they wouldn't have stopped at his lungs. So…

If they ate his lungs, and, at the same time, his lungs were drying out, and, apparently, turning into powder, then it would seem that the human tissue-to-powder process was faster than the wee beasties dining process. I'm obviously no authority on any of this, in fact, I'm not an authority on anything except, maybe, jam and peanut butter sandwiches, but I found this to be…interesting.

So, OK, his lungs dry out and, to the astonishment of the diners, starts to shower them with brown snow — I can't think of many things worse than *brown* snow — so, wouldn't that brown snow simply drop? Straight down? And all end up at the bottom of the pleural cavity? How does it also end up in the abdominal cavity? Blown by the wind that is keening across his body, five feet under the rubbish? Carried there by the diners leaving in their droves because they were being snowed on? If it was carried to the abdominal cavity by the diners leaving, then, wouldn't the brown powder also be in and on other parts of the corpse? Apparently not, because, to my way of thinking, if it was notable enough to mention as being in the pleural and abdominal cavities, then it would surely be notable enough to mention as being in other places too and the fact that it wasn't mentioned in that way, suggests that it wasn't in any other locations.

I know I don't know what I'm talking about and I know I'm out of my depth but, if something is noteworthy, then it's noteworthy for a reason. Maybe this kind of wording showed up in every case of a corpse like my brother. I didn't know, but, bottom line, for me, with regards to the PM report, was this; it was full of the kind of jargon I'd expect but with two noteworthy items that just seemed at odds, the mention of the bottles of urine and the brown powder-like substance.

I needed to ponder this info and instead of waiting for a suitable time, a part of my mind did what it does and went into some kind of hyper-drive. Were the two things connected in some way? Was the doctor making note of something that he expected to be questioned about? Did he have an idea as to what the brown powder was and why it was in two places? And if he was expecting to be questioned about it, from whom was he expecting those questions? From the family? Or the police? I'd already asked the question and been told it was 'most likely' from the mummified lungs, so effectively, I dunno, *held off.* I mean, the report was as dry and scientific as it could get, so, if you're going to go to the trouble of reporting something a little bit, *out of kilter* with that dryness, then why treat the enquiry of it as a 'bit of a nuisance'? While dealing with the corpse of my brother, there must have been lots of snippets of information, not really relevant to the essence of the report, so why, if there is, apparently, a normal and slightly mundane explanation for the powder, mention it at all? Was the pathologist expecting the police to ask the questions and been informed that those questions weren't going to be asked? Did he *know,* had he been *told*…but not necessarily in these words…that the police were *not* going to invest time and money into looking further into the death of a dirty little alchy who lived in a rat-infested tip of his own making? Was my imagination running riot here? Probably. Because, surely, surely, the authorities looked into everything questionable about the death of any and every person, regardless of their personal opinions of that person. Surely.

Later that day, after I'd packed the car ready for the drive up to Liverpool, I had a brandy and diet coke. It was about 8.30 p.m. and I was just on my way for a shower, when my phone dinged. It was Emily.

'Joe, we're really sorry, but it's the only slot we could get, our Dan's funeral is at 10 tmrw at Anfield Crem. Xxx'

Chapter 13 - Stunned

To say I was stunned would be wrong. To be fair, I don't actually know what I was. I don't really have a word to describe what I felt. I could say I was numb but, I don't think I was. I could say I was livid but I wasn't. I could say that I expected something like this to happen but I didn't. It was a bolt from the blue, as they say. I didn't see it coming at all and, if the truth be told, I was taken aback in a big way. I wanted to go on the attack but instinctively knew that it would be wrong.

Once again, Big Joe took control and my fireground head was on, the other one, the one containing a double brandy and coke, was tucked away somewhere, I dunno, somewhere nice.

'How come you're only just telling me now?' I asked.

'We both thought the other one had told you and it was only just now, while we were chatting that we realised you hadn't been told.' typed Emily, *'we're really sorry xxx'*

I didn't believe her. Them. I didn't believe them. Not for a minute. Not for a second. *'Ok, look,'* I typed, *'don't worry about it. It's been a very stressful time for all of us and there's nothing that can be done about it now, so, get some rest, you've got a big day tomorrow.'*

I couldn't think of a reason why they didn't want me there for the funeral but it was obvious they didn't. *'When did you book it?'* I asked.

Emily answered. Lydia was there, because her green blob was lit, but she was saying nothing. *'Tuesday xxx'*

'We spoke on here on Tuesday, how come you didn't tell me then?' I asked.

'We went to the funeral parlour after that chat we all had and we had to take the slot on offer, otherwise it would have been weeks.' typed Emily, Lydia still sitting in the background. *'We just wanted it done and dusted. We were gonna come home, have a bite to eat and let you know. Xxx'*

'So why didn't you?' I asked.

'Like I said,' Emily again, *'we both thought the other had told you.'* There was a slight lull, maybe 90 seconds or so, then she finished off, *'We had a bite to eat and a few too many drinks, and we just both thought you'd been told xxx'.*

It was insulting. Yes, it could have easily happened like that but I knew that it hadn't. Gut instinct, or something, I just knew they were lying, albeit in a plausible way. It was insulting to me that they apparently believed that I would fall for it…or not. Either way, it didn't matter to them. That was the really insulting part, that it didn't matter whether I believed what they were saying or not. What was going to happen was going to happen and there was nothing I could do about it and they had engineered it that way.

'Ahh well,' I typed, *'don't worry about it, get your heads into gear for tomorrow and I just hope the day goes well. Are there many people coming?'*

We chatted on for a few more minutes and then she went. I watched both their little green blobs disappear.

I left Big Joe in charge. I'm not sure who actually makes that kind of decision but, it doesn't really matter as long as it works. I had another brandy and coke…very unusual for me, so I assume it was the big fella who wanted it. It was very rare for me to have more than one drink. I liked the taste of it rather than the effect. Or maybe I just didn't like the effect of it, full stop, or maybe I was afraid of the effect of it. Not that it matters.

I've got to say, I felt safe with my other head on. I had a long drive coming up and needed my wits about me. I'd have plenty of time to think things through on the way up north. We always stopped overnight in Folkestone, had a decent meal, usually steak pie and chips, and then made our way up to the north of England on the following day. The best thing about my other head being in control was that Big Joe always, *always* knew how to turn a negative into a positive. He was a pretty slick operator.

Chapter 14 - Homecoming

The trip up to Liverpool passed without any problems. The Channel Tunnel was its usual smooth and hassle-free way of travelling over the Channel. Or under. Don't know why I said over when, clearly, I meant under. Our normal place to stay on this trip was, as usual, clean, and welcoming but cheap and the steak pie and chips was, as per the norm, delicious. So, everything was normal. So far.

We arrived at our little holiday cottage which turned out to be a bit bigger than we thought, and unpacked our stuff, leaving all my tools in the car.

On the Sunday morning, I dropped Pam at her daughter's place and drove over to Emily's to get my set of keys. She opened the door, still in her dressing gown and we greeted each other as though we'd only seen each other hours before. Her face looked tired and she still had make-up on, the mascara smudged around her eyes. We briefly hugged at the front door and she led the way to the kitchen. She smelled of alcohol. I sat down at one end of the table.

'Cup of tea?' she asked, filling the kettle, and switching it on. 'Or coffee?'

'I'll have a coffee please Em,' I said, 'not too strong but not too weak.' It was a little joke between us that had been running for years. She was supposed to say, 'So just perfect then.' And I would have said 'Correct.' But she didn't. And so, neither did I.

There seemed to be a bit of tension, but it could have been my imagination. I was possibly too sensitive at times and maybe misinterpreted little things on occasion but, as was always the case, I'd stick with my first impression until it was proven wrong. Was she embarrassed at the booking of the funeral, I wondered, and the fact that the booking had prevented me from attending? I thought we all had enough to deal with at the moment, so was never going to make anything of it. She went to the fridge and got milk out. The kettle started making its kettle noise and I thought, *that's a bit of a noisy fucker.*

'How's things Em?' I asked her. 'How did the funeral go?' Neither of my sisters had called me or messaged me to tell my how the funeral went, which I thought was quite bad but, at the same time, quite like us, our family. We were a strange bunch, no question. Not your common or garden everyday family. I think it would be OK for me to say that in all my years I'd never come across a family quite like mine. And, if the truth be told, I didn't really want to.

She started putting the stuff in the mugs to make the drinks. 'It was OK Joe, nothing unusual or special, just a funeral.'

'Sounds good.' I said, which was the kind of thing she would have expected me to say. My humour. Not to everyone's liking I grant you but usually it was to the liking of my sister. She didn't seem to notice it.

'Our Lydia got pissed and made a knob of herself.' she said, pouring water into the mugs. 'Do you want milk?' I nodded and she poured.

'Why, what did she do?' I asked.

She brought the drinks over and sat down at the opposite end of the kitchen table. She still hadn't looked at me.

Emily took a sip of coffee, opened the window behind her and lit a ciggy. She blew the smoke out and up, towards the ceiling and looked at me as she brought her eyes back down. Then looked away. 'She got pissed, but really quickly, like, just one drink really, y'know like Carla used to do?'

'Yeah,' I said, 'but…Carla was an alchy wasn't she so her one drink, the first one, was like a top up wasn't it, so…' the thought was making its way to the surface as the words were coming out of my mouth. 'Are you saying Lydia is the same as Carla and Dan? Alcoholic?'

'No,' she replied and took a drag on her ciggy, blew the smoke to the ceiling, and had a sip of coffee. 'No,' she repeated, 'I'm not saying she's the same, I actually don't know what she is Joe, I hardly see her these days so, I don't really know much about her, I'm just saying that she seemed to get pissed really quick.' She took another drag on her fag and exhaled the smoke as the spoke…ha-ha see what I did there? 'Maybe she'd had a few before she left the house. I dunno.'

'So, what did she do to make a knob of herself, apart from getting pissed after one drink?' I asked, taking a swig of my coffee. I was going to take a sip but it was cooler than I thought so I swigged. Not like you'd swig a cold pint of beer on a hot day, not that kind of swig, more of a massive sip of hot to warm coffee on a cold day, so maybe this was a massive sip rather than a swig. 'Got any biscuits Em?' I asked.

She got up and got the biscuit tin, opened it and put it on the table right by me. As soon as she opened the tin I could smell them. Custard creams. The queen of biscuits. Crisp little sandwiches of vanilla, er, stuff, a slightly toffee smell to them, a warm, friendly, homely smell. As you can see, I quite liked custard creams, loved them maybe, yeah, I did, I *loved* custard creams. I loved them. They were very, no, never mind very, they were *extremely* dunkable, especially in coffee. I lifted one out of the tin, away from its family, dunked it straight in and straight out of my coffee and bit into it, closed my eyes, savouring the release of vanillery custard with toffee undertones into my mouth and swallowed. I rolled my eyes at Emily, 'Vunderfuckinbar…' I breathed, slipping into German.

Emily laughed, or half laughed. It took 10 years off her in an instant. 'You daft twat.' she said.

I asked her if I could have another one and she told me to eat all of them if I wanted. I just took two more and put the lid back on the tin, slid it away from me.

'So, what did she do?' I asked again, 'Please tell me she didn't do a striptease.'

Emily told me how Lydia had seemingly got pissed after just one drink and then had draped herself over just about anyone who would stay still for long enough, telling them how she loved them and never saw enough of them and how *we should do this more often* which was kind of, I dunno, a touch inappropriate shall we say.

Emily gave me the two keys I'd need for gaining access to the flat and I studied them momentarily. Nothing had changed about a Chubb key. Solid feel to it, very distinctive shape. I would deffo know a Chubb key if you blindfolded me and put one in my hand. 'Were there three sets of keys Em, without having to get extras made?' I asked.

'Yeah,' she said, 'we've got a set each.'

We talked about the PPE stuff and Emily gave me a large cardboard box full of masks, the wrong type, paper suits and a box of latex gloves in a large size. We spoke about bagging up and she explained that the skip company didn't want stuff bagging up because it was easier for them to process the stuff without having to de-bag it all. I made sure that they knew we needed the open-ended skips, the ones with doors, you know the ones. Once sifted, I'd barrow the stuff out, dump it until the doors needed to be shut, then switch from a barrow to a large bucket, the plastic ones with two handles. We had a handful of them because the handles were notoriously snappable. What I'd do is fill three buckets and put them on the barrow to wheel around to the skip.

'Here's a thing Em...' I said, 'there's constant talk of paying for things *from the estate.*'

'Yeah, Lydia keeps saying that.' she said.

'So obviously we need to have an idea of what 'the estate' means don't we.' I said, 'We need access or at least knowledge, of what he has. I can pay for skips and stuff, but, at the end of the day, I need to get this money back. He, Dan, needs to pay to clean up his mess, assuming he has the necessaries. What do you think?'

Emily agreed with me. 'Yeah, I agree completely,' she said, 'but, Edward has already paid for the first two skips up front. Lydia said he's gonna pay for everything and get his dosh back at the end. Dan made all this mess, god love him, and if he's got the wherewithal, it should be used to clean everything up.'

I asked where Edward was getting all his money from, because I knew he didn't work on account of his health. Apparently a relative had died and left him a bit of a wedge, so, if it worked for Lydia, then it worked for me. It got me thinking though.

We spoke for a while about what we knew, if anything, about Dan's situation. Not the situation of having just been cremated, the situation prior to his death. It transpired that some bank documents had been found in the garden, so we had account numbers and stuff. Emily had been dealing with the bank, but, of course, we couldn't access funds until probate had been completed. She'd arranged for up-to-date statements to be sent out. 'I thought we'd already have them but, maybe this coming week.' she said. She lit another ciggy and blew smoke out. The cat scratched at the back door to come in. I hate cats. Always have done. Can't stand them near me.

Emily let the cat in and it immediately came to rub up against my leg. That sets my teeth on edge and I moved it away from me with my leg. It looked up at me as if to say *WTF*? She shooed it into the hall and shut the door. She knew I didn't like cats and wasn't bothered, whereas Carla, my dead sister, hated me for not liking cats, which I couldn't understand. I mean, I wasn't particularly keen on warthogs either but people just accepted that. And tapirs, what are they all about? Strangely ugly bastards. So, I wasn't exactly a tapir lover either but that was apparently OK. Not that I'd ever asked anyone. Mind you, warthogs and tapirs did have one thing in their favour, they didn't cosy up to you and try to rub themselves up your leg. Not in my experience anyway. Just the thought of a tapir rubbing itself up against my leg makes me shudder.

I asked Emily if she knew whether or not Dan had life insurance. She said that she was hoping his bank statements could answer all we needed to know in that respect and I nodded, 'Of course, so we'll just have to wait and see won't we.'

We chatted on about this and that for another hour, had another cup of coffee and two more custard creams, the queen of biscuits. Emily had two more fags and we went over the skip changing arrangements and that was it, I stood up to leave. As I put my jacket on, Emily's phone buzzed. It was Lydia, asking if I'd been and wanting to meet me at the flat the following morning, to coordinate what we were going to do. I wondered why she hadn't just messaged me, cut out the middleman, or woman. 'Yeah.' I said, Emily thumbing the word into her phone. 'What time?' I was amazed, always am, by my sister holding the phone in two hands and using both thumbs to type. You're probably amazed that I was amazed at this dexterous feat but, what can I say, it's just not something I could do. Or rather, I could, but the word I usually typed was Hdhakdyebffjfhrn, or something similar. Looks a bit Icelandic.

Emily walked me to the front door. As we walked past the living room door the cat popped its head out being nosy. I gave it a death stare and its tail went straight up into the air and it scampered back to its perch on the arm of the chair by the window. It looked over its shoulder at me as it retreated, and almost seemed to sneer at me. Emily's phone buzzed again. 'Ten.' she said and I nodded and said OK.

We briefly hugged at the front door and as I stepped out, I turned and frowned, 'Edward paying for all this stuff Em,' I said, 'Why would he do that, not knowing for certain that he'll get it back?' I walked down the path but after about two paces, maybe three, I turned around. 'Does Lydia know something we don't? Maybe?' I turned and headed for the car. 'Speak tomorrow Em!' I called out over my shoulder.

I got in the car and drove off.

Chapter 15 - The Midden

We left the cottage about eight o'clock and headed for Susan's place, Pam's eldest daughter. They were going shopping in the city centre, Liverpool city centre, meeting up with Kaitlin, Pam's youngest daughter and they were going to do some shopping, have a coffee, some dinner, or lunch if you're posh and generally do stuff they hadn't done together for quite a while.

It would be good for Pam to do something normal. She'd been shifting stone and mixing mortar, moving trees about, digging holes and just doing stuff that, how can I put it, was generally shite stuff to do. Always wearing work clobber, steelies, y'know, boots with steel toe caps, dusty jumpers, and battered work gloves. She deserved something different, so today, she'd put on a really nice dress, one I'd bought her a few years back, a sort of, erm, nice one, with a nice pattern that was very…nice and very Pam. She'd picked it, I'd bought it, that's the best way of putting it. She completed her ensemble with a nice pair of boots, long ones, knee length, and no, not kinky ones, just long ones. Again, she picked them and I, no, hang on, I didn't buy these boots, it was the steelies I bought for her, she'd bought the long ones herself. The get up was topped with a lovely coat and a lovely hat, woolly, but not the kind of woolly hat you think I mean, with a bobble on the top…no, this was like a sort of a cap, no not a cap, it had, like, a peak but, maybe it was a cap but anyway, it was quite…chic. Yeah, it was chic. I called it her Carnaby Street cap. Hat. Whatever. It all went well together anyway, and that's the important thing. She didn't get the cap in Carnaby Street by the way. I don't actually know where she bought it. Not that it matters.

It would be a nice day for all of them, but, I've got to say, I was glad I wasn't going. I can't stand shopping, can't stand traipsing around, especially with, hope she doesn't read this, Pam. Now don't get me wrong, I love the bones of her but, when she is shopping for, let's say a coat, she'll go to every possible shop and look at every possible coat, try them all on, and usually end up buying the first one she saw…nothing wrong with that, probably pretty standard procedure for buying a coat or whatever. It's not the *standard clobber-buying procedure* that I can't handle, it's the speed and the complexity that has me spinning. I always end up feeling car sick. Pam is fast. And I mean *fast*. Very fast. At moving around. She's not fast at making her mind up, in fact, she's very slow. If I try to keep her in sight, which I tend to do because I'm shopping with her, giving my opinion on her choices, and generally trying to be helpful, then within minutes of her starting to move between the aisles and displays, I feel travel sick. My head is spinning, I break into a sweat, my lips start to tingle and my gums go numb. It's like being track-side in Super Mario Kart. The next stage after numb gum is to vomit and once I'm at the vomiting stage, in order to *not* vomit, I need to be still, very still, for some considerable time, maybe as long as an hour. So, much as I love my wife, I hate going shopping with her.

When I go shopping for me, it's like a military operation. I know what I want, I know which shop sells it, I know how much it is and what size I want. I go to my car, drive to the shop, park up, get the item, go to the checkout, return to the car, drive home. Done. I call it blitzkrieg shopping. It works. Try it.

I dropped Pam at Susan's and set off for Dan's. During the drive there, I recalled the day he came around to see me at my first house, a little old terraced one. Built in the early 1900's, probably early to mid-20's, it was solid. Cold and draughty, rising damp, ice on the inside of the bedroom windows in the winter, but solid. And solid, apparently, was what mattered. My mum told me. 'Solid house that.' she'd say, then move onto the price of a loaf in Asda. I once asked her for an explanation of the *solid house* statement, expecting some olde-worlde wisdom on the way they used to build houses *'back in the day'* and she said that it *'wasn't gonna fall down in a hurry'*. Which was reassuring, though many of them fell down in a fucking *Olympic* hurry when the Luftwaffe dropped in. *It can fall down in slow motion all day long* I used to think, *as long as I can still move on fast forward.*

About 1977

There had been a knock on my door and as I approached it, I could see a man with a push-bike through the frosted glass. I knew it was Dan. I opened the door. 'Alright Dan.' I said, glad to see him but not betraying that fact with my voice. Strange family. As I keep saying.

'Hello Joe.' he said, in his quiet monotone, his eyes never looking into mine. He may have been happy to see me, I don't know. He took the bike clips off his jeans, hung them on the handlebars and parked his bike against the wall in the hall.

'Coffee?' I asked.

'Yeah.' he said. 'Yes please.'

'Go in and sit yerself down.' I said, motioning with my head to the living room. Sheba, my gorgeous German Shepherd had come out to greet my brother and they both went into the living room. I made coffee, milk no sugar for Dan, milk two sugars for me and carried them into the living room. I put his on the little table next to his chair and sat in the armchair opposite. Sheba stayed sitting next to my brother while he rubbed his hand in the thick ruff of her neck. Sheba liked that and seemed to smile. Everyone liked doing it, the fur was so thick and luxuriant. She was a beautiful dog, beautiful classic colouring, black as black could be and a deep tan brown. She had beautiful eyes full of expression and, above all, a marvellous personality. She was loyal as only a dog can be and I loved her and was, to coin a phrase, gutted when she had to be put down. Cancer. I've never got over it and for that reason I would never have another dog. I love dogs and I would love to have one, have toyed with it so many times, especially since moving to France, but I could never face that raw sense of loss again. Never.

We drank our coffee and spoke about the stuff brothers talk about. Work, family, everyday stuff. Dan was a lab assistant at a large pharmaceutical company. He wanted to be a biochemist and certainly had the wherewithal to do it but, our father wouldn't let him go to university. He had to be bringing money into the house, end of.

I said to Dan, 'You should just go to uni and fuck what he says Dan, it's your life you can do what you want.' He'd replied that it would cost too much and that he couldn't live at mum's and not bring money in and without money he couldn't get a flat or anything, so he was stuffed, basically.

I told him that he could live in my house while he studied, and it wouldn't cost him anything. But then he said that food costs money and he wouldn't be able to contribute and that he would feel terrible putting lights on and using hot water. And I just kept saying stuff like 'Well we'll cross that bridge when we get to it, don't worry about that kind of stuff, worry about doing your degrees.' But I knew that Dan was never going to do his degree. He was never going to uni. He had the brains in abundance, but Dan was missing something when it came to being decisive and resolute. Sometimes it was painful to see. I tried to get him to join the fire brigade. He had the strength and fitness and I thought that if he was in the same job as me, I could keep an eye on him, we could study together, pass our exams, and get up through the ranks, become the brothers that ruled the brigade. I always had big ideas. At first, he seemed to like the idea but then a cloud settled in his eyes and he'd switched off from it. That's what used to happen with my brother…he'd see a way forward and you could see it in his face, in his body language. And then something would happen. A cloud would descend. His eyes would become sort of, smoky. Distant. Like he was trying to eavesdrop on someone else's conversation. A faint, almost imperceptible vertical line would appear between his eyebrows. It was like another person was talking to him and telling him that he couldn't do that, that he wouldn't be able to do this or that, like he was constantly arguing with himself and his alter ego was so much stronger than him, it always won. Always. It was like he was bullying himself.

'I've bought a flat.' he said, lighting a ciggy. Sheba slunk off. She hated cigarette smoke.

I was...confused. I think that was the best word to describe my thoughts. I was happy that he'd been decisive, happy that he appeared to be happy with his decision. But then I was not happy because this meant that he was now tied to a mortgage and therefore his job, a job that, essentially, was beneath him. I was unhappy that I knew he was going to spiral down from where he was at that minute, based purely on the job he was doing and the job I knew he wanted to do. My brother was a scientist, a mathematician. My brother was someone who thought up experiments, not someone who carried them out. My brother was passionate about plants and animals, chemistry, biology and maths, and always had been. He was a proper boffin, was my brother. He'd start talking to me about this and that, and I had to tell him, constantly, that I didn't understand what he was talking about. 'Yeah, you do,' he'd say, and produce a pad and pen and scrawl all this stuff over the paper, much worse than hieroglyphics. All sorts of equations and symbols would appear, together with squiggles and shit and then he'd say, 'See what I mean?'

'Bought a flat where?' I asked, lighting a ciggy of my own. Sheba, who was lying outside the living room door in the hall, looked at me, a disappointed look on her face, got up and walked off towards the kitchen where I knew she would lie down by the back door. I imagined her tut tutting as she walked away.

'It's a new-build.' he said and mentioned a large national house-building company. 'Whereabouts?' I asked, blowing smoke at the ceiling.

'A one-bedroomed first floor flat on a brand new estate.' he explained.

'Where abouts Dan?' I asked.

'It's got its own designated car space.' he said, lighting another cigarette from his dying one and blew his smoke to join my smoke at the ceiling. Poor ceiling, I thought. 'For when I get me own car.'

'Where's the flat Dan?' I asked.

'West Derby.' he said.

I was relieved. West Derby was a nice area. A very nice area. 'Whereabouts in West Derby?' I asked.

He described an area that I knew wasn't West Derby. It was off a road called West Derby Road, that led to West Derby from city centre, but in no way was it West Derby. We talked more and I narrowed down the area of the flat he'd bought. I knew the area quite well. It was in the adjoining area to my station area. It was scum city. Full of drugs and crime.

'You do know that's not West Derby, don't you? It's off West Derby Road, but it's not West Derby.' I said.

'Well yeah, but…it's almost.' For the first time since he'd arrived, he looked directly into my eyes. It felt like a challenge.

Dan was my big brother, I loved him and for all my life he'd been my hero. He gave me my music, my love of photography, my love of mountains and walking in them. I'd looked up to him since, for ever. And that wasn't going to change. But the fact was, that it was not West Derby and was nowhere near being almost West Derby either. 'The main thing Dan, is that you're happy.' I said. 'So, when you moving in and what can I do to help?'

The approach to Dan's place was sort of 'around the back'. You went from the apparent front of the terrace and walked around the back, where the front doors to the upper flats were. A bit weird in my mind but there you go, 1980's Britain, where builders just wanted to fit as many dwellings on a piece of land as they possibly could, never mind the poor bastards who'd live in them, buy them even, as my brother had done.

It had been a long time since I'd been to my brother's flat. A very long time. I tried to work out when the last time had been. It was about 1988. Thirty years ago. Thirty years. That is a long time. A life sentence for murder. A whole career in the police or the fire service. Back then, the last time, was after he'd had the fire in his flat and been rescued by my colleagues from an adjoining station. I remember the occasion like it was yesterday.

1988ish

I was on a night shift at my station. We'd just had a body job. It was a strange job. A 'smell of smoke' call. People would call the brigade and say they could smell smoke and were concerned. We'd get turned out and would treat it as any emergency and this particular job was no exception and served to underline exactly why we treated a 'smell of smoke' call the way we did.

We turned out with two pumps, nine men. Blue lights, two-tones, donning BA en route, the normal stuff we'd do. We arrived at the address, a red-brick terraced street in Aigburth, on the outskirts of the city centre and dismounted. The people who'd called us came out to meet us and simply said they could smell smoke in their house but couldn't work out where it was coming from. We went in.

Sure enough, you could smell smoke, but you couldn't see it, there was no smoke haze at all. It was hard to tell what the burning material was. Usually, or should I say, often, you can tell what's burning by the smell. Like anyone can. But as a firefighter, you obviously get to smell a lot more than the average person. There are some things that have really distinct smells. Such as a pan of food. When a pan of food gets left on the gas ring and dries out, it burns. Obviously. But as well as the food burning, the pan itself starts to burn. And that smell is particularly noisome. It stays with you, on your clothes and in your nose for days.

At this incident, it was hard to say what was burning. It wasn't electrical. It wasn't a pan of food. It wasn't human flesh. It wasn't paper. That had a distinct smell too, especially newspaper, probably because of the ink, I dunno. Anyway, we searched the house, paying particular attention to the loft and there was nothing. So, we did a sweep of the back yards in the immediate vicinity. Nothing. We turned our attention to the immediate neighbours but again, nothing. We extended the search outwards from the immediate neighbours. Nothing. Smoke will always find a way into a building through the tiniest openings, but you can usually see something. Here, there was nothing. None of the adjacent homes had the smell, just the people who'd called us, we could only smell the smoke in their house and so we shifted our concentration back to them. We searched everywhere again. We examined everything but found nothing. And the smell wasn't going away. It wasn't getting any stronger, but it wasn't going away.

We decided to extend the search to the other side of the street. Strange things happen with smoke and drifting smells. Sometimes what should be obvious just isn't. One house on the other side of the street didn't respond to our knocks. There were no lights on. One of the lads opened the letter box and had a sniff. He said he couldn't be sure but there was maybe a faint smell of smoke. The boss knelt down in front of the letter box to get a sniff himself and as he did so, I shone a torch at the window. The curtains were drawn so everything was black but just as I turned away, I noticed a bead of water run down the inside of the glass, which was a little bit of a giveaway. I mentioned it to the boss as he was sniffing through the letterbox. He looked at the beads of condensation running down the inside of the window and told us to break in. We tested the door for a mortise lock, which was engaged, and then struck the door three times, once for each hinge, top, bottom and middle.

The door swung in and was manhandled out of the way and two of us, me and Den, entered in BA. Two others, Vic and Gerry, came in behind us, ready to shoot past us and search upstairs. We made sure we weren't going to incinerate ourselves in a backdraught and scuttled into the front room. Vic and Gerry went quickly upstairs and we could hear them talking to each other and clumping about, opening wardrobes, moving beds and other furniture. People can hide in places you wouldn't believe when trying to escape smoke. We were trained to find them.

We swept the room with our big lensed, powerful lights. There was a woman lying face down on the floor. A little black poodle was lying next to her with its muzzle resting on the woman's outstretched hand. The smoke had no density. It was just there, filling the room, like the bar used to be in pubs before the smoking ban. I dropped the hose and we bent to pick the woman up to take her out. But she was as stiff as a board. She was obviously dead. So too was the dog. And a pair of budgies in the bottom of a cage.

Dennis went out to speak to the boss while I searched for the fire. I found it very quickly. It was out. It had used up the available oxygen and simply gone out. A paraffin heater that had some folded-up clothes on top of it. The small pile of clothes had just got too hot, ignited and burned up through the middle but you could see that the burning hadn't been violent, the pile hadn't burst into flames. The ceiling above the fire wasn't burned, just discoloured by the smoke. The pile of clothes had just smouldered, probably for hours, slowly filling the room with smoke, spreading across the ceiling and mushrooming down the walls until it silently overtook the lady's face and slowly asphyxiated her as she slept in her armchair. She probably woke up fighting for breath, tried to get up and away but was overcome and fell to the floor where she died, her loyal poodle staying to the end. Not that it could have gotten out anyway. The two budgies, one green and one blue, had literally fallen off the perch and lay in the bottom of their cage, feet up in the air as if searching for something to hang onto. The paraffin heater ran out of fuel and the fire died away, the smoke slowly, ever so slowly dissipating and somehow, bizarrely, quite spookily, making its way across the street and into just one house there. I dribbled enough water from the hose onto the pile of clothes, just to make sure that they were dead. I didn't move them as the fire investigation would take place and obviously the more information that's visible, the better. I went out and serviced my BA, ready for the next job.

Within minutes the house was filled with people, firefighters, police, and paramedics. A doctor was called to pronounce the death. Probably more people than had been in the old lady's house for years. Her house was filled with noise and voices, some of those voices exchanging pleasantries, exchanging views on the football or the weather...life going on normally with death in the midst. Firefighters were upstairs, opening windows to vent the place. Doors were opened and wedged and a large fan was set up near the front door to blow the house through. Police officers were scouring the place for information as to who the lady was and who her next of kin were, going through letters and opening drawers, discussing the task, and exchanging the information they found. And all the while, the little lady lay there, seemingly peering at the floor, her little dog by her side.

After the doctor had done his thing and the police had done their thing, and all agencies were satisfied, we helped the undertakers to load the little lady into a body bag and she was taken out and put into the back of the dark grey van. The dog and the budgies were put into some black bin bags we found and made ready for the trip back to the fire station where they'd be collected the next day by the City Council for disposal, unless next of kin wanted to deal with them. Once the council security team had made the place safe, we packed up and went back to the station and a nice mug of tea.

It was while I was drinking that mug of tea that the phone in the mess rang and I answered it. It was the boss from one of the stations in Central Division. He recognised my voice, as we played footy together every week, and we exchanged a few words before I put him through to my boss. Three minutes later our station PA system clicked on and I was summoned to the boss's office.

It transpired that my brother, Dan, had just been rescued from a fire in his flat, situated in Central Division and had asked my footy mate to call me to come to his assistance. My boss told me to get off and sort things out and to come back on duty, if possible, otherwise he'd see me the following night.

I got in my car and drove the five miles or so to my brother's flat. I still stunk of the smoke from the old lady's house. You'd be forgiven for thinking that my mind was all over the place but it wasn't. I was still very much in fireground mode and would be until my tour of duty was finished, at least 36 hours away. The information I had was that a neighbour had smelled smoke and called the fire brigade. That station had turned out to a smell of smoke at more or less the same time as I had. They investigated, just as we had done and, as a consequence, had broken into my brother's flat. Two of my mates had gone in wearing BA, had done the same checks that I'd done and had found my brother lying on the settee. A smouldering fire in a pile of fishing magazines had done precisely the same in my brother's flat as it had done in the old lady's house. My two mates had found Dan very quickly and unceremoniously dragged him off the settee, down the stairs and out into the fresh air. The information was that he'd been very lucky...another five or 10 minutes and he would have been a body job. He was also considered to be drunk. Dan had sat in the back of an ambulance, taking in some pure oxygen for a while but had refused to be taken to hospital. Instead, he'd asked for his brother, a firefighter, to be called. The fire, I was told, had been caused by a cigarette falling off an ashtray onto the magazines.

As I drove through the dark streets, Queen's 'Works' *album on the CD player, I thought about the strangeness's that occur in life. There's me, wearing a BA set, crawling into a smoke-filled house, hoping to find either no-one or someone to rescue but instead, finding a strangely familial tableau of old lady and pets lying dead in the living room. Almost sounds like the title of a painting doesn't it, 'Old Lady and Pets'. And then, five or six miles away, at more or less the same time, my brother is heading towards the same fate as the old lady but is found and rescued by my mates from an adjoining station. Spooky or what? As I pulled up in the little car park by Dan's place,* 'Is This the World We Created' *had just started.*

The front door to his place was open. I shouted a greeting up the stairs and his voice, quiet, sounding a bit weak I thought, which was understandable, told me to come up. As I walked up the bare wooden stairs, I noticed that the smoke line, an almost straight-line discolouration of the walls, was down to about the fifth stair from the top, which means that he'd been lying asleep on his settee and the smoke had overtaken him substantially. He'd been breathing that stuff in for a long time. My brother was an extremely lucky man.

The stairs took you straight up and into the living room. As I walked in, he was sitting on his settee. Smoking a ciggy. At that time, I was also a smoker and so lit one myself and sat down in the one armchair after moving a stack of fishing magazines onto the floor.

'How are you, Dan?' I asked and he took a big deep breath before replying.

'OK' he said.

I studied the room. The ceiling and walls were coffee brown from the smoke. The old dresser in the corner was scorched up the corner where the smouldering magazines had been stacked, and the floor adjacent to it was burned. The windowsill had burned through in one spot about the size of a saucer. There was a ring of darker brown on the ceiling above the dresser, giving me a clear picture of the size of the fire. Again, my brother had been very lucky. The fire had been far enough away from the dresser to just scorch it. Apparently, it hadn't got properly going but had nevertheless generated a decent amount of heat. The place stunk of the smoke. Heavy and acrid. It was going to take some getting rid of.

'You've been very lucky Dan.' I said.

'I know.' he said and stubbed his cigarette out in an already full ashtray. It was a big glass ashtray and I recognised it was one I'd given him a few years previously. 'I feel stupid.' he said, lighting another ciggy.

'The good thing is mate,' I said, 'you have to be alive to feel that.' I got up to look around the flat. You didn't have to move from the living room to survey the whole place, it was that small. You came straight up the stairs and through a door into the living room. Two other doors led out of the living room. One led to a tiny space that contained another three doors, the left one led to the kitchen, the right one led to the bathroom and the one directly in front of you was an airing cupboard. The other door in the living room led to the bedroom. All the doors, apart from the airing cupboard had apparently been open, and every room was badly smoke damaged. There were streaks down the window where beads of condensation had run down the glass.

'I know.' he said. 'I'm glad someone called the fire brigade. I'll have to find out who it was and thank them. Your mates must think I'm a dick head. I'll bet they're laughing at me, aren't they? I wouldn't blame them.'

He was sitting there, looking down at the floor, his ciggy held in the fingers of his left hand. He was rubbing the thumb and forefinger of his right hand together, as if he was feeling the quality of a cloth at his tailor's. 'Do you want a coffee?' he asked, without looking up.

'I'll make it Dan.' I said, 'You stay there and smoke your ciggy, try to relax.' I went into the kitchen and put the kettle on. I had to wash a few mugs and a spoon. I looked in the fridge for the milk. There was none. There wasn't much of anything. A tub of butter, some plain yoghurts and what looked like some tomatoes, but they were covered in a silver fur. 'You carrying out an experiment in your fridge here Dan?' I shouted through to him. He laughed, which was good to hear. I carried the coffees through and sat down.

'So, Dan, you've got insurance, right?' I knew that he should at least have buildings insurance on account of his mortgage. I'd be willing to bet he didn't have contents insurance.

'I don't think I have.' he said, 'I think it lapsed a few months ago'.

'Are you certain about that Dan?' I asked, 'I'm pretty sure it's a legal obligation to have it where a mortgage is in place.' I tried to sound casual and matter of fact. Trying not to sound as though I was quizzing him. Which I was. I've got to admit, I was angry at him. I was trying not to show it because, y'know, he was my brother, I loved him, he'd been through an ordeal, a close call, albeit of his own making but, a close call is a close call and it doesn't really matter how you got there. 'In any case,' I added, taking a sip of my coffee, 'It is deffo a legal obligation to have buildings insurance for a property like this.' I said.

He looked directly at me and there was a flash of something in his eyes I couldn't quite put my finger on. 'What do you mean 'A property like this?' he asked. There was an edge to his voice. Belligerent. The thing in his eyes that I couldn't quite work out became more pronounced and I could now see what it was. It was the narrowing of the eyes and the overall set of the face. It was that part of him that was our father coming through...elbowing its way to the front...readying itself for...what?

I lit a cigarette, 'Only the type of property Dan, first floor flat, Leasehold, y'know, you don't actually have a footprint and anything bad that happens here usually has a direct consequence for your neighbours and so...', I let my statement tail away, hoping that not finishing it would seem less like me being a smart-arse or something. I sipped my coffee, took a drag on my ciggy and blew the smoke out.

The belligerence went out of him, his narrowed eyes relaxed, looked away and his shoulders seemed to sag to the floor. I thought back to just a few years ago and how on the ball my big brother was, how smart and in control he was.

'Is everything OK with you Dan? Work OK?' I asked.

He looked at me but his eyes didn't stay on mine for more than a second or two, then they flitted around the room, avoiding me. Fidgety eyes. That was a sign of something. I don't know what but, to me, it was a sign that something wasn't right. 'Yeah.' he said, 'everything's fine, apart from' he looked about his flat, 'this.'

'Well listen,' I said, drinking my coffee and putting my ciggy out. 'If you haven't got insurance, don't worry, I'll sort this out for you if you want.'

'That'd be good yeah,' he said. 'thanks.'

'I can get some chemicals from the Salvage Corp,' I said. 'get rid of the smell of smoke and clean the brown off everything.'

Dan nodded as he sucked on his ciggy. And that was it. I expected him to say something, but he didn't. I felt that something had changed in the few minutes I'd been in the flat. I could feel a barrier, I could feel...I'm not quite sure of the word but, hostility came to mind. A part of me said that my thinking was scrambled, that I was here to help, that I was his brother, his flesh and blood, that hostility had no place here and that I was being stupid. But I couldn't shake that feeling of not being welcome, that I was intruding even though I'd been invited and, apparently, wanted. He said nothing more and took to looking anywhere, at the floor, the skirting boards, the walls and furniture, anywhere but at me.

I wondered why he'd asked for me to be called. I guessed that he wanted to talk to me, y'know, properly talk to me but now that I was here, he'd changed his mind. I decided not to challenge him on it. Tomorrow was another day I thought. A new day. A sober day, though, to be fair, Dan didn't appear to be drunk to me. I couldn't see any signs, no bottles or cans, there was no smell on him, not that I'd stood very close to him, and of course, the smell of the smoke swamped everything. Having said that, if the lads who fished him out of his flat said he was drunk then, as far as I'm concerned, he was drunk. I realised, at that second, that the bond I had with firefighters was a very strong one.

Possibly, maybe even probably, stronger than the one I currently had with my big brother, my hero. It made me sad and I felt that part of me was becoming lost for ever, was sliding over the horizon, never to be seen again.

We made a plan for me to return to his flat in the morning and we'd work out how we were going to fix things. I left and drove back to the station to resume my duties. When I got back in the car, at Dan's flat, Queen carried on with 'Is This the World We Created.' I switched it off and drove back in silence.

The next morning, when I went back to my brother's flat, having spent a very busy night on duty, my brother met me at the front door to his place. He'd been watching for my arrival. 'It's ok.' He said, 'I went through my papers last night after you left. I have got insurance and they're going to sort it all out.'

'Well, that's good news Dan. Nice one. You getting the kettle on or what?' I said and rubbed my hands together, as if it was cold. Which it wasn't.

'I can't.' he said, looking at the sycamore tree in the small garden. 'I've, er, got to go out.'

I knew I was getting fobbed. 'Not even time for a coffee and a fag?'

'Sorry, no.' he said and looked straight at me. Straight into my eyes. His blue eyes looking into my blue eyes, not blinking, not flinching.

'Ok.' I said. 'I'll get off then.' He was already moving back into his place, getting ready to close the door.

'Let me know if you need anything.' I said as the door closed. As the gap narrowed, his eyes were still looking into mine. The latch clicked and I stood there for a few seconds and watched his figure through the frosted glass. He also stood there for a few seconds then he turned and climbed the stairs. I counted his steps on the bare wood and then I heard his living room door close.

So, here I was, approaching my brother's flat for the first time in over 30 years. I parked my car in exactly the same space I'd parked in three decades ago, got out and walked around the back of the little terrace of properties. As I walked away from my car, another car drove into the car park. It was Lydia and Edward. We greeted each other in typical Croft fashion and headed for the flat.

The pathway was covered in a thick carpet of red berries from a rowan tree that had been allowed to become too big for its position. The berries made the path as slippy as if it was iced up and Lydia nearly went tits up, which was dead funny, though she didn't laugh. Me and Edward did but Edward stopped rather quickly when Lydia shot a glance at him.

We moved around the back. Dan's door was two doors down. Each of the homes had a small garden and last time I'd been here, there were no divisions between them, no fences. I remembered Dan telling me that one of the conditions of the leasehold was that no-one could install a fence or a hedge or any other kind of division…and I remember saying to him that people wouldn't take any notice of such a condition. He argued that the condition was one of the reasons why he'd bought his property, that the condition enhanced the sense of community and that it would make people interact with each other, making for a happier, village-type environment. And I remembered his ire when I said that such environments didn't exist, except in an Agatha Christie novel. That was one of the differences between my brother and me...our mean streak, a streak that we both had but one that he didn't make use of and liked to pretend that he didn't have. We were the sons of our father and believe me, we had that streak. In our father, the mean streak was wide, as wide as the River Mersey and he was mean and vicious every day of his life. My mean streak was narrower than the narrowest tributary of the River Mersey, but it was there. To deny its existence was, in my opinion, pointless. In my opinion, to survive in this world, you need to be tough at times, you need to be able to be mean at times because otherwise, there are people who will take advantage of you and will be merciless in the doing. For me, having a mean streak is like having a good winter coat. You use it when you have to. It's a tool. For me, if you have a mean streak and attempt to stifle it for fear of maybe turning into your father, then you're deluding yourself, and denying yourself access to the attributes which make you, you. Balance was the key and Dan didn't strike that balance.

Dan had planted two sycamore trees in the tiny space that was his garden, and had failed to manage them...which, even I know that you just can't do because these things are worse than those damn Triffids and, I believe they were pretty bad. Sycamores, with their myriad whirly bird seeds that drop and spin all over the place, are deadly and you can take that piece of information right the way along to your bank. You *have* to manage them or they'll take over the world. Or at least your garden and next door's as well. Dan's sycamores were massive. I'd have hated to be one of my brother's neighbours. The whole area was covered in the leaf fall and I imagined the roof gutters would be clogged as well because the trees towered over the roof. They made the whole of the back of the terrace gloomy and dank.

Dan's little patch of garden was covered in refuse and litter and there was an indistinct smell that pervaded everything…sort of like a sour, mouldy, sweaty, rotting, rank smell, like I imagined a Tasmanian devil's lair to smell. I mean, I've picked on poor Taz there, probably because, subliminally, he was like a sort of anti-hero in the cartoon world of my childhood and, having seen a few wildlife programmes involving Tasmanian devils, they always looked sort of threadbare and dirty, and always seemed to be rummaging around in a corpse, pulling this bit of stringy tendon and that bit of bloodied bone stump with rags of meat clinging to it and gleefully chomping through it all. I'm assuming the gleeful aspect there in spite of their workmanlike faces. The smell wasn't overpowering but it sort of hung over the garden like a fog.

I examined the littered garden. It was easy to just see a garden full of refuse and look beyond it, simply registering the confusion of out of place textures and colours, letting them fuse into a general picture. But I knew that this stuff was here because my ex-colleagues had put it all here, moved it all out of the building.

From experience of being a firefighter called to such incidents, and knowing that my brother's home had been full of rubbish and that his body needed to be removed from the building, I knew that a 'clear way' had to be made and that would have meant whatever was causing the hindrance would have to be moved. The fact that it was strewn over the garden told me that it must have littered the staircase. It would have been thrown to the bottom of the stairs then jettisoned as far away from the entrance as possible. It was odd. It appeared as if no care had been taken on how this was done and, given that a person's corpse was involved, you could be forgiven for thinking that it could have maybe been done tidily, if only to demonstrate that you, as a firefighter, was treating this person with some dignity. Back in my day as a firefighter, there is no way that the rubbish would have been strewn all over the place and I knew that this wouldn't have changed. Some things would change but not this. It looked like a gas explosion had occurred, flinging everything into the air, for it to land in this haphazard way. I instinctively knew that this extended scatter of rubbish was not the pile that had been brought out by the firefighters.

The rubbish wasn't 'tidy', which I know sounds strange but I just knew that this rubbish had been 'gone through', searched. The wind could have blown it about but, to me, looking at the scene, there was a sheltered corner made by two walls, opposite the front door. Had I been the OIC of the incident, I would have had the rubbish piled as neatly as possible in that corner.

Once I could see that pile in my mind's eye, I could also see someone bending over the mound, searching it and throwing each item backwards, using both hands, I could see the pattern of spread. I could see two patterns of spread, two people bent over, facing into the pile from different angles, picking items up in each hand, examining each item and discarding it backwards. I could see the two fan-like spreads of litter that had then been moved about slightly by the wind.

Dan's garden was covered in a mixture of all sorts, all intermingled. Trousers, socks, shirts, underwear, what looked like a 1940's suitcase, god knows where he got that from, food stuff, green bread, milk cartons, empty food cans, cornflake packets, Jaffa Cake boxes. I love Jaffa Cakes, cake or biscuit? Biscuit or cake? There were half eaten sandwiches, lots of what looked like chicken bones, newspapers and magazines, shoes that looked like my grandad used to wear but all scuffed and twisted. There were what looked like jeans, at least half a dozen pairs of them, folded and crumpled and covered in what might have been tar or something else dark, sticky, and matted. There were letters and notebooks, what looked like old schoolbooks, some ornaments, a brass donkey and china figures, a dog with a man, could've been a shepherd. There was a set of old rusty spanners and cheap screwdrivers, a bike wheel, and a scattering of bike tyres, one hanging in one of the sycamore trees. There were DVD cases, a shoebox full of cottons of various colours, all filthy. There was a flattened box that had, at one time, contained an electric strimmer, there were spools of strimmer wire or cable or whatever it's called but no strimmer. Maybe it was inside the house. A variety of rusty garden tools were scattered about, a rake and a hoe and a little spade, y'know, like a lady's spade. Over on the far side of the garden, flung the furthest, was Dan's green five speed racing bike, minus a wheel.

He'd had that bike for years, since he was about 15. He'd got it for his birthday. He was the only one of us five kids that ever had a bike bought for them. I always wanted a bike but never got one. One year, there was a bike wrapped up in Christmas paper, stored in the coal hole, and as far as I was concerned, it must have been mine, me being the next in line age-wise, but it just disappeared and I still don't know whose it was or what it was doing hiding in our coal hole. My mum always said that I must have imagined it. Or dreamed it. Like you do. But I knew that the thing wrapped in paper, that looked like a bike wrapped in paper, at the back of our coal hole, discovered by me on one of my many

Christmas present hunts, had been a bike wrapped in paper and I knew that no dreaming had been involved. It had been there and probably had been mine, but my dad had discovered that I, or one of us kids had discovered it and consequently disposed of it. That happened a lot. A lot of secret discussions between us kids, especially the original three, me, Dan and Carla, took place on the subject of toys and games being found hidden in drawers and wardrobes and quite often those items never found their way into our pillow slips on Christmas morning. The looks of puzzlement and disappointment on our faces must have been a joy to our dad. Our dad must have had something against Christmas because he ruined every Christmas that I can ever remember from my first 20 years on this planet. I hate Christmas to this day and I always will. I've tried to like it, really tried. I've always made it just how it should be for my kids but, I'm not able to change it for me. Or maybe I don't want to, I don't know. I don't know why I wouldn't want to but, the thought of Christmas approaching fills me with a feeling close to dread, fills me with loathing and I always just want it to go away.

There were a couple of what looked like decent waterproof coats, or they'd been decent at one time and, bizarrely, for me anyway, dozens of empty two litre soft drinks bottles. There were letters, envelopes and writing pads, pens and pencils, a ruler, a protractor, an old logarithm tables book, it looked like the same one that had tortured me at school. I hated all that logarithm shit, hated it. I remembered being so puzzled about it that I thought about running away to live in the woods down in Halewood village, living off the land, in reality, people's doorsteps after the milkman had delivered all the stuff he used to deliver, milk, bread, log shaped butter wrapped in greaseproof paper, eggs, yoghurts and cream. Yeah, I remember thinking, I can do that, make myself a little den in the trees and live like an old fur trapper, whatever the fuck that was. My big brother had rescued me from this existence by sitting me down and explaining logarithms, showing me how to do it all. He was much better than my maths teacher, Miss Drake, at explaining it all and very quickly, under his tutelage, I got the hang of it and became very proficient at it, in fact I became the best in the class at logarithms. But did Miss Drake make any acknowledgment of my improvement? Anything? A word, a smile, a nod of encouragement? No. She didn't. She just found some other part of mathematics to torture me with and single me out. I once came up with a plan to make a bomb, put it in her brown leather briefcase and time it to blow as she drove out of the school gates on her way home, me sitting on Janice Jones' garden wall opposite the gates, smiling and waving at her as she passed me, but when I asked Dan to help me, he said no. Like he actually *knew* how to do it but had decided it wasn't a good idea.

All of this stuff, this refuse, must have been between the body of my brother and exit from the building and I imagined it must have been on the staircase. Looking at the amount of stuff, it must have filled the staircase completely and it had to be chucked out so he could be safely brought out.

Lydia was looking at the stuff with me. Actually, she was looking at me more than she was looking at it, maybe looking for a reaction of some kind. I'd seen it all before so there was no reaction. I had my fireground head on and no matter what, there would be no reaction to anything from me. My coping head was fully in charge. She unlocked the door and we went in.

The first thing to hit me was the smell. It was the Tasmanian devil's lair times one hundred. Make that one thousand. It was horrific, horrendous, truly mind blowing. This was not something I had ever experienced and boy oh boy I have experienced some god-awful smells in my time in the job. I'd been to fires involving tons of offal in a huge Liverpool abattoir (pronounced aba-tyre in scouse) and that had been bad, but this was on another planet. I'd had a job involving two tramps killed in a fire in a derelict building, cooked in their home for want of a better way of putting it and the smell of that had been really bad but this smell was very different. Very, very different. It was heavy, like a blanket that settled on you straight away. Like a heavy sodden blanket that drapes itself around you, moulding itself to you, preventing you from moving and too heavy to shrug off. It immediately made you want to stop breathing but when you did breathe, it made you gag, it made you baulk and retch, it made your eyes sting and I realised that the stinging sensation was probably from the overpowering stench of ammonia. You didn't want to breathe through your nose because it stung and made your eyes water and when you tried to breathe through your mouth it immediately dried the back of your throat making you feel as though someone had blown fine, bitter dust into your mouth. I retreated and told Lydia and Edward to come out and I took them to my car.

I'd come prepared for this and had three hi-spec masks for protection against dust and, more importantly, mould, and a jar of Vick. Also, some good grade disposable one-piece suits and a box of latex gloves. I donned a suit over my clothes, smeared a good dollop of Vick under my nose and put the mask on. They did likewise. I put a woollen hat on and pulled it down over my ears as well. I didn't want to get anything on me if I could help it. I thought about what I would have been wearing as a firefighter entering these premises and wished I had the same gear at my disposal.

The tiny hallway was filthy. A single light bulb on a short strand of cable hung down. The bulb was dark brown, as though it had been dipped in molten toffee. Amazingly it worked, though the light from it was next to useless. The walls had never been painted since the property had been built and they were filthy. They were covered in gouges and scrapes, handprints, like someone who'd been handling coal, were everywhere, like cave paintings. I half expected to see a bison being skewered by stick men with spears. There was a ledge to the left of the front door, about my chest height. It had a small window that had been boarded up, presumably to prevent anyone breaking in. The ledge was nearly a foot high in stuff that had been posted through the door, letters, bills, free newspapers, advertising flyers, political trifolds. The ceiling of the hallway had gone, just the rafters visible, with the plasterboard nails still in situ with nothing to hold. I wondered why the ceiling would be missing. I could think of only two reasons, a water leak or maybe someone trying to force entry through the small flat roof above the hallway. The corners were festooned in the thickest heaviest cobwebs I'd ever seen, coated in dust that made them dark brown. The staircase was uncarpeted, like it had been 30 years ago. It looked as though a regiment of troops fresh from the mud of Flanders had tramped up them. There were dog prints, prints from work boots or, most probably, fire boots. There was even, I keep using the word 'bizarre' but if you think that anything I've labelled as bizarre, wasn't, then this was *truly* bizarre, this was king of bizarrity (just made that word up)…there were even a number of dark, what looked like muddy footprints, as in bare footprints. They were underneath most of the other prints, but they were there, as plain as day. My mind flitted to the programme me and Dan used to love as kids, the Danish one, in black and white, Robinson Crusoe, starring Robert Hoffman I think, could have been Hoffmann. I could see us sitting on the settee, happy because our dad wasn't due in from work for a few hours yet and we were eating jam butties with our school uniforms still on and watching Robinson Crusoe. Life just didn't get much better than that. And the footprints in the sand that Robinson found one day were introduced in such a way as to add suspense and make the next episode a bit scary, even though we knew, from having read the book, that the footprints belonged to Man Friday.

The stairwell walls were dark and grimy, the cobwebs hanging in sheets from the ceiling and stacked down the corners. At the top of the stairs, on the one square yard landing, a dark toffee covered light bulb sat in a fixture on the ceiling that looked as though it had been involved in fire. Surely, I thought, that can't be damage from 30 years ago? Could it? I turned the light on but of course, it didn't work. Looking down from the top of the stairs I could easily see that the smoke line caused by the fire of 30 years previous was still very much in evidence.

I stood at the doorway from the stairs into the living room and looked in. In spite of my mask and dollop of Vick under the nose, the smell was overpowering. The sight of my brother's living room was…I don't know how to describe it. Dramatic springs to mind. But this was no theatre or film set. No producer or director of entertainment could dream this up, could think that this…scene, was a worthy one.

The living room was not visible as such. All I could see was refuse. Not belongings. Refuse. It covered the whole room, every inch. The floor was not visible anywhere except right at the entrance and a very narrow path, obviously the one cleared by the firefighters, had been cut through it in the direction of where I knew the bedroom to be.

The window, in the far corner, diagonally opposite the door I was standing at, was a tall window, with a low sill. The room was so full of refuse that only the top twenty-four inches of the window could be seen. There was a filthy net curtain at the window, grey and brown and hung with cobwebs, that disappeared into the midden.

Everything seemed black and brown and looked damp and sodden. What little light came in through the window was absorbed by the mass of detritus in the room, and it was difficult to determine what the mass actually was. I examined it.

There were what looked like islands rearing up out of it. In the corner, furthest away from us, was a fish tank, probably four feet wide, upside down. It seemed to be full of boxes and had what looked like food tins on top of it, some of them obviously empty, their lids peeled back. It looked like the fish tank was on top of the old dresser that I remembered from the fire but in the bad light, I couldn't be certain. The twisted legs of an upside-down ironing board stuck up and looked as though they were waving for help. There were the top half a dozen inches of what looked like a large hamster cage, with a newspaper stack forming a roof. Another island, I could see, was a microwave oven, lying on its back, just two inches of its dirty cream carcass above the surface. The last island, the one I'd reach first, was a cardboard box, white with what looked like black lettering on it. You could make out four black lines reaching up out of the refuse, two diagonals angling away from a point beneath the surface and two lines coming straight up. I reckoned the word would be Vodka. A box of Vodka bottles. Probably 12.

Scattered about the place, on top of and sticking up out of the refuse, like shell cases surrounding an artillery gun, were bottles, like the empty ones I'd seen outside in the garden, the kind that you'd buy soft drinks in, the two litre ones. They were full of something brown but I didn't for one-minute think they'd be filled with fizzy cola. These must be the bottles of urine that the coroner had mentioned.

I entered Dan's living room, taking a pair of latex gloves from the box I'd brought up with me and snapping them on. As usual, they pulled about 20 hairs off the back of each of my hands. Good job I wasn't putting one of them on my head because I definitely didn't have 20 hairs to spare there. I reached over to one of the discarded bottles and pulled it to me. Sure enough, whatever was in it was liquid. Dark brown and ever so slightly not as liquid as water, not exactly syrupy but, what's that word? *Viscous*, yeah, it was viscous. Dark brown and viscous. Like you would expect a bottle of blood to act, definitely liquidy but, you know what I mean.

The bottle was full almost to the top and around the shoulders of the bottle, a sticker had been, er, stuck on it. There was writing in big black marker pen. Capital letters but I could still tell it was Dan's left-handed writing. He was the only one of our family who was left-handed. Supposed to be a sign of intelligence isn't it but let me tell you, I've known some pretty dumb left-handers. Grandma always used to say that left-handers were dead clever but I reckon she might have changed her mind if she'd been standing next to me. There's no doubt that Dan *was* a clever man, no doubt at all, but, looking about the place, there was fuck all clever about what he'd done here. Fuck all.

There was a date, 9/7/18. And underneath that was what looked like some sort of notations, all numbers, letters, and strange symbols that meant absolutely nothing to me. I handed the bottle to Lydia. She didn't make any move to take it from me but instead, looked pained, disgusted, and just nodded.

'Looks like piss,' I said, taking my mask off so that Lydia could lip-read me, 'but I've never seen piss that colour.'

'It is.' she said, that same look of disgust creasing her face.

'It's piss?' I asked. 'How do you know? Did you taste it?' The fireground head came complete with fireground humour.

She laughed and shook her head. 'Edward burst one of them.' she said, looking at Edward and signing what she'd just said to me. 'He stood on one of them.'

Edward looked at me and twisted his face into a grimace. 'It was over there,' he said, pointing towards the bedroom. 'That's where he was. I didn't see it and stood on it. It burst and sprayed that stuff all over my legs.' He made a gesture, pinching his nose with forefinger and thumb. 'Stunk!'

'I'll bet it did.' I said.

'Definitely piss,' he said, 'very bad piss, very smelly, something wrong with him, with his insides or something.' He wasn't wrong there.

'So, these things are just about everywhere?' I said, holding up the bottle.

'Yes.' said Lydia, sweeping her arms wide, 'They are everywhere, so be careful where you walk.' She pointed by the door that led to the kitchen and there was a pile of bottles all the same.

As my eyes got used to the gloom, I noticed that, just as Lydia had said, they were everywhere, some stacked neatly, some just piled, and others randomly scattered about. Most of them that I could see appeared to have the same stickers on their shoulders, all with their notations in black marker. I continued scanning the place, taking it in.

Having advanced slightly into the living room, I could see into the bedroom as well. Both rooms were the same, both filled to a depth of over five feet with general refuse, including discarded food. The whole raft of stuff looked solid, looked very settled and permanent. This had taken a long time to collect. I was looking at years of hoarding *everything*. *Nothing* had been thrown away in this home for years. Nothing. Apparently not even his waste. Before I took any more steps into the place, I needed to know what he'd done with his shit. Pissing in bottles was one thing, albeit quite an horrendously bizarre thing but shit, that is a different thing altogether. What do you do with that? You can't get that into a bottle. Not that I've tried.

The more I looked at the midden, the more I realised that there was something odd about it all. I know that you have just thought 'What!? Really? You really think there is something fucking odd about all this shit, all this stuff? You should have been a detective never mind a firefighter.' I know I would have thought something like that if you'd been telling me this stuff.

The 'oddness' that at first I couldn't quite put my finger on was the snow. Or what looked like snow. There were patches of it everywhere, much more prevalent in some places than others. I bent down to look at the closest patch and realised straight away that it was chewings, gnawing's, whatever you want to call them. Mice or rats or both together had been chewing everything chewable, which, to a rodent, is more or less everything. In places it was maybe an inch deep. In the vicinity of the deepest snowfall, the area was sodden, you could see it. I think it would have seeped out if I'd squeezed anything.

I reckoned that the chewings alone, never mind all the other shit, could or would, fill half a dozen bin bags and I wondered how the fuck my brother slept at night with all that noise. This chewing malarkey hadn't been done by a single mouse or even a single family of mice. This was an army of mice that had done this. The whole place was one big shitty, pissy rodent nest. A picture of my brother standing by the kitchen door the last time I'd been here pounced into my brain, into my mind's eye and I was almost overcome with the horror of my brother's life. I fought it down. Pushed it to the back of my mind and got my fireground head back in charge.

Lying on top of the living room refuse was a wooden step ladder that had been my mum's…rickety, bearing paintbrush marks from the time me and Dan had been forced to paint our bedroom because our dad didn't like decorating. We were given wallpaper and paste and a couple of one-inch paintbrushes. We painted the ceiling and all the woodwork with those one-inch paintbrushes. We pasted the paper on the kitchen table downstairs and carried each strip up the stairs and stuck it to the walls, not even once managing to match the pattern. Dan was 14 years old and I was 10. We'd never done anything like it and so we fucked it up, as you would expect. It took us weeks, doing what we could after school and at weekends. Not once did our dad come to see what we were doing, not until he came in after it was finished. He laughed at us. Not in a nice way. It was a sneering, sly laugh…his eyes filled with contempt. He said that we were useless and that we would never be as good as him at decorating…like I gave a shit about that when I was 10. Or at any age come to think of it. I noticed one of Dan's hands trembling. I think our dad did too. He finished sneering at us, sighed and casually took his big leather belt off and beat us with it across our arses but the good thing was, we got to keep our kecks on. It didn't even hurt. Not that you could show that. I mean, you couldn't even show that you had *been* hurt either so what you had to do was learn how to look as though you had been hurt but were trying really hard to show that you hadn't. Without being 'cheeky'. Let me tell you something, THAT is a skill. It doesn't look great on your CV, which is why I've never put it there but nonetheless, it is a real skill. And no, I didn't have a book down my kecks, like in the comics, though I did try that with Mr Wentworth, our headmaster at St Paul's when I was sent to get the cane for battering the class bully. First year infants. Pretty proud of myself then and still am. But Mr Wentworth must have read the same Beano as me and caned my hand instead of my arse. Cheat. Six of the best, which is a ridiculous phrase for beating a child with a stick.

I got to like our patchy ceiling…I could see my grandad's face in it, like seeing faces in clouds…and I liked our mismatched wallpaper. It was unique I thought. It was also a good game of mine, discovering the best way to travel diagonally up the paper from one corner to the other, using as much of the pattern as possible. Weird I know but simple things amuse simple minds as grandma used to say. Dan always said to me that he would never decorate anywhere again, and he'd definitely kept to his word on that.

Getting back to the stepladder, it seemed strange to me that the ladder was on top of the refuse. I mean, a stepladder doesn't make its own way to the top of a rubbish dump does it? Obviously, my brother kept it there *in case* it was needed or because it *was* needed. So, I thought, *why* did he keep his stepladder on top of the refuse? What did he think he would need it for, changing a light bulb? I mean, apart from the light bulb on the little landing, which *needed* changing, you could reach the other light bulbs simply by walking across the rubbish dump. I went to the door leading to the kitchen and bathroom. Lydia and Edward followed me.

The door immediately in front of me was the airing cupboard. It was closed. The door to the right, to the bathroom, was ajar, ajar enough for a man to, say, put his arm through. I used the torch on my phone to look inside. The room beyond the door wasn't visible. I mean, you could see that there was a room there but nothing inside the room was visible except for rubbish. The rubbish was at the same height as my head. I'm not a tall man, five-foot-eight, the same height as my brother, but nevertheless, a room five-foot-eight deep in refuse is…is what? It's mind blowing, it's disgusting, it's upsetting, it's inconceivable in my world but then, quite obviously, my world was not the world inhabited by my brother. I found it hard to comprehend, I mean, I'd seen this kind of thing before, many times but not like this. Seeing things *like* this was not the same as seeing this…surely, I thought, *surely*, the whole room can't be this full of rubbish? Surely?

My mind was, what, I don't really know what my mind was, I can't really say. I simply haven't got the vocabulary to properly explain what I was looking at. Thoughts were coming so fast that they were speeding by me. Zipping through my brain. Shooting stars. There for a split second then gone, to be replaced by another then a flurry of them, then black sky then more flashes as another one streaked through. None of them were stopping so that I could read them. We talk about being able to read other people's thoughts and here I was, unable to read even my own thoughts. I was standing alongside the Formula One track of thought and I was failing to register the cars going past. I could *hear* them. I could *smell* them. My eyes could just about register them flying past, but I couldn't keep them in focus for long enough to see what they were. I was too close. I had to be further away from the track. I could write often used words, modern, everyday words like gob-smacked, and all other similar crap words, but they weren't good enough, not descriptive enough, not...*profound* enough. Not that you needed me to tell you that. I don't even know why I said it to be honest. Probably simply because I thought it. I do that a lot. Give voice to my thoughts. It's gotten me into trouble a few times. Anyway, I think I needed a word that hadn't been invented yet. I tried to invent one. As you do, spur of the moment thing, can't quite think what to say, so, *I know*! let's invent a new word! Needless to say, I couldn't. Instead, my mind decided to condense everything into one thought, one all-encompassing phrase. 'Fuuuck.' I said, 'fuuuck me...', followed very closely by, 'Whaaat the fuck?'

I stood, examining the room as best I could and all I could think of was making use of the toilet. Not me wanting to make use of the toilet but what my brother did when he wanted to use the toilet. What did he do? What on earth did he do? This room hadn't become chocked full of refuse overnight, this had taken a long, long time to get like this so...what in god's name did he do when he needed to go to the toilet?

I already knew that he was pissing in bottles, they were all over the place. But like I said earlier, it's not easy to shit in a bottle. And again, I underline this fact here and now…I have not attempted to perform this task. If it could be called a 'task'. *Aaah Croft, I have a task for you, now what I want you to do is…*

The question has to be asked here. Why would you do away with your bathroom? It's there, less than 10 feet away from any point in your home. Linear feet. I mean, if you were in bed and you needed to use the toilet, you'd have to walk the eight or nine feet to your bedroom door then the other 10 feet to the toilet, making, as you can see, 18 feet in total so, I am talking linear feet in this regard. Anyway, enough of that. Why bar yourself from using your bathroom? What thought process do you go through in order to actually do this? Surely at some point during your hoarding you think to yourself *hang on a mo…if I carry on chucking stuff in there, pretty soon I won't be able to use the toilet.* Don't you? In my world that question would be asked. What happened in my brother's world for that question to not get asked? Or, scary thought, maybe it did get asked…and answered. So, what would the answer be? Off the top of my head I couldn't think of one. Not even a sliver of one. Why on earth do you carry on using your bathroom as a dumping ground for refuse, knowing that you just might need it at some time?

A thought occurred. Maybe it was a storage room for treasures. Maybe I was looking at it from entirely the wrong perspective. My brother didn't keep this stuff because he wanted to store refuse. He was keeping it because, somehow, it represented value of some kind. Did my brother have so little real value in his life that he thought of his rubbish as valuable? Was he making some kind of statement to us, his family, standing in his home after his death? Was he saying to his family, the family he had shunned for decades, that he thought more of his rubbish than he did of us? Or was I trying to make this all about me by thinking these thoughts?

I turned to Lydia. 'What did he do for a shit?' I asked, easing my mask off again.

Lydia shook her head, made a moue and raised one eyebrow. 'I don't know.' she said, and then signed what had been said to Edward.

Edward signed something back to her then turned to me. He lifted his mask and let it settle on his head. 'Maybe he poo'd in the bottles.' he said and picked up one of them, holding it up into the meagre light, and inspecting it, like a sommelier from Hades. 'It's very brown and I've never seen wee that colour.'

Well…that explains everything, I thought and turned to Lydia. She made that same moue but raised both eyebrows this time, cocking her head ever so slightly in Edward's direction, as if saying that her husband had made a good point. I decided to just stay neutral and was about to say something like 'A good point well-made Edward.' when I changed my mind. I made my own moue, both eyebrows pointing down as I frowned. We were having a moue competition surrounded by our brother's midden. 'Mmmm good point.' I said to Edward, then raised one of my eyebrows questioningly. 'What would be the…errr… *mechanics*…of that operation? Do you think?' He looked puzzled.

While he was tossing that question around, I cast my mind back to the last time I'd been here. Three decades earlier. I remembered that a beige bathroom suite was fitted, bath, pedestal sink and low-level toilet unit. And the tile splashbacks were also beige. The walls themselves were just the cream or magnolia, in other words, beige, that builders used in just about every new-build in Great Britain.

I got my phone, held it up through the gap and snapped a picture of the room beyond to see if I could see what was what. Edward and Lydia gathered behind me to inspect the room beyond the gap. Sure enough, what we could see at the gap, extended to the full space. If anything, it was slightly deeper towards the back of the room and it was easy to see a hand reaching in and throwing a can as far as possible. They would pile towards the back of the room before becoming too heavy to resist the tumble and slide back towards the gap...looking for escape.

Nothing of the room was visible except that the top of a triangular shelf unit could be seen poking up an inch above the refuse, in the far corner where it was fastened to the walls. I knew that shelf unit and remembered Dan fitting it in the corner at the bath tap end. It had been in our bedroom when we were kids, a white, plastic covered wire corner shelf unit. I've no idea where it came from originally. Probably Garston Market. Tuesdays and Fridays. Our mum loved Garston Market. I went once and hated it. Too many people. Dan had used the shelf for aftershave and stuff when we were sharing a bedroom and, I remembered, it served the same purpose here.

'It looks like what's in there is mostly crushed beer cans.' I said. Lydia and Edward agreed. 'I think if we push hard on the door,' I said, 'we may be able to crush this stuff enough for us to start to empty the room, what do you think?' They agreed and so I put my phone away, put my mask back in place and tested the door.

I could tell there was going to be some give and so I braced myself and pushed…not too hard because there could have been something less giving behind the door that would have ended up going through the plasterboard wall and into the bedroom. There was definite give and so I braced my foot against the bottom of the airing cupboard door frame and exerted some real pressure. There was a lot of 'can movement' noise and the gap widened and as it widened there was a rush of cans out into the area we were standing in. The noise was deafening. I wouldn't have believed that a room full of cans on the move could make such a noise. And a small room at that. The speed with which the cans avalanched us was also ever so slightly disturbing. More for the thought of how they got there and who put them there rather than the physical threat. This was only a third of the room trying to spill through the gap and surround us but as the pile moved towards us, the stuff behind the door filled the void left by the escaping cans. It seemed to take ages for the noise and the movement to settle. We were up to our thighs in empty cans and food containers. A foil tray that had once contained Brain's Faggots, a meal that I love myself, one of the meals we were forbidden as kids, had come to rest right in front of me. The thick brown gravy that the faggots came in was still visible around the foil, it still even looked wet and could have been thrown away yesterday I thought, until a truly revolting smell, like a dead cat, made its way up and through my mask.

I turned and looked at the kitchen door, which was ajar in the same fashion as the bathroom one. The kitchen, I knew, was twice the size of the bathroom and you could see that the cans and refuse were up to within, maybe, 15 inches of the ceiling.

I motioned for Lydia and Edward to move backwards into the living room and as they did so a fresh can avalanche occurred, kicking off the deafening noise again. I quickly stepped into the living room as well…may as well get all the noise, for now anyway, out of the way as soon as.

I moved towards the bedroom door. The doorway was, apparently, where his body had been found, lying on a bed of refuse and covered with it as well. All the stuff that had covered him was probably strewn about the place and the stuff he'd been lying on was gone. Not for the first time, I wondered how he had become covered with the stuff and, also not for the first time, came to the conclusion that he must have burrowed in or lay down and swept it onto himself somehow. The bare wooden floor in the coffin shaped space had been covered with newspaper, which was sodden. Lydia saw me checking the dampness out with my boots.

'That's where he was found.' she said. 'We cleared the stuff he was lying on and that's where Edward stood on one of the bottles and burst it.'

So, the dark slimy damp was piss…plus all the body fluids of a rotting corpse that had seeped down through the rubbish. A mad thought flitted through my mind…'Piss Plus'…almost had a marketable ring to it. The situation was heart-breaking. As much as my brother had shunned me for over 30 years for no discernible reason, he was the boy I'd grown up with, the boy I'd had such fun with and shared tragic and traumatic moments with, he was the boy that I idolised and admired. He was my big brother and it broke my heart to think of him not so much dying in this place but living in it. My brother lay down here, in the doorway I stood in with my sister, somehow covered himself with refuse and died listening to the vermin chewing his 'treasures' into shreds.

I remembered my daft big brother, in our bedroom one summer's Saturday night. He was getting ready to go to Eric's house. Eric was his mate and lived in a posh house in a posh place just a few miles from us. We lived in a council house on a new Halewood estate near the Ford factory, a nice, roomy house with all mod cons like running water, an inside toilet and electricity in every room, and Eric lived in a terrace of quaint thatched cottages near the crossroads that would, in former years have been the hub of the village of Gateacre. The terrace he lived in had supposedly existed at the time of the great Doomsday census and, according to Dan, via Eric, via Eric's dad, who owned the whole terrace of about six cottages, a six-foot section of one of the walls of one of the cottages…was original to the Doomsday Book. My brother was very proud of this 'fact', whereas I, first of all, wasn't that impressed because the whole episode of the Doomsday Book had been 'taught' to me by one of the most, if not THE most boring history teacher in the history of history teachers, Mr Mount, who made every part of history as dry as anything you care to name that is as dry as fuck… and secondly, I immediately asked the question, 'How do they know?' Dan replied that Eric's dad said it was because he was a builder and knew these things, and I simply replied that you couldn't believe everything that adults said. I think I was born cynical. I probably would have doubted, at the time of my birth, that I'd just entered the room through *that* portal, had someone not wrapped me in a sheet and whisked me off for the weigh-in.

So anyway, where was I? Oh yeah, a summer's Saturday night and my brother getting ready to go to the Doomsday cottages of Gateacre.

He'd had a bath and had come rushing into the room with a towel around him. He shut the door and rushed over to the table between our beds and grabbed a bottle of talc. He put a load of it in his cupped hand and put a foot up on his bed. 'Joe! Joe!' he said excitedly, 'Watch this!' He put his talc filled hand under the towel and patted the powder up around his arse and then almost immediately farted. I was lying on my bed reading a book and was suddenly enveloped in a cloud of dust that smelled of Parma Violets and digested sprouts. I knew, at that moment, what grandad had gone through in the trenches of Northern France when the Germans gassed them. It was hilarious, not that grandad had been laughing at the time, and I just burst into uncontrollable laughter and so did Dan. He collapsed onto his bed and because he was laughing so hard, he kept farting little uncontrollable farts and each one of them expelled a smaller and smaller cloud of dust which made us laugh even harder. It was so funny. Crude, schoolboy humour but so incredibly funny. What was even funnier, almost, was me saying that I didn't know shoving a load of powder up your arse would make you sneeze it back out. I was actually being funny but Dan, the professor as I called him, really thought that I thought he had caused the fart by powder puffing himself. We laughed so hard we cried and after a while, the laughter subsided, and we lay looking at each other. Every now and then the memory would come back and cause more laughter. And then it went altogether. After all, it was Saturday and Saturday night in our house was lottery night. Saturday night was the night our parents went to the pub over the road for their 'night out'. It could end well, or it could end badly and there was no way of knowing. Saturday nights were my worst nights of the week but at least my brother had made a half hour of that Saturday evening into a golden memory. Years later, decades later, I still laugh about it. I still see the cloud of talc hurtling towards me, still see myself as my grandad, cowering in the trenches and panicking because I can't find my gas-mask, and I still see my brother twisted up on his bed laughing so hard he cried. And I still marvel at the fact that he must have thought this prank up and then practiced it in order to perform so well on the night. Dedication to science.

It was hard to *know* what I knew of my brother of yesteryear and to try to couple that with what I *now* knew of my brother of today. Impossibly hard. By the way, nowadays I *love* history. Absolutely love it. I was dragged back from that summery Saturday by Lydia. She was pointing at a suitcase that sat atop the bedroom of rubbish.

'Eh? What do you think?' she was saying.

'Sorry Lydia I was miles away. What do you mean?' I asked.

'The suitcase.' she said, 'It's full of mum's clothes.'

I looked at the suitcase. There were actually two of them. Old suitcases, from the 1950's I would say, maybe even the 1940's. They reminded me of the documentaries I'd seen of the Nazi death camps. They'd both been opened but then closed over…not latched or clasped or whatever you do with a suitcase, just closed over. I could see that they contained clothes.

'Mum's clothes?' I asked. 'What, like, what kind of clothes? What do you mean?'

Lydia shrugged. 'Mum's clothes.' she said. 'Just her clothes, dresses, tops, leggings, just her clothes.'

I was a bit taken aback. Our mum had been dead for nearly 20 years. What on earth did my brother keep her clothes for? What did he want them for? I was taken back to the night she died and the strange way that my brother had approached her as she lay in her hospital bed, hair nicely brushed back and her body composed and relaxed.

January 31st, 2001

I'd been called by my sister Carla at about half past one in the morning and had driven straight to the hospital, picking up my sister Emily on the way. Carla had gotten in touch with Lydia, who lived on the Wirral.

We got to the hospital in central Liverpool and gathered at the ward. A nurse took us into a small room and gave us chairs to sit on. I refused a seat and, instead, stood behind and slightly to the side of my sisters who all took a seat in front of the nurse. Another nurse tried to insist on me taking a seat, but I just gave her a look and refused. There are times when I feel as though I'm being manipulated and controlled and don't want to be. Sounds a little odd I know, as if there are times when I do want to be manipulated and controlled, and there are times when I feel that it is a good thing to allow people to think that they are doing this. Which gives me an upper hand. But equally, there are times when it becomes important to me to absolutely demonstrate that I won't be led, that I won't be told, and I won't be manipulated by anyone. There are times when I won't allow someone to dominate a situation and, rightly or wrongly, this was one of them. In this instance, I wanted to be able to, observe, is the best word. I wanted to observe the reactions of my sisters and I wanted to be able to observe the hospital staff when, in order for them to observe me, they had to make it obvious that they were doing so.

Does that make sense? I hope it does. The hospital staff couldn't observe all of us at the same time, which is what they wanted to do by sitting us all in a little row.

A nurse told us how our mum had died. And that it wasn't painful. That it was peaceful. She'd been on dialysis and, as they took the needles out, a procedure that she was scared of, she had a heart attack and died.

I don't know what reaction, if any, the hospital staff expected but what happened was this. My three sisters didn't flinch. They didn't cry or make any other sounds. They didn't stare in horror or wring their hands or do any of the things you would expect three daughters to do. You may have maybe *expected* one *of the daughters to be completely impassive but not all of them. There was not one flicker of hurt. Not one flicker. Not one tear. Not one word. I was exactly the same. Not a flicker of anything. I saw the two nurses exchange a very quick glance before they realised I was observing them and then they composed themselves.*

Of course, I was upset. I loved my mum. I would miss her. But I was not about to show myself to these people in front of us. And that is all I can put it down to. We were not going to show ourselves to anyone, not even to each other.

We all went in to see our mum. She just lay there. Obviously. I took her hand and it was still warm. The nurses had lied because my mum's face showed pain. And something else. Resignation. Acceptance. But above all, her face showed pain. You can brush hair as neatly as you like, pose the body in a relaxed way as much as you like. But you can't take the pain from the face of someone who died in pain.

We were given a room to sit in where we wouldn't be disturbed. A nurse brought a tray of tea in for us, but I refused to drink mine. Carla had been ringing Dan's landline, but he wasn't picking up. Dan didn't have a mobile back then. Eventually, he did pick up. I told Carla to tell him that I would come and pick him up. He was a stone's throw from the hospital. But he refused and said he'd come up on his push-bike...the one that now lay rusting in his garden minus a wheel.

Dan arrived and I hugged him. He was stiff and unresponsive. There was a smell on him. Blackcurrant. He was cold. As in temperature. It was January and he'd just cycled a mile or two. The cold, for some reason, always made the smell of alcohol seeping from skin, more discernible.

I went with him into the place where mum lay. I went to the far side of the bed and stood by her side. I looked up to where I expected Dan to be standing, opposite me, but he wasn't there. He was stood at the foot of the bed, with his back to her, and he was looking at her over his right shoulder.

'Are you ok Dan?' I asked. He ignored me. I don't think he heard me. 'Dan?' I said. 'Are you alright mate?' I said again.

His face was a rictus of what I can only think of as fear. Maybe it was something else, but he just looked frightened to me. He started to approach the head of the bed but did so in that same posture, backwards and very slowly, all the time looking at her over his shoulder. He seemed to be entranced, completely in a world of his own.

I stayed quiet and very still. I didn't want to break whatever spell he'd cast over himself. It took a good number of minutes and not once

did my brother turn to face his mother. He didn't touch her, didn't bend,
as I did, and kiss her on the forehead. He just stared at her face with
what seemed like fright on his own face.

And now here I was standing in my brother's flat, standing on the place of his death, looking at two suitcases full of my mum's clothing, lying atop Dan's treasure trove of refuse.

It was a hard thing to take in and almost impossible to assimilate right at that moment. I had no idea why he would keep all these clothes, but then, I had no idea why he would keep all this refuse. This is something I was going to have to examine and look into if I were to get my head around it. It was madness. To me, and, I think, to most people, what I was looking at represented madness. Insanity. Simple as that.

I thought about all the letters I'd sent him over the years. That was the only possible way I could communicate with him because he simply wouldn't open the front door. All the letters where I tried to get him to at least tell me why he didn't speak to me, why he would have nothing to do with me. I told him off in those letters as well. He treated my mum, our mum, badly by not having anything or certainly not having much to do with her. And he did likewise with my sister Emily. And I didn't think that was right and so I told him so. In my own way. Which can be harsh. I know that I was harsh. I know that. Standing here in this midden, his midden, standing on the piece of floor that was in the process of rotting through from the fluids of his body, I asked myself if I regretted the times I'd been harsh. I decided that it was a question that couldn't be answered in the frame of mind I was in and moved a step and a half into the bedroom, the furthest I could move without climbing onto the rubbish heap.

Just as you walked through the door, to the right, was his lovely desk, but not quite as I remembered it. It was, or had been, a beautiful piece of furniture. It was made of a lovely wood, don't ask me what because I don't know, I'm no good on that stuff, but it was browny-red with a very close grain. Teak probably. Or something else. I don't know why I proffered up Teak then but it's too late now, it's out. It had drawers down each side and a shallow drawer that slid out from the middle front, probably for putting your pencils and stuff or maybe for that manuscript you were working on. All the drawers were lockable. It was the kind of thing you expected to see in a minister's office in Whitehall or something like that. When I'd first seen the desk, all those years ago, I loved it and knew that it exactly summed up who my brother was…educated, smart, refined, handsome, funny, in short, my big brother, my hero. Maybe the brass desk lamp with the green shade that we'd talked about was here somewhere, buried in the rubbish.

The desk had stacks of books, magazines and tied up carrier bags filled, presumably, with magazines, going on the shape of them. The stacks reached almost to the ceiling. They were filthy and cobwebbed. They were also sodden, like they'd been rained on. And covered in snow. The mouse snow. Loads of it. Bags of it. It was like someone had spilled four or five big bags of sugar over everything. Some of the carrier bags had been burrowed into and every single book and magazine that could be seen was chewed. Every surface was sodden, presumably with mouse and rat piss. The rank bitter smell was overpowering, heavy and sickly and actually made your eyes water a little, like peeling onions. Along the front edge of the desk were two litre bottles full of piss, complete with their labels, all pointing the same way, all immediately readable, like they were standing on a library shelf.

I could make out some of the books. There were books on speaking German. Dan was fluent in German. I used to joke with him that I wasn't even fluent in English and he always found that funny. He was proud of his achievement and I was proud of it too. Books on fishing were everywhere. I guessed that most of the magazines would be on fishing as well. Fishing was his all-time passion. He'd been really good at it and, like I've said, tried to get me into it, but I was too…wired up for that, I had to be busy, busy, busy doing the stuff I was into, playing football mostly. Sitting watching a little float bobbing about was not my thing. I still went fishing with him because that is what I did when I was a little kid, I followed my big brother everywhere, I wanted to spend time with him. So, I fished for years but never developed a liking for it. I remember one time making a spear from a stick I'd found and asking him if I could shinny along the branch of a nearby tree, out over the water, and spear a passing fish. He'd said no. Or words to that affect.

There were books on flies, how to make them. He'd spend hours with his box of twines and feathers and varnishes, hours and hours making these lures that were supposed to look like flies. I was shocked that fish could be so dumb as to fall for it but fall for it they did. In numbers. Dan would practice his fly fishing in the back garden, constantly hitting his targets, saying to me 'What shall I hit now Joe?' and I'd point to a yellow flower and he'd hit it or at least come close. He would never let me have a go of his fly-fishing gear. Don't know why.

Dictionaries, Thesauruses, biology books, books on physics, mathematics, chemistry, astronomy, photography, books on art…but no novels. I was the novel reader, the daydreamer. We would have, and should have, made a good team. Our combined interests would have covered most bases.

In amongst the books and magazines were thousands and thousands of coupons, the little blue certificate type thing you used to get in a packet of cigarettes. You collected them and then traded them in for items from a catalogue. How cynical the tobacco companies were and still would be if they could get away with it. Why my brother kept all these coupons, I don't know. It's not like he could get anything with them now because they'd been discontinued years and years ago. Decades ago, probably. I wondered what, if anything, he'd been smoking towards.

I decided that I'd had enough and turned to Lydia. 'Lydia, I've had enough of this.'

'Ok.' she said, nodding an understanding.

'I just wanted to see what the job entailed and now I know.'

Lydia told Edward what I'd said. He nodded at me and gave me a thumbs up. 'Are you sure you don't need me to help you?' he asked.

Edward needed two sticks to walk, he got out of breath easily and wasn't the strongest of fellas. Also, he looked a bit green around the gills. I think the smell was getting to him. I mean, it was getting to me as well, but I had a little bit more about me than him in that way. I did need help, but Edward was going to be more of a hindrance. I shook my head and smiled at him. 'No mate. You need to look after your health, and this is no place to do that. There's all sorts of germs and shit here and you can't afford to get too involved. You've done more than enough already and thanks for that.'

I appreciated what Edward and my sisters had already done. This environment was shit and you needed a particular kind of personality to deal with it, one like mine. I needed to do this job as quickly and as efficiently as possible and I needed to do it my way and the only way of ensuring that was to do it myself. I could trust myself to follow my own instructions. Usually. In fact, I wouldn't even have to give myself instructions because I already knew what they were, so that would save time and effort. We moved down the stairs and outside. Lydia locked the place up and put the keys in her pocket.

We went to the cars and I got out of my paper overall, ramming it down into a black bin bag. It was never going to see the light of day again. I had a little stock of all the protective gear I'd need, so the gloves went into the bag too.

'I'll text you on progress Lydia, send you both photos as I go.'

'Ok.' she said, smiling. 'I'll see you soon.'

I nodded and gave her a hug, shook Edward's hand. 'See you soon.' I said and moved towards the car door. I was eager to get away now. Lydia and Edward moved towards their car. As Lydia was about to get in, she shouted over. 'Joe!' I looked up. 'Thank you!' she shouted. I smiled and winked, got in the car, and drove away.

Chapter 16 - The Letter from Mum

It was day one of the clear up. I parked the car at the front of Dan's flat and donned all my gear standing by the open boot. Walking around the back, I almost bumped into a bent old man walking the opposite way, who didn't even look up or acknowledge me. *Ignorant twat* I thought. 'Sorry mate', I called to his back as he walked away. After a few more steps he gave a hurried half glance over his right shoulder, turned the corner and was gone. I unlocked the front door and opened it. The smell came rushing out at me, like a guard dog. I realised I hadn't put a smear of Vick under my nose and grimaced inside my mask.

I got to the top of the stairs and entered the living room. Right in front of me was a stack of papers and magazines atop a large cardboard box. There was an old threadbare blanket on top of the papers, which had once been a sort of turquoise colour but was now mostly a filthy, shitty brown and looked like it had been burned in places. On top of the blanket was what looked like a letter, plain A4 paper, in one of those sleeves you can get, you know the ones. I could have been mistaken but I didn't remember it being there the last time I'd been here, just yesterday. It was square on to the top of the staircase and, on top of the pile as it was, quite prominent, like it'd been put there specifically for me to find as I entered. I picked it up.

It was a letter from mum to Dan. There were three sheets of A4 and I could see that they were a photocopy. There was something odd about them but I couldn't quite put my finger on it.

I read the letter. It startled me at the first reading and so I read it again. There was no date on it. My mum's address was at the top right-hand corner, like my brother wouldn't have known the address he grew up at, the one she wrote from. I thought that was odd…an address but no date.

Dear Daniel,

How are you? Why don't you give me a ring sometimes? Or better still call & see me? What's wrong with you? Why do you treat everyone like rubbish? No one has done anything to you Daniel, everyone is concerned & keeps asking, but if anyone came to see you, you won't open the door. If we ring you up, you've never got time to talk & when you do its only to hurt. Why don't you get that chip off your shoulder & start being a human being again & leave the booze alone before it destroys you. You were the only one who was worried about being like your dad & you are the only one who's taken after him except he was at least sociable & had a bit more feeling than you. You went to see Katie but you don't even want to know about Darren. Keith left Emily when he was 4 weeks old so she feels it even more. I'm still your mother Daniel and you have got a family who do care. You're not kids anymore & I do think you could make the effort, you might feel better.

Love Mam x

I couldn't quite believe what I'd just read. I was angry, I have to say. She couldn't possibly be that crass, could she? A voice in my head said, *she was one of us, from* that *house, of* course *she could be that crass.*

Nevertheless, her cold heartedness was, I dunno, *disturbing*. Yeah, the letter was disturbing.

I stood in my brother's midden, masked, suited, and booted, surrounded by refuse and bottles full of dark brown piss, standing just a few feet away from the spot where my brother had died, had rotted, almost through to the flat below, stood in the stinking, horrific place that my brother called home, that was his place of sanctuary from the world, the place that his own parents had condemned him to, and she, his *mam,* had sent him this letter that told him he was not as good as his father.

Not as good as his father. It was an abomination. My mum had thought this letter through, written it, put it in an envelope, bought and put a stamp on it, walked to the post box, slid the envelope through the opening and let go of it. This letter was *meant*. It had intent.

There were so many points in time at which she could have stepped back from it, reconsidered it, made it a letter where she voiced no more than her love and concern for her eldest child. But she didn't. Instead, she let her anger fuel an attack on her son. I understood her hurt, her anger. I'd been there myself with my brother. I'd used angry words with him in my own letters, but always mixed with expressions of love and admiration. For a parent to say such a damaging thing to one of her children, without any conscience of the part she may have played in the reasons for her anger…for my mum to make that statement, she had to absolutely believe it. Didn't she? Surely, she did. If she didn't believe it then she was acting from pure malice. For me to use the word abomination is to let her off lightly. Very lightly.

My mother believed that our father was better than my brother.

Not as good as his father. That phrase was stuck in my mind and kept going round and round, over and over. I was taken back to just a few years before my mum died, sitting in her living room, telling her how all five of us Croft kids were damaged mentally and that, in my opinion, at least two of the five were alcoholics and needed help, that they were on the edge of being beyond help, approaching their brink. Those two people, my brother and my sister Carla, were now dead.

I told her about the physical and mental abuse throughout all of our formative years and that such abuse takes a massive toll and that people don't just 'get over' such things. I told her that our wounds were the type of wounds that do not heal, no matter what anyone says, no matter what anyone does. The wounds are open and raw and the pain of them comes to spend time with you every day of your life.

I explained to her that being beaten with a leather belt, on a regular basis, for just about any misdemeanour, has a lasting effect. That that beating, when coupled with other stuff, doesn't just go away. That being made to cut the grass with a pair of scissors, not as a punishment, which would have been bad enough, but as a weekly chore, was not the way you teach your sons how to look after a garden. That being beaten with the leather belt for not cutting the grass short enough or not cutting the grass quickly enough or not picking up ALL the grass cuttings, is just not the way you bring a child up. That punching a young boy, with enough force to knock you on your arse, for no other reason than you weren't fast enough to appreciate a 'joke', is not exactly best practice in the child rearing stakes. That kicking a young boy with a steel toed work boot, causing the most impressively colourful bruising to a buttock, is just not fucking cricket.

Broken toys, ripped up clothing, being beaten for listening to Top of The Pops, being threatened for winning a game, having the exuberance and spirit of youth constantly attacked then crushed, then ground into dust…all of these things do not constitute proper child rearing.

I could have gone on about the brutal beatings meted out to her, that we were forced to witness whilst pretending that nothing bad was happening, beatings that resulted in teeth smashed so badly that the dentist had to take all of her teeth out in her 30's, black eyes too numerous to mention, smashed cheek bones, numerous broken noses, a broken jaw, stamping, kicking, strangling, all committed in front of the children…but I didn't.

I could have gone on about the sexual abuse. But I didn't.

The very act of voicing the things I'd voiced…to my mother about my father…had put me on a flight to despair and Big Joe took over and stopped me saying all of the things I should or could have done.

And after all that I *did* say, during which she looked at the floor in front of her and smoked a few cigarettes, you know what she said to me? You know what she said?

She looked me right in the eye and she said, in the most dismissive way imaginable, she said, 'Oh it wasn't *that* bad Joseph!' I even got the full name, the full name that she only ever used when she was angry with me.

Suddenly, without being summoned, not that he ever *was* summoned, Big Joe was in the room, looking out of my eyes…I was banished to the back somewhere and now, suddenly, he was in charge and he was calmly looking at her.

She lit another cigarette and blew the smoke in my direction, but slightly up towards the ceiling. The intent to blow smoke right at me was there but she stopped herself. Big Joe looked at her, keeping my face calm and expressionless, using my eyes to scrutinise her. She watched him, stared at him. Seemed to challenge him. He kept me calm, got my racing heartbeat under control. And then he told me to stand up and walk out. He told me to not say anything, told me to not slam any doors. He told me to go and get in the car, drive properly, safely, go home, and cook the tea for the family evening meal. He told me to put what happened in a box and slide it to the back of my mind for later analysis. And that is exactly what I did.

And now, standing in my brother's midden, the same thing happened. Big Joe took over and told me to physically put the letter in a safe place and never lose it, to mentally put it in the same box that everything to do with my mother was stored, and slide it to the back of my mind, to be pored over at a later date.

After I packed the letter away, both mentally and physically, I realised what the oddness had been, the thing I couldn't put my finger on earlier. There were actually a few oddnesses, a few anomalies. Why would my brother, who didn't appear to have a computer or printer or anything, why would he take this letter from his mother and get photocopies done? He had the original, what would he have been getting the photocopies for? This photocopy was placed very neatly on top of the shitty blanket facing the top of the stairs. Who put it there and why? It was clean and fresh looking, no mouse piss, no droppings, no chewings. The letter in its sleeve hadn't been there very long, which meant that someone other than Dan had put it there. Recently. Very recently. That person must have been Lydia or Emily. I didn't think it was Emily because I think she was so horror-stricken by the place that she would never come near it again, not until it was cleaned and the evidence of what happened to Dan had been removed. So, Lydia must have put it there. Which meant that it was her who had made a copy of it. Which meant that she must have the original. So, I texted her and asked her about it and she denied all knowledge of it. She said that she didn't know anything about the copy and she didn't have the original either. I texted Emily and she knew nothing and said that she hadn't been near the place since that first time, and wouldn't be coming near the place any time soon.

Someone was lying. But who? And why?

Chapter 17 - The OIC Interview

I'd just got back from day one of the clear up. I stunk. Having the PPE on made no difference to how the odour of the place got to you. It permeated everything, clothing, hair, not that I've got much, and your skin. I took my clothes off and put them straight into the washing machine, which, luckily, was in an outhouse, separate to the living quarters. I crossed the little courtyard with a bin bag around my middle and got straight into the shower.

Once in the shower I performed a little trick I picked up as a firefighter, to rid your nose of smells. You breathe a small amount of soapy water up your nose and then blow it out. If you do this three or four times, it tends to get rid of a lot of smells and crap. Sounds terrible but let me tell you, it's amazing the amount of dust and debris a firefighter gets up his or her nose, even with wearing the BA. Some of the stuff gets so far up your nose, you need to do something a bit out of the ordinary to get it back out again. Just one of those things.

I gave myself a good scrub and then made the water as hot as I could stand and just stood there, the water drumming on top of my head and running down my face. Let me tell you something, when I had hair, on my head that is, I used to think that rain, or being in the shower, sounded like a little crazed drummer inside my head, a Numbskull drummer. But now that I am bald as a coot, it's like having a full timpani team, section, squad, drumming away in there, it's an amazing noise. Or, just had a thought, maybe my head is a little on the hollow side. Yeah, that could be it. Hollow head. Anyway, I like to keep my eyes open in the shower, see how long I can go without blinking, keep breathing as best I can under the deluge, through my nose. Don't ask me why I like these things. I've probably got HHS. Hollow Head Syndrome.

I got dried and into a fresh T shirt and shorts. Pam was cooking our tea and it smelled pretty good. I went to see what it was. As I walked past the table, my phone dinged. It was Dennis.

He'd set me up with a Messenger conversation at 7pm with the OIC of the Dan recovery incident, a fella called Frank Stevens. I didn't know him and didn't recognise the name at all.

Pam had cooked spagbol, which was really nice. I loved spaghetti. A drop or two of a lovely smooth merlot and some of Pam's home-made garlic bread, which she does exceptionally well, made the meal memorable. There is nothing better after a trying day at work, than a good meal and a little glass of wine with someone you love. All I needed now was sleep.

As the allotted time for the Messenger meeting drew closer, I started to change my mind about talking to a fire brigade person other than a mate. I'm not sure why. Well, what I mean by that is that I know what goes on in my mind to make me not want to have the chat but, I wasn't at all sure about why this should be.

I thought back to something I once said, strangely enough, to my brother Dan. I think we were sitting in his living room, me in the armchair by his bedroom door, him on his settee by the window. He'd been saying how his job was beginning to bore him and he was looking to change and asked me what the fire brigade was like and I said to him that it was the best job in the world and that I loved it.

'What about dealing with bodies and all that,' he asked, 'do you get lots of jobs involving that kind of stuff or is it, I dunno, what do you deal with mostly?'

I remember feeling at the time that the question sort of 'intruded' but I'm not sure what it intruded into. Maybe it just intruded into a part of my mind that I didn't want to reveal. I wanted to answer him but at the same time I didn't. I knew that I would've been quite happy to answer this question with another firefighter, but somehow, I felt uneasy with the question coming from my brother. This 'intrusion' thing was something I'd never really had to put into words because it was something I just knew bothered me and I didn't really need to know why. But now he'd asked the question and I needed to answer it as honestly as I could.

In my mind I could see and smell my first 'body job', where two young women had died, where me and my mates were too late to save them. The sight, and smell of their scorched bodies lives with me and will do forever. All of the 'body jobs', as we called them, were vivid memories for me and always would be. People burned, drowned, crushed, torn by cars shredding themselves into other vehicles, trees, and lampposts, all of them, all these people, though they were dead, lived with me. Don't get me wrong, I didn't *see dead people* or anything, I wasn't obsessive in any way about them. They didn't dominate my life or my thoughts but they had a place in my mind where they all lived. And at odd times, for no apparent reason, one or more of them would come to the fore, briefly, just to make sure that they weren't forgotten and to, I don't know, help me get and keep other things in my life in some kind of perspective.

The thing about all these deaths, the thing that certainly occurred to me at the time of the incident, and occasionally occurs to me when the memories surface, is the overwhelming feeling of being an intruder into the event of their death, an event that, in my mind at least, should be a private thing, a thing between family and loved ones. I was always affected by the suddenness with which I, as a firefighter, became involved, sometimes quite violently, in someone's final moments on this earth.

When you enter a building to find someone lost in a fire, it's dangerous and when you discover and rescue that lost person, that feeling of having helped a person in dire need, is immensely gratifying. When you've done that, rescued someone, everything about that incident, the danger, the heat, the way the flames danced across the ceiling, the way the smoke embraced you, trying to find a way into your mask, the sounds of fire and things crashing around you, the finding of that person and the unceremonious dragging and carrying out into the street, to the safety of fresh air and lights and people…all become part of *your* story of this incident, part of the learning of your craft, part of what makes you, you.

But when things go the other way, as they do, when things don't happen the way you want them to and that lost person stays lost until it's too late, *that* feeling is very different. The incident itself, the things that happened, the heat and smoke, the dangers, they're all forgotten, maybe a few significantly insignificant things live strangely on in your mind, like the pink silk pyjamas one poor soul was wearing. What stays with you, what stays with *me*, is the incredible desolation created by the removal of this person from earth...of how you are not moving about in the place of a triumph of search and rescue, but in a place where, for whatever reason, you failed and, as a consequence, for me, you are intruding. If you rescue someone from a burning building and, as a result of their injuries they die later, in another place, that is one thing, but when the lost person is still with you, declared dead at the scene, and you're doing your job around that person, the sense of intrusion, for me, is very, very powerful and then, when that happens, you become part of *their* story...and in a way, sounds daft I know, but, in a way, that little part of *you* becomes lost.

I explained all this to my brother, sat in his living room, drinking coffee. I tried to explain it the way I've just done, but probably made a bit of a mess of it as I've probably just done here. It's not an easy thing to explain because it's so complex and so personal. In any case, my brother took a few moments of silence, looking into my eyes and then he sort of raised his eyebrows, lowered the corners of his mouth, glanced slightly to one side of me as though he was looking at someone just behind me, lit a ciggy and asked me if I wanted another cup of coffee. Which I did.

Cut to this Frank fella now, and I couldn't help feeling that he'd been part of this intrusion thing and, I know it's not right and probably not healthy but, I dunno, I sort of resented him. I can't help it, I just resented his presence in my brother's flat, resented him and his crew being part of the story of my brother. The thing was, of course, that I needed information from him and so I had to swallow that resentment and keep it out of this meeting, a job made easier, I thought, by the meeting being on a screen rather than face to face.

So, he was there, on my screen, his thumbnail photo with a little green blob on it, indicating he was also looking at me and my little green blob. I started typing.

'Hiya Frank, thanks for agreeing to speak to me mate. I don't think we know each other, do we?'

'Hi Joe,' he said, *'No I don't think we do know each other. To be honest...'* There was that phrase that always set my teeth on edge, even when I used it myself, *'I'm not sure what I can tell you about the incident, confidentiality wise. Why don't you tell me what you would like to know and if I can help I will.'*

'Confidentiality wise?' *Confidentifuckinality wise?'* A very brief battle exploded inside my head and the person who lives inside me, the one in charge of security, Big Joe, wanted to let rip on Frank, wanted to climb into the screen and wriggle through the ether, whatever the fuck that is, and emerge from Frank's screen to grab him round the throat and shake him about a bit. Just a bit. A little tiny bit. Honest. One of the other blokes inside my mind, the reasonable one, the one who used to operate me when I was a firefighter myself, said to me, *'I'll handle this mate, you just keep that other fella under control, OK?'*

'Fully understand mate, I know the score.' I typed, *'So, were you actually at the job Frank?'* I asked.

He answered straight away, '*Yes Joe I was the OIC'*. I had a quick squint at his thumbnail and, to be honest, honestly being honest, he looked too young, but, I thought, if he is the OIC, he has to be getting on for 30 or so, which, quick calculation, if he was around the 30ish mark that would mean that when I retired from firefighting, he was still at school, probably studying for his A levels. *Fuck*, I thought, *Joe mate, you're older than you think you are* and then I thought, *why, how old do you think you are?* and this other voice said *he thinks he's young enough to do the stuff he retired from doing cos he was too old to do it, that's how old he thinks he is. He's an idiot.* Enough! I said to myself, possibly out loud, and typed '*Nasty job to get mate. I hope you and your crew are all OK and fully recovered from it. I just need to know a few things with regard to the deceased, who, as you probably know, was my brother.'*

'*Yes,'* he replied, '*I'm sorry for your loss Joe. We're all OK thanks, you know how it goes.'*

I realised that this couldn't be an easy task for him and doubly realised that this was something he didn't have to do. '*Thanks mate,'* I said, '*I appreciate that. Is it possible for you to tell me which way round his body was, i.e., head towards the bedroom?'*

'*Yes,'* he said, '*his head was towards the bedroom, his feet in the room entered via the stairs.'* That agreed with my assessment of the photo Lydia had sent me. So, Dan *had been* lying the wrong way round, as far as I was concerned. He wasn't using the 'bed' as the manufacturer intended.

'*What about the alignment of his limbs Frank, did you see him fully?'* There were a few seconds or so of silence and then the little dots started flashing as he typed. They stopped for maybe half a minute then resumed and an eye blink later his reply appeared.

'Yes, Joe, I did see him fully, he was lying on his back with his legs straight out and his arms by his side.' In other words, like he was lying in a coffin, or should I say like an undertaker would arrange him in his coffin. I found this a bit strange, I mean, yeah, you can lie down to go to sleep like that and yeah you can lie down, go to sleep like that and suddenly die in the same position but, my head kept coming back to the fact that, as far as I was concerned anyway, he was lying in his bed, coffin, whatever you want to call it, the wrong way around. His head should have been at the wide end. That's not just me being pernickety, after all, it was Dan who'd made the bed, he made it that shape and he did that for a reason, and as far as I was concerned that reason was that it was just a logical thing to do even though the circumstances were completely illogical.

'What was your actual brief for the job mate? I know you were just assisting police but what did they ask you to do?' I asked.

'We had to clear the staircase, which was full of refuse, and clear a path from the top of the stairs to the place where the body lay, to make access for them easy and safe, you know the score, Joe.'

'Yeah, I do mate,' I typed, *'and so, was he under the rubbish or on top of it?'*

'He was under the refuse, maybe had about 4 to 5 feet of it on top of him, consisting of household items, papers, food wrappers. The police had identified where the body lay, more or less, and wanted as much stuff removing from on top of him without disturbing the body itself.

Once we cleared a path to the site, the removal of the rubbish from on top of him was a bit of a painstaking task.'

I thought about this for a few minutes, occasionally tapping a key just to make sure my little dots were flashing at his end so he didn't think I'd gone away. *'Was the rubbish a uniform depth Frank? Do you think he'd burrowed under the rubbish, or what? What's your gut feeling?'* I typed.

He was quick to answer this question, *'I couldn't in all honesty say I'm afraid,'* he typed, *'he could have burrowed but it could also have fallen onto him some time later. And yes, it was a uniform depth covering him.'*

Good answer mate, I thought, thinking back to my time in the job and the neutral stance that should be taken at times. *Good answer.*

'Ok Frank thanks. Mate, did he have hold of anything?'

Again, Frank was quick to answer. He probably had a good mental image of what he'd seen, an image that would live with him forever I thought. *'No.'* he typed, *'He was not holding anything.'*

'Ok Frank,' I typed, *'I think I'm just about done.'*

'I hope,' he said, *'that I've been of some help Joe and, once again, I'm sorry for your loss.'*

'Yeah, you have Frank, a great help and thanks,' I replied, *'just one more thing though,'* I felt like Columbo, *'the rubbish you removed, where did you put it all?'*

'We put everything from the stairs and the pathway to your brother in the garden and the stuff that was on top of him we put to one side.' he answered.

'Ok Frank, well that really is me done now.' I said. *'Thanks for all your help mate and if you would pass on my thanks to your crew, I'd appreciate it.'*

We said our goodbyes and Frank disappeared.

I put the laptop down and watched some TV. A documentary about whales. I needed something to drink and thought a hot chocolate with Horlicks would go down well. Pam had a cup of tea. If you've never had hot chocolate, say, Cadbury's Options, with a spoonful of Horlicks, try it…I'd give it an eight, possibly even a nine out of ten.

As David Attenborough waxed on about the blue whale, I was thinking about the conversation I'd just had with Frank Stevens and the position of my brother's body under the rubbish. What was it Frank had said? *'He was under the refuse, maybe had about 4 to 5 feet of it on top of him'*

So, the rubbish in the flat was in the region of five feet deep everywhere. It wasn't beautifully stacked, it was just, *there*. The beer can mountains in the kitchen and bathroom appeared random but they weren't, they were thought through, there was a sad logic to them. My brother had, for want of a better word, *constructed* a bed with cardboard as it's bedstead and squashed rubbish as it's mattress. He would need to cover himself for warmth at night and so used rubbish as a duvet. So, what were the mechanics of getting into bed. How did he do it? How would I do it?

Firstly, even though I am, to all intents and purposes, chucking my rubbish haphazardly about the place, I wouldn't do that. I would spread it about but I wouldn't let it get too high in the vicinity of my bed because I wouldn't want the task of clearing the bed on a daily basis of any avalanches. So, first things first, I would construct my bed in a place where it's easy to ensure its safety, which sounds ridiculous but, this is what he'd done too. His bed was in a doorway and was enclosed on one side by a wall and on the other side by his desk, which was the only place where the rubbish was piled in a structurally sound way. The rubbish on the desk consisted of stacks of books and magazines, which, are probably relatively stable, even to the height he'd stacked them. The books and the desk, were possibly, probably, maybe, his one remaining link to who he used to be, who he *was*, but locked away deep in his mind.

I would ensure as much as possible that rubbish was not going to cascade down onto me from the two remaining quarters, the head end, and the feet end, by evening it out, never allowing the rubbish to teeter over me. It's a rubbish tip but it doesn't have to be a *precarious* one if you get my drift. You have to *live* there, after all. Y'know, have you ever seen those bag ladies and bag men, who walk the streets with a mountain of rubbish contained in plastic bags, often piled into a shopping trolley or strapped to a bike or a pram? It looks as precarious as it's possible to look but, they never seem to have a problem controlling the stuff. Cut to India, have you ever been to India? And seen the men who cycle with absolute mountains of goods around them and behind them? When I went to Delhi, I was truly captivated by these people and their incredibly industrious and ingenious ways of overcoming transport problems that we in the UK would just get a man and his van to sort out. In some ways,

I thought my brother had applied a certain logic and deranged ingenuity to what he'd done in his home.

I reckoned that, if I was in the same position as my brother, I would have a bed area, that was 'safe' and a ready supply of, say, empty plastic bottles to pull over me at night for warmth. And those particular bottles, for me, would be in the vicinity of the foot of my bed, so I could just drag them up at night. Maybe even contained in large bags, just like a duvet.

So, I'm lying in my rubbish bed, how do I collect a uniform layer of rubbish on top of me to a depth of four to five feet? With my arms? How? I'm not Mr Tickle, so how did I do this?

Did it fall on me? If it did, and don't get me wrong, it's fine if it did, so, bear with me here, where did it fall *from*? My mattress is about a foot thick, a foot of trampled down, well established refuse. Then there's me lying there taking up the best part of another foot, so, for rubbish to fall on me during the night or over a few weeks, it would have had to be six to seven feet deep all around me and fall in such a way as to even itself out. Strange things happen in life, I know, but that just didn't seem feasible to me.

In my mind, for Dan to have been lying in his bed, and to have been covered, uniformly, to a depth of four to five feet with rubbish, he must have burrowed in or another person must have placed the rubbish on top of him, spreading it uniformly so that it looked the same as the rest of the room. If he burrowed in and died, that's fine. I mean, it's *not* but it is if you see what I mean. But if someone covered him up in such a way as to make him look like a room full of rubbish, then that smacks of something else entirely.

As I was digesting that thought, the blue whale going about its majestic swimming, Mr Attenborough's voice working with the hot chocolate and Horlicks, conspiring to send me to sleep, another question was answered from what seemed like years before…the brown powder from the post-mortem report, the brown powder that was, can't remember the exact words used but something along the lines of 'most likely' the dried remnants of the lungs.

The brown powder had been present in both the pleural cavity and the abdominal cavity, and I'd been a bit confused that dried out lung powder had somehow migrated to another part of the body, and to my way of thinking, must have done so with the aid of gravity or wind. I knew that, five feet down under a pile of rubbish, wind hadn't been the means of transport for the powder, and now, with the 'testimony' of Frank Stevens, I knew that gravity had played no part in this movement either. Dan had been lying flat, his uneaten lung remnants had dried out, turned to something resembling powder, and dropped into his chest cavity but also his abdomen. Didn't make sense to me.

I went to bed and, as was the norm for me, I got my thoughts into some sort of order, did a bit of pondering and fell asleep.

The next morning, the first thought that came into my mind was a yellow spot that I'd seen when I got up during the night to go for a pee. It had been about 3 a.m., maybe a little later, I think, and the picture I had was of a small bright yellow spot on the white rim of the toilet bowl. I went to the bathroom and investigated while I was there.

Sure enough, there was a small bright yellow spot on the toilet rim. It was obviously pee and obviously it was from me rather than Pam. I hadn't spotted it until I was stood there in the early hours of the morning and, being virtually asleep standing, had just gone back to bed. But it had stayed in my mind and now that I was inspecting it, it looked as though it had tiny little diamonds glittering in it. *Salt crystals* I thought. I rubbed my forefinger over the spot and it disappeared from the rim. I stood by the light from the window and looked at my fingertip really closely. The glittery stuff was almost certainly salt crystals, though I wasn't going to taste it. I hadn't even had my breakfast yet. I'm joking. I wouldn't have tasted it, though back in the day, the king of England had people, *physicians*, who regularly tasted his piss to see how healthy he was. Have you noticed that I refer to my piss as pee and everyone else's pee as piss? Interesting that.

I rubbed the yellow stain on my finger between finger and thumb. It was gritty. Felt like fine salt, like the *powder* of the salt rather than the little grains of salt. Are they grains? Yeah, I think they are, but if they're not, you still know what I'm talking about don't you? The dust off the salt. Rubbing the bright yellow pee stain between my finger and thumb felt like dust. Powder. The dried pee felt like powder. Pee, or, piss, dries into a powder.

The bright, almost fluorescent yellow, came from some tablets I took for my restless leg thing. Pam put me onto them. I take one every day, if I remember. And an hour or two after taking it, my pee is, like, *radioactive* yellow. If there is such a colour.

I wondered if piss drying into a powder would be on the internet and looked as I ate my breakfast. I typed the words *dried piss* into the search engine and to my complete surprise, opened a door to a world I didn't know existed. Did you know that you can buy dried piss on the internet? No? Well, you do now. Why would you want to? It's so obvious once you know, and yet it would never, ever, not in a million billion gazillion years have occurred to me…that you can buy a bag of dried piss powder that is guaranteed *Drug Free!* And what would you do with it? Re-hydrate it of course! There are various workers, students and, I dunno, all sorts of people who, at one time or another, might get their piss tested for drugs. Shocked is too strong a word but I was definitely somewhere on the scale of shocked.

So, if fluorescent yellow pee dries into a fluorescent yellow powder, what colour powder does dark brown piss dry into? It must be brown. Surely. It stands to reason doesn't it? It did to me. But then, with regards to the brown powder in the two cavities of my brother's torso, where did this leave me? I didn't know. I'd have to ponder it.

I finished my breakfast, brushed my teeth, checked to make sure I'd left no more little spots on the toilet rim and went to the flat.

By the way, while I was searching the internet for dried piss, I also checked this out:- **Coot**. An aquatic bird of the rail family, with blackish plumage, lobed feet, and a bill that extends back on to the forehead as a horny shield…or…this is probably more like it…**Coot**. A stupid or eccentric person, typically an old man.

Chapter 18 - The Kicked-In TV

The drudgery of the work went on. Pick up, look at if you need to, put it in the document box if wanted or the bucket if rubbish, fill the bucket, take it down the stairs, put it in the wheelbarrow, do it again until three buckets are full, take wheelbarrow to skip, empty it, start again. Over and over and over. Day after day.

The beer cans had presented a problem. I estimated that there were 20,000 beer cans in the flat, maybe 10 years' worth at about five or so a day. I didn't know what his consumption was but I reckoned five cans a day wasn't overcooking it for someone like my brother.

The kitchen, which measured about three metres by two, was full almost to the ceiling. The door was open a crack, just enough to put your arm in and flick a can up onto the pile. It's hard to envisage and, believe me, it was hard to take in.

It hadn't been an easy thing to do. He must have started to throw his rubbish into the room, starting at the window end. Maybe he started stacking it at the window end, on the worktop and just didn't get around to moving it and the pile sort of just took over, or the effort of moving it became too great. *But then,* I thought, *actually achieving this room full to the ceiling almost had taken effort and a certain amount of ingenuity.*

Getting it all out again also required a certain amount of, if not ingenuity then certainly resourcefulness. Just getting the door open enough to use the shovel wasn't easy. I pushed the door but it wouldn't budge, or rather, it moved about half a metre but then stopped dead. As soon as there was a gap, the cans avalanched out into the square metre of 'lobby' floor between the kitchen and bathroom. The noise was unbelievable, I'd never heard anything like it, not since I took part in a plate spinning competition on the quarry-tiled floor of the fire station kitchen. The speed at which the cans avalanched was also unbelievable, covering me up to my thighs in seconds.

As I shovelled cans into the buckets, making space, more cans cascaded into the little lobby until the kitchen cans mountain reached some kind of equilibrium and I was able to turn into the kitchen itself. The door was stuck on something and wouldn't open more than the half metre and I had to more or less wrestle shovelfuls out of the room. In the end, I brought my sledgehammer into play and attacked the door itself, hitting the hinge areas to good effect. I don't know why I hadn't thought of it earlier. One tap for each hinge, two whacks, followed by a door wrestling match and the door was out and in the skip. A clothes maiden had fallen behind the door, wedging itself between the door and a tall fridge, preventing opening. The equilibrium created by the door was released and another avalanche occurred.

Kitchen Can Mountain took an absolute shitload of buckets and barrows to empty. That's a lot of buckets let me tell you. The fridge-freezer was put outside for specialist removal after first being emptied of food that hadn't seen the light of day for god knows how long. To say that there was mould growing on it would be the biggest understatement since the Apollo 13 astronaut, Jack Swigert, reported some kind of problem to ground control or whatever it's called.

At the far end of the kitchen, under the window, I found the skeleton of a dog, lying in its little bed and covered by a sack. Judging by the size of the skeleton, the colouring of what hair remained and the under-bite, I took it to be Bertie, the Shih Tzu that my brother had bought for my mum and had reclaimed when she died. I wondered if, given the site of the 'burial', the death of Bertie had maybe been the catalyst for the hoarding to begin in earnest. We'd never know and, in the strangest of ways I just took it all in my stride and got through the work. My fire brigade head was well and truly on and it was only every now and then that I opened my mind up to allow stuff in and stuff out. When that happened, I'd have to usually take a little break outside by my car, sipping at a bottle of water or having a coffee, listening to the real world sliding by, buses, cars, people's voices, birds and whatever else makes normal everyday sounds. When I stood outside, I'd frequently look up at the windows of his flat and think about the world he'd created inside, and how those windows were the same as the windows of our bedroom in our childhood home, apparently like every other window on every other house, but, in reality not the same at all. Pieces, *panes* of glass, what, 6mm thick or so, separating worlds, universes, normality from abnormality, clever little words with massive meanings. And then I'd think about eyes. Dan's eyes, my father's eyes, my eyes. Windows to the soul, as *they* say. I wondered who'd first coined the phrase and wondered if they were just being poetic or did they have genuine reason to say it and then I thought *I actually don't give a flying fuck who it was or what they thought.* Whoever thought it up and first used it weren't important, weren't relevant. What *was* important, to me, was that, through the eyes of every person is a world different to the one behind your eyes and different to the world where you stand, looking in. The same thing applied to the windows of a house; different worlds existed on both sides of every pane of glass in every window of every house everywhere. And you could never tell what was real. Nothing was what you thought it was.

There were three wall cupboards above the worktop in the kitchen, which the mountain of beer cans had completely covered, all perfectly normal in that they were full of the things you'd expect to find in a kitchen wall cupboard, sauce bottles, salt and pepper, bottles containing herbs and spices, gravy makings, rice, pasta, tea, coffee. All normal, all filthy dirty and well out of date but all the kind of stuff you'd expect. And then there was a black A4 sized page a day diary.

I opened it. It was packed with writing, every page. Different coloured inks but mostly black, the writing obviously my brother's but different at different times. Some of the writing, no, lots of the writing was aggressive looking, agitated looking, some of it looked almost unintelligible. And, riffling through the pages, not reading anything but just taking first sight of it, some of the writing was very neat, not at all like his writing but at the same time still obviously his writing. It was intriguing, not least because it had been 'secreted' for want of a better word in a wall cupboard with the condiments of a normal kitchen. It was intriguing but it was something that would have to wait for later.

It took another shitload of buckets and barrows full of beer cans, food cans and packets to clear the bathroom, which presented the same problems of avalanching cans. The bathroom contained another dog bed, bigger than the Bertie bed, probably Midge's, Dan's Staffordshire Bull Terrier bitch, a beautifully tempered dog. There were dog leads, choker chains and collars, dog food bowls and the toys you'd throw for them to worry or fetch. I wondered why he kept all the stuff that was Midge's, even what looked like her bed blankets, manky as manky can be, hanging on a nail he'd hammered into the wall. There was also a full box of Jaffa Cake boxes full of Jaffa Cakes, if that makes sense. Apparently, my brother loved Jaffa Cakes the same as me. Or maybe more than me, though I found that hard to reconcile with my adoration of the cake sold from the biscuit aisle. God knows how he managed to buy a full box of boxes of them then seemingly forget what he had and cover them up with refuse. I had a little daydream about the Jaffa Cakes and wondered if I could eat a houseful of them. Probably, I decided.

When the bathroom was emptied of refuse, I discovered the toilet was also empty. Of water. The U bend was empty, dried up, evaporated. The way through to the sewers was open and obviously this had been a conduit for rats to enter the property. I pressed the flusher handle but the cistern was empty as well. I couldn't immediately find the stopcock for the water and needed to fill the U bend with liquid. I picked up one of my brother's two litre piss bottles, examined it like a wine connoisseur would, opened it and emptied it into the toilet bowl. The smell was utterly dreadful and I promised myself that I'd bring some big bottles of water and bleach the following day and repeat the procedure.

In the corner of the bathroom, above the bath, was the wire shelf unit I'd spotted the top of days before, when I was here with Lydia and Edward. It seemed like months ago. It still contained aftershaves, shaving creams, talc, and shampoo. I wondered if he'd ever performed

the talcum powder fart for Midge or Bertie and a stupid picture of the
two dogs sat on the settee, with a bowl of popcorn between them, a glass
of foaming beer in hand, laughing their socks off and spluttering in the
talc cloud, barking 'Again! Again!' leapt into my mind.

I took the top off a can of Brut and sprayed it into the air. It was Brut
and smelled just like it did decades before when I'd last smelled it. I
wondered when my brother had last had a bath. Washed his hair. Or his
clothes. Brushed his teeth, the teeth he'd always been so protective of, so
proud of. White and even. Film star teeth. Not like mine, crooked
because my mum wouldn't let the dentist put braces on me in case I got
bullied in school. Irony at its finest. Eventually, I got to where I was
now, somewhere between the bathroom and the place I'd nicknamed
Cardboard Box Island, in the Sea of Shite.

I picked up a string-tied stack of *Coarse Fishing* magazines and a
family of mice nesting underneath, squeaked in unison, and scattered,
making me jump up in the air about three feet to a metre. You may have
noticed that I use both metric and imperial measurements pretty much
intermingled and that is because I find them both useful and try to ensure
that they get used as equally as possible, without being a bit anal and
keeping a spreadsheet on the subject. Or to put it another way, it's
because I don't really care, and just leave it to my speech Numbskulls to
sort out, so, you can blame them if you're getting confused about it all.
You know what, I've realised what my grandad had probably realised all
those years ago, that when you get to a certain age, you can just think
whatever way you want and no one cares. Handy. Very handy.

As I worked through the square metre of rubbish where I stood, I
uncovered what looked like the corner of a TV. After another 10 minutes

or so, the TV was fully uncovered and I lifted it up and onto the top of the pile adjacent to me. It was a flat screen, maybe about 28 inches and it had a biggish hole right in the middle of the screen and a corresponding bulge and crack in the plastic casing at the back. It had been hit fairly hard with something, maybe a hammer. Or a foot. Maybe it had been kicked. Maybe there was something on it, a programme or news item that angered my brother and he'd kicked the TV. The second that thought blossomed in my mind I was whisked away to another world.

About 1961

I was sat on the settee. Dan was in an armchair, but not our father's armchair. We were both watching the TV. We'd not long been in from school and we were watching...I dunno, Torchy the Battery Boy or something like that. Whatever we were watching must have been good because neither of us even knew that our father was in the house, we were that engrossed. He didn't normally come in from work until teatime and it was probably about four o'clock or thereabouts.

He suddenly appeared, striding quickly into the room, went straight to the TV in the corner and kicked the screen in, turned and walked out. No words, no shouts, nothing. He didn't look at us, didn't speak to us, didn't slam any doors or anything. He just seemed to appear in the room, kick the telly in and walk out. When he kicked the screen, it exploded, or imploded or whatever it did. I don't know how those 1960's TV screens were manufactured but it made a hell of a bang when it was kicked. I seem to recall, now that I'm thinking about it, that there was a vacuum involved with the manufacture of the screens and that the explosion noise was actually an implosion noise. Either way, we were showered in glass fragments. We weren't hurt but we were shocked such that we didn't move. We didn't even look at each other. I just looked at the wooden box in the corner that used to be the TV. I was too shocked to even be scared.

After a few minutes, our mother came in and looked at the wooden box for what seemed an age and then she walked out. And when I say out, I mean out. Of the house. She got the pram with my sister Carla in and walked out. She slammed the front door and I heard her heels clicking off down the street.

Me and Dan still hadn't moved.

Our father came back into the room with a sandwich on a plate, a cup of tea and the newspaper under his arm. He sat down in his armchair, the one with the best view of the telly, and, putting his cup of tea on the arm, opened the paper onto the back page, the sports page, rested it on his knee and took a bite out of his sandwich. He didn't even look at us. He did, however, quite bizarrely, look at the telly every now and then. As he moved in the chair, the little pieces of glass on the chair crunched and squeaked. I liked the noise. I don't know why. I still like the noise made by grinding glass.

It was when he first glanced at the telly that my brother first glanced at me. A tiny sidelong glance made without moving his head. I copied him...glancing without moving my head. I didn't know what to do so I just sat and waited to see what my brother did and take it from there. No thoughts were on the move, no ideas taking shape, I just waited. And glanced about, my new skill.

My father ate his sandwich, drank his tea, and read his paper. He kept looking at the telly and the clock on the mantelpiece, the same clock that years later, in a moment of school holiday boredom, I decided to take apart to see how it worked, which was a big mistake but another story. I knew that he was checking the clock because he was going to go out. Probably to the pub. He finished his drink and sandwich, put the paper on the floor, got up and walked out. A couple of minutes later, the front door opened and closed. We still hadn't moved but were glancing at each other as though glancing was going out of fashion.

A few minutes went by and our grandparents, whose house it was, came into the room. My grandma got the two of us up out of our seats and started to brush at the glass fragments with her tea towel. My grandma always had a tea towel. Grandad just looked at the telly and at the mess and shook his head slowly. He kept sighing. 'By 'eck' he said. A few times.

'Grandma...' I said, 'can I have a sandwich please?'

They took us out of the room, and we were given a sandwich. I can remember the sandwich. Big thick slices of white bread cut off the loaf the way she used to do it, by turning the loaf around as she cut. I've tried to do it the grandma way and you, or rather, I, end up with a slice of bread that has a crust 2 inches thick at one end and half an inch thick at the other, with a kind of step in the middle. The sandwich had a thick spread of best butter — we never had any of that worst butter, I've never even seen it — a thick slice of the ham she'd cooked the day before and a serious dollop of yellow mustard, English mustard, the proper stuff, made by grandma from the powder. The mustard made my nose and eyes water, but I loved it. It's still one of my favourite sandwiches and I still put too much mustard on, like she did.

Nothing was ever said about the TV. And to my knowledge the same thing happened at least twice more, and nothing was ever said about those occasions either. By anyone. No-one in the family ever mentioned it to anyone else. Or should I say no-one in the family ever mentioned it to me, nor I to them. Weird or what? Actually, now I'm thinking about it, maybe it was just me that never mentioned it. Maybe everyone else was jangling about it all the time. Yeah. Never thought of that. Until now. I reckon a psychiatrist would have a field day with my family. I mean, he or she would be stumped for much to write about me but, the rest of 'em? Yeah…a field day.

And now, what, 60 or so years later, in my brother's flat, was what looked like a kicked in TV. I couldn't work out why he'd kept it. Again, I wondered if it was another of the catalysts that had provoked the hoarding of rubbish. Did he keep the TV to remind him of what he'd done? Or did he keep it, knowing that sooner or later, when he'd gone, someone, more than likely us, his family, would clear his mess up and find it and know what he'd done. Was it all part of some after-death message he wanted to send to us? I don't know. I couldn't start to think too deeply about it whilst working in it because, the chances are, if you start to think too deeply at the wrong time, you can get into difficulty. I've always thought that…leave the analysis, the debrief, until later, when things have evened out and calmed down.

Chapter 19 - The Diary of Daniel

The fish and chips had been…ok. I think my tastes had changed since leaving the shores of England. And I think chippy food had suffered the most. I love the smell of fish and chips and I love the crispy salty batter of the fish. I love the white chunky fish itself and I love the golden crispy salty chips. But somehow, I didn't love them all together on the same plate any more. It just seemed too heavy, too stodgy. *Could be down to my ageing gut*, I thought, rather than the food itself, or *maybe my palette had changed.* And then I thought, *well, it doesn't matter one way or the other does it because the bottom line is that you don't enjoy fish and chips as much as you used to, so, eat something else.*

I was always having these arguments, or discussions with myself and sometimes they were helpful and sometimes they weren't.

I started to browse the A4 diary. I had to do this outside because of the smell it gave off. After only 10 minutes I had to give up because the smell was making me think about ridding my stomach of the fish and chips.

I contacted my sisters on Messenger and we had a conversation about the diary and the feasibility of passing it around, like a family bible or something. I suggested I photograph every page, bin it, and send them copies of the photographs as soon as I'd finished. They agreed, though Lydia was hesitant and actually asked me if it was right and proper that we read his diary. My stance was that, for no known reason he'd not spoken to me for more than half of my life, he'd left a god awful mess behind him that I was in the process of cleaning up and that, I thought he owed me answers, answers that I probably was never going to find but, if a diary he'd left could shed *some* light, even just a glimmer of light, on anything, anything at all, then I was going to seize that opportunity. Emily agreed with me. I finished off by saying to Lydia, *Lydia*, I said, *I'll send you the photographs, then you decide whether you'll read them or not.*

I photographed the diary with my iPhone, Pam turning the pages and holding them in the breeze that had thankfully sprung up, carrying the smell of the diary away from us. I filled the frame with each photo and checked to make sure it was readable and when I'd finished, we bagged the diary up and put it in the bin.

I moved the photos onto my laptop and used the media viewer to read the pages. From the moment I started reading it, from the writing covering the inner cover, I knew that it was going to be hard work.

It started out with a list of phone numbers written on the inner cover. His family, including me, and a number of council offices, plus The Jeremy Kyle show, the BBC, Channel 4, and a number of taxi firms. It was a one year A4 page-a-day diary but he had used it to record two years of his life, 2003 and 2004, possibly with the start of 2005 from what I could make out at first glance.

To begin with it seemed as though this had been a success, but the more I looked through it, the more I realised it wasn't. I picked a random date, 28th May, and on that page were the entries for the 28th May 2003, with the entry for the 28th May 2004 written underneath but, at the bottom of the page, because he ran out of room for what he wanted to write, he started again at the top of the page, and overwrote part of the 2003 entry. It looked, at first glance, like a load of scribbling and it was only when magnifying the photo that I was able to see the two entries written, one on top of the other. It was difficult but with very careful scrutiny of the writing and applying the context of what had been written before, it was possible to decipher it.

Although mostly black ink, he'd used different coloured pens throughout, blue, orange, green and red. It was easier to read overlaps when the ink colour changed. *Maybe that's why he did it,* I thought, a certain logical craziness involved.

I started to decipher and transcribe the diary. It wasn't going to be a fast job.

Chapter 20 - Excerpts from the Diary

It took Pam no time at all to work out what all his figures meant. All the little lines under the day and date, like, for instance, *2nyt start 7pm 45 x 6 + 112.50*. She's good at research, smart at ferreting stuff out on the internet and putting things together.

It was obvious from the word go that the figures related to what he was drinking and I wondered if the diary had started as a means of monitoring his habit. If it did, it soon degenerated into, I'm not sure what you'd call it. It's a description of his day but it often paints him as a nasty, sly, manipulative person. At times he seems proud of what he writes and everything is very matter of fact. And then at other times he seems ashamed but soon bolsters himself. It's a strange experience reading it. Hard to reconcile with the boy I grew up with.

At times it seemed as if he was writing his diary for an audience, that he expected someone to read it one day, which, I suppose, is exactly what happened. It struck me that this particular diary was written years ago and I wondered if there had been others or whether he just did it for the span of this book, then gave up.

His drinking was truly horrendous back in 2003 to 2005, the period covered, and I shuddered to think what state his body was in during the time running up to his death. Such a waste. Such a fucking awful waste of a life.

Anyway, time for a little lecture, a *lecturette* I'm going to call it. All of the thousands of empty beer cans in his home were strong beers, the Supers and the Special Brews. They were 9 percent abv beers. Abv is an abbreviation for *alcohol by volume* and the number relates to the amount of pure alcohol or ethanol, in a given volume of an alcoholic drink, so, 9 percent of every mouthful of beer is pure alcohol.

Dan's '45', which crops up a lot, relates to the millilitres of pure alcohol in a given drink. All of his 9 percent abv beer cans had contained 500 ml of beer. To arrive at the '45' you multiply the contents, 500, by the abv, 9 percent and you get 45. This is 45 ml of pure alcohol.

Dan's 112.50 relates to a 750 ml sized bottle of 15 percent abv wine. You multiply the 750 by 15 percent, you get 112.50.

In the UK, the NHS recommended number of 'units' for an adult is not more than 14 units per week. One of Dan's 45's is 4.5 units, which means that to drink 'safely', my brother can drink about three cans of his special brew beers, *per week.* In an average week, my brother was drinking at least 30 of these beers, plus his 15 percent wines, plus his spirits. But let's just concentrate on the beers, let's just look at his beer can mountains. Dan was consuming 30 x 4.5 units which equals a staggering 135 or, about 120 units more than the 'safe' amount. Every week. For decades. Not including his wine and his spirits.

Looking at the stark figures, it was hard for me to understand that a *relative* of mine, my *brother*, the boy and man I had shared a bedroom with for the first 20 years of my life, it was beyond my grasp, outside my comprehension that this had happened within my family. I felt desolate. *I* felt desolate. *Me.* What did my brother feel? Anything? Or nothing? Did he simply become robotic…anaesthetized to everything except his base thoughts and desires and the need to fuel his addiction?

It was disturbing.

Sunday 26th January 2003

2nyt start 5:35pm 45 x 7

2nyt gave Bertie firmish slap on side 2 stop him from looking for piece of dog biscuit on floor, because he was in danger of causing landslide of cans, and he wouldn't stop looking when I told him to stop (several times). He walked away and looked at me. I told him to come here and jump up on chair. He did so, and I felt him and he wasn't shaking, i.e., not frightened. But he had been given a mild shock, i.e., he licked his lips and looked at me when I talked to him and stroked him. I went and got him another piece of biscuit, and pretended to find it by the landslide. He was ok about it all.

Wednesday 05th February 2003

2nyt start 7:24pm 45 x 5 + 112.50

This morning, b4 7am, started my car (started 1st time) and reversed to other car park, then decided 2 go for a spin. Had at least 45 x 4 inside me, will never do that again, even though my driving was fine. Had Bertie with me, untethered in the front seat. Blue Seat car was parked next to me B4 I went out, B4 7am. Who's car is it? Where do they go?

Came in after engine had warmed up and had another 45 x 3. Didn't put alarm on, and car has had no alarm on overnight into Thursday daytime.

Friday 07ᵗʰ March 2003

2nyt start 7.43 pm 45 x 6? + 112.50

Finished Disneys Atlantis this afternoon PS1

This morning (late) Bertie on the bed me in the toilet, Bertie screaming with pain, I shouted a lot. Bertie scratching his ear and screaming I assume. This afternoon Bertie same scenario but this time in lounge on chair. I was in kitchen. I lost it and battered him for a few seconds only. I don't know if I was controlling the fast slaps 2 his body (may have been 1 or 2 initial ones to his head, I can't remember, but I hope not), but I appeared to be fast and hard. I don't know if he jumped off chair or was "slapped off" chair, but he didn't cry once, in fact, the screaming from him scratching his ear instantly stopped when I started hitting him. He was very soon back on the chair, he didn't try to run away from me. I was shocked at myself, and soon went from kitchen back into lounge and apologised 2 him. I felt him and he wasn't shaking and seemed fine with me, maybe he thought I had helped him with his ear. 2nyt (or was it last night?) very late I heard a gnawing sound, quite loud.

Sunday 16ᵗʰ March 2003

2nyt start 5:33 pm 45 x 4

2day 12 – 12.30 pm took photos of my garden to show the mess left by Tommys fence erectors.

ASDA WAL/MART AGFA FILM iso 200

1ˢᵗ 4 or 5 of my gardens path mess

Channel 5 finished 5.38 2nyt says modern cars don't survive a 60 – 70 mph crash (head on) nearly as well as a 10 yr old car. Still a long way to go.

Bertie bites off tat on ryt leg.

Heard mouse distress calls about 5.30 pm 2nyt. Petered out about 6.30 pm. Crushed? Or trapped? Cans. Or babies wanting milk? By lounge door to stairs. Heard can/metallic sounds a few times. Is young one trapped with weight of cans above it?

Chapter 21 – Another Penny Drops

It just came to me as I was driving past Anfield, the stadium of Liverpool FC. I wasn't even thinking about it, I was thinking of a match I'd been to at that famous stadium what seemed like a hundred years before. And then it just sort of pinged into my head. I even think I heard a Ping! Like a microwave oven ping, though that might have been imaginary. Maybe one of my Numbskulls is a percussionist and, like I was as a 10 year old musician, adept with the triangle.

Piss dries into powder the same colour as the piss. A dead body is lying flat on its back. It's covered in maggots, beetles, flies and all the other little feasting beasts. You, a live person, standing up next to the corpse, want to know what state the corpse is in, but you can't tell because you can't see it for the things writhing around on it. In an ideal world, if I were in that position, what would I do? I'd pour water on the body and swill the maggots out of the way. And if there was no water? I'd use any available fluid. And if the only available fluid were numerous bottles of syrupy piss, then that is what I'd use.

The body has been opened up by rodents and their friends, and so some of the piss would wash into the chest or pleural cavity and some of it would slosh down into the abdomen.

And during the hottest summer on record in the UK, the brown piss would evaporate, leaving a brown powder-like residue and the beasts would simply return to the table to continue feasting.

And there you have it...the two strangenesses from the post-mortem report, the two things I found to be at odds with the dry scientific delivery of the pathologist's findings. There they were, with an explanation of their existence.

Could I prove that? No, I couldn't. Apart from anything else, my brother's remains had been cremated. And according to the post-mortem report, nothing had been kept.

So, the explanation was there *for me*. It satisfied *me*. But of what? That someone, some other person, had been monitoring the corpse of my brother. It seemed ridiculous. Because if that were the case, then someone was doing that for a reason. Who would have such a reason? Only a person who had some kind of, I really hesitate to say this but I'm gonna say it anyway, *ownership* of the body. *Like who?* I thought, like fucking *who*?

It was beyond weird. What kind of person would think that he had *ownership* of the body of my brother? Was he *killed* by someone? Someone who then *monitored* his body for its state of decomposition? Why?

If some random person killed him, then that person wouldn't monitor his body, they'd just walk away. I would. If I killed some random person for whatever reason, in his home, then I'd just leave and never come back. I mean, I wouldn't because I'm not a killer, but if I *were* a killer, that's what I'd do.

So, the person monitoring his body knew him. And had a reason to monitor the state of the body. What was the importance of the decomposition of the body?

My mind hurtled back to the post-mortem report. It had said that a neighbour, Walter Fitzgibbon, had alerted police to the fact that Dan hadn't been seen for five or six weeks. So, what was going on here? I couldn't work it out. I needed more time to let things filter through.

I parked up outside the flat and went to work.

Chapter 22 - Cardboard Box Island

I'd been steadily making my way to the first of what I had mapped out as 'islands'. The cardboard box. Cardboard Box Island. It was buried to within a few inches of its top and now I'd got there and uncovered it enough to remove it from the embrace of the midden.

It was, like the name suggests, a cardboard box. White with black lettering. It had once contained 9 one-litre bottles of vodka. I wondered whether he had bought it as a box of vodka, or whether he'd got it from his booze shop as an empty box to store stuff in. Not that it mattered.

Sifting the refuse was mind-numbing, it has to be said. But it was the kind of mind-numbing work that required concentration. I likened it to methodically working your way through a building collapse, where you had to be systematic. You can't just go at it, shifting stuff as quickly as you could to get to the injured and dying. You had to constantly assess each piece of debris, what effect moving it would have on the adjacent pieces, and therefore the general stability. It was a painstaking process.

Every piece of refuse in Dan's place had to be picked up and looked at, then discarded or not, as the case may be. The job wasn't a 'clear out'.

If it was, it would've taken me three days tops, grafting eight hours a day. This was a search. For various reasons, we needed whatever documents were in the place. I knew that there would be photographs, old family ones especially of our grandparents, because he had been a keen photographer. Photographs were vitally important to me, the most precious things you could leave behind. I'd taken thousands myself, but, of course, I had very few of my grandparents or, my brother himself. On top of every other document and photograph, according to Lydia at least, there was a will. Which I doubted.

It was quite a revelation to me that Dan's midden actually did contain photographs, not in packets or envelopes, just there, sitting, or lying, on their own, covered by old newspapers, clothing, CD's, empty food tins, full food tins, wrappers, letters from the bank, bank statements, books, you name it, it was here. Like he'd been looking at them and then just launched them onto the pile, only for them to get covered up with stuff as he went along. It was weird. I could imagine him sitting there, looking at one then deciding he didn't need it anymore and casually spinning it up into the air, maybe even aiming it at something, like you do with playing cards when you're exceedingly bored and just happen to have a pack of cards in your hand.

I found a photo of my grandma and grandad standing in their living room, by the fire, arms across each other's shoulders. Grandma, with her strong Yorkshire upright stance, shoulders back, staring proudly at the photographer, Dan. She was taller than grandad but grandad had Paget's disease, where your bones soften or something and his shin bones had buckled outwards, making him shorter.

I also, a good two cubic metres of refuse later, found another couple of photos, one of my parents dressed very smartly, sitting in a pub by the looks of it, looking impossibly young and happy. And one of my grandad, in his World War One uniform. He looked lean and fit, like you'd expect a soldier to look. His face was all clean lines and sharp angles, handsome, with calm, staring eyes. I wondered where Dan had gotten this photograph. Had mum given it to him? I'd never seen it before and I stared at it for a good number of minutes. It was hard to reconcile the photograph in my hand with the place I was standing. Here was a photo of a young man looking proud in his uniform, defiantly staring at the camera, full of the innocence and passion that would take him to the killing fields of France. My grandad was born in 1895, making him about 19 when World War One started. He was probably in the first draft of men called up to fight. He'd stood in the photographer's in Sheffield, maybe a day or two before he sailed off to whatever fate had in store for him, and now, here was that photograph, held between the latex-gloved finger and thumb of one of his grandsons, the grandson who'd plotted to steal a Numbskull from his ear and keep it in a matchbox, dressed in protective clothing, standing in a room that stunk to high heaven and back that his other grandson had both created and died in. I remembered me, Dan and grandad walking through the park on Stanley Road, climbing the witches hat merry go round, or rather, Dan climbing it and me clinging to it, while grandad sat on the bench, smoking his pipe and reading his paper.

My grandad had survived some of the great battles of the so-called Great War, had survived being gassed, been taken prisoner, and escaped, had somehow survived decimation of two regiments and gone on to marry and produce two children with my grandma, my Uncle William and my mum, Roberta.

Between the wars he'd moved from Sheffield to Liverpool, presumably in search of work, and his daughter had met my father. How proud must my grandma and grandad have been when their daughter and son in law produced their first-born child? My brother Daniel.

And now here we all were. All in the same room. In different forms, I grant you, but all in the same place, nonetheless. What would our grandad have thought, I wondered? And our lovely grandma, what would she have thought? I couldn't even imagine what they would have said. Sadly, I didn't care what my parents might have thought or said.

I extracted Cardboard Box Island from its anchorage, put it up on the Workmate and opened it up properly.

At one time it had contained 9 one litre bottles of Vodka. Now, it contained 7 two litre bottles of what was almost certainly piss. Dark brown and viscous, like the other bottles I'd come across, dozens of them. Most, but not all had labels stuck around their shoulders, with dates and scribblings on them. Either he ran out of labels or couldn't be bothered with the notations any more. Either way, it was disgusting and I photographed some of the labels for deciphering later, if at all.

There was a little section of the box that was too narrow to have fitted another of the bottles in but was, instead, stuffed with what looked like a plastic bag or plastic wrapping. I pulled the plastic out and it turned out to be a lot of little plastic bags crammed in together, like the ones you'd expect to see in a laboratory with samples of whatever in them. They had a little white strip across one side of them that you could write on.

All of the bags, and there must have been a hundred or so, contained a lock of hair. And every bag had writing in black marker on the white strip.

The locks of hair varied in colour, from very blond, to dark blond and light brown. I examined the notations. All of the notations were in black marker and all of them were in my brother's handwriting. I could tell. The notation on the first one I picked, a very blond one, said, *Front right 110368*. The next one, quite a dark blond, maybe fair or sandy, said *Top back left 190571*.

I sat on my toolbox, holding two handfuls of the little bags and let them slip and slide through my fingers, dropping to the floor between my feet. As they landed, some of them landed with notations up and some of them didn't. I don't know what I was doing, maybe just mentally resting, letting the weirdness seep in. Or out. The strange slipperiness of the bags sliding from my hands and the soft *plat* as they landed was quite soothing and when my hands were empty, I grabbed another two handfuls, and let it happen again.

I kept picking them up and letting them slide. I was thinking about my brother and the state he'd gotten into, using the soothing little bags as a backdrop to thought, like having pleasant music on in the background when you're reading.

The bags of hair had captured me, forcing me down the road he'd travelled to get to where I was, sat in his living room, his domain, his castle. I was inside his castle, holding some of his treasures in my hand

and letting them slide to the floor. What value were these treasures to him? What was their purpose? What were the numbers? Did he have a catalogue of them? If each lock was given a number, that must mean something. But what? There had to be a catalogue or a list, an inventory. Otherwise, the numbers wouldn't have a purpose, would they? Would they? Numbers are put on things to give some meaning. An item number. A catalogue number. A fleet number, a service number. And so on and so forth.

As I pondered, I carried on picking up and dropping. *Why did he cut chunks of his hair and bag them up* I thought? I spoke out loud to the room, to him, 'What were you doing mate?' I asked. 'What the fuck were you doing?' I heard a little movement of rubbish and caught sight of a tiny mouse scooting along the windowsill. It stopped when I looked at it, as if frozen mid step, two paws, front right, rear left, stopped in mid-air head cocked questioningly to one side. I think it was looking at me. I'm *sure* it was looking at me. It stood there, probably thinking to itself, '*As soon as I looked at that human it stopped what it was doing, mid movement and I think it's looking at me. I'm* sure *it's looking at me.*'

I dropped some more bags, the spell between rodent and human broke and the mouse went about its business. It winked at me as it moved on. I'm lying. It didn't wink at me but imagine if it had, how good would that have been?

I watched the last of the bags drop from my hands and picked a load up again, started to let them slide, watched as they landed. I wondered if more of them landed writing up or writing down…like buttered toast is supposed to always land buttered side down because it's heavier on the buttered side or something like that. I wondered if the side with the writing strip *plus* the weight of the ink, might make the bags mostly land writing side down. Sometimes I hated the way my mind churned on because now that the thought had crossed my mind, I was compelled to compare *writing up* against *writing down*. And now that I'd decided to keep score, I was compelled to keep records, because you couldn't decide anything on just a handful or two of drops.

'ENOUGH!' a booming voice shouted inside my head. Big Joe. 'KNOCK IT FUCKING OFF!' A quieter voice took over, though it *was* the same person, *you can't fool me* I thought, 'You haven't got time for this stuff, get on with the job and do your thinking later'. It took me a second or two to give an accepting nod to these words because, like it or not, they *did* make sense. I let the bags still in my hands drop to the floor and got a little carrier bag to put them in for the document box.

I stooped to pick them up and the top bag was lying writing up. *Middle back 210576* was written on it. I picked a handful up and dropped them in the carrier. 210576, I thought. 210576. A number I'd written dozens, if not hundreds of times in my life, on various forms, was 220576. My wedding day in 1976. 210576 was a date. The date before my wedding. The numbers were dates.

As soon as I thought of the numbers as dates, they started to make sense. Now, there wouldn't have to be a register or a list or anything. Everything you needed to know about contents of each bag was written on the bag. I wondered if the dates were significant ones or were they just random. I had a quick shifty through them. I felt Big Joe giving me a look. 'Just a few' I said to him. 'Just a few handfuls'. I did a few handfuls and in just those few, I picked out some dates that had significance. 010475, was the day I started my training to become a firefighter. 010375, was the day before I became engaged to my first wife to be, 230973 was my 18th birthday. Key to the door time. There were a number of Christmas Eves and Christmas Days, and a number of dates that seemed close to other family birthdays and things. Now, I knew that I'd *have* to go through them all…at a later date of course…and make some sort of catalogue, spreadsheet, or something.

I wondered why my brother would cut a chunk of his hair off the day before my wedding. Or my birthday. And what significance did my first day as a trainee firefighter have for him?

I thought of how meticulous or, to be more precise, *fastidious* my brother was, which, given where I sat, seemed a tad incongruous to say the least. When we were young men, he would take ages to shave, actually measuring his sideburns with a little white ruler. His eyebrows had to be just right and he would pluck any stray hair. His teeth were perfect and white and he practiced smiling in the mirror, asking me at times whether I thought his smile was lopsided. He used to measure the distance between the corner of his eyes and the lobes of his ears, he even kept a record of the size of his nostrils. I used to laugh at him and say he was mad. I used to take no more than a few minutes to shave and combing my hair was usually done with my fingers. I didn't care what my eyebrows did, they could go where they wanted, though, I did get slightly concerned when they decided to meet in the middle, making me look like something out of Sesame Street, and my nostril size was beyond my control so didn't concern me in the slightest. I could never understand the attention to detail he gave to everything about his appearance.

Looking around his flat I thought, *What was the point mate? What was it all about?*

Apart from the obvious, the bottles of piss, the bags of hair and the winking mouse, something was jarring with me. There was an anomaly. I put the rest of the bags away in their new bag and in the document box. The bottles of piss went on the skip and I got on with the sorting and clearing, next stop Hamster Cage Island.

Chapter 23 - Excerpts from the Diary

Tuesday 15th July 2003

2nyt start 6.14pm 45 x 5 + 26 + 26

This morning B4 8am took Bertie out. Got to Pat and Wills and there was a fast knocking on a window. I slyly looked but cud not see anyone. My first thought was that it was Will, either cos Bertie had been pissing on his garden and also not far from his front window, or to show me his bird book, or both. I cudn't see his car, and there wasn't any windows opened in his house. Bertie also heard the banging (but I don't think he looked at Wills window) and barked and took off past Brenda's. I end up going around the block. Bertie pulling to go across the road by the bus stop and I end up lifting from the ground on his lead and walking thru the opening into Cardiff Drive past a schoolboy and gently lowering him back to the ground. Coming back into my close Gary was going to his car, so I stopped. A schoolgirl early teens was coming down the pavement, so I went to walk back home and Bertie pulled against me, so I pushed him violently along the ground on his lead, and went past Garys car. I think Gary was coming back out, or something like that, so I walked, I think, to go back out of the close, towards Garys car, and I can't remember, but I may have pushed/thrown Bertie along the ground again on his lead, and the schoolgirl walked thru the close ~~past~~ towards Garys car and she turned her head and stared at me for pushing Bertie. I finally got back home and Bertie didn't seem particularly bothered by the whole episode. He didn't seem frightened, but he must have some thorts. I am feeling really, really bad about this. All this is down to u no what. I had dirty jeans and a dirty blue padded jacket on, I must have looked a sight. I didn't really want people to see me like that, and as well as u no wot, this also contributed to me acting the way I did. Shear frustration. If the knocking on the window hadn't happened, I wouldn't have left the passageway, and all of this wouldn't have happened.

Friday 08th August 2003

2nyt start 10.00pm 45 x 5

2nyt I shouted loud at Bertie because he was annoying me by sitting down by my feet again. I can't remember properly, but I think I pushed him, and he turned round and looked at me because he was surprised by my outburst. He then comes back and I shout my head off telling him to come up here! (onto the armchair) He comes up here, but stays facing the back of the armchair, annoying me even more! So I shout my head off again, and hit him on his back (top) leg hardish but controlled – don't know whether it was a full fist, a "palm fist" or a open hand slap. He moved and turned around and sat by me, licking his lips continuously. He was obviously alarmed but not that frightened. So I hadn't really had that much effect on him, which I'm glad about. I stroked him and said I'm sorry. He was ok with me, and still is as the night wears on. It is very hot and humid, his coat needs clipping, he must be suffering, but I don't know how much. I am too hot and I haven't got his fur, or even his shorn fur!

Wednesday 13th August 2003

2nyt start 7.47pm 45 x 6 + 1.5 x 112.50

Bertie 2nyt claws – push – accidentally hit face – hesitant to get on my knees – but he did with gentle coax.

Chapter 24 - Hamster Cage Island, Box 1

I had finally uncovered Hamster Cage Island completely and could properly get at it. It *was* a clever place to store something that you didn't want destroyed by the mice infesting the flat. You don't want the mice to chew your stuff, put it in a rodent cage and lock them out. Simple.

The cage was pretty packed with boxes, mostly shoe boxes. I don't know what it is about shoe boxes that intrigues me but something does. Maybe it's the regularity of them, or the way they look when they're stacked up in the shop. Maybe it's because when I was a kid, getting a pair of shoes was a big thing in your life, a really big thing and when you wore them for the first time, everyone, and I mean *everyone* noticed that you had new shoes on. You were temporarily famous. You could have a proper strut about back in the 'olden' days when you had a new pair of shoes on. *Or maybe* I thought, *maybe it's because, when you come across a shoebox in a non-shoe shop environment, you just* know *that it will contain* treasure *of some kind.* Yeah, maybe that's it, old shoe boxes are treasure chests.

As big as the cage door was, none of the boxes were going to come out of it. I half remembered, from Dan's white-mouse breeding project, aged 10, where I was his chief assistant, aged 6, that the top of the cage, the wire part, was joined to the bottom part by clasps. I imagined all such cages were the same and shoved the last bits of refuse away from around the cage bottom with my foot.

The cage bottom was the same colour as our mouse cage from yesteryear, sky blue, and the sight of it brought forward a memory from way back, a picture of my brother, holding a white mouse up by its tail. I was instantly transported to my grandma's back kitchen…

Early 1960's

It was about 1960, maybe 1961. Dan was 10 or 11 years old and I was 5 or 6. I don't remember how the breeding programme started but I remember our pet mice. We had one each. I've no idea what sexes they were or anything like that, I just know that mine was called Dixie and Dan's was called Pixie, after the TV cartoon characters. There was a cat as well, but I can't remember its name. I'll Google it in a minute.

We both had a little cage, each about the size of a shoebox. The bottom part was sky blue and made of tin and the top part was silver wire folded into the box shape. The door was like a little gangplank that dropped down to allow the mouse or hamster to walk up and into their little house, except when you wanted your mouse to walk up it, it wouldn't, no way. You had to grab it and drop it in the cage then whip your hand out and more or less slam the door. They usually escaped before you could get your hand out and you'd have to repeat the procedure over and over. A real pain in the arse, though I didn't know such phrases when I was 5. Or 6. For me, in essence, the whole thing of having little pets was just a chore. I liked the idea of having a pet mouse but, looking back, I don't really think I was a pet kind of lad. I loved watching my brother with the pets, how cool and calm he was about everything, how easily he got his mouse to 'go to bed', and, if I'm honest, I wanted to be like him, but I wasn't. I always wanted to be playing with my bow and arrow, my tommy gun or my soldiers and cars. Or I wanted to be galloping up and down the street on my horse, reins in one hand, controlling the beast, and my other hand smacking my own buttock, urging my steed to run faster. I would've tried that buttock slapping to improve my time on the Ford's 10k run but, it wouldn't have been a good look. Sometimes I'd put the pretend reins in my mouth, smack my buttock and shoot Melvin from next door with my silver revolver in my free hand. Like I've said before, I was a 5-year-old alpha male. Melvin, by the way, was really good at looking as though he'd been shot and falling off a horse. Really good.

Jinxie! Or was it Mr Jinks? Yeah, I think it was Mr Jinks…but I'm sure we called him Jinxie. The name of the cat just came to me and I didn't have to Google it. Pixie, Dixie and Jinxie. I think. I'm almost certain. I'll Google it later.

So anyway, the mice. I think we must have had different sexes because one day, we had a load of babies. Grandma told grandad to take them down the yard, which meant flush them down the toilet. I was having enough trouble getting one mouse back in the cage after play time so I had no idea how I was going to cope with another six but I thought flushing them down the toilet was a bit harsh. I had an idea.

'Can I shoot them grandad? With my bow and arrow?' I asked.

Dan backhanded me in the chest, making me cough and said that I couldn't and telling me that if I tried, he'd wrap the bow and arrow around my neck. Which, obviously, was preposterous, because the bow would snap wouldn't it, and, without using the word preposterous, which was probably beyond my young vocabulary, I told my big brother exactly that. He backhanded me in the chest again and grandma told him to 'knock it off.'

I'm not sure how the breeding programme came about because I went out for a gallop and a shoot 'em up with Melvin from next door, but what happened was this…Dan used his pocket money to buy a bigger cage and got a book from the library on mouse breeding. He got a book on mouse breeding and I got one on Douglas Bader. And so, we started breeding mice and when they were the right age, we took them to a shop in the city centre called County Pets, run by a man called Mr Jones and sold them to him. And we did that every two months or so and, because I helped him with the cleaning of the cages, he'd give me two and six, a whole half a crown.

Taking them to the shop was an adventure for me because my grandma would take us on the bus and when we got to town, she'd go to the market to get stuff and let me and Dan go to County Pets on our own, but NOWHERE else on pain of a thick ear.

It was dead exciting, we'd go up to the big main road, Stanley Road and wait for the number whatever it was, and we'd go upstairs but grandma would stay downstairs because she told me she had a bone in her leg. We'd try to sit right at the front so you could see everything properly. We'd both have a shoe box with the mice in, the lids fastened on with special elastic bands made for us by grandma. She used the same *elastic that she used for making the garters for our long school socks and so there was no way the mice were getting the lid off. One time my ones started to chew and scratch the box and Dan told me to shake the box, which I did. But it didn't stop them chewing. A woman in the seat across the aisle from us could hear the chewing and kept looking at me. Staring at me. I could feel the sweat running down my face but knew that I had to stay calm and try to appear unruffled. I thought she was going to tell the conductor and we'd get chucked off the bus but she didn't.*

When we got to County Pets, Mr Jones would always be happy to see us and would call us Daniel and Joseph. Just like that. He'd say 'Aaah Daniel and Joseph I see, and what have you brought me today?'

He'd open the boxes very carefully and count the mice, then open the till and give Dan the money. And then when we got home, he'd give me my half a crown, which spent some time in my pocket so that I could keep looking at it and then it would go in my piggy bank. On the way home, once we got off the bus, Dan would also buy us a bar of Caramac chocolate each and we'd eat it on the walk home, sharing it with grandma if she wanted some but usually, she wouldn't. We had to eat it all before we got home, which was never a problem, because if we took it home, mum wouldn't let us eat it because it would 'spoil our tea'...which it wouldn't but I get where she was coming from because I used to say the same to my daughters. When we were eating our Caramac, we'd stop on top of the footbridge at Glendower Street and wait for a steam train to come along so that we could get 'lost in the sky' as the cloud of steam enveloped us.

One time on this return journey, which turned out to be the last time for this particular journey, we stood on the bridge, our empty shoeboxes under our arms and waited for a train to come so we could lose ourselves in the clouds for a few minutes. Grandma had gone on ahead because she wanted a cup of tea and told us to come straight home after the train had been. The train came and there we were, stood on the bridge, lost in our own worlds, not speaking to each other, not even looking at each other, just two little boys standing on a footbridge over the Liverpool to Southport railway line, daydreaming in a cloud of steam from a passing loco, thundering underneath us.

When the cloud dissipated, we made our way down the steps into Glendower Street and our dad was standing talking to a man outside the Glendower pub on the corner. Our dad spent a lot of time in the Glendower. 'I'm goin' the Glen.' he would say. Sometimes he'd say to my grandad 'Coming down the Glen for one Albert?' Other times he'd use the full name of the pub, 'I'm goin the Glendower.' And somehow, I always knew that when the full name was used, there would be trouble.

If grandad went off to the Glen with our dad, grandma would moan to our mum about it, saying that grandad never lifted a finger around the house. I used to wonder where all the fingers were because I would have liked to find at least one and keep it in a matchbox so I could be popular at school.

As we walked past our dad outside the Glendower, he didn't greet us or wave or anything. He just carried on talking to this man but watched us walk past on the other side of the road. There was something about the way he was looking at us that frightened me but when he came in, smelling of cold and blackcurrants, he never said anything and he didn't hit us or shout at our mum so, maybe, I thought, maybe it was the man he was talking to who was in trouble and not us.

A few days later, when we got in from school, grandma had been crying, I could tell, and Dan must have just known what had happened because, straight away, he looked at where our mouse cages should be and they were gone. And our shoe boxes were gone as well. Dan opened the back kitchen door and went into the yard. He picked something up off the floor and put it in his pocket. All of the cages were on the floor and were squashed flat and the mice were nowhere to be seen. Grandma told us that they'd escaped. Grandad didn't say anything, but I could tell he wasn't happy because he wouldn't let me cut his baccy up with the penknife I loved. And wanted.

Dan never said anything to our mum or dad and they never said anything to us about the cages. Or the mice that had lived inside them. Ever. Part of me was glad that the chore of keeping pets was over but a bigger part of me was upset at the loss of our adventure on the bus and the illicit Caramac. We would make other trips together, just me and my big brother, but not that one.

'At least,' I always thought, 'we didn't get the belt.'

I picked hamster cage island up and put it on my Workmate, Black and Decker circa 1985, a bit creaky and battered, a bit rusty in parts and covered in splodges of plaster and paint, but otherwise still the best workmate I've ever had. Never had ideas better than mine, never argued about my sometimes dodgy DIY decisions and was always available for me to lean on.

I located the clasps, flipped them up one by one and took the wire cage off the base. The first shoebox, the one at the top of the pile, had an elasticated band around it, very like the one that grandma made for our mouse boxes all those years ago.

Almost involuntarily, I gave the box a little shake, hearing Dan's voice on the bus to County Pets. I slid the elastic off the box and put it in my pocket and in the act of doing that I saw, in my mind's eye, Dan picking something up off the ground in the yard at grandma's, standing in the middle of our squashed mouse cages. I took it back out of my pocket and examined it. I could tell it was old and I just *knew* that it was the one that grandma had made for us. A band of knicker elastic stitched into the perfect size for holding a shoebox lid on.

I was overcome with the nostalgia of the simple item in my hand. A band made from knicker elastic. I could see my grandma sitting on her sofa, stitching the elastic together, listening to the Billy Cotton Band Show on a Sunday while the dinner was cooking in the kitchen, filling the place with steam. I could hear the opening of the programme, 'Wakey Waaaaake…hey!!!', could smell the sprouts cooking and the juicy pork or beef waiting to be sliced. My mouth watered at the thought of one of my grandma's Sunday dinners, huge Yorkshire puddings, crispy roast potatoes and pork crackling, the gravy, the sauces, apple, horseradish, the salty dripping me and Dan would scoff on our after-school butties for the next week.

I was amazed at the memories flooding into my mind, dragged up from wherever they had resided for about 60 years, and here those memories were, as fresh as the day they were made, complete with pictures, smells and sounds, the smells so real that they made my mouth water.

I was amazed that my brother had picked this simple little item up off the ground and had kept it all this time, had used it to do the one and only thing it was made to do, hold the lid on a shoe box. I was amazed and grateful that my brother had recognised on that day, that a simple little token could be so valuable. Once again, Dan, my big brother, was my hero. I felt the band, rubbed it between my finger and thumb and the hairs on my neck stood up because I suddenly felt that my grandma was behind me, smiling, her needle and cotton in hand. I turned, stupidly expecting her to be there. But she wasn't. There was just Dan's midden, becoming less as the days passed, but still there.

I put the elastic back in my pocket and vowed that I would now keep it safe, in a shoe box, a length of knicker elastic stitched together by my grandma. I opened the box.

There was a brown envelope, A5 size, sealed, no writing on it. I opened it. Inside, were two colourful pieces of card. They were our RSPCA certificates that had been ripped to pieces by our father, 60 or so years before. I don't remember Dan picking up the pieces but he must have done. He'd sellotaped them together and put them in this envelope. When did he do it? Where were they hidden in the bedroom we shared for all those years? Why hadn't he mentioned them to me? Maybe he'd thought I wouldn't have been interested in them. He was probably right. I would have written them off, I *did* write them off and Dan knew it. I was so practical about all the stuff that happened in life and Dan was, different to me. Never as practical as me and yet, how practical was it to go and pick up the pieces and stick them back together? What would I have done with my certificate, had Dan given it to me? I'd like to think that I would've put it in an A5 envelope and stored it away but, I'm not sure I would. I may have done for a while but, knowing me, there was probably going to come a time when I would have just, on impulse, binned it. Now, I was glad that he'd kept it. It brought back painful memories of that beautiful sunny morning that the drawing pin had hit the potty under the bed, but I was glad that Dan had acted so defiantly at that time. Dan had demonstrated that people like our father, no matter how tough and uncompromising they are, no matter how ruthless and devious they are, can never extinguish human spirit. They can seriously damage that spirit but if even a tiny flicker of it burns on, then it is they who have lost.

Underneath the A5 envelope was a page from a fishing newspaper that was about Dan. He'd caught this carp somewhere in Bolton, had someone, probably Eric, his fishing mate, take a picture of him holding it and sent it in. I remembered him being all excited about getting an article written about him in a newspaper, about the hook size he'd used, the line poundage, the bait, the rod and reel, everything. Our father had come into our bedroom while we were out, taken the paper, and used it to line the bottom of the budgie cage and obviously Dan had just gone and bought another copy and kept it secret. Again, I loved that defiance. I wish I'd known that he'd done these things. I wish we'd had the chance to talk these things through. I wish he'd answered my letters and taken me up on my constant offers to sit and talk about our experiences, our lives. But he never did.

It was a truly strange thing about our upbringing. All five of us Croft kids never, and I mean *never* told each other what had happened on any particular day. I'd pondered that fact over the years and come to the conclusion that the events that shaped us as people, just happened. They were no more than everyday normal things. They just…*were*. There was nothing extraordinary about the things that happened and so why tell anyone about them? Why discuss things that were mundane and everyday? You can probably think of reasons why we would or should have discussed these 'everyday' occurrences but, for whatever reason, we didn't.

Underneath the page from the fishing newspaper were a couple of pages from a Beezer comic. I always felt very grown up when I read The Beezer because it was like a broadsheet, like a newspaper sized thing but for kids, though I *had* caught my grandad reading it once or twice. I'd seen him reading The Beano and The Dandy as well. I opened the double page up. It was the page with the Numbskulls and Colonel Blink the short-sighted gink, two of my favourite stories and characters.

The Numbskulls were a group of tiny men who lived inside a man, in various departments of the man, and everything that the man did was carried out by the Numbskulls. I'd like to say that it was kind of educational, teaching me, a little boy, how the human body worked. But it didn't. It just taught me that these little men really lived inside me and operated me when I wanted to eat or drink, and when I wanted to walk to the shops.

When I was sitting on grandad's knee, getting told a story about horse racing, or grass seeds, or why he had to use pipe cleaners on his pipe, a subject I found fascinating, I would sometimes angle myself so that I could see down his ear to see if I could catch one of the Numbskulls looking out, through the hairs my grandad had surrounding his earhole. He didn't have much hair on his head but he had a lot growing out of his ears. And his nose.

Grandma had told me that he definitely had Numbskulls in charge of his brain and so I was determined to catch one if I could. I already had a matchbox I was going to keep it in. It had some cotton wool in it, that I got off grandad. He used it to stick it in his lighter every now and then when he needed to clean it out. I loved the warm oily smell of his lighter, it reminded me of paraffin or something like that. He used to have these little pods like the ones you get cod liver oil in, and he would snip the top off them and pour whatever was in them into the bottom of his lighter, where you could see the cotton wool soaking it up.

When I asked him for some cotton wool, he wanted to know what I wanted it for and I told him it was to make a nest for a ladybird I was going to catch. I had to lie to him because I didn't think he'd be happy if I told him I was going to catch one of his Numbskulls.

Colonel Blink was dead funny. He was the short-sighted gink. Colonel Blink the short-sighted gink. He was little and round and had these dark rimmed glasses on and he couldn't see much so was always making mistakes. Sometimes when he made a really bad mistake or when he was exasperated, he'd exclaim 'Arf!' or Arf! Arf! I found this really funny.

One day, I'd be about eight or nine, my mum was telling me I couldn't go out to play because it was raining. I tried to persuade her that I'd be ok out in the rain because it would make me grow. When she said it wouldn't and told me not to be stupid, I said that she'd said that watering her plants made *them* grow so it must do the same for me. She got angry and said that if I didn't stop mithering her, she'd give me a smack and I did what Colonel Blink did and exclaimed 'Arf!'

Early 1960's

She went mad. She shouted at me, saying 'What did you say? What did you say to me? I'll teach you to use language like that with me!' She grabbed me by the arms and shook me about and said that she was going to scrub my mouth out with soap and water. She finished off by telling me that if she heard me using that kind of language again, she'd tell my dad.

That was the ultimate threat and so I decided there and then that I would never Arf! her again. Colonel Blink had a lot to answer for to me when I was eight. A lot to answer for.

The next day, I was sitting on the settee, reading a book. It was about King Arthur and the Round Table. My dad was in early from work. Dan was out and mum had gone shopping and taken Carla with her. I was trying to not be noticed by my father. I failed.

I was suddenly aware that I was being stared at. Don't ask me how that works because I don't know but, it must be some sort of primeval thing deep in your brain. You can just feel a presence. You can feel it across quite big spaces even, like in the supermarket or somewhere, you just know you're being watched and you have a quick glance about and sure enough there is a bloke or a woman or whatever, just staring at you like you've got two heads. Maybe it stems from when we were food for sabre toothed tigers and such. Maybe, people in India who live in tiger country, get the same feeling, and know they're being stalked. Stalked is a good word here because when you get this feeling, you instinctively know that it bodes ill for you, you know that it means trouble. I knew my father was staring at me. Stalking me. Like a predator. I was prey. I felt like prey. I knew I should run, for want of a better word but to do so was to absolutely invite trouble and who knew? Maybe my 'feeling' would turn out to be a false alarm. The trouble was, to wait for the outcome of the alarm was to err massively if it was a genuine alarm but then, to pre-empt the alarm and scatter, was to more than likely turn what might be a *false alarm into a genuine one. Also, to run for it if the alarm was a genuine one would only serve to make the outcome of the alarm that much more horrific.*

I was pondering my course of action whilst pretending to be absorbed in my book. Though 'pretending' is, I think, the wrong word but I just don't have the vocabulary for this explanation. I had to read every word, trying to memorize them in case he quizzed me, because, if he quizzed me, because he suspected I was only pretending to read, and it turned out that I couldn't tell him what was on that page, then I would be in serious trouble. Proper trouble. So, to guard against proper trouble, you pretended to be absorbed, to hide the fact that you were on high alert, but then, as a consequence of trying to do both things, had to split your resources. Not an easy task in the circumstances. And way too complex a task for a kid to be juggling with. The feeling in the pit of your stomach, the tingling, churning sensation deep in your insides, as adrenaline pumps into your system...that feeling...where you know you're in danger and, rather than running away from it, you're working out how to fight it, how to overcome it or how to just run with it and surf that wave of fright until it subsides, that feeling, is addictive.

That sounds weird, strange, I know that. But it is addictive. Very addictive. When I was a firefighter, I shunned promotion for over 30 years because I liked, no, loved, no, scrub that, I needed to be in the thick of things, in the forefront of the assault on fire and precarious rescues, not behind the lines directing operations. I needed to be in danger as often as I possibly could. On the odd days that we were quiet I'd become pent up and anxious. When I had to go on leave, I became agitated and fidgety the longer I was away from the station. I loved it.

Thrived on it. I was addicted to it. An addiction that I became hooked into when I was a little kid. Sitting in the living room of my world being stalked by my father.

I waited for the predator to strike, carried on reading my book, trying to memorise what I'd read before turning the page. I could feel the stare burning into me but daren't look up. It went on and on and I wanted to get up and leave the room, but I knew that was tantamount to me having turned to him and exclaimed 'Arf!', which I would never do. Ever.

Sometimes, if you were lucky and happened to bottle it and look at the predator, he would carry on staring at you for maybe three or four heartbeats, a flat, soulless stare, then, casually, contemptuously look away, much like a lion who's had more than enough to eat. Like he was saying, 'Later. I'll have you later. It's not like you're going anywhere.'

I heard his breathing grow noisy. There was a slight whistle coming from his nose when he breathed out.

Suddenly, he spoke, and I nearly jumped but caught myself in time. If I'd jumped, he would have asked me if he'd frightened me and if I said yes then he would proceed to give me something to be frightened for. And if I said no then he would call me a liar and quiz me. And then give me something to be frightened for.

'Joe.' He said in a voice that was sort of strained. Quiet, but had something in it that I couldn't quite work out. Like he was trying to speak when someone had their hands around his throat. Like I did when I gave Carla a piggyback and she was holding me too tight around the neck.

I looked up and he twitched his head and looked up at the ceiling which meant I should go up to my room. Which I did.

I sat on my bed, wondering why I'd been sent up here. I considered carrying on reading my book but just knew that doing so would be a mistake. Even though I hadn't heard him come up the stairs, my door opened, and he came in, closing it behind him.

He motioned with his head and eyes again and I knew that I had to take my pants off and lie face down on the bed. I hadn't seen him take his belt off, so I was slightly confused and was thinking that maybe my mum had told him about the Arf! incident and this was going to be no more than a scare for me and that he would tell me to get dressed, point his finger at me and warn me to never use 'that language' to my mum again. But that was just wishful thinking.

I hadn't even heard him move but from out of the blue he slapped my arse with his hand. Quite hard. It shocked me because I always got beaten with a leather belt and this skin on skin, was…very different, very shocking, in all, a very distasteful way to be beaten. I much preferred to be beaten with the leather belt. Much.

He continued to slap my arse quite hard, his hand lingering at times, his fingers reaching underneath me, touching me in places that, I really didn't want to be touched. By anyone. Ever.

I think he slapped me about 10 times or so, and when he told me to get up and get dressed, he stood and watched me, something he'd never done before. Another something he'd never done before. I found the watching to be as unnerving as the beating.

When he went out and closed the door, I sat on my bed and just looked at the wall. I didn't think anything. There was nothing going on in my head at all. It was just blank. I could hear cars going past outside, could hear people walking past, some of them talking. I heard some birds flutter past my window and then squabble about something down on the grass. And then I heard the front gate open and close and my mum came in with Carla.

Hearing my mum's voice downstairs brought me back down to earth from wherever I'd been. I came tumbling back into my bedroom, landed in a sitting position on my bed, in the house where I lived. Back into my world.

My mind did a strange sort of fizzing, leaping thing, jumping through and across tracks of logic and arriving at a conclusion too horrible to contemplate, too...awful to comprehend. Nevertheless, I unwittingly applied, correctly or incorrectly, the principle of Occam's razor and decided that the occurrence of least speculation was the correct one. I decided, in a few seconds of fizzing thought, that my mum had either been coerced into being out of the house or, worse still, had colluded.

I decided, there and then, at age eight, or thereabouts, that I would never read anything bought for me by my mum. I decided that I would only ever read books, comics, magazines, that either I or Dan brought into the house.

I still liked Colonel Blink though. He still made me laugh.

Once I became of an age where I knew swear words, I delighted, secretly of course, that my mum must have thought, when I exclaimed Arf! to her, that I was about to say 'AAAH fuck off!' but managed to stop myself in time. That has tickled me ever since it dawned on me. Tickled me and perturbed me at the same time because, y'know, I was eight. Did my mum really have, in the back of her mind that I just might tell her to AAAH fuck off!? Really? It continued to tickle and perturb me right up until the time I actually did tell her to 'Aah fuck off! Go on! Get the fuck out of my house!'

But that's another story.

I wondered why Dan had these Beezer pages in his shoebox. Maybe they were his favourite characters from the Beezer as well. I just didn't know. Maybe he knew about the Arf! to mum incident and kept the pages as a reminder of an amusing anecdote. But I could speculate all day and still wouldn't know so I moved onto the next item, which was fitted diagonally across the box, apparently too long to fit in any other way. Whatever it was, was wrapped in an old Llanberis tea towel. I picked it up and felt it. It felt strangely familiar. I started to take the tea towel off but before I'd got it half off, I recognised the item. It was silver, and encrusted with red, blue, and green gems. It was the plastic scabbard of my wonderful spring-loaded dagger.

Christmas Eve 1964

I was a kid and so, just like every other kid, or most kids, I was excited. I believed in Father Christmas. I'd seen him. Sat on his knee and told him I'd been a good boy. I'd even witnessed him sneaking into my bedroom one Christmas Eve. It was deffo him. I swear. Or 'swear down' as the kids say these days. I think they do anyway. They probably don't actually, so, feel free to discard that remark. Strike it from the record.

So, it was Christmas Eve and I was very excited. I was about, ohhh, 17. I'm joking, I was about 8 or 9. Which would make my brother Dan 11 or 12 and my sister Carla 6 or 7. At this time of my life, on this Christmas Eve, I loved Christmas. Loved it. Started looking forward to it immediately after my birthday, which was in September. After this particular Christmas, this particular Christmas Eve, I hated Christmas. And have hated it ever since. The more I think about what I just said, the more I feel as though I'm not using the right words. I do hate it but, I think the overriding emotion is fear. Yeah, I think fear is the big thing for me. Even now. I'm 63 but I'm still scared of Christmas. It's irrational I know. Daft. But there it is. I know that people will find that hard to believe and would maybe tell me to grow up or 'just forget what happened' but, I don't care what people might think or say. I am who I am and I am what I am.

My Auntie Julie and Uncle Barry were over from Manchester for Christmas Day and they'd come over for a Christmas Eve party in the pub over the road. I don't know what the sleeping arrangements were for Julie and Barry but what it meant to us three kids, was that the single beds of me and Dan were pushed together to make a big bed and the three of us slept in it. Carla in the middle of me and Dan.

We'd gone to bed before they came in from the pub and, in spite of my excitement I'd drifted off into a light sleep. I woke up when I heard hushed adult voices outside the bedroom door. I couldn't make out what was being said but there was some giggling going on so, y'know, there was nothing to worry about.

I pretended to be asleep. Facing the door. If this was Father Christmas coming in, then I wanted to see him.

The door opened and, against the light from the landing outside, I was able to make out a head peeping around the door. I think it belonged to my mum. On account of the hair. I mean, it could have been Harpo Marx but I don't think it was. The head disappeared and the door closed. The whisperings and gigglings resumed. I was disappointed. It hadn't been the big man, just Harpo Marx.

I opened my eyes properly and could see Carla looking at me. I couldn't tell if Dan was awake, but then, he was an expert at pretending to be asleep. Professional standard. I was just about to tell Carla to turn and face the other way so that she could see Father Christmas when he came in, if he came in, when I heard the door handle move. I shut my eyes again, so that I could peep through a narrow gap.

Harpo Marx appeared, stared at us for a handful of seconds then disappeared. The door opened more fully and there he was! The big man himself, with Harpo Marx dressed as my mum...and Auntie Julie leaning into the doorway. Father Christmas didn't look as fat as he was the last time I'd seen him but, that was about a year ago I thought. Maybe he was eating that Nimble bread and eating lots of celery like my mum was.

He came in and placed a heavy sack on the bottom of my bed and then Harpo Marx passed him another sack which he placed on the bottom of where Carla was sleeping. And then he did Dan's place and they all stood there for a minute and looked at us. One of them farted, I'm guessing it was Father Christmas because my grandma had told me that women didn't trump. And when that happened, they all started giggling. Dan moved in the bed, as though he was being roused from a deep sleep. Told you, he was a pro...and Father Christmas, Harpo Marx and Auntie Julie melted away, Harpo closing the door quietly. Then I heard them all go downstairs and I supposed they were letting the big man out.

About 15 minutes later I heard the adults going to bed, saying goodnight to each other on the landing, the lights going off and bedroom doors closing.

It was dark but I thought I could see Carla's eyes open. You know the way ordinary things can look terrifying when you can't quite see them properly in the dark? It looked like my sister's eyes had dark rings all around them but the eyeballs were huge and staring right at me. I thought I could make out her mouth moving as well, like she was trying to bite me. Again. She'd bitten me a few times in the past, drawing blood on one occasion. I was getting a bit worried so I kicked her. She moved and said ow! Dan moved as well.

'He's been!' I whispered.

'I know.' whispered Carla, 'I felt him putting something at the bottom of the bed.'

'I did.' I whispered, 'Did you Dan?'

'Yeah' he whispered. 'Have a look, Joe.'

I didn't need telling twice. I very quietly moved and reached to the sack at the bottom of the bed. I got a handful of it and gently pulled it up the bed towards me. Every time it rustled, I stopped and waited. When no lights came on, I carried on, moving the sack stealthily up the bed. When it got to within reach, I felt it, trying to make out shapes and sizes, reporting back to Carla and Dan. Quietly.

'Get something out.' said Dan and so I reached in and had a stealthy rummage. You can't beat a stealthy rummage, even now I enjoy the odd stealthy rummage. I eventually found what I knew to be a selection box...and knew it to be full of chocolate. I reported the facts.

'Have some chocolate' whispered Dan and so I did. I opened a chocolate bar and took a bite.

We'd been whispering the whole time. I'd moved everything so quietly. No-one could have heard the rustle of paper. No-one had hearing that good. No-one. No lights had been switched on. No door handles had moved. No doors had opened. No floorboards had creaked or squeaked. No clothing had rustled. No sound had been made. Which only served to making the bedroom door crashing open and the sudden flood of light as the switch was thrown all the more shocking. My mouth was full of chocolate and I didn't have time to swallow it before the man wearing white 'Y front' underpants, white vest, or singlet as my grandma called it, and Father Christmas's hat, rushed at me, picked me up and threw me across the room.

I landed on the floor in the corner, trying, knowing that I had to swallow the chocolate before I choked on it. I managed to swallow half of it before the man grabbed the sack containing the gifts from Santa and, picking it up like a sack of loot from the Beano, slammed it into the floor over and over and over. I could hear things breaking and smashing. The sack became more and more limp as the things inside lost their shape and I, bizarrely, quite fucking bizarrely, chewed up the big lump of chocolate in my mouth and swallowed it, suddenly feeling safe. From choking at least. The things that go through your mind at the strangest times.

The man in the Father Christmas hat was breathing heavily and glaring at me. I was terrified and my eyes took in the tableau that was my, now, Christmas Morning bedroom. My brother was looking at me, his face absolutely still and calm, his eyes wide and staring. Carla was looking at Father Christmas and was seemingly attempting to make herself look smaller, actually appeared to be shrinking. Father Christmas was standing in white underwear and red hat, his chest heaving with his exertions, his eyes burning into me and behind him, silhouetted in the doorway, the landing light having now been turned on, was Harpo Marx, wearing my mum's dressing gown. And behind her was my Auntie Julie in what I now know to be a babydoll nightie. Her face was a mask of horror, her eyes wide and staring and her mouth making a large black letter 'O'.

Time seemed to stand still. We were like a photograph. You could almost hear decisions being made. Father Christmas suddenly moved towards me, picking up the selection box I'd opened and raising it above his head like a club. I thought to myself that I was going to be beaten to death with a selection box and, again, in super bizarre fashion, found it ever so slightly amusing, though amusing is the wrong word.

As Father Christmas raised his chocolate bludgeon, my Auntie Julie screamed in a massively loud voice, 'Charlie! NO!'

So, *I thought,* it wasn't even Father Christmas.

My dad, Charlie, stopped dead in his tracks and glared at me. He squashed the selection box in his big hands, turning all the chocolate bars to pulp and hurled it at me. It hit me in the face but didn't really hurt. Even if it had, I would have made no sound.

He turned and stormed out. Harpo Marx looked at each of us in turn, turned out the light and closed the door. My Auntie Julie moved her head in line with the reducing gap as the door closed, watching me.

The landing light went off and we were back in complete darkness. There were little pieces of chocolate and paper all over me. I ate a piece. Of chocolate, not paper, and I sat on the floor in the corner until I thought it was safe to crawl back into bed.

When proper morning came, Dan and Carla sat up and started opening their gifts. I crawled to the bottom of the bed and, laying on it, stared down at my ruined Christmas sack, like a boy peering into a pond for sticklebacks. After a while I reached down and had another rummage. My hands found something that felt like a jewelled dagger, the one I'd wanted, the one that I would use when I played Robin Hood with my mates. I took it out and held it up. It was silver and big, bigger than I'd thought it was going to be. The scabbard was encrusted with jewels, blue, red, and green. I unsheathed the weapon and tried it out, stabbing myself in the belly with the blade...which, being spring loaded, disappeared up into the handle.

It was the only one of my gifts that survived. I spent the whole of Christmas Day stabbing people with it. I loved it. And y'know what? Chocolate is chocolate is chocolate. It doesn't matter if it's all mashed up, it just tastes the same. Mind you, I did have trouble sitting because of the bruising to my left buttock from landing on the bedroom floor. Good job I had two.

That incident was never mentioned, not to me, not by me. Funny that isn't it? Sometimes I wonder if it actually happened. I know it did but…it sometimes doesn't feel like it did.

I took the rest of the tea towel from the scabbard, hoping to find my spring-loaded dagger. I could feel a definite hilt through the towelling but it wasn't my dagger, though I once again recognised the item. It was my mum's bone-handled carving knife. I slid it from my jewel encrusted scabbard and examined it.

It was old and well worn. It must have been sharpened a million times. I tested the blade with the ball of my thumb and it was sharp. Very sharp.

I turned it over and over in my hand and recalled the time when I decided to kill my father.

1970'ish

Life was just too hard. From waking to sleeping again, life was tense and filled with worry. I worried about my safety, my mum's safety, the safety of my siblings. I wanted to do something to protect everyone but, in a nutshell, I was too scared.

Like I've said a number of times, no one spoke to each other about what happened in our daily lives and, looking back, I find that almost impossible to believe. But it's nevertheless true.

Me and my brother shared a bedroom for over 20 years and in that time, we'd both been abused horrendously. Physically beaten and assaulted, sexually abused, mentally abused on a daily basis and yet we never spoke about it. Never. We never discussed anything that happened, never told each other what had happened while they had been out of the house. The most we did was to exchange glances, looks, the kind of look you might give someone who sat in the condemned cell with you, who knew what you knew, that punishment or worse was looming and one of you was going to be first.

On our estate, on Saturdays, Mr Ogden from one of the farms down the lanes, would drive his van around the houses, selling fresh fruit and veg. Dan was his gopher. Dan would run to all the houses, knocking on the door, and taking the orders. He'd bring them to Mr Ogden who would stand at the back of the van, weighing out the produce, bagging it up and Dan would then deliver it.

On the same Saturdays, I would play for my school football team in the morning and then come home and usually have dinner then go out with my mates to climb trees or play footy, or marbles or whatever.

Also on those Saturdays, my mum would do the shopping and take Carla, and the twins with her.

Sometimes, if things hadn't gone to plan in the tree climbing department, I would be in the house on my own and about three in the afternoon, my dad would come in from the pub and the bookies. He'd spend Saturday doing that…pub, bookies, pub, bookies, pub. bookies. If he'd won in the bookies or won playing cards in the pub then he was a happy man. If he wasn't a happy man, you knew he'd lost. If he wasn't a happy man, we all lost. He'd take his losses out on us. And on a Saturday, when no one but me was in the house, I would be his first port of call, the first to suffer the consequences of the bookie beating him, or someone at his card school beating him.

Sometimes he wanted me to box with him. He'd been an army boxer and he really wanted me to be a boxer. When I was little, he'd get on his knees in front of me and tell me to hit him, to punch him. He'd prod his chin with a fat forefinger and tell me to hit him, to punch him. Of course, I was scared. And so, I didn't want to hit him.

After many of these attempts to get me to box, I started to believe that he really did want to teach me to fight and I began to think that it would be ok for me to hit him. Eventually I plucked up the courage to hit him but did so with a half-hearted blow to his cheek and he looked happy but with an edge to his voice, he told me to hit him harder and I did. He told me that what I'd just done was better and this was praise, praise from my father. It was unheard of but it was good. Really good. I wanted more. Suddenly a part of my mind became free and I felt alive and, I don't know, bigger, stronger. I suddenly felt worthy.

He prodded his chin with his sausage forefinger and before he'd even finished telling me what to do, I landed a solid punch on his nose. A proper, solid punch, bang! Right square on his nose.

He reeled backwards on his knees, like Mr Wobbly, the man with no legs but a huge arse, from my Noddy books, and when he came back to upright, he'd changed. Something frightening had happened to his face and it had nothing to do with my right hand. Something indefinable had happened and he didn't look like my father. He looked like the man on the ledge from a childhood nightmare, his face looked pointy and his eyes were expressionless and black.

For a split second, still high on the praise he'd sent my way just moments ago, I thought he was joking, but then he hit me with the flat of his hand, not a slap but like he was pushing me away. He hit me right in the middle of my chest, hard, like getting kicked by a horse must have felt. The blow took all my breath away and knocked me backwards, very

fast. I fell and banged my head on a copper coloured wastepaper bin my
mum had at the side of the fire. It sounded like the dinner gong in school.

I struggled for my breath for what seemed like an age. His arm was
still outstretched, his hand bent upwards like he hadn't made contact yet.
He looked like he was frozen in time, and his eyes were black slits but I
knew he was staring at me. I wanted to cry but knew that I shouldn't. As I
got my breath back and started to move, he relaxed, got up off his knees
and sat in his chair, still staring at me, his face deadpan. When he picked
up his newspaper and started to read it, I knew it was safe for me to
move. I went up to my room and looked at the world outside my window.

One of the ways I escaped from the world I lived in, especially when
circumstances meant I had to be in the house, was to slide sideways into
a parallel world. In that world, *my* world, I could be me, the real me,
exuberant, competitive, boisterous, funny, outgoing, in other words, a
normal, everyday child, a normal, loud, full of beans, inquisitive boy. My
world allowed me to escape the world I lived in, where I was not allowed
to be any of the things I actually was. I wasn't allowed to be competitive,
or to be more truthful, I wasn't allowed to be competitive enough to beat
my father at anything. Being funny was the domain of my father. If you
let your mask slip a bit and became who you were, even for just a
second, his eyes would narrow and he would stare at you, his jaw
muscles working like he was chewing something really…chewy. And
you knew that you had to withdraw, had to return to being a nonentity
and you had to do that pretty quickly.

When I side-slipped into my world, it was never, *could* never be
complete immersion. It was imperative that you kept at least one eye and

one ear on the real world. To not always be aware of your surroundings was no more than courting disaster.

Like I said, life was just *too* hard. Fraught with danger at just about every level. Life in the real world wasn't helped by having a sister, Carla, who would get her own way by threatening to tell *him* of your misdemeanours, like listening to music on the radio, eating more than one biscuit, not washing the dishes when our mum told you to. And if she didn't get her own way, on whatever it was she wanted, then she *would* tell him. Even when our mum implored her not to. Both me and Dan received many a beating based on something Carla said. We'd get quizzed by him, right out of the blue, right in the middle of him talking about what was on telly or something, he'd shoot a question at you. Your natural response is to lie because you know that you shouldn't listen to the pop charts on the radio and when you did, he would call Carla in and ask you why your sister had lied about you. Carla would start crying because she felt that she was in trouble and so you, the big brother would come clean and take your punishment. There were times when both me and Dan may have been listening to the pop charts but she would only tell on me. I could never understand that. At those times, Dan would be looking terrified but trying to act as though he wasn't concerned with the kangaroo court currently in session. I never gave him up. And he never thanked me or even spoke to me about what had happened. It's not what we did. We simply never spoke about anything. Ever.

I'd be ordered upstairs with a movement of his head. I'd go up and wait in my bedroom. Sometimes he would come up straight away, other times he wouldn't come up for hours. Sometimes, he'd come up, use the bathroom, and go down but then return a few minutes or hours later. And all the time, you didn't know if your punishment was simply to be sent upstairs or worse.

When it was worse, he would come in, close the door and take his belt off. He'd look at your trousers and nod which meant you had to take them down and lie on the bed. He could then take his time and leather you at his leisure, which he often did. There was no such thing as 'six of the best'. You got what was on the menu for that day, for that minute, dependent on, probably, a million things going on inside his head.

You were not allowed to cry out. If you did, then you were given *something to cry out for*, which could mean anything. You had to take your punishment quietly, even though it was horrendously painful and left you bruised and striped with welts.

All of this was bad enough, but often, the punishment would seem to end. There would be a lull. No words would be said, no movement detected. You would think that it was over and sometimes it would start up again. But that feeling, of laying half naked, with someone behind you, armed and dangerous so to speak, let me tell you, that is not a nice feeling. You had to have nerves of steel to not move. Because if you moved, things could, and often would, get a whole lot worse. For others as well as you. Sometimes my father was like a whirlpool. He could start spinning and everything around could be dragged in, people, furniture, belongings. All could become beaten, battered, and smashed, seemingly on a whim. And if that happened, and you had moved, then *you* were the cause of it.

Like I said, life was just *too* hard. For everyone. And so, I decided that I would kill him.

If I went to Borstal, then so be it. If I ended up in prison, then so be it. I decided to kill my dad because he made my life and the lives of all my family so unspeakably, fucking miserable. Life was dark and grim and, at home anyway, was not worth living. And deep in my mind I knew, or at least felt, that he, my father, my protector, *would kill someone, probably my mum, and then, once he'd done that, would just kill all of us. So, I decided on a pre-emptive strike. The question was, how?*

After lengthy deliberation, I decided that it could only be done while he was asleep, but this couldn't be his night-time sleep because he would hear me coming into his room, wake up, recognise the threat, and kill me. The only other time I saw him asleep was when he fell asleep in front of the TV, in his chair. But this sleep was a particularly dangerous sleep. Usually, he fell asleep in his chair because he was drunk. Sometimes he could be in a drunken good mood, fall asleep and stay that way for hours. But then when he woke up, it was like someone had switched the circuits around inside his head, and he could wake up accusing people of things that ended in violence. Or he would want his meal, which he'd already eaten, and if he didn't get it then things would end in violence. Or the programme he was watching had finished while he slept and that would end in violence. When he fell asleep in his chair, drunk, no matter what his pre-sleep mood had been like, your immediate future was dependent purely on how he woke up. So, to kill him during this sleep had to be swift and sure. Failure was not an option.

I'd read a book about the Romans. I can't remember what it was called. But in it, I learned that a favourite *way of executing someone…like you could or would have such a favourite…you know, like, 'By the way, Quintus, what is your favourite method of execution?'*

'Well I don't know really; beheading can be quick but rather messy and so I've always sort of favoured hanging...what about you Julius?'

Forgot where I was now, due to Quintus. Bastard. Oh yeah, I know...a favourite Roman method of execution. I think it was a military method and was done with a gladius, the short Roman sword. The gladius was used by the Romans as a stabbing rather than a cutting weapon. The method was to have the victim, or the executionee, just made that word up, kneeling and the executioner, standing behind, poised with a gladius. The point of the gladius was positioned to the left side of the neck and, when the order was given, thrust down hard and through the heart. Fast and simple. And relatively non-messy. Now, all I needed was a gladius and a chair to stand on behind his chair.

Amazingly, in the cold light of day, back in the 1960's, early 1970's, at age 15 or so, I decided that execution by gladius, would be the easiest way for me to kill my father. Now, I am filled with sadness at that thought. I have no guilt or remorse at making such a terrible decision, just a bewilderment that a father can engender such desolation in the mind of his child that the only way out of the wilderness for that child, is to commit murder.

I reckoned, as there was no gladius to be had, that mum's carving knife was long enough and sharp enough to do the job. A gladius was maybe two foot long or thereabouts but I measured mum's knife against my own chest from the shoulder and decided it was long enough, especially if, once the blade was thrust down with all my weight, it was 'wiggled about' inside the wound, cutting and slicing everything there. The knife was razor sharp and I thought that it would do the job.

The occasion arrived. My dad was fast asleep in his chair and, cool as you like, I got up and went out to the kitchen. I got the long carving knife out of the drawer and felt the blade with the ball of my thumb. It was, as I expected, razor sharp. And then I stood in the kitchen and leaned, with my back to the sink, knife in hand, thinking through what I was about to do. Going through the motions in my head, like football training, rehearsing a corner kick, defence onto attack, four onto three, over and over in your mind until it's perfect.

It would have to be fast, giving no time for anyone in the room to react and cause an alarm, waking him up. If that happened, I may as well use the knife on myself because that is what he would do. I had to walk in swiftly and quietly, knife hiding up the length of my right arm, walk behind him, place the point of the knife next to his neck and thrust my whole weight down onto it. As soon as the blade was buried to its full length, I had to move it about as violently as I could to cause the most amount of internal damage as possible. The attack had to be fast and devastating. By the time any alarm was raised, as it would be, it had to be too late.

What happened afterwards was what happened afterwards. Simple as that. 'Que Sera, Sera', whatever will be, will be, as my parents were fond of singing in duet. I started to move away from the sink and immediately stopped.

What if I made a noise entering the room? What if he was already awake and just about to exit the room? What if he was looking right at me as I walked in? What if someone reacted much faster than I imagined they would? What if my aim was poor? What if he woke up just as I was about to plunge the blade in? What if I didn't kill him and he got up and killed me? Would he then kill all of us? Would my act of protection and defiance prove to be the end? For my brother and sisters, for my mother?

I started to shake, deep seated trembles that shook my whole body. My breathing became fast and hard and sweat ran down my face. I could feel my eyes staring, becoming really intense, my jaw was set so tight it hurt my face. I felt like I was going to be sick. The trembling became uncontrollable and I knew that I couldn't go through with it. I put the knife back in the drawer, went upstairs to my room and lay on my bed.

I shivered and trembled as if I was frozen to the core, staring at the ceiling, looking for my grandad. He wasn't there, it was just a very badly painted white ceiling. I could hear the TV downstairs…the end credits of Coronation Street. I imagined the music waking him up and seconds later I heard the living room door open. He came upstairs and went to the toilet. He came out of the toilet but I didn't hear him go downstairs. Nor did I hear any other door opening or closing. I knew he was standing right outside my door. He was listening for something. I don't know what. Maybe he was trying to hear me listening to some illicit music. Seconds that felt like hours passed. I had psyched myself up so that I wouldn't jump when my bedroom door crashed open yet still manage to look startled. I calmed my trembling and very quietly got hold of my latest book, opened it above my face and made it look as though I was reading. I made a point of quietly clearing my throat, a sound I thought of as very natural. I also deliberately rubbed one page of my book against another, a quiet sound but one that he would hear and hopefully consider as normal. I also quickly read the page I was turned to because it would be like him to burst in, grab my book and quiz me on the page I was on. I could hear Dan's little clock ticking over by his bed

and tried to count the seconds along with it. I did ok up until reaching 10
then thought I heard a tiny movement outside. I held my breath and
listened harder but there was nothing. I resumed breathing and sniffed
quietly to hide the sound of a deeper breath. And then I heard stealthy
movement and he went downstairs and into the living room.

Did he know? How could he have known? Why did he stand outside
my room for so long? What was he listening for? I couldn't possibly
know the answers to these questions, but my mind wouldn't let them go.
And then a voice inside my head said, calm as anything, 'Stop. This is
your life. Live it. Read your book.' And that's what I did. I decided to kill
my father, bottled it, and read my book.

The last item in the shoebox was a tin. A tobacco tin. Green and
gold. I picked it up, shook it. There was a muffled sound, feel, to the
shake and I wondered if I'd find a mummified Numbskull or two inside.
I opened it. There was a tissue. I took the tissue out and opened it up.
There were two teeth in it, two front teeth, one of the top front ones, you
know, the Bugs Bunny ones, whatever they're called, and one of the ones
next to the Bugs Bunny ones. Whatever they're called. I'm not doing
very well in the tooth naming stakes here am I. Suffice to say they were
two front teeth and I knew where they'd come from. They'd come from
Dan's mouth. They'd come from his mouth on the day our father gave
him the punch that maybe defined my brother, that, looking around the
flat, had quite possibly, or more than likely, killed him. I remember it
like it was yesterday.

1969ish

Dan was probably about 15 going on 16 and that would make me
about 12 going on 13. My sister, being two years younger than me, was

tucked up in bed and the twins were less than two years old, so were in bed.

I don't know how it kicked off, probably over nothing, like it usually did. A big thing for my mum was my father being late in for his tea, usually because he was in the pub. She would have cooked a meal for the family, and we would have had ours at our teatime, usually between five and six. If my father wasn't in at the mealtime, she would put a plate over it and either put it in the oven on a low light or on a pan of simmering water.

When he came in from the pub, he would be drunk. I always knew when he was on his way because I could smell him coming. I'd get this sudden overpowering smell of oranges and would go into a semi panic, mainly because it meant that my deepest wish, the one where he would have been killed by a bus or died in a car crash, had not come true. 'Here's dad.' I'd say.

Someone would dash to the window and peep out and after a few seconds would confirm that his car had just turned into the estate off the main road or that he'd just come out of the pub at the top of the road. No one ever asked me how I knew that he was on his way and I always assumed that everyone could smell what I could smell but I was simply the first to mention that he was seconds from arriving.

We would all 'compose' ourselves into a 'normal' looking family scene and try to act as though we weren't afraid for our future.

When his key was heard going into the lock there was an extra second or two where everyone surreptitiously checked their demeanour and stole a glance at others to make sure that you didn't stand out for any reason.

He would enter the house and close the front door. If he slid the bolt home straight away, you knew, beyond doubt, that there was going to be trouble, that there was going to be violence. He was 'thinking ahead' and simply putting an obstacle in the way of anyone's attempt to get out of the house quickly. If that happened, you had to act as though you hadn't heard him doing it and even if you had heard it, well, it meant nothing, you had nothing to be scared about. To show fear, to show anything except 'normality' was to invite him into singling you out. I always likened it to being blindfolded in front of a firing squad and hearing the soldiers sliding a round into the firing chamber…if you were brave, like in some of the books I'd read, then you didn't flinch from what you knew was coming your way, you acted as though getting shot by firing squad was an everyday occurrence, you showed no fear. If he didn't slide the door bolt home, that didn't mean that everything was going to be ok. It meant no more than he hadn't slid the bolt home.

So, he'd close the front door and then he would hang his coat up on the gas cupboard door. We had a cloakroom, an actual proper cloakroom, pretty fancy-Dan for a 1960's council house but there ya go. We didn't have any kind of heating except a gas fire in the living room, but we had somewhere to hang our cloaks. My father was the only one who could use the gas cupboard door to hang his coat on. If anyone made the mistake of doing it, their coat or jacket would get flung down the front path, sometimes ending up on the pavement. If a coat was hanging on the cupboard door, that wasn't one of his, then this might cause real violence in the house and then again it might not. But if you'd mistakenly hung, say, your school blazer on the door, forgotten about it and then not *suffered violence because of your misdemeanour*, then it was easy to not even think about your blazer until it was time to go to school the next morning, couldn't find it and then realised that it was out in the street and had been there all night. In the rain. Like I did.

Having hung his coat up, he'd come into the living room and we had to go through this act of being surprised at our father walking into the room...like we hadn't heard him come in...and we all had to sound really happy to see him, we all had to say 'Hiya Dad!', the dilemma for us being, do you instantaneously blurt it out and run the risk of not being heard properly, because of someone else saying it at the same time, or do you wait for a split second and blurt it out *just after everyone else*, like my sister Carla used to do. Whatever you opted for, it had to be done with feeling and if it wasn't then you ran the risk of the consequences. He never replied of course. Never. He usually wouldn't even look at you. But you had to wait for a few heartbeats at least, to see whether or not he decided *he was going to look at you, because if he did look at you it* meant that he wanted something and you were the one who had been granted the favour of getting it for him. And if you weren't actually looking at him when this happened then he would have to use your name to issue his instructions, and having to use your name quite often put him in a bad mood.

So, on this particular night, the night he set in motion a string of events that, in my opinion, killed my brother, I'd smelled the oranges, issued a warning and he'd come into the house and hung his coat on the gas cupboard door.

My mum was in the kitchen and I heard them having words. I could tell from the tone that my mum's words were…hostile. I caught the word 'slaving'. She would usually use that word when referring to him 'drinking with his mates' while she was slaving, doing whatever it was that warranted her use of the word. Whenever she used words like that, I would be saying to myself 'Shut up mum, please stop it.' I knew that if she let it go, we all might escape but if she carried on then we would all suffer in some way. I used to think that my father was dangerous when he was drunk and that it was simply the best thing to just leave him to be drunk. If you left him alone and you still ended up with a beating, or worse, then so be it, that's life…but to actually encourage it seemed…foolish to me.

He came into the living room and me and Dan 'Heil Hitlered' him. That's what I likened it to. He was a vicious dictator and it's what we had to do to survive. We had to conform to his rules, we had to placate him, had to make it look as though we respected him, loved him. He ignored us, sat down, and took his work boots off, which was good because that meant if you got kicked it would only be with a slippered or stockinged foot. The smell of my dad's feet, sour and rancid, filled the room within seconds but I kept my face composed, knowing that I'd give it 20 minutes or so, to ensure that he didn't think I was offended by his feet, which could prove costly, and disappear to my bedroom to read. Dan was already reading a book, 'Chemistry made Simple', which, in my book of strategies was a mistake, because he now only had 'going to bed' as a get out.

He crossed his legs and started to read the evening paper, starting with the back page, the football page. I was watching something on the

TV, and he told me to switch to another channel, which I did. He carried on reading the paper. I now extended my 20 minutes to at least double that. If I left the room after the 20 then I would be making silent comment on him changing the channel. Which I wasn't going to do. No way.

After a few more minutes my mum brought his tea in and put it on the chair arm that he normally ate from. She handed him his knife and fork. He said nothing but carried on reading the paper for 30 seconds. My mum sat down and picked up some knitting she was doing. My dad made ready to eat his food and spoke to me. 'What's this about Joe?' he asked. I knew that he was going to do that and had been paying attention. 'Something to do with apartheid.' I said. 'Oh yeah.' he said, 'What about it?'

I was just about to answer, as best I could, when I saw him start to cut the pork chop that was on his plate. I could see that it was tough, dried out. As were the potatoes and the peas. The gravy had a thick skin on it, and I saw his face change. I saw him glance at the book that Dan was reading, not at my brother but at the book he was reading. He picked his plate up with the thumb and forefinger of his left hand and at first, I thought he was going to take it to the kitchen but he transferred it to the palm of his right hand, stood up and launched it, full force, seemingly straight at my mum.

It went over her head and slammed into the wall, making a noise that was too much for what it was, splattering food everywhere. I watched, in slow motion, a glob of gooey gravy sail across the room and land on the head of a brass flower seller on the mantelpiece, instantly drooping down over the head like a shawl. I almost fatally laughed. Both Dan and my mum jumped. My mum's knitting hands spasmed so that she looked *like me knitting and, bizarrely, I found that funny as well. Dan turned towards our father and he looked really angry and glared at my dad and because of that my brain went into a kind of shutdown, where you only think of the things you need for survival and your body gets itself ready for flight, adrenaline surging like a wave into your system.*

My mum reacted instantly and wrongly. 'What the bloody hell did you do that for Charlie!' she shouted. Wrong! Wrong! Wrong! I thought. In my mind, this was the kind of thing that would get us all killed. I actually thought those words. I knew that he was dangerous and, somehow, I just knew that he had such disregard for us that he could explode and kill one of us in a blind rage, maybe not even intending to do it and then think...Aaah y'know what?...and kill the rest of us. And somehow, I always knew, or thought I knew, that if he did that, *then he would* not *go the whole hog and kill himself.*

In an instant, he covered the ground to her and grabbed a handful of her hair, dragging her up to her feet. She started to protest but as soon as she was standing, he punched her in the face, knocking her back down into her chair. A split appeared across the bridge of her nose, not the first time this particular split had been opened, and blood cascaded down her face and onto her clothing. The sound of fist on face was a brutal sound, nothing like the movies. This was a sickening blunt thud of something heavy and hard hitting something made of...us...of people. It sounds ridiculous to use such words because obviously it is one of us hitting one of us, but even though you know that, it's still not easy to reconcile the sound with what your eyes are seeing. It reminded me of the dull, heavy, meaty thud you would hear in a proper butcher's shop when he was hacking into a side of beef on that big solid block of wood.

When my mum landed back down in the chair, the whole chair moved a few inches backwards and as it did so, I noticed the dinner plate, which was sliding slowly down the wall, stop, as if it was startled and wanted to know what was going on.

It was only a split second after the blow and my mum hadn't got to the stage of reacting to it, assuming she actually could, when he pounced, that is the only word I can use to describe his action...he pounced on her and dragged her back to her feet, two hands grabbing her clothing at her chest height and bodily picking her up, moving easily into the middle of the room with her. His left hand kept hold of her clothing and his right fist, a large, calloused, strong hand, balled into a fist with huge round knuckles, slammed into her stomach, once, twice, then he let go of her with his left hand and she crumpled to the floor in front of me, falling so that she landed on my feet. He shot a calm, flat glance at me, his bright blue eyes looking almost black and I acted as though I was totally absorbed in the question of apartheid, my eyes glued to the screen as if nothing untoward was happening. The transition between a sort of half peace and this brutal beating of a little woman...my mum was four foot eleven...was...shocking. A word that doesn't begin to describe what was happening but one that describes the effect on me, on my brain, on my instincts...which were telling me to run while at the same time telling me to stay still, perfectly still, make yourself small, absolutely non-threatening, absolutely not even interested *in what was happening. I was shocked into furious thinking and total surrender.*

My mum was on the floor but was beginning to get up and in my mind, I pleaded with her to stay on the floor. He was standing over her, as if ready for a dangerous adversary, his arms outboard from his body, his hands clenched into fists, his breathing was deep and calm, his eyes fixed on her, like a cat fixes a mouse in its stare.

Dan still had his book open at the page he'd been reading but he had turned his whole body to face my dad and his expression was one of pure unadulterated hatred, one of massive anger and I got the impression he was going to intervene. I prayed that he wouldn't. It sounds terrible that I did not want to intervene or want my brother to intervene…but…I didn't. I'm not proud of it and I'm not ashamed of it. When terror strikes, you do what you have to do. You do what some ancient part of your brain tells you to do. You survive. It was this day, this event, that made me, at age 19, become a firefighter and put my life on the line for others, put my life on the line to rescue people from their own version of the terror I felt at age 12 going on 13.

My mum staggered to her feet and made for the door…heading towards the unbolted front door. Amazingly he watched as she staggered past him. I could see his jaw muscles working, like he was chewing something, his blue eyes so relaxed and black, his stare like the stare of a predator. She got past him and as she presented her back to him, he put his foot flat on her arse and pushed as hard as he could. She went flying into the living room door, collapsing into a heap in the corner. As she flailed into her collapse, her hand caught the light switch and turned the lights off. The room was now lit only by the black and white TV in the corner, the programme about apartheid still on.

My dad followed her, dragged her up to a standing position, turned the light back on and turned her around to face him. He put his left hand tightly around her throat and slammed her backwards into the living room door, her head banging violently into it. And then he raised his right fist and hit her hard again in the face, smashing her head into the door. She was like a rag doll. No sounds from her, no response at all and I thought she was dead.

And then my brother, my big brother, my all-time hero, threw his book on the floor and rushed towards them. He was bellowing. Bellowing. Bellowing at my dad to stop it.

It was maybe three or four steps that Dan had to take to get to them, but by the time he reached them, his arms raised to grab hold of something, anything, my dad turned to face him, still holding my mum up by her throat, with his left hand, his eyes fixing Dan with deadly intent...assessing the threat, working out what he needed to do to fight off this uprising...and brought his right fist, massive and bony, square into Dans face, Dan running onto it almost.

The fist hitting Dan's face made a noise that I remember but don't want to. It made a noise that sounded like the meaty butcher's block noise but with an underlying crunchy crackle. Blood spurted all over me, a spray of it, like freckles, covering my nose and cheeks. Dan flew backwards, like he was running but falling over at the same time. He crashed into the corner of the room, the opposite corner to my mum and slid down the wall, right next to the dinner plate that was still making its way to the floor. The plate stopped its descent again, as if upset that its moment was being stolen from it by my brother. Dan's nose was bleeding, his lips were bleeding. He was conscious and stunned and obviously in pain. He spat blood onto his shirt, a feeble, fat-lipped spit, full of hurt. Two teeth spilled out and slid down his shirt on a river of blood, snot, and saliva. I felt something on my lips, realised it was Dan's

blood and involuntarily licked at it, like you do in the sugary doughnut
game where you try to eat it without licking the sugar from around your
mouth. I wiped the back of my hand over my mouth but didn't look at it
in case my dad saw me do it.

My dad still had hold of my mum's throat and his right fist was still
in mid-air, at the spot in the room where it had connected with my
brother's face. My mum's hands came up and tried to wrestle my dad's
hand from her throat, but it was like he was frozen, staring with his flat
black eyes at my brother.

I watched the anger fade, watched the black of his eyes change to
bright blue. He let go of my mum's throat and she slid to the floor,
gasping, and rubbing at her neck. My dad sat down in his chair, crossed
his legs, picked up the Echo, aimed his head at the TV and said, 'Still the
same programme Joe?' I nodded.

Over the years, in an attempt, to explain the behaviour of my brother,
I've often thought about that punch. Bone on bone, hard, made doubly so
by the speed with which Dan approached the accelerating fist, that
landed right on his mouth, knocking the teeth out and splitting his lips.
Did the trauma of that punch cause my brother's brain to crash into his
skull? The front of his brain crashing into the hard bone of the skull, is
that enough to cause brain damage? Just one punch? I don't actually
know that answer but my belief was that it probably did injure his brain.
Dan was a youth. And our father was a trained fighter with fists like
hammers.

Now, in the hell-hole that was my brother's home, and not for the
first time, I wondered if damage to the front of the brain, the frontal lobe,
could cause my brother to believe that saving rubbish was a good idea,

that doing away with his toilet was clever and that drinking strong alcohol in large quantities over a very prolonged period was the way to go. Did my father kill my brother with that punch? I think he did. But then, what did I know?

I re-wrapped the teeth in their tissue paper and put them back in the tin.

In the bottom of the cage was a long black *thing*. I picked it up. It was heavy, flexible, thick, like a truncheon. I had a vague memory of it but couldn't quite place it. It looked like a piece of cable but not like any cable I'd ever seen.

I sat on my big plastic toolbox by the door to the stairs and had a drink of water. I put the piece of cable on the floor between my feet and stared at it.

1968ish

It was about two, maybe three o'clock in the morning. I was dreaming about my dad chasing me through a dark forest. I couldn't see my dad, but I knew it was him because I could smell the oranges, rich and tangy, but with a rancid underlying smell of rot. He was gaining on me and I knew that if he caught me, I would die. I was trying to wake up because I didn't want to die aged 14, but I couldn't. I knew that if I was able to move part of my body, anything, just twitch my finger even, that such a movement would rescue me, leaving the monster to hunt the forest for someone else to slaughter. I also knew that the best thing to do was to relax and then try to take myself by surprise, kick out or twitch, but to do this required me to slow from a sprint to a jog. And that would allow the monster to make up ground. I concentrated really hard and slowed my running, readying for the twitch of my finger. I could feel the thud of the heavy footsteps getting closer. The smell of rotting flesh was beginning to overcome the orange zest and I knew that the beast with the face of my dad was right behind me, reaching out to grab the back of my neck in an iron fist, when I just opened my eyes and looked at the ceiling of my bedroom, right at a spider crawling across it, or walking across it.

We always say that a spider was crawling, but do they? Crawl? Or do they just walk? I reckon if I was a spider I'd be put out if someone described me as crawling to work, or wherever spiders are on the way to when you happen to spot them. And how funny is it that as soon as you look at them, they stop, like they know you've just looked at them. Which is what this one did. It stopped dead. Just above me but to one side. So, I asked myself, fresh from the nightmare of a monster dad chasing me through the forest, was this spider walking across my ceiling, on his way to work, two of his eyes locked onto the dark hollows that were my sleeping eyes, the other six just swivelling about taking in the scenery, happy to just trundle along when suddenly my eyes sprung open and battened straight onto the movement above me that happened to be him? Had I now become the monster in his waking nightmare? Did spiders even dream? And if they did, did they have nightmares? About people chasing them with a shoe in hand?

Funny how your mind just churns on, thinking shit, asking questions, looking for information, analysing stuff and generally just…working away. Perpetual motion of your cogs. Yeah. Cogs. That's what I had. Churning cogs. Lots of 'em.

I looked away from the spider and it carried on with its quest. I turned and looked at Dan. I knew he was awake because I couldn't hear *him breathing and I was slightly incensed that he'd been here, in the world of our bedroom while I'd been getting chased through the dark trees by a monster in another world, and he hadn't woken me up, hadn't* known *my predicament.*

I could see that Dan was on his back, looking at the ceiling, and I could tell he was tense, as if ready to leap out of bed. And then I heard it. My mum's voice, quiet, but urgent.

'Come back to bed Charlie.' There was a base rumble as my dad replied but I couldn't make out the words, just the tone. He was angry. Aggressive.

'There's no one there Charlie, come back to bed.' My mum's voice was very quiet but I could nearly always hear her, even when she was being quiet. She was pleading with him.

I heard him moving about. It sounded like he was looking for something. I heard drawers being quietly opened and then closed, one after the other. And then I heard the rumble of his voice and was able to make out one word, 'kill'.

My mum's voice became more insistent, urging him to come back to bed. He said something too quiet for me to hear and then I made out that he was shushing her, but she persisted, pleading with him to get back in bed, that there was no one there, that no one was coming to get him.

I was becoming more tense as I strained to pick out the words, not moving, hardly even breathing. I could tell that Dan was doing the same. I wanted to talk to him but daren't break the silence for fear of attracting attention and for fear of losing information from my mum's bedroom.

A car went past outside, its lights piercing the narrow gap at the top of the curtains and travelling from left to right across the ceiling. I knew from the route of the lights that the car was travelling from right to left, driving down into the estate from the main road. Someone on their way home from work, going to a house in another world. I wanted to be in the back of that car, going to that other world but I was trapped in this one.

The noises from my mum's bedroom suddenly changed. I could tell that there was a struggle, that two people were struggling. It was a soft, rapid sound, no hardness. No edges. I knew that my mum and dad were struggling on the bed. Not doing the things that adults do on a bed but struggling like me and Dan did when we were wrestling. But more urgent. Much more urgent. To me, at age 14, I somehow knew that someone, another person, another human being, my mother, was fighting for her life less than 10 feet away from me. I also knew that she was losing that fight because the struggle was becoming less frantic. There was a voice, no words, but a voice, or a voice noise, noise made by air and vocal chords, it was sound, human sound but not human. It was there, I could just about hear it and I was very frightened. More frightened than I'd ever been, and I had been pretty frightened in my short life so far.

I knew that my eyes were wide open, as wide as it was possible for them to be…funny how you open your eyes wider when you want to increase the power of your hearing…and my mind started to race. My heart quickened and my muscles started to feel warm. I assessed the clothing I was wearing, underpants and vest. Singlet as my grandma would call it. I'd given up on the pyjamas because I was too old for them.

It was a thing. *At my age. In my school. Wearing pyjamas was for cissies. If you were a man, then you went to bed in your undies.*

I went through my escape. I'd rehearsed it in my mind many times before, but I just made sure of what I would do. I'd get up and rag the curtains aside, open the window wide in the same movement as climbing onto the wide windowsill. I'd get one foot onto the sill outside and jump down onto the grass, remembering to land with both feet together, let my legs buckle and roll, on landing, like I'd read about parachutists on D-Day. I knew that I'd land just to the right of the rose bush that grew in the centre of the grass and so my parachutists roll had to take me away from the bush. I didn't want a load of rose thorns up my arse. From there I would turn right and sprint across all the front gardens, making sure to keep to the grass because I would be barefoot, avoiding Mrs Hall's roses, Mrs Smith's rockery, Mr Hewitt's motor scooter then coming out through Mrs Kane's front gateway, which I knew would be open because someone stole their gate last bonfire night. Not me. I'd then be well ahead of any chase and would run all the way to Parkfield Lane Police Station. There were two phone boxes between our world and the police station but, I wouldn't take the chance of stopping at one of them and being caught.

I knew that Dan wouldn't follow me through the window because I knew that he'd stay to try to protect everyone. That's one of the things that made him better than me. But I also knew, deep down in my heart, that he would die with everyone else and I knew, or thought, that the best chance of protecting anyone, was to get help.

All the noises ceased, and everything went quiet. Not a sound, not a movement. Nothing. I could hear my heart in my ears. My breathing was increasing, and it was an effort to keep it quiet. After a few minutes that seemed like hours I heard movement. A soft sound. And then, even though I hadn't heard the door of my mum's bedroom open, I heard a tiny creak that I knew was a slightly loose floorboard right outside my bedroom door. Either my dad had somehow managed to open his bedroom door without making a sound, which I found hard to believe, or my sister Carla had come out of her bedroom and was coming to our room. If she'd been going to mum's room the natural route wouldn't have brought her into contact with the loose board. I was now completely thrown into turmoil. If Carla entered our room, she would make noise because our door creaked. Only slightly, but enough. And that would bring him, our father, like a ferocious dog, bursting out of its lair, to see what was going on, to see what misdemeanours were being perpetrated in his kingdom. If Carla came through our door, I would either have to make a run for it now, right now, or stay to face my fate with my brother and my eldest sister.

And then I heard another noise. It was another tiny creak which I knew was the 5th stair from the bottom. I couldn't work out what was going on. Was it Carla and if so, where was she going? Carla was about 11 or 12 at the time and could easily be on her way out of the house, to do what I intended to do maybe. But then, I heard movement, rapid movement in my mum's room and I heard bare feet stumble past my door and then mum's voice, hoarse, weepy, 'Ohh Charlie, Charlie, come back to bed there's no one there, please stop this, please come back up.'

'I'll kill them.' he said. 'All of them.' I heard the bolt being slid open on the front door. I thought that there must be someone outside, but I hadn't heard anything. Maybe I'd been too wrapped up in listening for

other things. Maybe our house, our world, was coming under attack from someone. I got out of bed, ready to fight. I considered putting something on then decided against it. I grabbed one of my football boots as a weapon, pictured myself using the studs in a raking motion and went out of my bedroom door, ready for anything.

My mum was standing about three steps down from the top of the stairs and my dad was behind the front door, as if waiting for someone to come through, a large, ruthless looking knife in his right hand.

My mum turned and saw me. She was startled and half frowned at the football boot in my hand. She told me to go back to bed, but I wasn't paying any attention. My dad hadn't heard her or if he had, he was ignoring her. He ignored me too and I realised that he hadn't seen me. I realised that he was not currently in my world. He was somewhere else. Somewhere where people were coming to get him. The kind of people that he would kill to protect himself, which, to my mind meant that they were people who would kill him if they got to him.

'Here they come!' he said, his voice hoarse, scratchy. 'That's them outside the door now!'

'There's no one there Charlie, no one. Put the knife down and come to bed...please put the knife down.'

He ripped the front door open and rushed outside. I briefly thought about running down and slamming the door shut but quickly dismissed it. I could see him standing outside on the path in the same clothes that I was wearing. It must have been uncool to wear pyjamas in his world too. He was standing, peering this way and that but there was no one there. He came back inside and walked up the stairs, the knife hanging down by his side. He walked past my mum, barely glancing at her, then walked past me, his hard eyes sliding over me as he walked past. He went into his bedroom and closed the door. I heard a clatter, presumably the knife dropping to the floor and then I heard him getting into bed.

My mum went down and closed the front door, slid the bolt across and then did the exact same as my dad had done. She walked past me, her eyes sliding over me, went into the bedroom and I heard her get into bed.

Not one word was ever said about what had happened. Not one word. When they were out of the house I searched for that knife because I wanted to see what it was, but I never did find it. It must have gone to the same place that our mysteriously vanishing Christmas presents went to. I did, though, find a very heavy, truncheon sized piece of electrical cable just under the bed, right where my father could reach it in a hurry.

Recalling that incident, especially when my parents walked past me in turn and looked at me as though I was an intruder, unsettled me. It was their eyes, the way they slid over me. Sly, dismissive, contemptuous and with a promise of violence just a blink away.

I went out to my car, took my gloves off and poured myself a hot coffee from the flask in the boot. I sat on the low wall sipping the hot liquid. One of the neighbours came out and asked me how things were going. Strangely, his name was Dan and, also strangely, he seemed to be an alcoholic as well. I told him it was painstaking work, slow and pretty filthy and I apologised for the smell created by the rubbish in the skip. He didn't seem fazed by it at all and I wondered if his own place was similar to my brother's.

He told me that he would have a little drink on occasion with my brother and said what a nice bloke he was, really clever. 'Yeah,' I said, 'He was a clever fella alright.'

Dan lit a cigarette and offered me one. I told him I didn't smoke but even if I had, there was no way I would have taken one off him. His hands hadn't been washed for a very long time by the look of them and the ciggy packet looked like he'd dug it up from somewhere.

'Can't believe he's gone to be honest.' he said, blowing smoke towards the sky. 'I've known him a long time, gotta be, ohhhh,' he took a big drag on his ciggy while he was thinking, 'twenny, twenny five years lar.' He took two more massive drags on his ciggy, inspecting the glowing tip after each drag, 'Gotta be a quarter of a century I've known him.' One last giant drag then he flicked his ciggy into someone's garden and blew the smoke after it.

I was getting bored with him now and also, I'd just caught a whiff of him, a sharp, sweaty, dirty smell, someone who hadn't put clean clobber on for months. I'd come out of the midden for a change of air but now, I preferred the midden to the neighbour. I drank the remains of my coffee and put the cup back in the bag in the boot.

'I still think I keep seeing him, fuckin weird it is, fuckin weird.' he said, shuffling towards his front door, right beneath my brother's living room window, a little flat roofed porch similar to the one Dan had at his front door round the back.

'Bet y'do Dan.' I said, walking alongside him but not too close. 'You know someone for that long, only natural you'd miss them. Mind plays strange tricks sometimes, doesn't it?'

'You're not wrong there lad, y'not wrong there, see you later…' he said as he got to his door and pushed it open.

'Yeah.' I said, thinking, *not if I see you first you won't, y'smelly twat,* 'Take care mate.' I said as I reached the corner.

Chapter 25 - Excerpts from the Diary

Tuesday 9th September 2003

2nyt start 8.40pm 45 x 5

No bed. Bad pains + diaorea

Wednesday 10th September 2003

2nyt start 7.34pm 45 x 6

pains – diaorea

This morning, 7 – 9am, couldn't keep eyes open, finally went to bed about 9ish am, got few hours sleep, woken up by Bertie barking from downstairs by the front door. Got up, looked at myself in mirror in bathroom, and was surprised to see how different I looked — much better! Was he barking this morning, or Thursday morning?! I can't remember now! I know I had bad dreams in this sleep, stabbing someone, a man. I may have woke up because of these. Tonight, after drinking what I did, about 10 – 11pm, I almost puked by bringing up a load of half-digested liquid, so I went to bed. Left the TV + PS1 + light on, didn't take Bertie out.

Thursday 11th September 2003

2nyt start 10.26pm 45 x 3 + 112.50

This morning woke up about 6 – 7am 8am(?) was Bertie barking downstairs by front door? I felt absolutely awful, and looked absolutely awful! Just shows you what I have been doing to myself for years! Still a few (only a few) pains today, although this morning, stools normal.

Saturday 13th September 2003

2nyt start 8.11pm 45 x 5

Got up around 12pm ish Sunday and wasn't hungover, but felt tired and in a bad mood.

11pm! Bertie!! The SLAM!!

Sunday 14th September 2003

2nyt start 7.42pm 45 x 5 + 112.50

1.30pm this afternoon in garden, yanks on lead and Bertie! He instantly annoyed me, and I shudn't have reacted the way I did. I yanked him a few more times on Kittys garden. He can instantly annoy me by going around a tree/object and pulling in the opposite way that I want him to go/come back. I think he gave a few little moans. He seemed ok with me a short while later.

Monday 15th September 2003

2nyt start 6.37pm 45 x 8

Tuesday 16th September 2003

2nyt start 9.18pm 9.20pm 45 x 7 + 112.50

Wednesday 17th September 2003

2nyt start 5.42pm 45 x 10½, other ½ poured down sink.

2nyt outside near on path I shouted at Bertie to shut up and Brenda shouted allright Dan! I think because Patch was barking. Bertie wouldn't shut up and I think Gary saw me yank Bertie hard, and Bertie went flying along the grass of Wills garden. I think Bertie gave a little moan. I think he had lost his footing and he fell/rolled. He immediately got frightened and ran to the wall, and to my front door for safety. I coaxed him round and went up the path again. He looked at me and wagged his tail a few times, as if to show subservience to me. I talked to him and we (he) seemed OK and friends. Is he? or is he friends with me thru fear? Bertie originally started barking when I was trying to talk to Bethany, telling her not to run out looking for her dad.

Chapter 26 - Having a Moment

My phone rang. It was Pam. 'How's it going love?' she asked. 'How are you?'

I wanted to say *I'm not so good really*. I wanted to say that my mind wouldn't be quiet, that it wouldn't let me out, that everywhere was barred to me except here, where I was, where it wanted me. I wanted to say that my brother kept talking to me and seemed to be laughing at me when I wanted him to laugh with me. I wanted to say that I was angry at him for not trusting me or wanting me in his life, that I was angry at my father for not acting as a father should, that I was angry at my mother for not protecting us, for not protecting me. I wanted to say that I was angry at myself for failing to be the brother I maybe should have been. I wanted to say that I was despairing of how my sisters acted at times and how they could be so ruthless in their pursuit of self. I wanted to say that I was tired of the constant storm in my brain, the insistent, never ending vigilance, watching shadows, listening too carefully to words, scrutinising too deeply for that *look*. I wanted to say that I was sorry for the intensity from which I lived my life, that I knew it was frequently intimidating to some people. I wanted to say that I needed to live in the world that I sometimes saw in the mirror, the one from where the real me could sometimes be glimpsed behind the blue veils that could snap shut in a blink. I wanted to say that I didn't need my security team any more, that they could take a long holiday. But I knew that I *did* need them. I knew that they would never take leave, never relax their vigilance, never let a stray word or an interpretable glance go without examination and analysis. I knew that they were with me, in charge of my protection, for ever. I wanted to say that I was glad but sad that they were needed and that there was just too much stuff I needed to say that couldn't be said but instead I said, 'I'm fine thanks love, but more importantly, how are you?'

Chapter 27 - Hamster Cage Island, Box 2

The next box was also a shoe box and, at one time, had contained hiking boots so was quite big. Scarpa boots. Size 9. I remember copying him and buying the same boots myself because he'd said they were the best. To be honest, truly honest, they weren't the most comfortable boot for me to wear but, for some reason, I persisted with them because Dan did and I just assumed they were meant to be uncomfortable. Dope. I remember eventually ditching them and buying a pair of Zamberlans and cursed myself for the stupidity of my loyalty to my brother's choice of boot. The Zamberlans were not just good, they were *exceedingly* good, like a Mr Kipling cake, especially the French Fancies. Let me tell you something, I could eat a serious number of Mr Kipling's French Fancies, maybe even a houseful of them. A normal sized, three bedroomed semi, not your country house mansion or anything daft. You've got to be sensible with such claims, so, for future reference, the claim of being able to eat a houseful of a particular confection, or, indeed, savoury because a Morrison's sausage roll has just popped into my mind…the houseful claim *always* refers to an average semi-detached house.

I opened the box. There were a number of items inside and the first one just jumped out and smacked me straight between the eyes. Stunned me. Stopped me dead in my tracks and set off an alarm in my mind. I put the box down on the floor, stood up and backed away from the toolbox I'd been sitting on, keeping the boot box in sight. *Could it be the same one?* I thought, *Why would he have it? Why would he keep it — in this box? A box of keepsakes.*

The item was a hairbrush. A plastic hairbrush, light green, with a reddish-pinky kind of soft *pad* with the black, thick, stiff plastic 'bristles' sticking out of it. The 'bristles' had little balls on the end. My mum used it to brush Carla's hair. I remembered my first wife, Lucy, buying one to use on my daughter's hair and I'd stolen it and disposed of it. She'd bought another one when the first one went missing and I'd done the same thing. Lucy eventually gave up buying the brush and made do with something else.

The brush, the green one, the one in the shoebox, had been used to beat me about the face by my father.

About 1960

Chewing gum. Chewie, as it was known in Liverpool. We, us kids, weren't allowed chewie. Like a lot of parents, me included, you don't want your young kids to have chewing gum, for various reasons. My reasons, once I became a parent, were hair, as in my daughters, and car seats, as in my car seats. My grandma used to say that it was dangerous to swallow chewie and that if you did, it would stick to your lungs and kill you. Another Liverpool version of this was it sticking to your heart and doing the same thing, killing you. Heart, lungs and chewie...not a good mix.

One night, must have been a Saturday night, because my parents were out, probably at the Glendower and grandma and grandad were in charge of us. We were in bed and I had chewie. Dan had given me a piece when we went to bed. Pink, fragrant, probably a Bazooka Joe. I loved Bazooka Joe chewie, loved it, though I couldn't eat a houseful of it.

Anyway, I was furiously trying to blow a bubble like my brother who was the best bubble blower in our street, shifting the stuff around in my mouth trying to get it so that I could stretch it with my tongue like I'd been shown a hundred times. I just couldn't get it right and the more I tried and failed, the more agitated I became. But I wasn't going to be beaten by a Bazooka Joe. No way. Suddenly, I have no idea how it happened, it just disappeared from my mouth and I swallowed it. Panic was instantaneous. I was going to die, right now. This Bazooka Joe was going to do its thing and stick to my lungs, they'd stop working and I was going to die, and it was as simple as that.

I leapt out of bed and dashed downstairs to my grandma, and she was dead cool about it. She tut tutted a few times and took me to the kitchen where she ripped a two inch piece of crust from a loaf of bread and told me to eat it. When I swallowed it, she gave me some water to drink and when I'd done that, she declared me to have been saved. I dashed off, like a lunatic, like your pet dog when you let it free after it's had a bath, sprinting up the stairs, full of vigour because now, I had a future, I had a life to live when just a few minutes ago I'd only had seconds to live.

So, the hair brush…it was a warm sunny day and I'd been playing out in the street with my mate from the house on the corner. He didn't live there but visited his grandad once a week and we'd play together.

His name was Robin and he had bright ginger curly hair and an angelic face. Scrubbed and shiny with pink cheeks, bright blue eyes and ruby lips. I've got to be honest here and say that, at the time, I didn't think of his face as being angelic, it's only now that I've seen angelic faces of, er, angels, in pictures that I can apply that adjective to Robin. Back then, Robin was what I now know to be quite posh and his clothes were always perfect.

On the day in question, m'lud, he was wearing a hooped tee shirt in those two colours that, according to my grandma, should never be seen together, blue and green, but I liked it and couldn't think why blue and green should never be seen. But that's what she would say and who was I to argue? He had navy shorts and some sandals with crepe soles, white ones. The soles, not the sandals. The sandals were brown leather with a pattern of little holes in them, like brogues but sandals, you know the ones I mean. Posh. To us, they were posh. I had a pair of latticed plastic sandals, the ones they call jelly sandals these days. I even used to go to school in them. Anyway, to me, Robin looked like one of the kids out of my Enid Blyton books, posh hair, rosy cheeks and perfect clothes.

On this day, he had chewing gum, chewie. A big pink one. Smelled like a Bazooka Joe. Every time he spoke to me or laughed, I got a whiff of it and it was lovely. His grandad came out and called him in for his dinner and he spat the chewy out onto the pavement. Right by me. It sat there in the sun and I could smell it. I wanted it but knew that I wasn't allowed it. I looked about and there was no one around. I did another thing that I wasn't allowed to do. I picked it up and put it in my mouth. Just as I did that, my brother came out and sat on the pavement next to me. He picked a lolly ice stick up from the gutter and poked at some muck in between the stone setts of the street surface. An ant scurried away.

It sounds disgusting, me picking up the chewing gum and putting it in my mouth but, y'know, I was probably about five years of age at the time and didn't really know any better. It tasted just how it smelled, sort of fruity and pink. I was giving it a right good gnashing, getting every bit of flavour out of it. Dan noticed and said, 'Have you got chewie?' I nodded, chewing vigorously. 'Where did you get it?' He asked. I told him that Robin had spat it out. He shook his head at me and said that I could get germs. I thought he'd said Germans and was puzzling over that, thinking of bombs and tanks and soldiers. Dan went back into the house.

I was contemplating blowing a bubble, a skill I hadn't yet mastered, but sooner or later I would. I was just about to have a go, doing some strange face contortions as I manoeuvred the chewie into the right place. Before I could get my tongue into the middle of it, like my brother had showed me, my father appeared at my side, as if by magic and picked me up. I hadn't heard him or even sensed him, he was just suddenly there. He plucked me off the kerbstones as easy as anything and carried me into the house, into the parlour that was our part of the house. He stuck his big fingers in my mouth and pulled out the chewie, and then picked up the hairbrush off the chair next to him and grabbing me by the upper arm, swiped me across the face with the brush. Hard. And then he did it again. And again. And again. And again. And he kept on doing it even though I was crying and screaming and in real pain. He beat me across my face with a stiff hair brush, then picked me up under his arm and went up the stairs, very fast, two steps at a time, threw me onto my bed, knocking the wind out of me, slapped my arse really hard a few times and slammed the door on the way out.

That night I wasn't allowed any food or anything. No one came to see me. My face was burning hot and I could feel little dimples all over my cheeks where the balls on the end of the bristles had dug in. I cried and cried and when it subsided and I could cry no more, I just whimpered and sniffled every now and then.

It got past tea time and I knew that no one was coming to get me, so I got undressed and put my pyjamas on. I got into bed and because it was still light enough to read, I looked at the pictures in one of my Enid Blyton books. Robin was there, going about his adventures in his posh sandals with his rosy cheeks and all I could think of was what had he had for dinner when his grandad called him in.

And now, here, in the stinking midden that belonged to my brother, wearing a paper suit with the hood up, a pair of latex gloves and a facemask, I was looking at that hairbrush from nearly sixty years ago.

Questions leapt into my mind. What was he doing with it? How did he know there was significance to it? How long had he known? Who else knew? Did my father broadcast to everyone what had happened? What he'd done? Did my mum know? Grandma or grandad? Why was nothing ever said about it by anyone? Ever? And why the fuck was my brother saving it in a boot box full of mementoes? All questions that I would never have answers to. Or so I thought.

I picked the brush up and threw it into the current bucket, the one waiting to go to the skip. I picked it up, took it to the skip outside and upended it, waiting until the stuff slid and settled and when it had and I could still see the brush, I climbed into the skip and kicked rubbish over it.

I went back upstairs to the midden and looked into the boot box and the next thing I picked up was wrapped in a blue handkerchief. I unwrapped it and the item in my hand acted like a magic portal, instantly drawing me back into a strange place where two pictures flashed and clashed with each other, *fought* with each other, vying for dominance. The first picture was a happy one and the other picture…wasn't.

The item was a snow globe. Inside the snow globe, quite bizarrely, was an igloo and a little fir tree and, granted, nothing too bizarre there, but, instead of a Father Christmas or a polar bear completing the scene, Popeye and Bluto were poised, ready to knock seven kinds of shite out of each other. Now *that* was bizarre.

I loved the snow globe and remembered that my Auntie Marie had bought it for me. It had lived on my little bedside table for quite a while until I threw it away in a fit of, I dunno, temper? I don't think so. Anger? Again, I didn't think so. I threw it away, I think, because I *needed* to. I'd seen something in the snow globe that I didn't want to see and once I'd seen, it couldn't be unseen and so I chucked it out.

And now here it was. Back in my hand.

1965

It was a summer's day but cool and slightly overcast. The council had been clearing some ground up at the top of our road, next to The Grange. The Grange was a big, rambling sandstone house that, at one time, before the 1960's Liverpool slum clearances, must have been an incredibly imposing residence. But now, it was black, like sandstone goes after years of exposure to stuff in the air. Black with emerald green 'spillages' of moss down the walls from leaking gutters and dripping gargoyles that sat atop the corners and various eaves of the roof. The gargoyles were scary when you really looked at them, which was something I did on a regular basis. All protruding eyes and huge canines, and one of them had horns, like the devil. I was always studying things up above me, I don't know why, especially clouds, rooftops and treetops. I still do. Looking for snipers, *my mate Tich used to say. His name might not have been spelled like that, but that's the way I'm going to display it here. His real name was O'Reilly...but he became known as Tich because he wasn't very tall. His first name was David, not Dave, never Dave. No-one used his first name except his mum, and only ever the full version. David. Tich was small, but I'll tell you what, he was a tough, strong little fella. Really strong. I was bigger than him, just, but didn't get the better of him very often in a wrestling match. You don't see young lads wrestling like we used to do back in the day. Wrestling was something that, as a young boy, you just naturally did, almost from the time you could walk. In fact, to be honest (NOT a lie coming up), I can't actually remember a time when I didn't wrestle as a youngster. I seem to have a memory of me wrestling my mum when she was trying to change my nappy. Mind you, I* was *twelve. Just kidding. Funny how some kids do that though isn't it. Try to escape from getting their nappy changed. I can remember both my daughters doing it. Really funny it was but amazing how strong a little baby can be. I don't wrestle too often these days, unless Pam has attempted a coup on the TV remote, which she does from time to time. She's another little person who is tough and strong. Little tiny woman, very strong. Like Mighty Mouse. Not that I've ever wrestled with Mighty Mouse. Tich was my best mate for a number of* years. He had an elder brother who he used to wrestle with a lot so that could explain why me and him nearly always ended up like some strange eight limbed beast with two heads. In a stalemate of grips and holds that couldn't be broken. Good fun.

Tich's dad was fond of the pub, like mine. A heavy man with an ugly face and greasy dark coloured hair. Straight out of a Dickens novel he was. He stunk. Greasy, beery, sweaty. A dangerous smell. I was scared of him. As I was of all men. I mean, I'm not now but back then I was. Very wary of men, very wary indeed. Mind you I am still very wary of men. And I hope that some men are very wary of me too. That is the air I try to give off anyway. I don't necessarily like it but that is…just me. I'm built that way. All part of the defence strategy, I think. Probably a head doc could put me right on that, not that I need putting right because I'll still be me but, maybe better educated. Knowing the whys and wherefores would probably not stop me from doing what I think I need to do in life.

Tich was a strange fella when I think about him. We were always climbing trees. Before the slum clearances we, by which I mean us kids, not me and Tich, used to climb on top of the yard walls and run along them, leaping across the back entries. We used to come out of our own house, climb onto the wall and run down it, turn sharply along it when you got to the entry, run along the entry wall, leap the entry itself if you needed to, then run to the back wall of your mate's house, turn up the yard wall and run up to the back kitchen window and knock on it. Invariably you could see down into the back kitchen and your mate would look up at you, you'd motion with your head for him to come out and he'd come out and sort of slide up onto the wall next to you. It was

all a bit surreal when I think about it now but back then, you spent a lot
of time on the walls. It saved opening the gates I suppose.

Once we were cleared from living in the slums and shipped out to the
country, as we thought of it, there were no walls. Just hedges and fences.
We tried to climb them but it wasn't easy. They don't keep still for long
enough. But we could climb the trees and climb them we did. We spent a
lot of time in the trees. There was one particular road that had a row of
trees. I can't remember what type of trees they were. Wooden ones
probably. I never knew what they were called, so it's no wonder I can't
remember what they were. They were just trees. There must have been
twenty of them. It was always our aim to travel along the whole road
without touching the floor. Not many of us managed to do it. My brother
Dan was the first. I seem to recall that he did it at the first attempt as
well. He was brilliant at climbing trees and the only thing I ever wanted,
or so it felt at the time, was to be able to climb a tree like my brother.
Eventually I managed it but I had to grow a bit to be able to reach across
some of the gaps. Tich was a champion tree climber. The fastest tree
climber in the whole of our part of Halewood. Plus he was not afraid of
anything. Not even death. Many's the time we would shinny up a big tree
and climb up to quite a height quite fast. But Tich was always up there
the fastest, and often, when you caught up to him, he would then move
higher into it, daring you to follow him. I only ever went as high as my
capability and my courage would take me. But Tich would just go up and
up, sometimes so far up that he could stick his head out of the canopy at
the top. When he was there he would sway the branches madly, almost
like he was trying to shake himself out of it. It was scary to watch but he
became friends with some of the bigger lads through his daring. Another
of his daring tricks was to climb up on the wall of a railway bridge and

sprint along it, jumping off at the end. And when I say sprint I mean just that. Me? I wouldn't even climb onto the wall never mind sprint along it.

So anyway, it was a summer's day but cool and slightly overcast. The council had been clearing some ground up at the top of our road, next to The Grange and had made a large hill of rubble and compacted earth. It was probably supposed to have been moved away but stayed there for months. And it was heaven for us. We played on it and around it, all day, every day. We even walked up and over it on the way to and from school...it was that tempting. One of our favourite games, if not the favourite game, was King of the Castle. There was a song or a chant that went with this game. It went,

'I'm the King of the Ca-stle,
Get down you dirty ra-scal!'

The idea of the game was that a load of you 'assaulted' the hill and once at the top you fought for dominance of the hill by throwing everyone else down it, usually, if you had the breath, shouting out the chant and trying to time the 'Get down you dirty ra-scal!' line with the actual throwing of an opponent. It was a great game and we loved it and would play it for hours, ending up filthy and sweaty. You could play it as an individual or as a team. I always preferred the team game. Me and my brother Dan were World Champions...absolutely unbeatable. Me and Tich were a good team as well. But when me, our Dan and Tich were on the same team, well, we were like a Viking horde, a Roman Legion and the Desert Rats all rolled into one. No one could take that hill from us when we were at the top. No one. And if we weren't at the top, well, we just took it off you. Just like that. Some teams, when they were working out how to eject you from the top, came up with fancy Dan ideas of outflanking and making swerving runs designed to split your forces. We never did any of that stuff. We just went for the full blooded frontal assault. Straight up the hill, straight into the massed ranks of the enemy (there was only room on the top for three, maybe four but to us they were massed ranks) and throw them straight off the top. It got to the stage where, if we came along, if we were just walking over to the newsagents to get some chewie and a team was on the top, they would just come down and slink off into the long grass. We were like lions coming to the kill made by a pack of hyenas. The hyenas sloped off and watched from afar. Occasionally a few brave ones would attempt to take the hill from us but we were just too good.

And on this cool, slightly overcast summer's day, exactly that was occurring. We three were Kings of the Castle and a pack of hyenas were trying to take it from us. We were throwing them off and pushing them down and wiping the dust and sweat from our faces with the sleeves of our tee shirts. We were chanting the chant and completely dominating the hill when I caught sight of a man walking down the road, towards where we lived. The man didn't look over or show any interest in us but I recognised our father. It was too early for him to be coming home from work but I knew it was him. He had a folded newspaper sticking out of his pocket. He used to do that on a Saturday when he was off work and going over to the bookies and pub, have the paper sticking up out of his pocket, folded to the racing pages. It was definitely him; I could tell from his straight-backed almost regal way of walking. Head held level and shoulders square, his gait measured and steady, eating up the ground without looking fast. I told Dan that dad had just walked past. He hadn't noticed and told me to never mind and get on with defending the hill. I was worried because the folded newspaper and the earliness of him *showing up, signified things to me. It told me that work had finished early, he'd been sacked or laid off or was on strike. It told me that he'd had time to study the horses, maybe even been to the bookies. Which, to me, meant that he'd had a drink or two. Maybe not but maybe so. Nevertheless I got on with defending the hill, just like my brother told me to.*

A minute later, our younger sister Carla came running up fast. 'Me dad wants yer.' she shouted.
My hope was that he wanted Dan, not me. 'Who?' I shouted, as I threw an enemy down the hill and wiped sweat from my forehead.
'Both of yer.' she said.

We instantly stopped what we were doing and walked down the hill, not saying a word to each other or anyone else. We didn't even look at each other. We were now locked into our own worlds, intent only on getting through the next minute and when that one was dead, the one after that. As we walked away we heard the howls of mixed delight and indignation as Tich was picked up and thrown down the hill by the new Kings of the Castle.

On the way to our house, maybe a hundred and twenty yards, my instinct told me we were in trouble, but I couldn't think why. I knew our bedroom was clean and tidy because we'd done it that morning. I knew the grass was cut because we'd done it only a day or two before, Dan on the shears, me on the scissors. I still had the remnants of the blister on my thumb. So I couldn't think of any reason we'd be in trouble. Logic, my friend, and enemy, often in equal measures, therefore told me that we were being summoned to be congratulated for being such heroic Kings of the Castle. Almost as soon as that thought bloomed in my head it was rejected. Our dad never congratulated us on anything so it couldn't be that. It wouldn't be that. Before another useless thought bloomed in my head, we were in the world of our house and the door was closed behind us by our mum. Her face was flushed. She told us to go up to our bedroom.

At first, I thought we had been sent to bed and was relieved, even though it was only mid-afternoon. Getting sent to bed was a punishment in itself and if I was going to be punished, even though I'd done nothing wrong, then getting sent to bed was a sentence I would happily carry out. Much better than the alternatives.

Dan went into the bedroom first and as I followed a step or two behind, I saw his body tense up in front of me and knew that our dad was already inside.

He told us to take our trousers down and lie face down on the bed, which we did. Then he told us 'Underpants as well'. Which we did. Lying next to my big brother on the bed, bare arses looking up at the ceiling, I felt incredibly vulnerable, incredibly exposed, which, of course, I was. Nothing was happening behind us, which puzzled me. I heard the door open very quietly and then close and I thought that he had gone, that it was some kind of joke, which, if it was, I would have had to laugh at and find hilarious. But I wasn't going to be the one to turn around and check. My big brother could do that. That's what big brothers are for.

And then I noticed that Dan was looking at the snow globe on the little table at the side of my bed, the bed we were lying on. Popeye and Bluto were squared up to each other in the globe, just about to have a set-to. Popeye was a hero of mine. I wanted muscles like him, especially the ones with the battleships firing broadsides. And as I looked at the snow globe myself, I could see what Dan was looking at. It was something you could either see or you couldn't, one of those things where you can either see one thing or the other but not both at the same time. In this case, you could either just see Popeye, Bluto and the igloo or you could see that both my mum and dad were standing behind us reflected in the globe. Just standing there.

The belt landed on me first. Hard and sudden. Sharp and stinging. I almost cried out, which would have been a really stupid thing to do. My fists gripped the yellow candlewick bedspread and, with each stripe laid onto my body, twisted the fabric into tight little folds. I noticed that my brother's hands didn't move, his fingers remaining perfectly spread out. Relaxed looking. I copied him, letting go of the bedspread. I even started to surreptitiously straighten it out but I think my dad noticed and laid the next stripe with more of a sting. I had to be content with the calmly spread fingers. The striping stopped and the room was silent. I heard a little click and then the door opened and closed very quietly. The little click, I knew, was the noise my mum's ankles made sometimes when she moved or turned. I now know that the noise is most commonly caused by a tendon slipping over the bone. Wikipedia. So I knew my mum had left. I checked in the snow globe. She had gone but our dad was still there, just looking at us. What seemed like an age later, he turned and walked out, leaving us lying on the bed.

We got up and dressed ourselves. When we were dressed, we looked at each other. I picked the snow globe up and gave it a good shake. Popeye and Bluto glared at each other in the snowstorm. My arse and lower back were burning, and I could feel the ridges under my shirt. We couldn't sit down so we stood by the window and looked at the world *outside. Funny how people can be walking past smoking a ciggy or talking to a companion, ordinary things going on just a few feet away in a world that is different from the one you peer out of. Funny how life just keeps happening but yours sometimes stops. Tich was sitting on the pavement outside our garden gate, throwing little stones into the road. He must have felt us watching because we made no sound, but he turned and looked up. He motioned with his head for us to come out. I shook my head slightly. Dan just stared out. Tich raised his chin almost imperceptibly, a knowing acknowledgment that we were 'indisposed'. He stood, put his hands in his pockets and sauntered off up the road.*

I could hear sounds coming from another part of the house. I couldn't quite work out what kind of sounds they were, but they were human sounds. Sounds of a voice or voices but heavily muffled or quieted. We both silently crept towards our door though we weren't brave enough to open it. We put our ears to it and strained to hear. It was hard to make out anything but in amongst the sounds I heard a word which I thought sounded like 'Charlie', the name of our father. I looked at my brother and could tell that he had heard the same. We looked into each other's eyes for a few moments, his blue eyes looking into my blue eyes, not blinking, not flinching, then Dan moved his head in the direction of the window and we returned to watching the world slide past our house.

We never played King of the Castle again. We never even mentioned it. But we retired as unbeaten champs. Tich, my little friend, never got to be a man. He was killed by a train on the Hunts Cross line. The local newspaper reported that the train driver said he ran along and then jumped off the parapet wall of the bridge.

I sat on my toolbox and thought about Tich for a few minutes. I could see him, his wavy fair hair, bright blue eyes and slightly protruding teeth. As a person, he was very quiet and thoughtful, and, really, was a great mate to have, though I had managed to spoil that friendship by being stupid. I hoped that he had died as a result of misjudgment rather than a desire to die.

The boot box was turning out to be a bit of a Pandora's box. There were some old birthday cards for my mum. I opened the first one and it simply said, "Happy Birthday Mam, Dan, xx". I put it into our document box. I thought my sisters might like to see it. Underneath the cards, was a travel chess set and I picked it up. I remembered it well and opened it. I couldn't believe it was the same set from all those years ago, it looked so new. Even the cardboard sleeve that the set was in looked like new.

Early 1960's

So, every Friday, and I don't know why Friday was the day for this…event…so don't even bother to ask me why…every Friday was chess night. My father would have his tea, eating with his plate on the arm of the chair, drink his mug of tea and smoke a roly, then say to me 'Get the chess board out then Joe.'

The chess board was Dan's little travel set, pocket sized, and contained draughts and chess. Each square of the board had a hole in the middle of it and each piece had a little peg that fitted in the hole. Dan was brilliant at draughts, but I don't think he could play chess. I don't ever remember him playing it. I certainly never played him at it anyway. I never beat Dan at draughts, not even once. I didn't even come close. I never saw our father play Dan at draughts. He may have done but I never saw it happen. There was never a conversation between Dan and me about it, so I assume it just never happened. Dan, as far as I'm concerned, was lucky if our father didn't play a one on one game against him because it was horrible. I hated it. It scared me.

So anyway, my father had learned that I was in the school chess team and decided that Friday, after he'd had his tea, was chess night. And once he decided that something would happen, then it would happen. No matter what it was or what time it was or whether or not something else was happening...it didn't matter...if my father decided something would happen, it happened.

I was pretty good at chess. I learned it because my girlfriend could play it and she was in the school chess club. So, I joined, either to be with her or to impress her, or to make sure no other lad muscled in on her. I can't exactly remember which. We were ten.

My girlfriend, Margaret, taught me to play and I beat her in the first game we played. She called it beginner's luck. *I thought she was saying* beginners, look, *luck being how we pronounced look, and I didn't have a clue what that meant. I'd never come across it before. Mind you, even if I'd known she was saying* beginner's luck *and not* beginners look, *I still wouldn't have known what she was talking about because I'd never come across* beginners luck *before either. Anyway, we played another two games and I won them both. And then I beat Clank. Clank was a tall freckly lad with a mop of gingery hair who just reminded us of a cartoon robot from one of the comics, the Dandy, I think. The robot's name was, you guessed it, Clank. Clank was the captain of the school chess team. And so, Mr Carstairs, the boss of the chess club, wanted to 'measure' me and Clank was to be my yardstick. I beat him, Mr Carstairs was impressed, and I was in the school chess team. I don't know who I deposed from the team because it just didn't occur to me to find out. I was only there to keep an eye out for my woman. I'm thinking now that it was probably Margaret that I deposed because soon after I was named as a team member, she dumped me. Or started hanging about with someone else, I can't remember who. Probably Clank.*

Chess was something I took to very naturally. Layered thinking is the key. For me anyway. Layered thinking is what I do. I'm not saying I do it well or even successfully, but it's what I do. As you may have noticed. I haven't played chess for many years now so would be useless probably and, to be fair, I was never a great chess player. But I was good. Ish. Yeah, goodish probably sums my chess career up quite well.

So, like I said, my father got to know about it somehow. I certainly didn't tell him. My father, our father, wasn't the kind of father you would rush home to so that you could excitedly tell him you did this or that and got a gold star for it. My father just wasn't the kind of man who took pride in his kids doing anything well. My father wasn't the kind of father that, as a kid, you even spoke to if you could get away with it. I was always scared having anything to do with my father, on any level. I could easily be part of a group of people having some sort of relationship with my father but one on one... that was really difficult. Horrible. Scary. Mostly terrifying. Yeah, that sums it up. Mostly terrifying. I hated finding myself in the position of one on one with my dad. In fact, I hated my dad. I would have killed him if I could have gotten away with it.

Anyway, the Friday night chess game. He beat me every time. Every Friday night it was the same story. He beat me. But I was getting better. I was playing a lot of chess in school and in matches against other schools and I was improving all the time. My layered thinking was becoming more and more layered.

When I learned the game in the chess club, I was taught to always shake the hand of your opponent and always say the same words, whatever the outcome. I was taught to say, 'well played'. I was taught to never gloat after a victory. Mr Carstairs used to say to us that there was only one thing worse than a bad loser and that was a bad winner. And so, I have carried that simple little maxim through my life, losing and winning with dignity. Always.

My father won the Friday night chess match all the time and every single time he would wink at me and smile, sometimes laugh and say something like, 'Gotta get up earlier if you wanna beat me Joe' *or* 'you'll have to be a lot smarter than that if you wanna beat me.' *Never once did he shake my hand or say, 'well played'. Not even once. But I was getting better. And better.*

And so, inevitably, it happened…we were playing the Friday night game. The travel set was on the arm of his chair and, as usual, I sat on a little foot stool in order to play. The game was well under way. He was being his usual cocky self, making his moves fast and then sitting waiting for me to work out what I wanted to do. If I took too long, he would make little noises with his mouth. Or take a deep breath and expel it noisily from his nose. Little signs of annoyance that would always worry me. I mean, properly worry me, properly scare me.

I saw the possibility of a trap…but it seemed to be too obvious. Nevertheless, I set the wheels in motion and started to set the trap. I think, looking back, that it started life, the trap that is, as a snare to get one of his valuable pieces but, as the game moved on, I realised that he hadn't seen it. That he was too intent on his own moves and was being dismissive of mine. Or maybe, I thought, has he sussed out what I'm up to and was setting a better trap of his own? Was I walking into his trap? Getting too excited about my own?

I studied the board. Hard. I could see what he was up to and, it was nothing that I hadn't already seen...there didn't seem to be any cunning plan under his obvious intentions. But then, I couldn't believe that he hadn't seen the trap I was setting for him. And so, I studied the board even harder. He started his usual tricks when I was taking too long. The nose breathing. The little fidgets. He even rolled himself a cigarette and blew the smoke over me, which, to be fair, I didn't mind because I liked the smell of rolling tobacco smoke and had ambitions to become a smoker.

I decided that I was 'in charge' *of his plan against me and turned my full attention to my attack on his piece. It became apparent that if he carried on with his intended target that, not only would he clear the way for me to carry out my planned attack but, in so doing, would also make a possible fatal error and open the way for an attack on his king.*

I made my next move and, sure enough, he unwittingly blundered on with his plan. I made my following move and now, suddenly, he became aware that he was in trouble.

He had made a fatal move and I could see that a check mate was just a handful of moves away. And I could see that he could see it as well. Now, the boot was on the other foot. The glove was on the other hand. The hat was on the other head. Now, he was taking a long time over his move. For the coup de grace to not happen, it would need me to have not realised the position of the game and make a wrong move, letting him off the hook, or to bottle it and shy away from the win because I was scared of winning.

And he set about making me too scared to win. He started a 'campaign' to worry me. That's the only way I can describe it. He blew smoke over me. He clamped his jaw tight. He breathed steadily and audibly. He stopped looking at the board and stared at me instead. Jaw muscles working. Hard eyes. Unflinching. Unmoving. Steely blue eyes. Not blinking. Just staring. He ground his cigarette out slowly and with more force than was necessary, as if telling me what he would do to me if I carried out the obvious moves.

He made his next move, the only move he could make. And I made my move. I didn't wait. I didn't study the board. I just moved. Then he moved and I took one of his pieces. A smooth action. No faltering. Ruthless. I just took his piece off and dropped it in the plastic lid of the travel set. It made a little plasticky click. 'Check' I said. I know now and, I think that deep down I knew then, that dropping his dead chess piece in the lid, rather than placing it, will have really got right up his nose. Such an action would be an affront to his 'masculinity'.

He studied the board hard again. Rolled and lit another cigarette. Blew a cloud of smoke over me. Sighed. Blew smoke out of his nose noisily. Spat little pieces of tobacco out. One of them landed on my left cheek. I left it there. He moved a piece to block the check...the only move he could make and now I had a serious decision to make.

I could make the killing move, or I could bottle it. I pretended to study the board, but I was just thinking. Debating. My heart was racing, beating so hard and fast that I thought it would jump out of my chest and splatter the chess board. I knew that he wouldn't take the checkmate well. I knew it or I thought I knew it. I couldn't see him taking it well. I couldn't see me making the move. I could only see me bottling it. A voice inside me was telling me to checkmate him and to hell with the consequences. Another voice was telling me to not *do it...was telling me that the consequences could be dire, not only for me but for my mum, maybe for all of us.*

I could feel the colour draining from my face. I could feel a tremble beginning in my whole body, deep inside me. I knew that this was terror. I knew that he would be able to see the tremble and I knew that he would like that. I knew that he would feed off that and as that knowledge dawned on me and the thought itself raced through my mind, my hand moved all on its own and made the killing move. 'Check' I said. I knew it was checkmate. But I said check. *I drew the line at saying the word. I was brave...or stupid...but I wasn't* that *brave or stupid.*

He sat there and studied the board. For ages. And ages. He didn't move. Didn't make any noises. It was as if he'd stopped breathing. After a long time, in the quietest voice I've ever heard him use, he said 'That's checkmate that Joe.

I acted surprised. 'Is it?' I asked in an incredulous voice and studied the board. 'Oh yeah, it is.' I said.

He picked the Echo up and started reading the back page. Crossed his legs and turned away from the board. I asked him if he wanted another game and he simply said 'No.' He didn't even look at me. I put the travel set away.

I stood up and stooped to kiss my mum goodnight. 'Night mum.' I said and she responded with a 'Night' that sounded a little bit cut off, a little bit curt, like she was unhappy with me. I did the same with my dad, but he didn't lift his head from reading the paper, not offering his cheek, making it almost impossible for me to finish the act, but finish it I did. To not finish the act, no matter how difficult it was, would have been no more than an invitation for my dad to visit me. And I didn't want him to visit. So, I somehow contorted my body to kiss his cheek. 'Night dad.' I said. He made no reply. Didn't acknowledge, in any way, that I was even in the room.

I didn't know what to do. Do I say it again? Which might attract the wrong attention from him, or do I just walk away and go to bed? Which might attract the wrong attention as well. I decided to meet my fate halfway. I walked to the living room door, opened it and, turning to the room, said 'Night then.' No one answered me and I left, closing the door as quietly as I could.

I brushed my teeth and went into my room. I got undressed and put my pyjamas on. I'd been contemplating ditching the jarmees and sleeping in underpants and vest. Like Dan did. It seemed more grown up I thought. I switched my little lamp on and got into bed. Got my current book off the little table and opened it at my page. The Haunting of Toby Jugg, *by Denis Wheatley. Dan had told me to read it, said it would scare me.*

I was engrossed in the story, reading about the giant spider stalking Toby when my bedroom door crashed open, swinging with such force that the door handle smashed through the plasterboard and one of Dan's paintings fell off the wall, luckily landing on his bed.

My father walked into the room and stood over me. His face was contorted and angry and his eyes blazed at me. I was shocked and immediately started to tremble, my book was fluttering madly. I couldn't think, couldn't blink, couldn't move. I was terrified. He stood glaring at me, breathing heavily, noisily. He lifted his hand and pointed at me. His voice was hard and threatening, 'Don't you ever…' the ever, was shot out, his face twisting into one of pure malevolence towards me, 'get that game out with me again.' He moved closer to me, stooped over, the pointing finger touching my nose. Pressing on the side of my nose. I daren't try to move away, not even an inch. Not even a fraction of an inch. If he felt me try to move away, he would hit me and hit me hard. To move would invite retribution. To even change my expression or to utter a sound would invite further trouble. He glared at me for a minute, maybe two. I could see the battle going on in his eyes. I could see him arguing with himself, could see him deciding whether to beat me up, punch me, slap me, or just leave me. I could see the turmoil in his face. His eyes seemed to turn from blue to black then back to blue. 'Do you understand?' The words were quiet, hard, flat, delivered with an expression of pure menace. His words were absolutely understood. There was not a single chance that I might have misunderstood. Not a chance in hell. I understood perfectly. To mention even the word chess to him would have been tantamount to suicide. And so, I never did.

He glared at me for another minute, his thick finger still at the side of my nose. He suddenly flicked his hand sideways, swiping my nose and head violently to one side, walked to the door and turned to glare at me again. I could feel blood running from my nose and dripping onto my pyjamas. He slammed the door so hard that another of Dan's paintings fell off the wall.

As he went out, I heard voices on the landing and knew that my mum had been standing outside, and all I could think, now that my brain had unfrozen, was that Dan would blame me for his paintings being off the wall.

My mum never did ask me how my pyjama top got to be full of blood. And Dan didn't blame me for the paintings being off the wall. He never even mentioned them.

I put the travel chess in the skip bucket and now I was down to the last three or four items and started to think that maybe I should stop looking through stuff and get on with the clear up. That I was wasting time. And then I thought that all I had was time, and it was mine to waste and if I wanted to waste it on looking through my brother's stuff, then I could do exactly that. And this little argument went back and forth and while it did so, my arse parked itself, all of its own accord, on my toolbox, probably my Numbskulls making decisions of their own for Their Man. The Scarpa boot box lay between my feet, open, the contents, just stuff, stuff that would mean nothing to anyone but one of us, to Dan, me, Carla, Emily, and Lydia. Maybe Roberta and Charlie. Maybe even Grandma Anita and Grandad Albert, whose real name was Frederick. I suddenly felt like I was adrift in some way. I could see people, my wife, my children, my friends, I could see them going about life in their world, a world of colour, laughing and chatting. I felt like I was in a world of darkness, of gloom, of stench, a world of black, white, and sepia. I was adrift in my own mind and I needed to cling to any and every piece of wreckage that drifted by me. My world was as remote as the Southern Ocean and, in the distance I could hear voices, voices that sounded like those of my sisters, of my brother, calling out. I looked about the room and it became a sea, with islands set in it, the island I was at, Hamster Cage Island, and the island in the far corner, my next port of call, Old Dresser Island. My brother had made this sea, had lived on it, had somehow survived without many of the things we take for granted for survival. He had set himself adrift, had shipwrecked himself. The wreckage of his life, the stuff in these boxes, were the driftwood of my life, and I had to reach out and grab anything and everything because maybe one of them, just one piece of his wreckage could prove to be my lifeline to something approaching normality. My hand went into the box and pulled out a brown envelope.

Inside was a notebook, quite an old one by the look of it, an old schoolbook from St Paul's, our school from Kirkdale. It was dark green with Liverpool Education Committee across the front of it. I opened it and flicked through the pages. It was full of his writing.

Sometimes it was hard to make his writing out. He was a scruffy writer, it's got to be said. He should have been a GP. He was left-handed and left-handers sort of angle their writing hand a bit strangely I think, because they can't see what they're writing through their own hand. Or something like that. I'm glad I'm right-handed, though there has been the odd, very odd, discussion over the years about it.

Someone once said to me that I tie my shoelaces left-handed. I didn't even consider that tying shoelaces *could* be 'handed', and I'm not even sure left handed people do actually tie their shoelaces differently, plus, bottom line, WTF does it matter? The only thing of any note that I really know about tying shoelaces or rather, me tying shoelaces, was that I was beaten by my dad and stopped from playing out until I could tie my own shoelaces. I was about 4 years of age. I remember spotting my grandma behind my dad one time when he was standing over me, watching my latest attempts. She was biting her bottom lip or, y'know, not exactly biting it but…tucking it into her mouth and then dragging her teeth over it as it came back out again. Sounds a bit weird when you see it written down but it's the kind of thing you do when you're willing someone to succeed at something, like when England are taking a penalty against Germany. He would show me how to tie the lace by tying his own while sitting opposite me and I would copy him exactly. Or nearly exactly. I reckon it was the last little bit, when you've made a loop and you wrap the other bit around it, thread it through and pull it into another loop. That was the bit that had me stumped. He did it too fast for me to see that it wasn't just a little conjuring trick and that was the bit that would get my head slapped. Quite hard as well. Hard enough to set off a horrible buzzing sound inside my head that I thought everyone could hear, which, I subsequently found out, they couldn't. I learned that when his breathing started to whistle slightly through his nose that a slap was on the way. I tried to get ready for it but, to be honest, it just didn't work. A 4 year old head versus a man's hand? Not much of a contest.

I got the shoelace thing in the end. But in the end, it was my grandad who showed me that the last little loopity-loop bit wasn't a conjuring trick after all. He did it in slow motion for me and as soon as I saw it done like that, it clicked into place. My grandparents told me not to tell anyone that they helped me. You're the first to know. I've kept that secret for over 60 years.

The next time my father stood over me, I was successful. He didn't even have chance to get to the whistling nostril. I thought he'd be happy and cheer or something, but he didn't. He just had a good pull at the bow on my shoe, like he wanted it to come undone and when it didn't and I was ecstatic, he just turned and walked away. So, maybe I tie my shoelaces, sort of like in a mirror image or something like that. I don't really know because, basically I can't be arsed thinking about it too much. I just put my shoes on, tie the laces and get on with the day. It was other people who brought it up. Not me.

The thing about the left-handed question though, is this...take cricket...hate the game but used to play it at school because we were made to during the summer...well, my most comfortable side to bat from is, apparently, a left-handers stance. I'm only marginally more comfortable from that side, so can switch hands or sides any time I want...not that I've had the need to do so too many times in my life.

I'm the same with a golf club. I naturally hold a golf club in a left-handed way. Apparently. Not that I've ever played golf but I've had a practice swing or two with my mate's clubs. It was him who told me I would be a left-handed golfer. There was a time when I would have liked to play golf but, for various reasons it passed and now it's too late. I know you've just said to yourself 'It's never too late!' or something like that but, believe me, it is. And just like the cricket, I could quite comfortably play golf from either side.

Strangely though, it's not the case with any kind of racquet game. I've never played tennis but I've played squash and badminton quite a lot in my life and can only play right-handed. And writing...I can't write with my left hand to save my life. I'd give it a good try if my life depended on it but, I think I'd die. It's like I'm not human when I try.

So anyway, where was I? Looking through Dan's little dark green notebook from yesteryear. This book...it was sort of a diary but not a diary. There were little notes with dates on them but there were others without dates on them so, it wasn't strictly a diary. I'm not sure what you'd call it to be honest. A Journal? Yeah, I think so. Maybe. A Journal.

So, I was looking through this Journal when I came across this entry…*Was allowed to stay up late tonight to watch Danger Man. Joe had been sent to bed after he got his face smacked with the brush. Must have hurt. He was still crying a bit when I went to bed. I pretended to get to sleep dead fast. He broke the rules and you shouldn't do that. Dad went to the Glen and bought me and Carla some crisps.*

He knew about the brush. He *knew* about it. He'd known about it for, I dunno, 60 years or thereabouts? And that brush was here, or *had been* here but was now in the skip. He had kept the brush in this box with other mementoes. Why had he never said anything about the brush incident?

My father went to the pub, the Glendower, to buy them some crisps. He would've had a pint or two while he was there so he must have been gone for half an hour or so. Why had no-one come upstairs to see how I was or bring me some food?

Why didn't my mother come up to see me? Did she go to the pub as well? I don't think so because if she had, then grandma would have come up to see me. She would have brought me a slice of bread cut thickly from the loaf and slathered with dripping and salt. Sounds terrible and to be honest, it is, now, looking back. But I was brought up on bread and dripping and I loved it. Especially the brown crunchy bits. I wouldn't eat it now for a gold clock but, y'know, I didn't know any different back then.

I couldn't understand why no one had come upstairs to see me. I looked back to that time, lying in my bed, snuffling and sniffing, starving, thinking of eating one of my fingers, following the cracks in the ceiling, straining my ears for the sound of someone coming to rescue me. I could hear the birds outside. Could hear the soft mumblings from my grandma and grandad's gaff. I just called it a gaff because I wanted to be a bit hip there. A bit trendy. Me grandad's gaff. It's got a ring to it. I could hear all the sounds and smell all the smells. I could *feel* that house, that time. But I couldn't understand why no one came to see me. If he was out of the house, why wouldn't someone come to see me?

And then it dawned on me. Slowly at first but when the thought started to emerge, it was a like a foal being born. I saw it on the telly one time, a foal getting born. Alien, gangly legs covered in slime and blood, then an eruption of…stuff, and then this thing got up, wobbled about a bit, and galloped off. And that is what my thought did. These alien legs sprouted from my mind, gathered momentum, erupted into being and once it existed, just like the young foal, it was not going back to where it came from.

No one came to see me because…Dan wasn't going to do it, he seemed positively happy with the brush incident, had agreed that I had broken rules and should be punished, he may have actually *witnessed* the brush incident, maybe even instigated the event that led to the brush incident…Carla was just a toddler…and my grandparents and mother didn't come because they knew that if they did…that information would get back to my father.

There had been a stooly in the house. A stool pigeon. And that stool pigeon *must* have been Dan. My brother. My hero. I couldn't think of any other explanation.

I thumbed through the pages to another entry. Again, there was no date but I could more or less pinpoint it to about summer 1965, because I remembered the incident quite well.

Had to stop him from murdering Phillip. It was hard to get him off but I am much stronger than him. I through him and he landed in the roses. He was scratched badly. Dead funny.

Phillip was one of the boys from next door. He was bigger than me, older than me and he'd done something to my sister Carla that had made her cry. She was about 7 years old and had come into the house crying her eyes out and I reacted. I reacted because I wanted to do for her what my big brother had done for me.

Back before we moved to the countryside of Halewood, in our street not far from the north docks of Liverpool, a boy at the top of our street, Lenny, had stolen my Bronco Layne cowboy hat, took it right off my head and put it on the head of his dog, a cross breed Alsatian called Sooty. Sooty was lying in the middle of the street, chewing on a big bone and, fearless as ever, after all I *was* Bronco Layne, I went to get my hat and Sooty, probably believing me to be trying to steal his bone, bit me on the wrist.

I ran home, crying, blood oozing from a couple of puncture wounds on my right wrist and my brother asked me what had happened. No sooner had I told him than he went out of the house, up the street and knocked on Lenny's door. When Lenny answered it, Dan dragged him out into the street and set about him, beat him up and made him retrieve my hat. That was the day that my big brother became my hero.

And so, when my little sister Carla came into the house crying because a lad bigger than her, bigger than me, had made her cry, I went in search of him, knocked on his door and when he answered it, eating a jam butty, raspberry, I could smell it, I grabbed him by his school tie, wrapped it around my hand a few turns and dragged him out onto the front garden, got him in a headlock and wrestled him to the ground. As part of the process of doing this, his jam butty became trapped against his mouth by his tie and smeared raspberry jam all over his face. Once I had him on the ground I jumped on top of him and beat him up and while I was performing the beating up procedure my brother intervened, and, though I clung on, mashing the jam butty into the face of my sister's assailant, he, my brother that is, managed to pick me up and throw me into the rose bush in the centre of the garden, whereupon I got scratched to fuck. Your Honour. Don't really know why I had to put that 'Your Honour' bit in but it kind of finished off the paragraph quite well I thought.

Sitting in the midden on my toolbox in 2018, and sitting in our living room in 1965, I couldn't see any difference between what Dan did for me with Lenny and what I did for my sister with Phillip. But apparently Dan could.

I'd had enough of looking through his Liverpool Education Committee notebook and put it in the document box. I'd maybe carry on reading it later. Maybe. I was pissed off to be honest. It was a good job he wasn't here with me.

In the bottom of the boot box was another tea-towel-wrapped item. I picked it up. It was heavy. It felt like a hammer and sure enough, once unwrapped, it was a hammer. A ball pein hammer. A 2lb ball pein hammer. It was stamped on the hammer head. The last time I'd seen this hammer it had been in my house in Halewood.

31st December 2000

So, the day he died, new year's eve 2000. A day that lives long in my memory. It lives long in my memory because it had been a day I'd waited for, longed for, virtually all of my life.

I'd been on days at the fire station. I got home after my shift and had been in no more than five minutes when the doorbell rang. It was Mick, my sister Carla's husband.

Mick was a nice lad from a nice family. He was pleasant and well spoken, had a good sense of humour. Pretty good at taking the piss and pretty good at having the piss taken. I liked him.

He was on his own and was carrying a small blue bag, like a sports bag but tiny. You could imagine a leprechaun using it for his gym stuff. I could anyway. It looked a bit battered and old, faded, with cracks in the vinyl handles.

I asked him in and he came into the hall…but wouldn't come any further into the house. He was fidgety and said he was in a hurry, had to get home because Carla had his tea on.

He held the bag up to me, 'This is yours.' he said, 'Carla told me to give it to you.' I looked at the bag. I'd never seen it before and I said so. 'Never seen it before Mick. It's not mine mate.' He laughed nervously.

'Sorry, I didn't mean it's yours, I meant that it's being given to you. It's from your dad's place.'

'My dad's place?' I asked, 'What do you mean?' He looked really nervous now and I sensed that he was worried.

'Your dad's place,' he said, 'erm, his flat. Where he lived?'

I was looking at Mick with a semi-vacant stare, but it was dawning on me what he was saying.

'You know your dad's dead?' he asked.

'No I didn't mate, when was this?'

It was Micks turn to stare at me now. Which he did for the count of, I dunno, three or four. His eyes were big and round, like an owl. His mouth had shrunk into a letter 'O' but a little tiny one. I didn't know a human mouth could look so small. But Mick's did.

He shook his head slightly as he spoke. 'Didn't Carla ring you? She said she'd spoken to you this afternoon. Don't you remember?'

I laughed. Not in a good humoured way. 'No Mick I don't remember because there's nothing to remember. Carla didn't ring me. But anyway, thanks for letting me know about the death.'

I actually didn't care about the death of my father, other than I would have liked to have been sitting on his bed when he drew his last breath. I'd have liked to watch the lights go out. I'd have liked to watch that final feeble struggle. I'd have liked to see him at his absolute weakest. Am I cruel? Nasty? Vicious? Yeah I am. Where my father is concerned, I am all of those things and probably more. I felt deprived.

I opened the door for Mick to leave. He didn't. Instead, he held up the leprechaun's gym bag. 'Do you want this?' he asked.

I made a face. 'What's in it Mick?'

He opened it and looked inside. 'A few tools,' he said, rummaging around 'a pair of er, pliers,' he said, holding up a Mole Wrench, 'errr, some screwdrivers,' another rummage and then he held up a hammer, a ball pein hammer with a broken shaft.

I knew that hammer, that ball pein hammer, with '2lb' stamped on its head and its short handle. As I looked at Mick, I could hear the crunch of breaking wood as it destroyed my mum's prized sideboard with the 'cocktail bar' in the middle of it, I could feel the explosive, implosive percussion of a TV screen being smashed. I saw our teak mantelpiece and fire surround reduced to splinters, the Sahara gas fire dinged and pulverised but miraculously still working, the door to my sister's bedroom with five big round holes in it, the handle bent. I heard the booming of this hammer as it rampaged through my life, through the lives of my whole family, shattering and destroying. I could once again see the ten, or was it eleven, I can never remember properly, so let's say ten World War Two aeroplanes, British, American, and German fighters and bombers, Airfix models, all made and very badly painted by me, all in a cardboard box under my bed, smashed into tiny pieces, the box undamaged. It was never the smashing of the models that was the problem, though it really should have been, it was the fact that he'd gone to the trouble of taking each plane out of the box, pulverising it, then putting it back in the box and replacing the box under my bed. A little surprise for me. I left that box under that bed when I moved out just before my wedding. All of this flashed through my mind in an instant.

My father was a pipe fitter welder by trade. In his home tool kit, which was sparse, was a 2lb ball pein hammer, the one Mick had just gotten out of the bag. The hammer was in his home tool kit, instead of his work one, because the handle was a bit short. Only by three or four inches but...short. It looked like it had been snapped at some time and then the raw edges smoothed off. Not that it mattered. What did matter was that it was part of his home tool kit. And it mattered because it had a place. A place that it could not be moved from unless he was the one moving it. To my knowledge, nobody, apart from him, ever did move it. Which could have something to do with the fact that he told us he would use it to crack the skull of anyone who touched or moved his hammer. Y'see, he had to always know where that hammer was because when the urge to use it came upon him, he could go and pick it up and not have the time to lose his inclination.

My father used the hammer to smash furniture. Or toys. Or TV's. Pots, pans, even the bathroom sink. That was a good one, when everyone had to wash and brush their teeth in the kitchen sink while we waited for the council to come and replace the smashed one. I've often wondered, what...what was going on in the mind of a man standing at the bathroom sink, shaving, when, mid-shave, he stops, puts his razor down, goes downstairs, face half covered in shaving soap, goes to the special place of the hammer, picks it up, goes back to the bathroom and smashes the sink, still full of water, into little pieces...and then, as if nothing has happened, put the hammer back and complete his shave in the kitchen sink. He even shouted for me to go and get his shaving mug. Thankfully, my mum never said a word on that occasion.

Mick dropped the hammer back in the bag and put the bag on the floor, made as if to leave then turned to me and blurted out what he'd really come for, the question of who was going to pay for the funeral. He said that him and Carla couldn't afford to pay for it and that he thought it was very unfair if others didn't put their hands in their pockets.

I looked at him. Face like a button, his owls eyes and tiny round mouth. I felt something come over me. There was a warmth deep in my belly, that seemed to radiate quickly through my body. I felt something change around my eyes. Felt them become somehow very intense, too intense, focused solely on the man in front of me. My eyes started to take in information at an incredible rate, the set of his shoulders, how his feet were arranged, what his hands were doing, what his eyes were doing, where they were looking, how his mouth looked. My own body started to respond to this information, my feet shifting slightly, moving into a position to move me rapidly. My shoulders and arms started to tingle as blood coursed into the muscles and my hands closed into almost fists. My weight was imperceptibly shifted to allow fast movement towards my brother in law. My body was flooding with adrenaline and the hall of my house evaporated and was lost from view as the world closed in on Mick. Mick was all I could see, Mick was all I was interested in, Mick was everything to me at that moment and I, me, the real me, now buried somewhere deep inside my mind, was suddenly afraid for him and screamed at my protector to stop. At first, he wasn't listening and simply continued his preparations.

Suddenly, Mick's demeanour changed and he seemed to shrink in front of me. He looked down and fidgeted a little. He started to move towards the door, but I stopped him, 'Take that with you mate,' I said, pointing with my head at the gym bag, 'I don't want anything of his.' He picked it up, 'Ok well thanks Joe, sorry to be the bearer of bad news, erm, see you...' He was gone. I heard his car door close and he drove off.

I stood there for what seemed an age, holding the front door open. My fingers started to relax and my hands opened. I felt my eyes become different, bigger, and the adrenaline surge dissipated. The world of my hallway became real once more and I closed the door. I went into the house and headed for the kitchen.

My wife, my first wife, Lucy, was just putting a meal out for me. Spaghetti Bolognese. The delicious smell of garlic bread wafted form the direction of the oven.

'Who was at the door?' she asked.

'Just Mick.' I said.

'Oh?' she said, 'What did he want?'

'Just came to tell me my dad died today.' I said. 'Do you want some wine with the meal?'

And now, sitting on my toolbox in Dan's place, I hefted the hammer, lost in my thoughts and memories. Obviously the hammer had been given to my brother once it had been rejected by me. Why he'd decided to keep it I would never know, couldn't even begin to guess at. Not that it mattered.

The hammer felt malevolent. It felt like I could smell him, hear him, see him. It felt like he was looking at me, watching how I would react to holding this tool. It felt like he was smirking at me. I looked up, away from the hammer, and looked directly into where I knew his eyes would be and held them there, daring him to do something. Daring him to come and talk to me. Daft thing to say but, I knew that had I been able to, right at that moment, if I could somehow slide into a parallel universe, I could easily have smashed the hammer into his head, and kept hammering until it was reduced to mush. Easily. My loathing of the human being who sired me was complete and undiminished in spite of my advancing years.

I'd like to be able to say that the hammer in my hand hummed or vibrated or did something equally mystical, something to indicate its power and maleficence. But it didn't. It just sat there. An old hammer in an old man's hand. Dumb as fuck. The hammer, not the man. A two pound lump of steel and hickory.

I stood up and went outside, walked to the skip, and dropped the hammer in. I went to the car, got a bottle of Evian, and went back to Hamster Cage Island and its treasure.

The last thing in the box was a small black cloth bag with a drawstring opening. Like you might expect to get from a jewellers when you bought something in the erm, jewellery line. One of those bags. But quite a biggish one. I turned it over and it had the word Mitchell and a fancy-Dan logo on it. I had a vague memory of Mitchell being something to do with fishing reels but it was no more than that.

I opened the drawstring and poured the contents into the boot box lid. I stared at what had come from the bag and thought *WTF Dan, WTF mate, what's your game here.*

I took a swig of water and picked up the remnants of a smashed Kodak 110 camera. My camera. Dan had been the one who got me interested in photography. Dan was the one who got me interested in everything. He'd bought a Zenit-B single lens reflex camera and was forever trying to explain to me what all the dials and buttons did, what all the jargon meant, how it worked. I was genuinely fascinated and loved his Zenit-B but, I was still at school and didn't have the money to buy one and if I had the money to buy one, I would have spent it on the best pair of Adidas football boots instead.

I turned the smashed camera over and over in my hand. I could still see, even smell, the tangy grease from the inside of the little machine and wondered what on earth it could be, for it to endure for so long. The tanginess was quite distinct and also quite strange, sort of sharp and sweaty, reminiscent of underarm sweatiness and yet I liked it. Or half liked it. Whatever that means. I mean, I hate that rank underarm smell you get from gorillas and certain people, but this smell, intrigued me. Yeah, that's the best way of dealing with this. I was intrigued. Mind you, I obviously wasn't intrigued enough to find out what the bloody stuff was so strike the word intrigue from this account. D'you know what, I've dug a hole here and now I'm going to get out of it. The smashed camera had a strange smell.

I suppose I'd better go back to the gorilla thing. Gorillas stink of underarm smell, the rank kind, not the vegetable soup kind. I only know this because I got close to one at a zoo in France a few years ago. I actually thought it was the woman next to me but it wasn't, it was the gorilla.

1960's

It was coming up to my birthday and I asked my mum to get me a little camera, a Kodak 110. It was too expensive she said so I suggested going halves and she agreed. I had a paper round and always saved my money, so I gave her half of the price and on my birthday, I got this camera. I loved it. The film was in a little cassette and you just shoved it in and away you went, snapping everything.

That night, the night of my birthday, can't remember how old I was but...maybe 13...yeah that sounds about right. 13 or 14. Could've been 15. Or was it 16...naah I'm messing with you. I was about 13 or 14. Maybe 15. So, where was I...yeah...that night, I put my camera, which had been in my hand all day virtually, on the mantelpiece. On the corner, next to my mum's miniature brass candlestick. There was a matching one on the other corner. I say miniature because, I reckon you could've only put a birthday cake candle in them, they were that small.

Next morning, I came down...it would be about quarter to six...paper round, remember? I went into the living room for something, again, can't remember what, and there, on the corner of the mantelpiece, next to my mum's miniature brass candlestick, was my camera, just where I'd left it, the exact same place...but it was smashed into pieces, crushed, and bent. It looked like it had been stamped on. I stared at it for a few seconds. I know my mouth was open...or agape, though I don't really like the word agape, so revert to open. My mouth was open, and a sudden, massive wave of anger flooded my head, pushing all other thoughts out, swamping all reason. For the briefest of moments, I was actually, physically moving towards the stairs, moving towards the bedroom where my father slept...and then someone inside me, some other person, my man, my aide, sometimes my boss, gripped me tightly, drew me into a great bear hug that I couldn't escape from and spoke soothingly to me, told me that to do what my anger wanted, was to commit suicide, was to invite a wrath from the man upstairs sleeping with my mother, a wrath like no other, told me that there was more than one way to skin a twat.

I knew it had been my dad. I couldn't begin to think what his motive was, but then chastised myself for even considering that there actually was any possible motive for destroying his son's birthday present. I picked up one of his stinking, sweaty work boots, his right one, and turned it over. There was a tiny sliver of silvery grey plastic stuck in one of the treads. A voice inside my head told me to take the boot, just the one boot, out with me and when I got to Mackets Lane railway bridge, throw it down onto the tracks. The other voice told me to not be stupid.

I put the boot down, but not before angling it such that I could yocker into it. If you don't know the word yocker, it means to spit. I got a big mouth full of spit and yockered it down into the toe of his boot. Then I went up to Mackets Lane shops to do my paper round.

I left my camera on the corner of the mantelpiece, next to my mum's miniature brass candlestick, just the way it was. I didn't touch it. I didn't say a word to anyone about it, and, typical of the family I was born into, no-one said anything to me about it.

Two days after my birthday, I went into the city centre, on the 78 bus, to W. H. Smith, and I bought the same camera. I went home, took the film cassette out of the smashed camera, and examined it. Miraculously, it was undamaged. I put the cassette into my new camera, binned the smashed one and put the new camera in the exact same place on the corner of the mantelpiece. I didn't say anything to anyone, nor did anyone say a single word to me about the rebirth of my Kodak 110.

I left it there, on the corner of the mantelpiece, next to my mum's miniature brass candlestick for exactly one week, and then I moved it to my bedroom. I resolved that, if he smashed my new camera, I would just continue to say nothing and continue to replace it...and if I had to keep doing that for the rest of my life, that was what I would do.

And now here it was, 50 or more years later, hidden in the midden. What on earth was my brother doing, why did he retrieve my smashed camera from my mum's copper coloured waste bin by the side of the fireplace? And why did he not speak to me about it? I couldn't fathom it.

I threw it into the bin for the second time, shook my head and decided that tomorrow was another day and that I'd had enough of this one.

Chapter 28 - Excerpts from the Diary

Tuesday 18th November 2003

2nyt start 9:54pm 45 x 6

2nyt late, another Chicken leg on My garden this time! I shouted fuckn ell! And didn't hit Bertie, I just "jumped" him up and down a few times, and he let go. (lessons learned?) I eventually put it in Kittys bin.

Wednesday 19th November 2003

2nyt start 5:11pm 45 x 6

Bertie poo 2nyt Cardiff Drive on the corner where Citreon usually parked (but not 2nyt approx 10.20 pm) Another chicken piece on my garden 2nyt! Saw it after walk (above) when Bertie went for poo no. 2 on my garden. Every chicken piece from start have been covered in some kind of coating and are very greasy. They all have a bone inside which you can feel when u press, and they feel rubbery and return to shape when u stop pressing. The bone feels like a leg bone, but the chicken pieces are different shapes, some look like drum sticks, others look like (thighs?)

Tuesday 27th January 2004

2nyt start 7:15pm 45 x 7

2nyt shouted (the worst yet) at Bertie cos he knocked "my ordered chaos" of mags PS1 games, clutter etc on the floor by jumping down in response to Katy barking. I told him to stay there (if he jumped down he would possibly have caused damage to what was on the floor) and he did. I don't think he was frightened or shaking, but he must have been alarmed and wondering what was going on. It took me about 15 minutes to put them "back" in the nearest "order" I cud.

Tuesday 3rd February 2004

2nyt start 9:22pm 45 x 6 + 112.50

Late morning, went out with Bertie, checked 3 bins, 65 Cardiff not full, 67 Cardiff full + extra box, checked 18 Middleton, and extra bin bag (clearish) put in, + kwiksave x 2ish bags also. Extra bin bag taken out by me and put into 67 Cardiff bin. I slammed hard several times all 3 bins. Met Kitty on her garden she said I gave her a fright. Having trouble with sticking door offered me the key to try. Bertie barking so I cudnt talk. I yanked him up to my head level on his lead and sed shut up! I don't think I dropped him, I think I lowered him. He must have been quiet cos Kitty said "at least he's quiet now", and I spoke to her about door sticking and keys/locks. She had laft. I went in and dun 3 or 4 carrier bags of rubbish + dog shit off no. 10 garden in to Kitty's bin. Bertie has been fine with me from here, so I don't think I dropped him. If I had dropped him Kitty would have sed Arr!

Thursday 5th February 2004

2nyt start 8:52pm 45 x 6

2nyt bin gone, 11am – 12pm out with Bertie by Brenda's, white haired man walking on W. Derby Rd pavement past Middleton Way towards Tuebrook and is looking and staring at me, so I "head bobbed" and looked mad, deranged, and was obviously affected by the alcohol inside me, although I wasn't obviously drunk.

Sunday 25th April 2004

2nyt start 9:39pm 45 x 6 + 112.50

Bertie didn't cry or whimper. 6am. Once again Bertie is frightened of me. Come here! X so many. Wall, "jumping" him up and down caused by him pulling "this and that way" and stopping i.e. he won't go where I want to go. He heads for the wall where he feels safe and immediately heads for the front door and "safety". Of course I am sorry about what I have done. I cannot trust myself when I am under the influence. I have a terrible personality change which I don't like. Being stressed at the same time doesn't help either. 2nyt I cut grass for first time this year. Finished at 9.03pm by sweeping up cuttings. I started at aprox 8.08pm, it was heavy going because of the amount of growth in some places. My grass and Wills grass was long at the time of "jumping". And Wills grass was in full bloom of dandelions masses of them all over.

Wednesday 28th April 2004

2nyt start 9:11pm 45 x 6 + 24 + 112.50

Mind Out!! Bertie Mind out! at top of my voice and cycle bag (complete with heavy lock and chain) raised, then and only then, did he mind out, onto his chair whereas he had just been turning round and round each time I sed "mind out!" I don't think I wud have hit him. But the more I do these type of things, the closer I get to actually doing something and hurting him. I have got to get a grip on myself.

Chapter 29 - Regression

I'd reached the window, sifted, and shovelled the millionth shovelful of the shite into the buckets and skipped them. Now I stood in front of the window looking out on the world and wondered how long it had been since someone had done what I was doing. Five years? Ten? Longer?

I realised that I'd never stood here before, so I was looking at what he'd looked at for the first time. I was seeing his view of the world from his living room window. I looked down at my car, parked in the same place that I'd always parked in when visiting him and suddenly remembered a time when Dan and I had stood down there, next to the car, on a bitterly cold night, smoking a cigarette and having a conversation that had troubled me at the time and that I'd re-visited on a regular basis.

Now that I was looking down at the place, I remembered the conversation like it was yesterday. I'd called at his home, just because I fancied a cup of tea and a smoke with my brother. As was the norm at that time, he didn't answer the door to my knocks. I knew he was in because I could see his bike through the glass. And when I opened the letter box and looked through, I could hear movement, so I knew he was there. And when I shouted through, 'Dan! It's me! Joe!' everything went quiet and I could picture him frozen in mid whatever he was doing, a look of annoyance on his face. He usually answered once he knew it was me but this time, he didn't. I knocked a few more times, careful to keep the knocks 'friendly' and eventually I walked away and round to the front, where I got in the car and lit a ciggy. I was just about to drive away when he appeared at the side of me. He had his coat on and looked freezing. 'Hello Joe.' He said in his quiet, unreadable way. 'I didn't know it was you, I thought it was someone else.'

Someone else called Joe, I thought.

As usual, he never made eye contact with me. They say…those bastards who are always saying stuff…that the eyes are the windows to the soul or something like that and, for me, my brother avoided looking at me because he knew I'd be looking into his eyes and if, as they say, the eyes really are windows to the soul, then Dan didn't want me to see inside, where *he* was, the real him. He didn't want to run the risk that I'd see him. I got that. I understood it very well. I did it myself but, in a different way. I nearly always made direct eye contact with people but also nearly always allowed Big Joe to look out, thus hiding myself from scrutiny. It was very rarely actually me that you were looking at when you looked into my eyes. So…I really got why my brother didn't look at me.

I got out of the car and we exchanged the usual pleasantries between brothers. It was freezing and I only had my car jacket on, so I asked him if he was going to invite me in for a cuppa but he said *no*, that he was *just on his way out*. I asked him where he was going and he said, *just out*.

So I asked him if he wanted to sit in the car where I could put the heater on but he said *no* and that he was going to have to get going *in a minute.*

I asked him what was new and he said that *nothing* was, that *work was work and life was life.* After a while I said that I'd let him get to where he was going and did he want dropping off and he said *no, I prefer to walk.* I said that I was going to have to get going because it was too cold to stand in the street and he said *ok.*

As I was getting in the car he said, 'I've been seeing a psychiatrist y'know.' I got back out of the car and asked him should we go inside but again he said no. I said that maybe we should sit in the car but he persisted with no. He obviously just wanted to stay where we were, on the pavement by the car.

He lit a cigarette. 'I've been regressed and was taken back to when we lived in Germany.' he said, blowing smoke into the cold air. My mum, father and brother lived in Germany before I was born. My father was stationed there with the army. 'I was in the bath and my dad decided to get in with me but I started crying. He got out and grabbed me by the ankles and pulled my feet up into the air and I slid under the water. My arms were too short to reach the rim of the bath and I was drowning.'

All the time he was telling me this he was looking at the ground, one hand in a pocket, the other holding his ciggy. His voice was monotone and flat, very matter of fact. I didn't quite know what to say. I *always* knew what to say but, on this occasion, I was semi stumped. 'What do you mean regressed?' I asked.

He was staring at the ground, motionless, the smoke from his cigarette spiralling up to his face. 'You get hypnotised.' he said, 'Then they take you back to your childhood and it's like you're back there, like watching a movie and it's you.'

I was intrigued and horrified at the same time. For a start off, I didn't believe in hypnosis. I thought it was a load of bunkum. But then, this was my brother in front of me and he'd always been able to educate me, always been able to open my eyes to new things. I needed him to satisfy me about this so I did what I always do. I asked questions.

'How do they hypnotise you? Hold a watch up and swing it in front of you?' He looked at me. Briefly. Then looked back at the ground.

'No.' he said and then stayed quiet. I waited, thinking he was going to tell me, but he didn't, he just looked at the ground. I could see his jaw muscles working, like he was chewing something, like our father used to do.

'So how do they do it Dan?' I asked.

'He talks to you.' he said. 'Gets you to relax.'

'Do you go asleep?' I asked.

'Not really.' he said. 'You're aware of where you are but...' He paused for what seemed like an age. I thought he'd forgotten what he was talking about. His jaw muscles were still grinding away at something. He didn't move and kept staring at the same place on the ground. I waited, conscious that I shouldn't interrupt. He inhaled deeply and looked into my face though not into my eyes. He was staring at my mouth. He finished his sentence as though he'd only just started it, '...you're somewhere else as well.'

'So do you keep your eyes open?' I asked.

Now he looked into my eyes. For maybe the count of five. I could see inside for five beats. I could see him and I didn't like what I saw. I saw many things through those windows, things that I never expected. I saw contempt, I saw loathing and rancour. I saw malignancy. I saw my father. For the briefest of moments my mind was cast back to a passage from a Stephen King book that had made the hair on the back of my neck stand up. It was in *Salem's Lot* where one of the Glick brothers, now a vampire, hovers outside the bedroom window. I can't remember which of the Glick brothers it was… but I think it was Ralphie. For just the tiniest of moments, the hair on the back of my neck stood up as I looked through the windows of my brother's eyes, and into his soul.

'You know you were his blue-eye don't you?' he asked, dropping his eyes back to the same place on the ground.

I suddenly felt as though I shouldn't be there and wanted to get back in the car and drive away. I felt as though I was in danger. I felt like I did when I'd been inside a burning building, protected by all my equipment, when the heat suddenly and massively intensified, which, for various reasons, it does sometimes, signifying immediate danger to a firefighter. I knew I should move away from him and leave but that natural, normal, sometimes stupid combativeness that resides in me made me quash my instinct and respond the way I did.

'Whose blue-eye Dan?' I asked, my tone accompanied by a frown, my own eyes boring into him.

'Dads.' he said, once again looking directly into my eyes, once again showing me something I'd never seen before in him.

Of course, I knew that he meant I was our father's favourite. And equally I knew that it was bullshit. In a flash, my mind weighed up everything that had happened in my life as a child under the 'protection' of our father and I was bewildered and appalled that my brother could think what he thought. Appalled that my clever, intelligent brother, the boy, the man who had taught me so much in my life, who had shown me so many things that were good and lasting in my life, could actually come to the conclusion that anyone, any child, any *person* on this planet could be a favourite of the man who was our father. No one person was favourite to our father except our father. In a flash, I understood that my brother was struggling to rationalise his own life and was attaching a certain amount, quite possible a *huge* amount of blame to me…because…apparently, I was our father's blue-eye.

'I'm not sure how you've come to that conclusion Dan,' I said, knowing that now, Big Joe was looking out of my eyes, 'because as far as I'm concerned, that fuckin cunt didn't have any favourites except himself.'

He looked away. Back down to the same spot on the ground. He'd dropped his cigarette and both hands were in his pockets. Fidgeting. I got the strong feeling that if he took them out of his pockets, there would be trouble and I mentally prepared myself for an assault.

Unfortunately, in spite of my loathing for the 'man' who sired me, I had his genes, massively repressed but they were there, at the back of my mind, lurking and skulking about in the darkness like a pack of Hyenas. I say the back of my mind but, y'know, I need a brain specialist here, to tell me in which part of my brain this thing, this, *corruption* of the human psyche resides. Suffice to say that, here, standing in the freezing car park,

I felt as though the meeting with my brother was on the verge of becoming confrontational, that the twat in me wanted to press the point. 'Did your *psychiatrist* tell you that one Dan?' I asked, infusing a large amount of bile into the word psychiatrist. 'Or have you made that one up all on your own?'

He suddenly looked like a balloon with a slow puncture. His body seemed to sag and I was ashamed of how I'd spoken, of the ruthless, hard edge I'd managed to get into my words and radiate from my eyes. I hadn't meant to deflate him the way I had, I'd only meant to defend myself and challenge his perception. I decided, for about the millionth time, that I needed to work on my diplomacy skills.

He took his right hand out of his pocket and looked at a watch on his wrist that wasn't there and said that he had to go. 'I'll see you Joe.' he said, not looking at me, and walked away.

I watched him for a handful of seconds, a stack of mixed feelings whirling about in me…relief that the meeting hadn't erupted into full blown confrontation, relief that the feeling of imminent danger had suddenly left me and a desperate desire to wash away the evident wretchedness that emanated from my brother in abundance. I got in my car, lit a cigarette, and drove off. A few moments later I passed Dan. He was walking quite fast, his head downcast and shoulders hunched against the cold. As I drove past and looked at him, he looked straight at me and I felt like I could see the whites of his eyes.

Chapter 30 - Excerpts from the Diary

Tuesday 11th May 2004

2nyt start 8:09pm 45 x 7 + 112.50

Bertie and bin bags This morning either 5am or 6am 2 bin bags tree cuttings into Kittys wheelie, I took 3rd one to Margs wheelie but it was full, probably with soil etc from gutter, so brought it back. I only have one bin bag of tree cuttings left to dispose of now. Whilst I have a bin bag in my hand and Bertie + lead in other going to Kittys bin, he annoyingly pulls on lead as if to say I'm not going that way! Or possibly black bin bag may have put him off for some reason? Anyway he pulled several times and I think I pulled him back either fully possibly sharply, but not violently, or part way, and shouted at him but not loudly like Sunday 25th April 2004. I shouted something like "come here!" I think, and I think I also said "you are a naughty boy!" Anyway he quickly went to the wall again, walking quickly and following wall to my front door. I don't know if he was frightened of me, or of me and the anticipation of being "jumped" on lead, or just the anticipation of being "jumped" on lead, or not frightened at all, but felt uncomfortable and wanted to go home quickly (he obviously feels "safe" inside). I let him in, put lead on stairs, I think I shut door with yale lock, and did my bin bag tree cuttings to Kitty wheelie bin and Marg wheelie. I finished and went in and up and Bertie was ok with me no shaking or other signs of being frightened. I sat down next to him.

Friday 14th May 2004

2nyt start 8:39pm 45 x 7 + 112.50 x 1.5

2nyt went out about 11 pm back by 11:15 pm and Bertie either frightened by me or unsure about me. He only had a few pisses for some reason, and then went on "wall walk (shallow V in kittys garden, which he has done several times now over the last several days, I can spot this routine) to front door, to get in. He wants to go in, as if he feels uncomfortable for some reason, but I do think he wants more pisses but won't go for them. I didn't shout at him, but I did "almost shout" at him, saying "come on!" I didn't call his name. I may (only may) have been heard by Brenda, Ken (light on) and Tommy (light on). I also said in a nice voice, "come on," and "this one!" He slightly wagged his tail but didn't go to the tree for a shit + a piss, but just did the "wall walk I'm going home"

Wednesday 02nd June 2004

2nyt start 7.48pm 45 x 8 + 112.50

Both cars gone by 6.05 pm one had gone by 5.46 pm but I can't remember which one. Gold one back by 6.08 pm parked tight by No 4, gold out again don't know when, but back by 8.19 pm parked tight against no. 4. This morning coming in from garden I left tools outside and wanted to come in for something and wanted to go out fast, and I was saying "Bertie mind out!" over and over. I raised my hand at him to move him and he quickly ducked and moved. I don't think I have ever raised my hand to him B4. I wudn't have hit him, and he wasn't affected later on in the morning.

Sunday 11th July 2004

2nyt start 5.00pm 45 x 8 + 22

looked out at 6.08pm and Goldie at No 4. No cars been here until now today, except at roughly 12.30pm when there was a dark to mid-blue car at No 4 + 6 (halfway between the 2), looked like an escort, reg possibly a W, cudn't see properly. Don't know when it came, don't know when it left, but it wasn't here long after first seeing it. Blinds are not open, and they have been in the same position (including now) since Friday nyt (Vertical gap in front bedroom blind – on left hand side at the end by vertical frame – has remained the same since Friday nyt).

This afternoon with Bertie outside I yanked him from a bumble bee on the path, and he immediately thought of the comments I was making from last nyt, he immediately took his "path" via walls and Kittys garden to the front door. I coaxed him back, and he also showed other signs that I may or may not have written down before, the best one is standing on 2 legs (back ones) with his front legs on my legs and looking at me. Other signs are stopping and not wanting to go, but to go in, and looking at me intently and constantly as if to try to watch that I "don't do anything to him", and to get back inside, where he thinks its safe (I think he thinks that there is less chance of me doing something to him when he is inside. He is a very intelligent little dog, and I love him to bits. He still sleeps next to my head every nyt, and cries when he can't get up on the bed.

Thursday 15th July 2004

2nyt start 8.08pm 45 x 6

Smiths clock reset this morning to BBC News was about 2 minutes now only 2 seconds slow plus fast a few seconds. Early hours this morning 1.45am, I nearly lost it with Bertie outside. I didn't drag him or do anything, but I did several (stifled) "Commmme Onnn!" cos he doing his highly irritating stopping dead, looking at me and pulling back, to go in. One or two stifled shouts where done on path outside Kittys, I hope Brenda didn't hear me. One or two stifled shouts were done on path by Wills garden hope Brenda or people in Cardiff didn't hear me. In the end I took him back in, once again his misinterpretations have cut short his pissing outings.

Saturday 17th July 2004

2nyt start 8.59pm 45 x 7

2nyt lost it with Bertie outside on path in garden, side path and even outside Brenda, hope she didn't hear me, I myt even have lost it outside Kens, I can't remember, but he may have possibly heard me from Brenda's. The "lost it" was controlled, I didn't shout full blast, it was stifled but a **loud** stifle. I may even have been heard round the back by Tommy. What set me off was going out with Bertie then a half strong shout — I can't remember what I said (probably fucking Hell!), I was totally pissed off with myself for getting all the way downstairs and out the door only to realise I had forgotten my left hand work glove.

Chapter 31 - Old Dresser Island

Having finished the corner with the window, I'd finally reached the old dresser in the corner of the living room. It was an old brown thing, very 1950's maybe 60's. Listen to me, like I've got even the foggiest idea about furniture. Suffice to say it was old looking. A bit crap. Like something you'd throw on a skip. Which is where I was going to throw it. It had drawers in the middle with a door either side of them. On top of the dresser was a rectangular fish tank, quite a big one, upside down. And under the tank, safe inside, were a number of boxes. There was a King Edward cigar box and I remembered him going through a phase of smoking King Eddies, looking like Churchill, though I seem to recall from some book or other that Churchill didn't actually smoke King Eddies, preferring some fancy-Dan Cuban ones called something or other. See, sometimes I have the facts but not the details and sometimes I have the details but not the facts…and it's probably fair to say that I quite often have the facts and the details together, but not necessarily on the same subject. Anyway, my brother had a phase of smoking cigars. He had his pipe phase as well and had a bit of a pipe collection. I reckon he thought smoking a pipe made him look scholarly, which he was, but still would have been without the pipe. His favourite pipe, for a while anyway, was the one Sherlock Holmes used to smoke. Not the exact one of course. Is it a meerschaum? Maybe. I think it was but this could be one of those cases of facts and details from different subjects. Y'know, I say that Dan smoked a pipe in order to appear scholarly but it could just as easily have been that he smoked pipes because our grandad smoked pipes and he had a collection of them as well. Grandad, that is. I loved watching grandad doing all the 'bits' of stuff he used to do with his pipe, especially the bits with his penknife. Have I ever mentioned the penknife before? The one that I wanted?

Dan used to get his tobaccos from a fantastic little shop down some steps off Water Street in the city centre. I loved that shop. I loved the smell of Dan's pipe tobacco, a lot more pleasant than the shite grandad used to smoke. Looked like a dried up turd and needed cutting up. With that penknife. It smelled nice in the baccy pouch but once he set fire to it, well, it wasn't for me. I had a little go of smoking a pipe but used to cheat by just putting ciggy tobacco in the bowl. And then I couldn't see the point of taking the tobacco out of the paper tubes it came in — a fiddly job — and putting it in this little wooden bowl, so the habit of pipe smoking never caught on with me. I never even thought of buying rolling tobacco, which would have saved me the task of extracting the tobacco from the paper tubes.

Anyway…there was a red OXO tin box as well and also a shortbread biscuit tin with a picture of a castle on the lid…the Eilean Donan Castle in north west Scotland, one of my favourite parts of the world. I'd been there myself, to the castle that is, once or twice and even bought some shortbreads there, in a tin, very similar to Dan's tin. I think Eilean Donan was probably the most photographed castle in Scotland after Edinburgh Castle. And I think I'd taken about two thirds of them, some of them quite good, even though I say so myself.

Shortbread biscuits had once lived inside Dan's tin and suddenly I wanted a nice big mug of coffee, hot and milky, one and a half sugars, and some good quality shortbreads. I couldn't stand the cheap shortbreads you can get around Christmas time from virtually everywhere. Too greasy. Good quality ones were buttery and crumbly and just melted in the mouth, especially if they'd been dunked in coffee. Some of you will probably call me a shortbread heathen now, but y'know, each to their own, and I like dunking shortbreads. I like them without dunking too but a good dunk was my favourite way with them.

Underneath the OXO tin was a Patrick shoebox — I remembered him buying the trainers — quite expensive and he loved them but I didn't. Adidas were my favourites. On top of the shortbread tin was a flattish box, quite ornate, maybe A4 sized. It looked like mother of pearl type stuff but dark purple in colour, quite an attractive looking thing.

I made space and readied myself to lift the fish tank. I knew it would be heavy but I didn't realise it would be as heavy as it was. I suppose smashing the glass would have been the easiest way of dealing with it but I didn't think of that. It weighed an absolute ton and getting it to a sufficient height to clear the boxes was a bit of a struggle but, I did it in the end, though if I hadn't have had rubberised work gloves, I reckon I'd have ended up smashing it into handleable pieces.

I picked the cigar box up and examined it. Nothing out of the ordinary, just a thick cardboard cigar box, a picture of King Eddie himself on it, looking a bit smug as only a king could. According to the box lid, it had contained fifty King Eddies but now it felt way too heavy to contain cigars. I opened it and was both surprised and delighted but then puzzled…hang on, you can't be doubly somethinged when there are three somethings, so, I was thriply surprised, delighted and puzzled to find five Dinky cars inside. Puzzled because they were all mine. Had been some of my favourites. I didn't know what had happened with them once I left our house to set up a home of my own. I'd looked for them in my mum's loft once our father had left but I never found any of them. And now here they were.

There was a black taxi, an Austin FX3, my all-time favourite taxi. Cos everyone has a favourite taxi don't they. My Uncle Jack used to drive one and I loved it. I always wanted to travel, stood in the 'cubby hole' next to the driver, the cubby hole that was open to the elements but he would never allow me. I didn't get to travel anywhere in that taxi, come to think of it. But then, I was about 5, where was I gonna go? One of the tyres was missing. Off the toy, not the real one. I remembered that when I wanted to play with it I had to change one of the tyres from another car to cover for the missing one.

There was also, probably my all-time favourite Dinky car…a Standard Vanguard sedan, black, the one that curved all the way to the back bumper. I loved that toy car. As I turned it over and over in my hand, a memory started to resurface. It had gone missing, and I became convinced that my little mate, Tich, had nicked it. Me and Tich had scrapped about it, y'know, wrestled. I'd accused him and he'd denied it and he wanted to fight and so that's what we did. I rarely ran from a challenge. In fact, I *never* ran from a challenge. Actually, I've just thought of one challenge I *did* turn away from and funnily enough it had been a challenge from Tich...the sprinting along the parapet wall of a railway bridge challenge. I seem to recall that Tich won the wrestling match or was definitely getting the better of it on this occasion. I think I told you, he was a strong little fella, very strong.

The more I thought about it the more I became convinced that it was my brother who'd told me he'd seen Tich putting the Vanguard in his pocket one day. I couldn't swear to it...the memory was there but every time I tried to properly look at it, it sort of slid away again but, I was almost certain Dan had pushed me down the road of accusing Tich. My brother had broken up the wrestling match and I remembered he'd been a bit rough with me when he grappled me from Tich's grip, yeah I remember that because he bent my ear, which was quite painful. What am I saying, discount the *quite* painful, insert *very* painful. Bent ear...try it. You'll see what I mean.

Me and Tich were never the same as mates after that scrap. Understandably so. I'd accused him of something he hadn't done and then fought him over it. But I genuinely thought he'd nicked my Standard Vanguard. I'd been told that he'd nicked it and he hadn't. It was here in my brother's King Eddies cigar box. If I could speak to Tich I'd tell him I was sorry but, that was never gonna happen on account of him being dead. I looked up at Dan's smoke stained and beer splashed ceiling and said 'Sorry Tich'. A little bird landed on the windowsill and seemed to look through the glass at me for two heart beats then fluttered off.

There was also a Rambler Cross Country, an American car with white tyres. I've never been able to make my mind up about white tyres or whitewalls as they're called. Too, I dunno, *fancy-Dan* for my liking.

But I liked the car, loved it in fact, mainly because it had twin headlights and I always liked twin headlights for some reason. I think I still do.

My silvery bluey grey Bentley S2 coupe was there as well. I always loved that car and promised myself that when I was older, I'd have a Bentley. I'm still working on that. Got a long way to go.

And last but definitely not least, my beautiful Dinky Pullmore Car Transporter, or the tractor unit for it anyway, which was the important piece of it for me. I bought it myself at a jumble sale. The fella, freckly face, blue piggy eyes, head like a boulder, short brown hair cut in the style of a monk but without the egg in the nest, wanted 2/-6, two shillings and sixpence, or half a crown. A half crown was a single silver coin. There were eight of them to a pound and at my age, if you had a half-crown you were minted. Loaded. But I didn't, I only had a two bob piece, or two shillings. The proper name for a two bob piece was a florin and there were ten of them to a pound but, y'know, anyone could have a florin whereas anyone who was anyone had a half-crown and I wasn't anyone who was anyone, I was just someone who was no one, but I had two bob on me and I'd gone to the jumble sale on the hunt for toy guns or Dinky cars and a toffee apple.

The toffee apple was sixpence or a tanner and I was going to get one of them once I'd secured my firearms. But then I saw the Dinky car transporter and I loved the tractor unit because of its beautiful mudguards that curved over the front wheels. I don't know why I loved these mudguards but I did. It was why I loved the Austin FX3 taxi as well, those mudguards. I tried to get the price of the car transporter down to one and six because of the toffee apple but boulder head was having none of it. He drove a hard bargain and took my florin off me and as he did so I caught him looking in the direction of the toffee apple counter, the bastard, and that was me done for. No toffee apple today. But at least I had my transporter. And now here it was, my transporter tractor unit sitting in my hand having just been taken out of Dan's cigar box.

I turned my attention to the OXO tin box and prised the lid off it, which came off with a pleasant little cerlick! Which is like an ordinary common or garden click but with that little extra *cer* that gave the overall sound a bit of class. A posh click. It's like the difference between the sound of a Ford Popular door closing and, say, a Rolls Royce. Not that I've ever heard a Rolls Royce door closing, so, let's say a Daimler door closing, cos I've heard one of them cerlicking shut. I travelled in one of those to my grandma's funeral. And again to my grandad's funeral.

There was a sheet of cotton wool across the entire box and I lifted it up. Underneath the sheet was a whole set of 48 '00' scale World War Two British soldiers. Hand painted. Quite badly. Correction, *very* badly. The set had been mine. I recognised it straight away because of the paint job. I remembered sitting at my grandma's table with a page of the Echo laid on it, my paints and brushes spread out. I remembered thinking that it wouldn't take long cos they were only little. And I remembered trying to paint a face of a soldier when the paint on his tunic and helmet hadn't yet dried and grandad telling me I had to wait and be patient. I remember thinking how this painting was stealing my life away and how, out there, on the deadly streets of Kirkdale, there were adventures of every kind just waiting for their missing ingredient, me. I remember getting all panicky because the clock on grandad's mantelpiece kept ticking and every tick was laughing at me because I was a prisoner to my World War Two '00' scale soldiers. And when the sun came out and lit up the room, the ticking got louder and the rest of the soldiers just got more or less dunked in the paint and put to dry. So yeah, I recognised these soldiers from over half a century ago.

The soldiers, in case you don't know, were very collectable to us kids in the 50's and 60's, maybe still are, and I had lots of them back in the day. They came in a nice cardboard box, which I liked, (beginning to think I've got a bit of a thing for boxes and lids), that showed, like, action pictures of the troops within. You could use these pictures to give you clues as to how the little plastic troops would look if you painted them, which, being dead small, was not an easy task, especially for someone like me who was just too impatient for fiddly tasks. I'd only painted mine because Dan had bought a set of Bedouin troops, that were made of white plastic, and had painted his, all 48 of them, camels and all, and had done it brilliantly. He was really good at painting and stuff, really good, whereas I was really good at hunting down opposing troops in *real* life, even at six, and killing them with weapons made by my grandad or even, say, the sleeve of my jumper, which when pulled off one arm and stretched, acted as a pretty good garrotte. My mum used to discuss my stretched sleeve with my grandma when they were talking knitting tactics, blaming the wool from *that shop* on Stanley Road.

Anyway, back to the painted troops. I lifted my badly painted set on their bed of cotton wool and underneath were Dan's brilliantly painted Bedouin fighters. They still looked bright and colourful, like he'd only just finished them. *Very impressive* I thought. I lifted them out on their cotton wool bed and underneath was a matchbox. For some reason, I turned it and checked the sandpaper on the side. It was well streaked. *Been a lot of matches struck on this box*, I thought. Why on earth I checked that and then went on to report it here, I don't know. So don't ask. I slid the box open and it was filled with tiddlywinks. *My* tiddlywinks. My Shoot! football game tiddlywinks. I tipped them out into my hand, the blues and the whites and was instantly transported back to the 1960's.

Sometime in the 1960's

Back when I was a kid, as soon as I was old enough, I became a paperboy. I loved delivering papers. I was always well liked by the proprietors of the newsagents because I ran my round...even my Sunday rounds with the big heavy Sunday supplement papers. On a Sunday I'd stagger along the first street, maybe two, until the weight became easier to manage and then when it did, I'd start to run. Because of this running, I'd be back in the shop in no time and often, when one of the other lads hadn't turned up by the allotted time, I'd be asked to deliver that round as well for double pay. There was one occasion when I delivered three rounds, one after the other. I used to imagine various things that would make me run harder and faster. I was never just delivering newspapers. They were secret documents. And someone was chasing me, trying to stop me from delivering them to my boss. Or I was running because I had to be at the football ground to play for my team in a cup final, like Raven in the comics, who was a hero of mine and looked a bit like George Best. Or I had to complete my round by a certain time or my beautiful girlfriend would be killed by the sadistic swine, usually in a Nazi uniform, who'd kidnapped her and demanded a ransom, which was inside the last paper in my bag. And so on and so on.

I used to go to the barber's in Hunts Cross, Frank Tadini's. He was a great barber, my only other experience of a barber being my grandad and his big pudding basin, and knew precisely what I meant when I asked him for a Kevin Keegan. I was the first in my school to get one and I must have made Frank Tadini a fortune because inside two weeks everyone who was anyone had a Kevin Keegan. Next to Tadini's was a newsagents called Lathom's. When I'd had my hair cut I'd go into Lathom's and get a Marathon and a Kit Kat and eat them on the way home as an appetiser for my dinner. Sometimes I'd get an Aztec bar instead of the Kit Kat. I was standing waiting to get served, scanning the top shelf, the Christmas shelf, when I spotted it. Shoot! It had a picture of a fella who looked like Roy of the Rovers, scoring a goal, blasting it into the net, and I just wanted it. I had the woman get it down for me. She wasn't happy because she had to get the ladder and then climb up it and everyone could see her bloomers. When I say everyone, there was only me. But if everyone had been there they'd have seen what I saw…which was not a pretty sight. Sort of a dull, grey colour, looked a bit bobbly like an old blanket.

I had a look at the game and decided to get it. I put a deposit on it and then went back every Saturday to pay a little bit off and then I got it in time for Christmas.

Shoot! was a game of football played with tiddlywinks. It was brilliant. And I became really good at it but never beat my dad. Ever. Not, that is, until the day I did.

Over the months I'd managed to scrounge a piece of pegboard from the newsagents where I worked and an old blanket off my mum, no bobbles, which was perfect thickness for playing tiddlywinks. I covered the pegboard with the blanket then covered that with an old sheet my mum gave me and I drew the football pitch on it. It was probably about *five feet long and half as wide, perfect proportions. I played it a lot, against my mates, when they were allowed in the house, which wasn't often, and against my dad quite often, but mostly I played it against myself. Everyone used to say that I couldn't play it properly against myself but my theory was this…as long as I had rules which made it fair for both teams, and as long as I played by those rules, and as long as I played every move to the best of my ability, the outcome of each game was the right outcome. And the bonus was, that in one game I was able to perfect attack and defence in every move I made. It was like playing two games in one. So I started to get quite good at it in a tactical sense.*

If I played against my dad he would win every game handsomely. But then, the better I got at playing and the better I got at stifling the way he played by positioning my players tactically, the closer the scores became until one night, not only did I beat him but, I thrashed him 3-0. He didn't even get close to scoring. I don't think he even had a shot on goal. He wasn't happy. He didn't speak, didn't congratulate me, didn't look at me. He told me to go to bed. As I started to put the game away he told me to leave it.

I expected him to come to my room, like he'd done when I beat him at chess, but, amazingly, he didn't. I hardly slept that night, waiting for the door to crash open. The next day I got up and went down. I was getting my breakfast and my mum was looking at me funny. I thought my hair was sticking up from sleep or something and I said 'What?' She said that my dad had left something for me in the coal hole. The coal hole was a little room off the cloakroom, where we used to hang our cloaks, that, when we had a coal fire, was used to store coal. And the hole of the coal hole came from when we used to live down by the docks and coal was tipped through a hole in the ground in front of the front door, landing on a brick built slope. That hole was, you've got it, the coal 'hole'. And so now, everything to do with a place where coal was stored was called the coal hole, even when no coal had been near the hole that wasn't a hole for a long time.

Something my dad had left me? *I thought.* This was unusual. A present! From my dad! What could it be? *I put my breakfast down and rushed to the coal hole, slid the bolt, and wrenched the door open. My football pitch had been snapped into three equal pieces, and the goals, plastic, had been mashed up, the sticks that had a diving goalkeeper attached to them and extended through the back of the goal, had been snapped and the tiddlywinks, dozens of them in different colours for different teams, were strewn across the coal hole floor. The box with the brilliant picture of the fella scoring the goal was ripped into little pieces and scattered in with the tiddlywinks. It looked like confetti.*

I shut the door and ate my cornflakes. 'He said to tell you to put it all in the bin.' *My mum said. And I simply said,* 'I'm not touching it. If he wants it in the bin he can put it there himself.' *This was something that, if reported back to him, would result in a serious beating or worse. But this was something that, there and then at least, right there and then, as I chewed my cornflakes,* this *was something I was prepared to die for.*

I never did put my Shoot! game in the bin. I never even looked in the coal hole to see if it had been moved. And I practiced and rehearsed what I would say if and when he asked me if the task had been carried out. I would have said 'No.' *and if he'd have asked my why, I'd have said* 'If you want it in the bin, you put it there.'

Of course, the question was never asked. And I think deep down I knew that it would never be asked. And of course, deep down I knew that I would never say what I wanted to say. Nothing was ever said about the Shoot! incident. By anyone, ever.

And now, here I was, sat in my brother's living room, Tich looking on, the used matchbox in one hand and the two teams that had fought out that match in the other. The sky blues, my team and the whites, *his* team. My brother had picked just those two teams up from the floor, had sorted through all the colours, the reds, the dark blues and greens, the crimsons and yellows, he'd sorted them out and extracted just those two teams from that famous night in the cauldron of Boddington Road stadium and put them in a matchbox. Why?

My joy at finding these toys and bits from my past was beginning to wane as I pondered why he had them. He must have been into my mum's loft and got all this stuff out. When did he do this? Why hadn't he said anything to anyone? Why the secret?

The Shoot! game...how had he known that the two teams involved were the blues and the whites? He hadn't been in the crowd on that memorable night, so how did he know which two teams to put in the matchbox? When did he go into the coal hole and collect the tiddlywinks off the floor? Was it him that threw my stuff in the bin when I'd refused? I just don't know. I just didn't know. I was never going to know. I was puzzled.

I opened the Patrick shoe box. His View-Master 3D viewer was inside, wrapped in a soft yellow cloth, like the stuff you get in your glasses case from the opticians. The grey plastic View-Master was in absolutely pristine condition and stacked alongside the viewer were maybe about twenty of the envelopes containing the reels or discs, again, all pristine, looking like they'd just been bought. I leafed through the envelopes, remembering most of them but not all and then, towards the back end of the collection one of them stopped me in my tracks — Wonders of the Deep — a picture of a big shark cruising past on the front. He'd bought it. I couldn't believe he'd bought it.

1966ish

I'd be about 10 or 11, which made Dan about 13 or 14. He was allowed to go to town on the bus on his own. But he could also take me as long as he kept his eye on me. One day, during our summer holidays, it was raining heavily, Dan decided he was going into town to buy a new View-Master disc and mum said he should take me with him, probably because I kept asking her when it was going to stop raining. We got the bus from the top of our road and sat upstairs at the front because we loved the view and I could pretend I was driving the bus, though no-one ever knew I was doing this because I did the steering secretly with my forefinger on my thigh, sort of 'drawing' the turning circle as if I was turning the steering wheel. I'd studied the drivers turning the wheel and copied the speed and everything, but, y'know, scaled down to the size of a half-crown.

We went to the big department store in Liverpool with the naked man above the main doors. Not a real naked man, a statue. At the View-Master counter, Dan was turning the sales carousel around and around as he couldn't make his mind up. He could be a bit dithery at times, the complete opposite of me. He wanted the Wonders of the Deep, but he also wanted Animals of the Galapagos.

The woman behind the counter got bored with him and went off to serve someone else while Dan made his mind up. I was also very bored and wanted him to hurry up because he said we'd walk down to the Pier Head bus terminal to get our bus home, which meant I'd get to see the ships on the Mersey, and get a hot dog at the bus station with my pocket money. With onions and mustard. I loved watching the ships on the river, especially the ferries as they battled the tides, and I loved hot dogs and he just needed to get a move on.

Dan asked me if I thought I could steal the Wonders of the Deep if he bought the Animals of the Galapagos. As usual, full of bravado I said yes and he dared me to do it. At first, I refused because I could get into trouble but he laughed at me and said I was a chicken and that he knew I was just talking big. In a flash, I picked up the Wonders of the Deep and pocketed it. The woman behind the counter didn't notice and Dan bought the Animals of the Galapagos.

We walked to the bus station through the busy city centre streets, the sense of freedom quite exhilarating, all the people and all the trucks and buses. And the taxis. Dan bought us a Topic each at a booth by Central Station and we ate it as we walked. I liked Topics, though they weren't my favourite choccie bar.

When we got to the bus station we got our hot dogs and ate them while we watched the ferries scooting across to the other side of the river, dodging the big ships that travelled upriver to the oil terminal at Dingle. As soon as we got in, mum made us some cheese sandwiches with a bowl of soup. She didn't know we'd had hot dogs and, more to the point, didn't need to know. I'm not sure what kind of soup it was. Soup was soup in my mind and I only ate it because I'd get told off if I left it, because the kids in Africa were starving. My mum and grandma were always saying that.

My mum asked Dan which reel he'd bought and he got them both from his coat and put them on the kitchen table. 'I thought you only had enough money for one?' she asked him and, to my complete astonishment he told her that I'd stolen the Wonders of the Deep. She went mad, shouted at me and ragged me round by my shirt collar, stinging my neck where it rubbed me. She slapped my head a few times as well, told Dan to take me back to the shop and told me to put the reel back. She gave Dan the bus fare and told us to come straight home afterwards.

When we were walking over to the bus stop I looked up at him, 'What did you do that for?' I asked, 'What if she'd told me dad?'

He looked down at me and there was a strange look on his face. 'You shouldn't have pinched it.' he said, 'Mam' he always called her mam but I called her mum, 'knew I only had enough money for one, she's not daft y'know.'

'But you could've just put it in your box and she wouldn't have known would she?' I said, then asked 'So what are we gonna do now?' He didn't answer and we got to the bus stop and looked down the road for the bus. I got an idea. 'Why don't we just put it in the bin and pretend I've put it back?' I said.

He shook his head, looking past me for the bus. 'No.' he said. 'You pinched it and you'll have to put it back.'

I argued that he'd got me to pinch it but he said he was just talking, he wasn't trying to get me to pinch it. I knew he was lying but I couldn't work out why at the time. I've often thought about it since that day and *the only reason he would have done what he did was to get me into trouble. But, to me, it didn't make any kind of sense. I would never have done it to him but then, I suppose, I would never have persuaded him to rob something in the first place.*

He took me back to the shop and pretended to be looking at all the slide shows in their envelopes, spreading them on the counter top, the same as before. I had my hands in my jacket pockets, the Wonders of the Deep *in my right hand. When the woman got bored and turned away to do something by the till, I just made the thing appear and pretended to be reading the back of the envelope, then I put it down with all the others and that was it, he said he couldn't make his mind up, the woman got a shirty look on her face and we left and got the bus home. We didn't walk down to the river this time.*

On the way home I chattered about this and that and tried to convince him that I could eat a house-full of Milky Ways but all he kept saying was shut up. *And after all that, he'd gone back to the shop at some point and bought the* Wonders of the Deep *anyway.*

I picked up the shortbread tin and studied the picture of the castle. It was a beautiful castle, no doubt, and in one of the most beautiful parts of the world as far as I was concerned. I shook the box and it sounded like photographs inside. Biscuit tins…a traditional place to keep family photographs.

Our Dan was dead keen on photography and, as was normal for my brother, he was *very* good at it. To be fair to him, and I know this is probably not the first time I've said this to you, anything he turned his hand to, he was good at…which was why I put him on a pedestal my whole life, always talking him up, almost bragging about how smart and clever my brother was. I loved the fact that my brother was, I dunno, *my* brother, that he was connected to me, that we had the same blood running through our veins. Or something like that. He was my brother and I thought he was great. There ya go, put it in a nutshell for you. The venerable Daniel Croft, hahaha, now I am officially talking through my arse.

I opened the tin. I expected the photos to be of grandma and grandad and Avery Street, where we lived with them, y'know, the house, no electricity upstairs, a toilet at the bottom of the yard, the famous 'brick shithouse' and a single cold-water tap in the kitchen, and maybe the debris at the top of the street by the sidings wall. The debris, usually called the 'oller' by scousers but for some reason was called the debris by us, was made by the German bombers when they were trying to destroy the railway sidings on the other side of the wall, but instead, these particular bombs destroyed the top half of the street on our side. Just one more bomb in the stick and our house would probably have got hit. Maybe Dan would've taken some pictures of our old mates in the street or our school, St Paul's, or Mabel's, the sweet shop where the man with one arm and the red beret worked.

Maybe there'd be photos of Whisky, our black and white border collie, named after a well-known brand of booze, Black and White. We used to have a black and white cat with the same name as well, though, thankfully, a passing lorry removed the feline Whisky, thus saving the utter confusion that would have prevailed. My grandma said that it had been a lorry delivering booze to the Glendower pub on the corner. How's that for being in the wrong place at the wrong time, with the wrong name? I've often imagined that grandma saw the cat strolling across the road as the truck came around the bend and shouted *Whisky*! And the cat turned round in its haughty way, as if to say, *you talkin t'me?* And the rest is history, as they say. Years later, Robert de Niro used that line in a movie and shot to fame.

I fully expected the tin to be full of old family photographs. But they weren't. They were pictures of my wedding. My first wedding. I'd never seen them before. Lots of formal ones, y'know, the ones you take at any wedding plus lots of informal ones or candid ones as they're called. I was, yet again, stunned. The thing was this, when my wedding day was looming in 1976, and I'd been fretting about scraping the money together for a photographer, Dan had asked me if I wanted him to take them. Of course, I agreed to this and that is what happened, Dan acted as the official photographer. But didn't, but, apparently had. Sounds confusing.

May 1976

Towards the end of the day, still at the reception, though I'd had enough of it all and was looking to get off home, he came to me and we had the strangest conversation.

'Joe,' he said, 'I don't know how to tell you this but, I've just found a roll of film in my pocket.' He held it up between forefinger and thumb.

'Have you?' I asked, thinking, so what Dan? You're the photographer.

'Yeah.' He said, looking me straight in the eye.

'Is that a problem Dan?' I asked him.

'Well yes and no.' he said, 'It should be in the camera y'see.'

I wondered if he was pissed but he didn't sound it and I wondered where the hell this conversation was going. 'Ok.' I said, 'So, put it in the camera then?'

'It's too late.' he said.

I looked at my watch and said, 'It's only half six Dan' and thought what fuckin difference does the time make to anything?

'Yeah but I can't take the photographs now can I?' he said.

I genuinely couldn't make out what he was talking about and said so. 'I don't know what you're getting at Dan, what's your point?' He held the film up in front of me…

'It should have been put in this morning but I forgot.' he said.

The penny dropped with a massive clang. Or clink. Yeah, a massive clink rather than a clang. 'You mean you haven't taken any photos?' I asked.

'Yeah.' he said.

'None?' I asked.

'Yeah.' He said, moving his feet nervously, 'None.'

'Not even one?' I asked.

'No.' he said, looking me straight in the eyes, his eyes wide and slightly wild looking, a bit scared maybe, 'Not even one.'
'How did you forget?' I asked, frowning a question mark.

He sighed, his eyes searching mine. 'I don't know.' he said. We looked at each other for a minute or two. His eyes never left mine. He looked like he was ready to run.

'Well,' I said, 'there's fuck all we can do about it now mate, so don't worry about it.' and I wrapped my arm around his shoulders and hugged him to me. He was stiff and resistant to my hug, a bit stand-offish. 'We'll get some from somewhere,' I said, 'loads of people have been taking them so we'll just cadge some.' I laughed and said, 'What are we like eh?'

He'd looked crestfallen. Bewildered. I thought, then, that he'd been truly devastated by his mistake and had thought that same thought ever since and laughed about it ever since. Both me and Lucy, my first wife had laughed about it dozens of times. All those poses, all those smiles, smiling until our faces hurt, and there was no film in the camera. Neither of us were bothered by it, neither of us cared that much. The wedding day was no less memorable because there were no 'official' photos. I know a lot of people wouldn't go with that sentiment but, we genuinely didn't care that much.

Now, looking at the photos of my wedding day, May 22nd 1976, looking at the 'official' photos of that day, the ones taken by my brother's camera, the ones taken by my brother, my mind was in turmoil. Why did he lie? What possible reason was there for this subterfuge? I couldn't think of anything.

I sat there with the biscuit tin on my knees, a clutch of photos in my hands. In my mind's eye, I could see him standing in front of me on that day, his suit perfect, the white flower of the best man's buttonhole almost luminescent against the black of his suit jacket. We'd both bought black suits because it was what I wanted for myself and Dan decided to follow suit...so to speak. The black probably went against the grain for some people and I distinctly remember my mum having a lot of a moan about it, but I was the man getting married and my wife to be was happy with my choice and my choice was black, so, just get on with it mum, *I said to her.* And what if everyone wants to wear whatever they choose? *She spat back at me, at which I simply laughed and said that as far as we, the bride and groom, were concerned, everyone* could *choose to wear whatever they wanted, that is what we wanted, for people to not be dictated to and to just do what they wanted.* Will you at least wear a silver or grey tie? *She asked, or* begged *would be a better word. We both, groom, and best man, wore navy blue ties. Looking at the photographs now, sitting in the gloom, the groom in the gloom, it looked like the brothers Croft were at a funeral. And now, at age sixty something, looking back over those years and having more of an idea about what my life up to the moment of my marriage had been like, I asked myself a question, if I'd been raised in a healthier environment, with normal family values and the normal hopes and aspirations that come with those values, would I have dressed more traditionally, more in keeping with the occasion? Yeah was the answer, almost certainly yes.*

The mind's eye picture from that day, of my brother standing in front of me, was bright and real. I could see, smell, and hear the memory flooding out from wherever it resided. Like being at the movies. It was like a slow motion camera tracking my brother's body and movement, his expressions, his demeanour.

He stood square on to me, not too close, his hands up in front of him, using them to express and emphasise what he was saying. I'd always thought that he looked as though, once he'd told me there had been no film in the camera, he was ready to run but he wasn't. His demeanour was not that of a man getting ready to run. He looked sharp and alert, his eyes flitting across from my face to my hands, my shoulders, my feet. He was assessing me. Dan had not been in flight mode on that day, he'd been very much in fight mode. He was poised...he'd wanted to fight me on my wedding day. He'd engineered a situation that, presumably, he thought would make me want to strike out. He wanted me to attack him on that day and he was ready for me, his feet positioned well, his hands were up and ready to parry and strike. Not only was he ready to fight me on that day, I thought, but, he was ready, poised, to 'put me down'.

A spotlight suddenly bloomed in my mind, illuminating an anomaly that had skulked in a dark corner for 42 years, an anomaly that had lain dormant, gathering dust, and been forgotten...my mind's eye camera rewound to the point of him holding up the film that should have been in the camera. It was in front of me now as I sat there and I studied it.

It didn't have a tail. It didn't have that two to three inch tail of film that gets slipped into the slot of the film take-up spool. The film that Dan held up in front of me on that day had been rewound into the canister. It had been a used film. Exposed. He'd been holding up, for anyone who happened to be watching, the photographs, as yet undeveloped, of the wedding day.

He and I were the only ones party to the conversation about the missing film and the photographs actually existed...which, surely, meant that, had I attacked him on that day, my reason for doing so would have been a fit of anger caused by his failure to put film in the camera and that he'd *ruined* my wedding day, whereas, he would've been able to scotch that claim, *prove* it to be wrong, by holding up the film from his pocket and claim that I'd attacked him for some other reason that he already had waiting in the wings. Had my brother tried to lure me into a wedding day fight, with dozens of people as onlookers? It seemed he had. It seemed that he'd been willing to ruin one of the most important days of my young bride's life, mar the day for everyone, the bridesmaids, the mothers, fathers, the guests…all my fire brigade mates. That one simple little lie of my brother's, a lie that he could prove beyond doubt he *would not* have told, would have set me up in the eyes of everyone, that I was some kind of, I dunno, some kind of irrational, sickeningly violent bully, someone who could and would explode over nothing and start lashing out. Just like our father.

Why had he tried to do that? What would it have achieved? And why, having failed in his attempts to have me attack him, had he kept the photos. If the roles had been reversed and let me tell you, the roles would *never, could* never have been reversed, I would not have kept them. They would never have been developed, would never have seen the light of day. He'd kept them. Had left them in a tin in a glass case, safe and secure. Where they there for the protection of his mementoes or where they, as it seemed, there for the protection of something he wanted to, I hesitate to use the word, *taunt* me with? It didn't matter to him now, on account of him being dead, but now, the truth was out. The truth was known. Where they some sort of trophy for him? A physical reminder of how he'd *got one over on me?* The smallest biggest question kept buzzing away in my mind…why? Something else nagged at me and I tried to focus on it but couldn't. My mind kept returning to the photographs and the lie of 1976. I had to leave it alone for now, analyse later.

Finally, I picked up the purple mother of pearl type box. It was about eight inches long, five inches wide and maybe an inch and a half deep. I had a good look at the box but couldn't make my mind up what it was made of. It could have been plastic but I didn't think so. Not that it mattered what it was made of. I opened it. There was a sheaf of papers in it. The top one was an envelope addressed to Dan. It looked like my sister Carla's handwriting. It had been slit open and I took the letter out and unfolded it. I read it and it shocked me but not because of its content, though the content was, or should have been truly shocking. What shocked me was the flat, emotionless delivery of the words. And it shocked me because it sounded like me.

Dear Dan,

Remember I told you that dad had sex with mum in my bedroom that time, well hes done it again now quite a few times. She doesn't want to and tells me to turn away, which I do but I can still hear everything and feel everything.

They have had a big row about it and he punched her in the face again and cut the bridge of her nose. It needed stitches but she wouldnt go the hospital. She just wore a big plaster on it for ages and now shes got a wide scar. I don't think the twins know what goes on in my room.

The other night they were rowing when they came to bed and I could hear her pleading with him not to. They came into my room and she was trying to get away but he punched her and she landed on my bed. He sat on top of her and poured a half bottle of whisky into her mouth. He held her nose so she would swallow it but she spluttered some and it splashed on my face and I could taste it. I thought she was going to drown and was really scared.

She tried to stop him doing it and I think she crossed her legs but he punched her twice in the stomach I think cos I heard it. He raped her. What do you think I should do Dan, love Carla xxx

PS. Answer your phone please Dan

The letter wasn't dated but obviously it was after Dan had left the house to live on his own, but before our parents got divorced, a divorce which became Absolute in early January 1982. So, let's say 1980/81. That would make Carla about 23 or so. The twins would be about 14.

I read the letter two, three, maybe four times. I wondered why I hadn't been told about this. I wondered why, to my shame, I didn't feel anything beyond the words. Had this letter been about my daughters or someone I knew outside my birth family, I would have been outraged and baying for blood. But somehow, for some reason, when it came down to my birth family, I was not outraged. It was like I simply accepted such stories. They were normal. It was just the way it was. It was our life, our way of life. How could we, me, have become so desensitized to such suffering? How is it possible for me, a man, a human being, to shrug off my own sexual abuse by my father? How is it possible for me to put it in a box and cover it all with the phrase 'It wasn't my fault, I didn't cause it.' How is it possible for us all to go through what we went through and hardly even talk about it to each other? I had no answers to these questions. Nothing. For most of my life up to the time I became a firefighter I think, life was perfectly normal to me. I hadn't known anything different, so why would I question things?

Most of the time, our school friends were not allowed in our house, and if they were, they were absolutely not allowed to go upstairs. If they needed the toilet, which was upstairs, they had to go home. And going to a mate's house was rare for me. Going to a mate's house usually involved coming into contact with other parents and I never wanted to do that. On the odd occasions I did meet my mate's parents I was very suspicious of everything said to me and found it very hard to engage in chit chat. And on the extremely rare occasions I came into contact with the fathers of my mates I was always on alert, ready to flee, and usually just left straight away. If a male parent spoke to me I viewed everything they said with suspicion and, in fact, never engaged once with any of them.

Getting back to the letter from Carla, I wondered what, if anything, either of them had done about this force feeding of alcohol followed by rape. I'm assuming nothing was done because I would have got to know about it. Or would I? It took me the blink of an eye to know that I *would not* have got to know *anything* about this horrifically normal occurrence. I wondered what I would have done about it had I been told and, again, rather swiftly came to the conclusion that I would have done nothing. It's shameful to say that, but…and I know there shouldn't be a 'but'…what would I have done if I'd done something? I would have taken my mum to my house where she was safe, but after a week or two she would have gone back because she always did. I could have told the police but they would have done nothing, or if they'd have done something and investigated, my mum would have denied that it happened and Carla would have been called a liar. There would not have been a case to answer, no evidence, but Carla would have now been in mortal danger. Or, I could've taken the law into my own hands and 'sorted him out'…except I may not have been able to 'sort him out' and had I attacked him, he would have got the police onto me and everyone in that house would have backed his version of events, because to do otherwise was to attract attention you did not want to attract, to do otherwise was to place yourself in mortal danger and people tend not to do that. If they can help it.

Looking back now, the people who lived in that house were conditioned to simply accept *everything* and *anything* that happened in it. If you've never been 'conditioned' to accept bad behaviours then, thankfully, you can't know what I'm talking about and I'm sure you'd argue your side vehemently and in almost every way you'd be right…but that's not the way this particular world works…this particular world works exactly the way the perpetrator wants it to. Usually. This is one of the reasons why people who live in such homes rarely speak about what goes on there, and if they do, they do so in a flat dispassionate way, which in turn, either makes the listener disbelieve or treat the person relating the events as, I dunno, a bit of an oddball. The funny thing is, when you come across someone from another household who has been or is a victim, you often recognise each other. It's sort of telepathic in some way. And when you do recognise each other, you tend to talk about your life, something you don't do with your own family, your familial fellow-victims. It's a really strange, not to mention difficult thing to describe but, there you have it. In a nutshell.

A 'for instance' is an anecdote that one of my sisters told me just last year, some, what, 36 years after it happened. The divorce was well under way and my mum, three sisters and Whisky the border collie, had been temporarily moved out of their home, the one I grew up in, for their own safety. They were placed in a tenth floor flat in the heights on a different estate. My father had been left in the family home until things were sorted out. According to my mum, it was illegal at the time to take him out of the home because he was the tenant and the promise from Social Services or someone, was that, once the divorce was made Absolute, he would be evicted and my mum made the tenant and then a restraining order would be placed on him.

He wasn't supposed to know where they were living but somehow he found out. Probably one of his cronies in the pub mentioned that they'd seen his wife in the heights. One day he waited until he saw my sister coming home from school and he followed her, somehow worked out what floor they were living on and what flat number and knocked on the door. My sister answered and he forced his way in. He questioned her as to where our mother worked and she refused to tell him. Brave girl. He opened the door to the small balcony, grabbed hold of Whisky by the scruff of the neck and held him out over the hundred foot drop. The dog screamed and pissed himself, squirting a stream of droplets into the air. If you've never heard a dog screaming, and I have, as one burned to death at a house fire I attended, then it is a sound that you really don't want to hear too many times in your life. In fact, if you've ever heard any kind of animal, including human, scream in fear for their life, a very different scream to any other, it's something you never want to hear twice. He, my father, held the dog that was his, that he had named after his favourite tipple, with one hand, out over the drop, until my sister told him what he wanted to know and then he brought Whisky back in and dropped him onto the floor, where the poor dog skittered off to cower behind the couch, whimpering. He left the flat by slapping my sister around the head and slamming the door. But, get this, he never came back. However, and this is the really disturbing part of a really disturbing incident, imagine the terror felt by my mother and three sisters who lived in the flat, for every single second they were there. Imagine the terror they felt every time there was a knock at the door, every time they heard the lift doors opening, every time any kind of noise was heard out on the landing. Just imagine that. That little story can go in the nutshell along with the other stuff that we put there a little while ago and if I were you, I'd flush that nutshell down the toilet.

I sat, in the dark, dank, stinking room, feet away from where my brother had rotted right through the floor, feet away from where the rats and mice had feasted on him, from where the maggots and coffin beetles had finished him off, burping in appreciation of the food, apparently quite normal in certain countries. Or so I believe. I wondered how I could sit there and make my comments and jokes that weren't funny but, actually *were* funny in a part of my mind that didn't even laugh at them. I'd need a head doctor to tell me why I was the way I was and, at the end of the day, what good would it do me to know why I am me? How would the answers benefit me? I would still be me. I'd still be dispassionate about myself and my birth family and our history in that house. I would still be me.

I slid the letter back into its envelope and put it in the upturned lid of the box. There was another letter underneath, but this one was un-enveloped. Just made that word up I think. Yet another word made up by me that could very well find its way into popular vernacular. I unfolded it. It was the letter, the original letter from my mum, the one that had been photocopied and put in a clear A4 sleeve by the living room door, the first day I came to work here.

I pondered that for a few minutes. Here was the original, in a box, inside the fish tank, as far away from the front door as you could get in this home. How long had it been here? In this box? Why had it been photocopied and by whom? The photocopy had to have been made some time ago but how had it presented itself here on day one? Who put it there? It was a mystery. If it wasn't one of my sisters, who the fuck put it there? Why? I couldn't work it out.

I'd read the letter a few times when I first found it and I did the same thing again. It seemed to get worse the more I read it. I couldn't believe that a mother, this particular mother, *my* mother, had written this letter to her son. This particular son. I'd have loved her to be in this room with me right at that moment. I'd have loved her to be sitting next to me in the gloom and damp, sitting next to me in the reeking swamp that was her son's living room. A room that he had made, seemingly, in the image of his own mind.

Had she been here, I would have said to her, gesturing around the room, do you see this? Do you smell it? Your son lived here, surrounded himself with rubbish, did away with civilisation in here. This is how he thought of himself, as ugly, as rubbish, as not worthy. You told him in your letter that he should return to being human, so, in your mind, as you wrote your letter, what *was* he to you? Your son, your first born child, what *was* he to *you*? An animal? You told him to leave the booze alone before it destroyed him. Mother, the booze was the shit-icing on a cake made of turds, the booze didn't *destroy* him, it was you and that devil who spawned him, you and that devil that spawned all of us that destroyed him. You told your son in your letter, that his father was a better man than him. Your husband was a better man than your son, you told him that. A man who beat you for three decades, who broke every bone in your face with his fists, a man who dragged you along the floor by your hair, who kicked and stamped on you, who raped you, who took sexual pleasure from most if not all of his children, who beat and degraded his children, a man who wilfully set about the destruction of the human spirit residing in every infant brain, this man, this monster, was *better* than your son. You said so. In a letter. *Your* words, formed in *your* mind and set out, by *your* hand, in *your* letter, a letter you then made his, that he could keep, to read over and over again. Let me ask you this, *mother,* what was it that you expected to achieve with your letter? And also, *mother,* how dare you sign this letter off with the words *Love mam* followed by a single kiss. How very fucking dare you?

That is what I would have said to her had she been here. But she wasn't, so I refolded her letter and put it in the lid with the Carla letter.

Underneath the mother letter was an A4 sized brown envelope folded in half. I took it out, it was the last item in the box. I opened it, put my hand in, pulled out a sheaf of papers and started to look through them. They were all mine, or rather, all to do with me.

There were five 'birthday cards' from St Paul's Sunday school, one for each of my first five birthdays. The card for birthday number one had a little boy sitting in a high chair surrounded by three little angels, making them three little dead children come back to life if what I've heard, on the grapevine, was anything to go by, that little children die and go to heaven to become a little angel. All three seemed to be about the same age as me, maybe a year older, all blonde girls, all fussing about me, one with a bowl of food, looked like porridge, could have been gruel, and the other two were amusing me with toys. There was a short verse on the other side, basically telling me, not that I could read at age one, that 'I will fold your hands and pray'. I'm not sure who the 'I' was, Jesus maybe?

The second birthday card had me wearing a golden romper suit and posh sandals. I had a toy car in my right hand. There was an open garden gate behind me and I was standing on the edge of the road. A teenage angel was holding my by the shoulders, either teaching me to cross the road or about to push me into the road. I was smiling but my eyes looked dead and I had golden hair peeping out from under the hood of my suit. The back of the card taught me a prayer that asked the Heavenly Father, for the sake of Jesus Christ, to help me be a good child. Maybe that explains why my mum and my grandma were forever saying things like, *aaah Jeesus Christ!* And *God give me strength!* whenever I started asking questions about stuff.

The third birthday card had me standing at a table, brown kecks, green shirt and posh sandals, being taught to read by a blonde adult angel with massive golden wings and on the back, it told me that on the day of my baptism, which was 13th November 1955, I was made A MEMBER OF CHRIST. What on earth did that mean? There were two prayers as well, a morning one and an evening one, the first asking the HF to help me to be obedient because I belong to Jesus Christ and the second asking the HF to forgive me for being naughty and to always make me very sorry for being so. *ALWAYS MAKE ME VERY SORRY FOR BEING SO.* Fuck.

The fourth birthday card had me quite big now, and at last wearing an Everton shirt. I was kneeling by my bed having a good pray and there was a pink winged angel kneeling with me, looking all starry eyed at the ceiling, probably bored shitless. There was a teddy bear sitting up by my pillow, which was a lie cos I never owned a teddy bear. Dan did, but I didn't. Sometimes I'd beat his bear up when he wasn't looking. On the back I was told that on the day of my baptism I'd been made THE CHILD OF GOD. Not A child of God, no, THE child of God. So I was on a par with Jesus. And I was only four. That is a rapid climb up the promotion ladder let me tell you. I was also taught The Lord's Prayer. Thank God. Where on earth would I have been without the Lord's Prayer.

The fifth birthday card had me standing in church, apparently while everyone else in the picture was sitting down, apart from the angel behind me. I had a book open in front of me and was looking up to where you would expect there to be a plaster cross with Jesus hanging off it, front centre. I had a blue proper overcoat on and proper lace up shoes, brown leather by the looks. The back of the card informed me that on the day of my baptism I was made AN INHERITOR OF THE KINGDOM OF HEAVEN, followed by a long paragraph which ended with *As soon as I get into my place in Church I will kneel down and say very softly so that only God can hear me:*— followed by a prayer thanking the HF for calling me to the church and helping me to pray.

I held all these cards in my hand, a holy running flush, and thought, so where the fuck were you, HF, JC, and all you blonde angels, all giants of the religion industry, where the fuck were you when us Croft kids needed you, eh? Where the fuck were you? I put the holy propaganda in the lid with the letters.

Next up was my Holy Baptism Card. Which was truly astounding but at the same time not at all astounding in my family. It showed that I had been baptised on the 13ᵗʰ November 1955 and showed that I had three godparents, my mum's brother William, my father's brother Terry and a woman called Phyllis Hughes. I knew the two men but not Phyllis, though I had come across her name somewhere but couldn't remember where. The non-astounding astounding thing was this…my mother had told me on a number of occasions that I had not been baptised. She told me, on a number of occasions that none of us had been baptised. Why would she do this? I'd have to ponder that one but, I couldn't think of any reason why this would become a secret. Surely she didn't forget it?

There was a first birthday card from Phyllis with four kisses. Presumably Phyllis my godmother. The card was a good one for me though, a picture of a boy cowboy riding a horse like billy-o, hat nearly blowing off in the wind and a pair of silver six-shooters strapped around my waist. And last but not least was an 'Out of the everywhere — into here' card, whatever that is. It had a picture of a fat naked baby on the front and inside were all my birth details, weight, name, eyes and hair colour but the interesting thing was this, I mean, it's interesting to *me* anyway, I was born at 5.10 p.m. or, on the 24-hour clock, 17:10. Nineteen years later I would join the Fire Brigade and would be given the service number 1710. How weird is that?

What was even weirder was the fact that my brother had all these documents. I remembered going to my mum's and asking if there was anything from my childhood that might be useful for compiling a family tree and she directed me to a box in the loft. When I found the box there was nothing for me in it. Lots of stuff relating to the other kids but nothing to do with me. She was mystified and couldn't explain and then, when she died and we were all there, all five Croft kids, in the same room for the first time in a quarter of a century, someone started sorting out all the 'baby papers' as we called them but there were none for me. None. No school reports, no cards, nothing. It was like I'd never existed.

Yet all that time, those documents *did* exist. They existed in my mum's loft box but Dan had searched for them and taken them away. Why? When? And why was there an upside-down fish tank in his living room that protected all this stuff of mine from the chewing of the rats and mice? Why did he feel the need to deprive me of these documents but then preserve them?

It was almost like he put them in that safe place, deliberately for me to find. Did that mean that he had planned for me to be here, doing this job? Surely it couldn't, because that would mean that he had planned for him to create a midden and then die in it, and somehow know that I would turn up to sort it out. It seemed ludicrous but, in my tired state, in my emotionally tired state, I couldn't see anything else.

I sat there and, I'd like to say that I pondered but I didn't. I just sat there. My mind was empty or seemed to be empty. Had I been able to use my mind I would have known, would have recognised that often, when my mind seems to be empty of all thought, there is a grenade about to go off inside my head, but, as usual, when the grenade did go off, it took me by surprise even though later I would know that it wasn't a surprise. I know I don't make sense sometimes but, how can I put it, I do to me.

The grenade that went off sent me to the document box. I got the bag out containing the bags of hair and I sat there on my toolbox and sorted them all out chronologically. They all had dates on them and the grenade focused me on a date, a significant date that I'd spotted earlier, 210576, the day before my wedding. The thought that blossomed with the grenade was that this date, the 21st May 1976, was the last time he'd cut hair off his head. I arranged all of the bags into date order and it was a fact…210576 *was* the last time hair had been cut off and bagged up. But that hair was mine. It was all mine. He'd been cutting hair off *my* head. The last possible time he'd been able to do this had been the day before I moved out of the family home for good, the day before my wedding, 210576.

Chapter 32 - Excerpts from the Diary

Friday 20th August 2004

2nyt start 9.16pm 45 x 7 + 112.50

roughly around 6ish pm, took Bertie out B4 Kwiksave. Just B4 took him out, adjusted harness, but obviously wrongly. His front legs are always slipping out of harness, cos harness is 2 big. I took him out, and harness didn't look right, but everything ok until I was at Brenda's front. I had decided not to let him go to tree or W. Derby corner cos I'll be seen by T50. Then I thought, well he wants to, so I won't go to tree but corner myt be ok. As we passed Brenda's front, Katy was in garden and a short barking session started. My reaction wasn't bad, but it wasn't good, it cud have been better, obviously my mind and mood were affected by u kno wot. I lifted him out of the way to try to rush him on to the corner, but the harness slipped down his body and must have put pressure on his penis, because he reacted immediately by pulling away, he must have been uncomfortable. It was obvious we weren't going to make it to the corner, and I tried to guide him back down the passage, but he kept pulling away. It flashed thru my mind to pick him up, but I didn't, and tried to pull him towards me, but he kept pulling away, looking at me intently, as if he was trying to tell me that all was not ryt. I was instantly annoyed and shouted at him. I didn't shout loudest, but it was medium loud, I had half lost control of my voice because of the annoyance that I felt, but shouldn't have felt. If u no wot wasn't in me, I wouldn't have reacted that way. I shouted something like "Come on!" and pulled him gradually down the passage, I didn't pull him violently, and I myt have said "come on" loudishly one or more tyms. He did his usual and hugged the wall and quickly walked down passage and into kittys garden hugging garden towards Brenda's window and I think — I'm pretty sure — that I shouted "come on" or "come here" one or more times, again loudish, cos I was still agitated, but quickly calming down, and I didn't want Brenda to hear me or see me as being cruel. He came over to me on the path, and he sat down I think, anyway I think I said to him "Naughty" or "Naughty Boy!" in a loudish voice, just in case Brenda was listening and or watching. I then stroked his head, and didn't pull, but walked slowly towards mine. This was to create the impression that he had been "naughty" at Katy and I wasn't being cruel. Got to the front door, went in and Bertie was having trouble getting up the stairs, going up one awkwardly, sitting down and looking at me. I shouted – not too loudly – "Go up!" He went up one or two more, in the same fashion, and then the harness slipped off him altogether, and he ran up. I can't remember if I examined him then or after Kwiksave, but he was ok and not in pain or damaged. The harness must have been very uncomfortable and or causing pain. He was ok with me. This episode wasn't too bad as regards to ill-treating Bertie. But I still have to work on myself to have a better — and back to normal (when was that - years ago?) frame of mind.

Saturday 28th August 2004

2nyt start 8.54pm 45 x 7

Fell over, lost balance early hours! Write about it! Shouted my head off! Had to rearrange my left hand build-up of games + letters, found missing memory card for ps1, Logic 3, no. 2, missing for months as a result of an earlier landslide due to Bertie jumping down towards the left, probably as a result of Patch barking, or he has heard some other sound.

Monday 29th November 2004

2nyt start 7:42pm 45 x 6

Last Monday Bertie/lead chair boing shout, frighten him but, no quivering I come close to breaking down mentally?

Saturday 18th December 2004

2nyt start 8:38pm 45 x 5 + 39.6 x 2

2day between 11am – 12pm out with Bertie and Janet was talking to me outside her gate about the garden back door at no. 02, and Bertie wouldn't stop barking, so I shouted (but not too loud, I tried to control it, cos of other people hearing me, and also disturbing no. 6) at him and "bounced him" a few times on his lead.

Sunday 26th December 2004

2nyt start 7.46pm 45 x 6 + 39.6 x 3

Went to bed at 6am Monday morning slept till 11am on and off it was good but light sleep. Dreamed about fighting with a man with blood all over me. Xmas nyt (25/12/04) it snowed heavily. Sunday morning around 8-9am (it was light) I took Bertie out and on my garden and Kittys garden he pulled very fast and heavily, away wide to the left onto Kittys trees (I think) and he nearly overbalanced me on the icy top layer. I don't know why he did this, was it cos Kitty had come out with a bin bag? Or was he excited about the snow? Or both? I was immediately enraged, I can't remember if I pulled him back but I immediately said in a loudish controlled but intensely annoyed voice "What are you doing" and a few other things and probably swore and, I think, "come here!!!" barely controlling my voice. I don't know if he was frightened or not, and I can't remember how long he was out for. But he has to realise this business about being on the lead, also, barking at people, whether they talk to me or are just near me. He can be intensely annoying, and when you shout "shut up" or say "shut up" or say "be quiet" or shout "be quiet" and all the time he won't take any notice, it makes you want to shout into the air "fucking bastard hell !!!" "why won't you bleep bleep shut up???" Kitty was wary about putting her bin bag in the bin in case she slipped so I said to her that I would do it, and I did.

Chapter 33 - Wall Drawings

Six whole days of my life had disappeared into my brother's rubbish tip. Six whole days that I'd never get back, but it had now been stripped and lay bare and empty. All the rubbish, every single piece, had been painstakingly picked up, looked at, put into the document box or bucket, in which case, it went to the skip outside. My brother's home was now completely empty.

The latest rubbish skip had now departed and a new skip delivered ready for the strip out of floors, walls and stuff. The smell of the refuse still hung heavy over the close, somehow clinging to the fabric of the buildings and trees. I knew that the strip out of floors and walls would add to the saturation and wondered how long it would take to disperse.

Some of the walls were covered, from ground level, up to maybe two or three feet, by drawings. All of the drawings were in, presumably, pencil. Maybe charcoal. In places, they overflowed onto the woodwork. My brother was quite talented at drawing and always had been whereas I could just about draw the curtains.

There was a drawing that recurred all over the rooms, of what appeared to be a dark forest on a dark night. It was almost completely black. The tops of what looked like fir trees packed closely together were silhouetted against a slightly lighter sky. And that was it. On some of them, there were two points of light in the trees, though *light* is not the right word. They were more like little holes in a dark fabric with a slightly lighter fabric backing, if that makes any sense. They were easy to not see, if you get my drift. It was like the artist needed them to be included in the drawing but didn't really want them to be seen.

After a while studying these forest drawings, there must have been twenty or thirty of them, I realised that there was a sequence. They started in the bedroom, behind where the head of the bed had been and they reoccurred all the way around the room, disappearing into the built-in wardrobe where there was one up on the ceiling, the only one not at floor level. They went from the bedroom into the living room but, it was very weird, there was a drawing that had been started in the bedroom but finished in the living room. It even covered the door frame and had to have been done with the door off its hinges. I had to take my hat off to my brother, because *that* represented dedication to his art in my mind. Strangely, in both the living room and bedroom, it stopped either side of the window, no drawings at all underneath the windows.

I realised that the fir trees were the same ones in every drawing. This wasn't a random set of trees, this was something that he *knew*, that he saw all the time. This was the same section of trees from the same forest, reproduced almost perfectly, albeit in different sizes, every time.

The points of light didn't appear until the drawing moved from the bedroom into the living room. In fact, the first time they appeared was the drawing that crossed the threshold, the one that was done with the door off its hinges. And both points of light were on the living room side of the drawing.

As the drawing moved around the room, the points of light changed slightly and it took me a little while to realise that, as they neared the door to the stairs, the centres of them seemed to have a slightly darker centre. Almost like eyes but not quite. The drawings stopping just short of the doorway to the stairs, the last of them being behind this door if it was in the open position.

I pondered the significance and realised that I could ponder for the rest of my life and get nowhere. Maybe he had a thing about being watched or maybe he liked skulking in the trees and watching other people. Maybe someone *was* actually watching him. Maybe he just felt as though he was constantly under scrutiny, which wouldn't be at all surprising growing up in the house he grew up in. I often felt as though I was under scrutiny by the world at large, as though everyone was waiting for me to fuck up so they could punish me. The way I usually dealt with such feelings was to pull my shoulders back, look the world in the eye and say '*Well, I'm here, this is me, this is what I've got, what have you got?*' Possibly why I often appear to be confrontational I suppose. Maybe the drawings were my brother's way of telling the world that he knew what they were up to, that he knew they were watching and waiting. I don't know. I'm trying to be some kind of psychoanalyst here when, in reality, I haven't got a clue what the drawings were about. They were odd. That's about the only thing I really *knew* about them.

I'd told my sisters about them and photographed them properly, well lit, well framed. Dan would have been proud of me. *No he wouldn't*, a voice inside me said, *he hated you.* The voice was probably right. It was obvious from the stuff I'd found that he had *a thing* about me. Maybe it was this sibling rivalry bollocks gone mad. I'd never looked upon any of my siblings as a rival in any way unless we were playing a game or wrestling. I didn't get the sibling rivalry thing at all. That didn't mean it didn't exist, I got *that*, but it was hard for me to grasp. Maybe he'd suffered from that First Born Syndrome, not that I really knew what it was, though I could guess from its title that it wasn't good for me, being the second born. Again, I'd never know and *so*, I thought, *by all means ponder, but don't get drawn in, cos you'll lose out in the end, believe me.*

There were no drawings in the kitchen. None. I checked the bathroom, already pretty sure there were none there and it was the same. Nothing. I was just turning out of the bathroom when I noticed a darkness under the filth on the floor in front of where the toilet had been, now just empty floor and capped pipe awaiting a new one.

The water being turned off, I dropped a gob of spit onto the floor and rubbed at it with the toe of my boot. There was a drawing under the dirt. I went out to my car and got a bottle of drinking water. Back in the bathroom I dripped some water onto the floor and rubbed it with my boot. Slowly but surely, I rubbed the filth away, revealing a forest drawing on the floor, as if the artist had been sat on the toilet. Had you been sat on the toilet, the eyes, now distinctly definitely eyes, would have been looking up at you between your legs.

What had been going on in the mind of my brother? What on earth was the drawing in front of the toilet for? How had he done it? It was perfect in every way and to draw it from a sitting on the toilet position, would have been…difficult to say the least. It must have represented something important to him, but what? I couldn't for the life of me work it out. I'd love him to be here so I could ask him. Not that he'd answer me. He'd probably have said, *just drawings*, and lit a ciggy. I cleaned it and photographed it.

There were drawings other than the dark forest. Not too many of them, maybe six or seven. They looked like targets and were on the walls of the same rooms. All at the same height as the forest drawings, all different sizes, ranging from a couple of inches across, to maybe eight inches across. They all looked identical. All rings of black and in the middle a black bull's-eye. I counted the rings. Nine of them. Every target had nine circles. In every drawing there was a black dot drawn on one of the rings, a different ring in each drawing. The last, or could have been the first, ring drawing was behind the door leading to the stairs and had its black dot on the seventh circle. The targets meant nothing to me, and I could speculate till I was blue in the face as my grandma would say. They'd been photographed and I had the rest of my life to ponder them.

I was tired. Fed up. I'd had enough, went out to my car, got out of the paper overalls, threw them into a bin bag in the boot and drove away.

As I drove through the streets to the cottage, pondering on people and their worlds, my phone rang, showing up on the nav screen as Pam. I pressed the button on the steering wheel to answer, thinking, for about the billionth time how I would have loved my grandparents to be in the car with me at that moment. A phone. In a car. And a satnav screen with a little woman talking to you. I reckon my grandad would have loved it all but my grandma would have thought it was witchcraft or something.

'Hiya love, how you doing?' I asked.

As always, the sound of her voice, happy and alive, made me feel good. 'Fine thanks darlin, I was just wondering what time you'll be home and shall I make a nice curry for tea?'

Now that was a question I liked and I liked my answer even better. 'Yeaaaah,' I said, 'Curry it is. And a beer.' I loved curry but not too hot. I couldn't see the point of food that was so spicy you couldn't taste it. I loved a good curry but I knew I couldn't eat a houseful of it.

I told her I was en route and would be about forty minutes or so and that I'd have a shower and get changed before eating. Before we cut the connection, and knowing how she liked a puzzle, I described the target or ring drawings I'd found. She surprised me by saying there was something about rings that she thought she knew about but couldn't quite drag it to the surface. 'I'll have a little browse.' she said before hanging up. Pam was good at that and not for the first time I thought that she had a talent for research. A broad, non-specific knowledge base and a memory packed with information was a decent start point, and, apart from her beauty and general loveliness, that sort of summed up my wife.

I got back to the cottage and did my normal disrobing before entering, went in, and headed for the shower. 'Hiya love!' I said to Pam, 'I'm starving.' She blew a kiss at me and said, 'Nine circles of hell.' I frowned a question at her and she said, 'Your targets…they could be the nine circles of hell.'

Chapter 34 - The Missing Keys

The last day of clear up had finished and I was back at the cottage. Showered, clean clothes, bottle of Leffe next to me, Pam busy making the sweet and sour chicken with rice that would very soon be in my belly.

The flat was completely clear of rubbish. It had taken me longer than I expected and I've got to say, it was one of the worst things I've ever had to do. I had no understanding of what drove a person to hoard rubbish, refuse, piss and locks of hair. I wanted my brother here, in front of me so I could ask him what he was doing. It must have been perfectly normal to him but, y'know, it wasn't normal was it? It just wasn't.

I was, how can I put it ...*intrigued* about his toilet. His bathroom. What was his train of thought that ended with him getting rid of his bathroom? How do you even function properly as a human being without use of a toilet? I know we used to do without toilets, back before they were invented by whoever it was, but I think that even then, we used to designate a place for our 'business' as my grandma would call it. '*Have you done your business?'* she'd ask, before we went on the train or the bus, *'Best do your business while you can.'*

I needed my brother to tell me how he went about his *business*. *Where* did he do his business? He had to go, so, how? What are the mechanics involved?

I wondered if a latter-stage alcoholic actually *does* business. Or maybe, because they probably mainly take sustenance of a fluid variety, they don't actually excrete solids? I mean, how does it all work? *Your bowels still function though*, I thought, and your bowels empty out through, sorry, I'm about to get *scientific* here, that little hole at the bottom of your torso, so, even if you are emptying liquid from the little hole, you can't exactly aim it, not precisely, so, what on earth do you do? Use a funnel? With its spout in the neck of, say, a Coke or a 7Up bottle? I don't know about you but y'know what Dan? That sounds like really hard work and, at the end of the day, you already had a perfectly good funnel, leading into a perfectly good funnel and spout…it's called a toilet coupled with a drain. Call me a…whatever you want to call me bro, but I just think that whatever you *were* doing to vacate your bowels was just simpler sitting on your toilet and I really struggle to understand your logic. I understand that there *must* have been a logic train running in your mind but I don't think it was calling at the right stations.

Judging by the amount of refuse in his bathroom, he'd done without a toilet for a considerable time, so what had he been doing? Why even start using the bathroom as a refuse tip? Doesn't something click in your mind and a little voice says *'Whoa…hang on a mo…I'm gonna need this room aren't I…you can do without some things in life but a toilet is not one of them'*. Doesn't that happen? Apparently not. Or if it does, something else in that mind is stronger and more pressing, strong enough to overcome the most logical, the most human thing. How does a person get to the stage in life where storing refuse overcomes the requirement of a toilet?

Our family, just a handful of generations before, had lived in the squalor of the Courtyards, the infamous Liverpool Courtyards, where one privy and one cold water pump was used by dozens of families. It's hard to imagine, impossible to comprehend how you lived a normal life. What we would consider to be a normal life that is. Even us, me, my brother, my sister Carla, we started our life in a house with no electricity upstairs, going to bed like Wee Willie Winkie, with a candlestick. We had a potty under the bed...a gazunder...as some called it. We didn't, to us it was just a po or poe, obviously short for potty. There was no bathroom where we lived our early years, just a tin bath hanging on a nail in the back yard. There was just one source of running water, a cold tap in the kitchen, running through lead pipes into a stone sink. All your hot water had to be boiled on a stove. Our toilet was 'down the yard', a squat, brick building with two huge slabs of Welsh slate resting on top of the brick wall, canted down to shed the rain. The walls were white-washed inside and the toilet seat was scrubbed planks of wood with a hole cut in it. A small paraffin heater was used during the winter to stop the pipes freezing. Our toilet 'tissue' was squares of newspaper rammed onto a nail sticking out of the wall, but even this was pure luxury at side of what my brother had lived with for...how long? How long had he been living like this and why? Dan...mate...brother...how the fuck did you get into this state?

There's an obvious follow-on question to all this and that is, could I have put a stop to it, could I have intervened and helped him out of this hole he got into?

I thought back to the time of the fire in his flat and how, when he was inebriated, he'd needed my help but then, as soon as he was sober, he didn't. Not only did he not need my help, but he was particularly shameless in telling me so. He, to coin a rather industrial but apt phrase, fucked me off, and, as it turned out, what, about 25 years later, he *did* actually need my help because his home still bore the marks and damage that the fire had caused. So, could I have intervened and helped him out of this mess? I don't think I could. I don't think he would ever have accepted help or even admitted that he needed help. It's possible that in his world everything was ok as it was. What am I saying, I think 'possible' is the wrong word to use here, maybe probable would be the better choice, yeah, it would maybe be better to say that in his world everything was *probably* ok.

So anyway, his flat was clear of refuse and, for me, there were some startling finds or, to be more precise, non-finds. I hadn't found a will. Not that I expected to. A mind that logically arrives at the point in life where a toilet is not required, is not the mind that thinks about writing a will. If there was a will it was stored somewhere else. There was nothing, no document, that signified a solicitor acting on his behalf, so, if he made one, then it was maybe lodged with his bank. I don't know. *But then*, I thought, *his bank now know him to be dead so if they had his will, they'd tell us wouldn't they*, which meant that I was back to square one, there was no will.

So, no will. Nor were there any keys. Or rather, there *were* keys, a few bunches of them, but none that fitted the locks of his front door. I was a little bit of an expert, though 'expert' is probably stretching the description, on locks and keys. Many years before I'd owned a lock shop and fitting service, plus I could cut any key you wanted, mortise, cylinder, pipe, flat, double sided, single sided, you name it. So, when it came to locks and keys, though I wasn't exactly an *expert*, I was, shall we say, knowledgeable.

The remnants of Dan's front door was on the grass in the garden. The police had smashed their way into his flat on the day his body was found. I'd examined the remnants of the door and discovered that the locks on it were the very ones I'd fitted for him a lifetime ago. They'd been very expensive at the time, probably still would be today. He had a lot of glass in the door and so I'd fitted a Yale twin cylinder night-latch and also a Chubb Castle 5-lever mortise lock. I remember saying to him that as long as he used the locks in the prescribed way, anyone wanting to get into his house would have to smash the door to bits. And I was right because that was exactly what the police did.

An examination of the door remnants…listen to me, I sound like I'm on the stand here don't I…anyway, an examination of the locks showed that both of them, the last time they'd been used, *had* been used in the prescribed way. Both of them had been deadlocked. They could have been deadlocked by the occupant of the house, or they could have been deadlocked by someone leaving the house.

A night-latch, or cylinder lock, more often than not a Yale lock, can be easily opened by someone breaking the glass in a door, reaching in and operating the lever. Hence the twin cylinder lock, which has two cylinder locks, one of them being fitted in the lever on the inside of the door. Operating this lock deadlocks the lever, making the breaking of glass a waste of time.

All the locks on the front door remnants were fully operated. The operation of these locks requires two different keys and those keys should have been in the home, but they weren't. Which can only mean one of two things, either he locked himself in his home and disposed of the keys outside the home, so, he opened a window and threw them out or gave them to someone or something along those lines, or someone else locked the door from the outside and walked away with the keys. I couldn't think of anything else that could have happened. The police and the coroner didn't find any keys on him so, where were they?

I was convinced I'd missed something so I went through it all again. Door properly locked. This needs keys. Dan was the last person to lock the door or someone else was. If Dan, then keys should still be in the house — but they're not. If he locked the door and threw the keys out of the window, then, why? Doesn't make sense. I know a lot of what he did made no sense, but nevertheless, there *was* a stream of functionality, and throwing his keys out of the window made no sense, so, he didn't do that. If he locked the door and gave the keys to someone outside, dropping them from his window, then, who? When? And why? And where is that person now?

Or…someone else took his keys, locked the door from the outside, and walked away. And they still have the keys or not as the case may be. But, again, who was this, why did they do it and where are they now?

I found two bunches of keys in the house, but I could tell, as soon as I found them, that the Chubb keys were not present. I could tell a Chubb

Mortise lock key from a good distance, possibly even tell a Chubb key with my eyes shut. There was not a single Chubb key in the house. There *were* a couple of Yale type cylinder keys, but none of them fitted the twin cylinder Yale lock.

So, bottom line…Dan is dead inside his flat, his front door is dead-locked and there are no keys inside the flat. Explain.

Apart from the obvious, I couldn't explain. The keys were not in the property because they are outside the property, which must mean that someone other than Dan had locked the door. That is the only possible explanation in my opinion.

What was it Sherlock Holmes said? '*When you have eliminated the impossible, whatever remains, however improbable, must be the truth*' or something like that.

I'm sure a fertile mind could come up with a variable or two here, could come up with a good number of 'what-ifs' but, for me, any questions raised can't be answered sensibly. Did someone other than Dan, lock the door and simply walk away, leaving Dan with no way of getting out of his home and never come back? Ever?

Did Dan lock himself in, throw the keys out and if so, why? To stop himself from getting out? Like Dr Jekyll? Was he protecting the world from *him*?

I thumbed a message into Messenger, into our joint conversation. '*Hiya Lydia, hiya Em, I know I've asked this before but I need to ask it again. Dan's keys…do we have any knowledge of them?*'

A few minutes went by. When I'd opened up the conversation, Lydia had been there because her green blob was lit. As I watched, her blob went out and Emily's blob came on. She was typing. *'No, I have no knowledge of them. I was hoping you would find them in the flat. I take it you haven't?'*

I replied that the flat was now empty and that there were no keys that fitted the locks. Lydia's blob lit up. *'You've thrown the door on the skip now haven't you?'*

'Yeah' I replied.

Another message from Lydia flashed up. Lightning thumbs. *'And has that skip gone?'* she asked.

'Yeah' I replied, *'Ages ago. Everything off the garden went in the first skip.'*

Her dots wiggled about. She was typing. *'So even if we find keys in the stuff we brought away that first day, we now won't be able to try them in the lock will we?'*

That question, to me, felt aggressive. I'm not sure aggressive is the right word but the tone of the question was definitely on the scale of aggressive…maybe half way up that scale, possibly two thirds.

'Yeah' I replied, *'we will.'*

'How xxx' she asked.

'Because I kept the stile.' I replied.

There were two minutes were nothing was said. No typing was going on. Both their blobs were lit. *Were they having a private conversation?* I thought. Or were they just waiting for me to elaborate?

Emily's dots danced up and down. *'What's the stile Joe?'*

I couldn't help myself. I'm a firefighter. Thirty years of answering questions fully and informatively, made me someone you maybe didn't always want to ask a question of. *'A door is made up of parts,'* I typed, *'basically, stiles, rails, mullions and panels.'*

Lydia flashed a question into me, *'Dan's door didn't have panels, it was glass.'*

'Glass panels.' I typed, *'In a wooden door. The construction is the same. Anyway, the stiles are the long pieces down each side of the door, the hinge stile, where the hinges are fitted and the lock stile, where the locks and latches are fitted.'*

I let that info settle and then I finished off my explanation. *'I dismantled the door and threw it all on the skip…but I kept the lock stile with the locks in situ.'*

'Why did you do that?' asked Emily.

I thought it was fairly obvious why I'd do that so I was a tiny bit stumped by the question. *'Because I didn't want a smashed glass panel door hanging about but I did need the locks to test any keys I might find in the place.'* I typed. *'It just made sense to me.'*

'Good thinking fat head.' typed Emily. Fat Head was sort of a family nickname for everyone. We were all Fat Heads. Can't remember how it came about because we haven't actually got fat heads. We haven't got

skinny heads either, we've got what you might call bog standard heads. Fat Head was an endearment. A strange one but, there ya go, families.

Lydia's green blob disappeared.

Chapter 35 - The Missing Wallet

So, there were no keys, something which seemed to bother my sister Lydia, though I can't think why it would so was probably wrong.

I didn't find a wallet either. My brother always had a wallet. What I mean there, is that, *up until him stopping talking to me*, he always had a wallet. I know that he stopped talking to me a long time ago and that in the intervening time, he could have ditched the wallet but, it was his *habit* to use a wallet and, maybe *I'm* just someone stuck in *my* ways, but I believe that some habits are hard to get rid of and I think that a man using a wallet is one of them. You go out of the house, you need to take your driving licence, your bank card, credit card, your folding money, appointment cards and so on and so forth. I believe he would have kept to the habit of owning, carrying, and using a wallet. Dan was a creature of habit…he never threw anything away, not even his rubbish…he even had his clothes from 50 years ago. He'd been a smoker for over 50 years, he was a drinker. All habits. He didn't seem to have dropped any of his other habits so, why drop the habit of carrying a wallet?

But let's assume he *did* ditch the pointless habit of carrying a wallet, where did he keep his bank card, his driving licence? In his pocket? His rucksack? In a box? An envelope? What? Where?

Not only had I not found a wallet, but I hadn't found any of those things that I've just mentioned, the things that you carry in your wallet. So, where were his bank card and driving licence? There was nothing. Nothing that you would normally carry around with you…in your wallet…that would identify you. Nothing. Where were they? I mean, I wasn't entirely certain that he used a bank card but, he probably did, didn't he? Doesn't everyone use a bank card? How could you function these days without a bank card? Functioning without a toilet is one thing, a damned big thing admittedly, but, surely in this day and age, functioning without a bank card is right up there isn't it? He was a driver, had been for decades, where was his driving licence?

I texted into the joint conversation on Messenger, wondering if Lydia would show up. *'Hiya Em, hiya Lydia, did Dan have a bank card or what?'*

I got a reply within a few seconds. It was Emily. *'Yeah he did. Just got the last three months of transactions on his account this morning but only just opened them…been at our Nick's minding the baby all day…he last used his card on 29th July'*

The 29th of July. I got the calendar up on my laptop. It was a Sunday. My youngest daughter's birthday. His body was found by the police on 14th October, also a Sunday. I worked the difference out…77 days. Seventy-Seven Sunset Strip. Don't know why I said that, it just jumped into my mind. Seventy-Seven days. Exactly eleven weeks. Eleven weeks during the hottest summer recorded in England.

I texted the conversation. *'Thx Em. What did he buy on 29ᵗʰ July…and where did he buy it?'*

She replied straight away, *'Didn't buy anything just got cash out'.* This was followed by another text, *'200'*

Pam came in with the food in a bowl, TV eating. Just what I needed. I typed a response to Emily, *'Ok thx Em, food just arrived, I'll speak later ok?'* I got a big blue thumb. I ate my food, pondering and watched the telly, a game show.

Halfway through the food, which was lovely, one of my favourite dishes, my phone dinged. It was Emily, but in our private WhatsApp chat. *'Something not right with these bank statements Joe, you need to see them.'*

'I'll be there in 60.' I said.

'OK fat head' she replied.

Chapter 36 - The Bank Statements

I parked outside Emily's house about 65 minutes later. On the way there I was thinking about my exchange of texts with her just over an hour ago and the previous conversation about the keys.

The rigmarole we had to go through to get hold of the statements was, I dunno, *unpleasant* in as much as it was paperwork and ID's and proof of your ID and it just seemed to go on and on. I mean, don't get me wrong, I understand it has to be done like this otherwise any old Tom, Dick or Harry could just get hold of whatever they wanted so, I get it, but let's just say it was…stressful.

A question was in the front of my mind…it seemed to me that Emily was agitated about something. She'd messaged me in WhatsApp, which meant she wanted what she'd said to be private. I was intrigued. Not for the first time recently.

I locked the car and walked up the path. The garden was looking a bit overgrown I thought but then decided to not say anything about it. I knocked on the door. My normal 'rent man' knock. I call it that because that's what my mum used to say about me knocking on the door. 'Knock like a bloody rent man!' she'd say. I wouldn't mind but I've never heard a rent man knock on a door…before my time I think. I knocked again. The door opened. Emily looked like shit. Eyes red, like she'd been crying. Face a bit puffed. Hair a bit…bedraggled. Oh! to have hair to get bedraggled! That is something I would change about me in an instant. I often wished I hadn't lost my hair. Not that I stressed about it or anything, in fact, I embraced it with the shaved head look. It was the fact that you were robbed of choice. The only choice I had was to grow a ring of hair around three sides of my head with nothing on top or in the front. I would love to have the choice of looking bedraggled, not that I would choose that look because I wouldn't. And no, before you ask, I haven't ever thought about hair transplants. Ever. And yes, before you say it, I *have* given thought to all the people, mostly men, who have mental problems because they've lost their hair and I genuinely feel for them…as I do with every person who has mental problems because of their own bodies. I reckon I'm just lucky in that all my mental problems lie in other places.

'Hiya Em,' I said, stepping in. 'Don't know who looks worse, you or the garden.' In the blink of an eye I'd gone against my own decision of two seconds ago, to not mention the garden. Best laid plans and all that.

'Hiya Joe' she said. She sounded tired and gave me a little hug. Which was unusual. We weren't an overly demonstrative family. Not physically anyway. We could certainly hold our own when it came to having words. Which I suppose *is* physical isn't it? Is it? I dunno. Anyway, we weren't really a hugging kind of family. Actually, when I think about that, we weren't familial huggers but were quite huggy when it came to mates. That's something I've never really given much thought to but now that it's out in the open I'll have to ponder on it for a while. I'll maybe get back to you about it but probably won't, so don't hold your breath.

I closed the door and we walked down to the kitchen, the centre of all family discussions, and I sat at the table.

'Coffee?' she asked, switching the kettle on. I nodded and she got mugs out and put coffee in both. I looked out of the kitchen window at the back garden. It, too, was looking a bit bedraggled. I decided to say nothing. It also looked as though my comment about the front garden and her bedraggled look had passed her by.

The kettle finished boiling and she poured water in the mugs, put milk in, a healthy dollop in mine. I like my coffee to be milkyish but still hot. She spooned sugar into her mug and raised her eyebrows at me and pointed with her head at the sugar bowl. 'No thanks Em.' I said and she brought the mugs over and sat at the table.

'I know the gardens look a bit untidy but, to be honest, I can't be arsed.' She lit a cigarette and blew the smoke towards the open kitchen window. I caught a whiff of the smoke and thought, not for the first time, how nice it smelled. I gave up smoking about…let's see, now…OMG was it really that long ago? Getting on for 35 years? Unbelievable! How time flies. How fast is my life disappearing. How fast am I approaching…I stopped the train of thought that was my 'norm', my constant, life-long train of thought…that my life was going to end and that I had to 'be quick', that I had to 'hurry up', that I didn't have time for this and didn't have time for that. Anyway, I gave up smoking on my eldest daughter's 5th birthday. An 'extra present' I called it, her dad around the place for an extra 20 or 30 years or so. Hopefully. And I've never had or craved another fag in all that time. But every now and then, I get a whiff of the smoke from a freshly lit one and I like it. I took a sip of coffee.

'So,' I said, 'where are these bank statements?' I was all business and workmanlike. My default position in life, treat everything like the fireground, like it's all just a puzzle that needs organising into a proper plan of action. Do this before you do that otherwise you'll come unstuck when you try to do that and so on and so forth. All very logical, all very…'efficient' I suppose. It was the way I approached everything. I don't know whether I was a good firefighter because I was like that, or whether I was like that because I was a good firefighter. Probably a mixture of both come to think of it. Now that I see it written down. Seems logical.

She put a large envelope down in front of me and I took out the sheaf of bank statements. There were about a dozen maybe, including the ones that have all that stuff about interest rates and overdraft rates and all that shite. Stuff, I mean, not shite. *I'll have to do something about my swearing,* I thought, immediately followed by the thought, *aah fuck it.*

I flipped through them. And then I flipped through them again to make sure I knew that what I was *about* to say was what I *should* say. 'He was loaded Em! What the fuck?

'I know.' she said.

'How long have you known?' I asked.

'Since an hour ago when I opened them and told you.'

I looked at the statements. He had three accounts. His current account had £23,000 in it. His savings account had £800 in it and he had a £20,000 ISA account. Plus, the mortgage on his property was fully paid up. Plus, he was paying life insurance.

I waved the statements at Emily. I was angry at my brother. Again. 'Why was he living in shite, with all this money Em? What the fuck was he doing?'

'I don't know.' she said, 'But, the first thing that came into my mind was what you said last time you were here, remember?'

My mind sprinted back to not long ago and a question I'd posed to Emily as I was leaving her house. 'You mean the question of, *Does Lydia know something we don't?*'

She nodded. 'Yes.'

'So, it seems that possibly she did, or does know something we didn't but do now.' I said.

'Yes.' she said.

'So, the only way she could know is if she'd seen the statements or he'd told her.' I said. I could see that Emily was fighting back the tears and I could also see why she looked as though she'd been crying when I arrived. I imagined she was upset at how, in her mind, two of her siblings were colluding behind her back about money, that her twin sister could act like that towards her. Emily had this thing that twins were somehow different to other siblings, somehow connected in a spooky way, knew what the other was thinking and feeling. It didn't wash with me. I didn't think anything other than if you spend a lot of time with someone, anyone, and you get on really well, that you are almost automatically going to know how they would finish a particular sentence and all the other stuff that twins come out with to make themselves feel special.

'Em,' I said, 'I can see all this upsets you and it upsets me as well.' She nodded at me and it was like my words had given her permission to let the tears flow. 'The thing is Em, from my point of view anyway, is that you have no control over what other people do or think. If people want to conspire and collude behind your back, there's nothing you can do except be aware of it, and because there are *always* people around you that *will* connive or *are* conniving to take something from you, money, things you own, space you occupy, be it on the road or in a supermarket aisle, then you should always be alert, always aware, and...I dunno, maybe try to anticipate it.' I took a gulp of coffee. 'You only ever have control over what *you* think and what *you* do. And that's it. For me...I always expect people to do me wrong. Always. If they don't, it's a pleasant bonus and if they do, well, it's no more than I expected anyway.' I had another mouthful of my coffee. Emily was looking at me with the saddest eyes I'd seen since I caught Sheba, my beautiful German Shepherd, with half a Marks and Spencer's leather slipper held between her paws. 'For me Em, and I can only ever speak for myself, I always try to say and do the right thing. I'm not saying I always manage to achieve this because I know I don't. But I *try* to. And if I fail, then the only accusation that can ever be levelled at me is that I'm...' I paused, searching for the right word, 'fallible,' I said, 'human.'

Emily had lit a cigarette during the latter part of my speech. 'That's pretty bleak Joe, that's not the kind of world I want to live in, never trusting anyone.'

I laughed. 'You're right Em, it does sound bleak, but it's not. It's not as bad as I've made it sound.'

'Really?' she asked.

'Yeah really…' I said, 'What it means, to me, is that I always have a realistic sense of the world around me, it means that, just like everyone, I get caught out, but, maybe because I always have at least a half expectation of getting caught out, it doesn't…erm…' I finished my coffee while I thought, 'hit me as hard as it might have done, and, because I expected it anyway, it's easier to get past it.'

Emily stared at me and blinked a few times while she was digesting what I'd said. The good thing was, the tears had stopped. Her Numbskull foreman probably said, 'Pack it in lads, wasted on this fella…' She lit another cigarette. I thought about how many ciggies I would've smoked while I was sat here, if I still smoked. I was glad I didn't.

'Did you find a will?' she asked.

I shook my head, 'No.' I said, 'But, let's be honest, did you really think Dan would've made a will?'

'Not really.' she said. 'But…' she glanced at the statements, 'it seems obvious that Lydia and Edward knew there was enough in Dan's account to start lending money to it, so to speak.'

'Yeah.' I said. 'Or…' A little light was blinking away deep in my mind, one of the many anomalies stored away in my, erm, anomaly store, was nagging at me. There was a conversation, *part* of a conversation that had bothered me at the time, I couldn't quite grab hold of the words but I knew where they were. 'Hang on a sec Em.' I said, and got my phone out, opened up a joint conversation the three of us, me, Em, Lydia had had a while ago in Messenger. 'There was a conversation Em…' I said, scrolling backwards to the beginning of all this. There was a lot of conversation to scroll through. Emily made a fresh cup of coffee while she waited.

'Here it is.' I said, and placed my phone on the table for Emily to see. It was Lydia 'speaking'. It felt like years ago. We'd been talking about Lydia's apparent panic at wanting to get a funeral booked and paid for and I'd said that maybe she should just take a step back and let things settle down and Lydia had typed, *'No. Edward is willing to pay for the funeral and we will pay him back once the'*

Lydia's sentence had finished abruptly, as though she'd suddenly realised she was typing something she shouldn't.

'What am I looking at Joe?' asked Emily.

'There,' I pointed, 'that sentence just ends with the word *the.'*

Emily looked at it, then questioningly at me.

I pointed to the time of the following comment, then rested my finger back on what Lydia had said, 'Look, over two minutes elapse between her saying *that* and the next thing said, which was by me, and I was basically saying the same thing that I'd said before, that there was no need to rush into things, no need to panic.'

The same question was written in Emily's expression.

'So, look what she says next…' I said, resting my finger on Lydia's next statement and read it out, *'No. Edward is willing to pay for the funeral and we will pay him back once everything is sorted.'*

Emily eyes were scanning the words on my phone screen, flitting through the four comments, two from me, two from Lydia.

'See?' I said, pointing to the two things Lydia had said, 'Here she says, *and we will pay him back once the* and then *here* she says, *and we will pay him back once everything is sorted.'*

I caught a glimpse of dawning in Emily's eyes. 'So what you're saying is…' she had a little think, got her words sorted out, 'that the first time she said it, she was about to type, *we will pay him back once the* will is found.'

'Exactly.' I said. 'Her statement is about money, Edward paying it out, then getting it back. *We will pay him back once the*, what? Once the what? The *money* comes *through?* The *cheque* gets *cashed?* The *box* gets *opened?* it's *something* having *something* happening to it, see what I mean? I could be wrong but, that's what it looks like to me.' I sipped at my new coffee and Emily lit a new ciggy. We sat there, Emily apparently having a ponder and me pondering Emily pondering. I had a look at the current account statements.

He'd made his last transaction on 29th July. Two hundred pounds drawn from an ATM. Looking up the list, he'd drawn a lot of cash out over a relatively short space of time. Examining the statements back to the previous November, it appeared that he was buying his booze, or to be more precise, spending with his card in a shop called BoozeMart up until late April, when he appeared to stop doing that and started withdrawing cash instead. I assume he was still making purchases in BoozeMart, so, for some reason it appears as though he wanted to buy in cash rather than have the transaction 'traceable' so to speak. If that was the case, why would he want to hide his transactions? Who was he hiding it from? Himself?

I didn't get it. 'See this Em?' I ran my finger down a list of consecutive transactions at BoozeMart then pointed at a list of consecutive ATM transactions, 'He's changed his method of buying booze here, y'see?'

Emily moved her chair to sit next to me. 'Hmmm.' she said. 'So what Joe?'

'Well do you reckon he's still buying booze or what?' I asked.

'Yeah of course he is...he's alcoholic isn't he, he's not gonna stop buying it. He *can't* just stop buying it.'

That phrase hit home. The fact that he was so far gone down the alcoholic route that it was, at best, possibly dangerous for him to just stop. Not having booze close to him wasn't an option. 'I wonder why he changed his method of buying it though...is he trying to hide it d'you think?'

Emily moved her chair back to the other end of the table. 'Who from?' she asked.

'That's what I'm saying.' I said. I looked back at the statements, scratched an itch on the back of my neck. 'It looks like he's trying to hide what he's spending his money on but he's only hiding it from himself isn't he? Maybe that's what he's doing, hiding the facts from himself, I dunno — it just seems strange to me, this sudden change in buying habit.' I thought about the word 'habit' after I'd said it. He was like a drug addict, no, he *was* a drug addict. Alcohol was his drug, one of his habits, and his method of paying his dealer, BoozeMart, was to go in and use his bank card, get his stuff, and go home. That was another habit. But he changed it, changed his method of paying. I found that strange, I have to say. It was *noteworthy*. An anomaly.

Emily lit yet another ciggy and looked out of the window at the bedraggled garden. She was in a half silhouette position. She inhaled deeply and started talking as she exhaled, 'I just don't know what to think Joe, I don't think my brain can take all this stuff in properly. I mean, are you saying that Lydia is up to something, that she is…I don't even know what I'm saying. Dan wasn't exactly 'with us' if you know what I mean. You've only got to look at the state of his place to know that, so, I don't know whether we can look at a change in his habit as anything too…*important*. I don't think we can apply any sort of, I dunno, *normality* to anything, y'know, not what *we'd* call normality. D'you see what I'm saying?' As she'd been talking, she was exhaling smoke and, once again, I was amazed at just how much smoke came out and for how long. Five exhalations it took for her to stop breathing smoke out. And then, as soon as she did stop exhaling smoke, she took another drag and set the process in motion again.

I did know what she meant. And it was hard to apply our logic to things he did or didn't do. 'I see what you're saying Em.' I said. 'For me, I just try to cover all bases and, I dunno, it's like, when you're playing a chess game for instance, and you're trying to think about what your opponent is going to do next, you don't think about that from *your* perspective, using your logic, you do that thinking from *his* perspective, using the logic that you think *he* applies to his moves.' I picked my coffee mug up but, a slightly fuzzy head told me that I'd had too much coffee and went to the sink for a cup of water, speaking as I got it. 'You look at Dan's place and it looks like utter madness, it *is* utter madness, but only from our viewpoint. There *is* a logic to it, granted, not *our* logic at all but nevertheless, it was *worked* out. The mountains of beer cans, the cardboard bed he died in, the bottles of piss with their notations, the bags of hair and suitcases of mum's clothes…all madness to us, but to him, it all meant something, it was all put in place by him for reasons known only to him.' I drained my cup of water and got another. 'There were reasons for everything he did. It all looks as random as fuck…which is as random as you can get…but it wasn't Em.'

I looked at the last statement, the last transaction that he'd ever made. Four days previously, he withdrew £180. Two days prior to that he withdrew £160. I added up his withdrawals for July…they came to £1700. That was alarming. June was £1200. May, £750, all drawn out between the 23rd up until the end of May, so, what, a week.

On the 19th May, he used his card in BoozeMart to the tune of £45 and after that transaction, he switched to withdrawing cash only. Except for one transaction. One day prior to his last ever transaction, the £200 cash withdrawal on the 29th, he used his card to top up a mobile phone to the tune of £30. I'd cleared the flat and hadn't seen a phone anywhere.

'What happened to his phone Em?' I asked.

She took a last drag of her ciggy and stubbed it out in the ashtray. Took a sip of coffee. 'Well the old one,' she said, 'the one he got off mum when she died, remember it? I don't know where that one went. He probably threw it away because it kept breaking down and the battery wasn't charging properly.'

I did remember that phone and said so. I also remembered a conversation he'd had with our cousin Shirley, sometime early in the year, and recalled that I'd heard from her in April.

Emily lit another ciggy, inhaled deeply and spoke the smoke out. 'He bought a new one from Asda.' she said, 'Only a basic Nokia, almost the same as the one of mum's that wouldn't charge up.'

'Where is it?' I asked.

She put her cigarette in the ashtray and stood up. 'It's in the blue box of stuff that Lydia brought round that first day she went there, remember that day when she just went to have a look from the outside? Before the door got fixed?'

She went out into the garden, 'It's in the shed Joe, it absolutely stinks so I won't have it in the house. Stay there while I go and get it.' She walked off down the garden to the little shed at the bottom and I could see her rummaging around in a blue plastic box. While she was rummaging I had another look at the bank statements. On the 30th April he spent £40 at Asda Mobile. That was probably the purchase of his new phone. The only other mention in the statements of anything to do with a mobile phone was the Top Up that he bought with his bank card on 24th July. I was pondering that information when Emily returned with a plastic zip lock freezer bag and gave it to me.

The phone was quite obviously new. A Nokia 105, probably the cheapest Nokia you could buy. A typical 'burner' phone they were always going on about in cop shows on the telly. I tried to turn it on without taking it out of the bag and it wouldn't. No charge probably.

'Have we got a charger Em?' I asked. She shook her head. 'Didn't you find one in there?'

'No,' I said, 'I didn't find anything to do with any kind of mobile phone.' I turned the bag over in my hand. 'Did you put it in this bag?'

'No.' She said, 'That's how Lydia found it.'

I was surprised and held up the bag. 'In this?' I asked.

She lit another cigarette from the one that was virtually burned out in the ashtray and nodded. 'Yes,' she said, 'Edward found it outside in that bag. The firemen must have thrown it out when they were clearing the way for the police.'

I shook my head, 'Really?' I asked.

'She said that it was right by the front door, as plain as anything.'

I held the bag up again. It was clear, see-through plastic, with a blue plastic zip at the top. It looked quite new to me. I sniffed it. It smelled of nothing, like a plastic freezer bag. I unzipped it and stuck my nose in. The smell of Dan's place wafted out. I zipped it back up again and sniffed the bag. Nothing. 'I don't think this bag has ever been in his flat.' I said. 'It's too clean.'

Emily blew smoke at me and apologised. 'I'm only saying what Lydia told me, I don't actually know.'

I was a bit non-plussed. I slid the back off the phone without taking it out of the bag. There was no battery in it. I checked inside the battery compartment and there was no SIM card either.

'Did Lydia take the battery and SIM card out?' I asked.

'What do you mean?' said Emily, 'Hasn't it got a battery?'

I slid the bag across the table to her and she picked it up and examined it. 'Dan must have taken them out.' she said. And then a frown creased her forehead, 'Why would Lydia take them out? No, Dan *must* have done it.' A line from an old film I loved, 10 Rillington Place, flashed through my mind, *'Christie done it.'*

'Yeah but, why would Dan do it?' I asked, and held up the bank statement. 'The last proper purchase he made with his card was a £30 top up to his phone, *that* phone.' I said, pointing at the bag in Emily's hand.

Emily sat looking at the phone in the bag.

'And the SIM card...' I said, 'Why would you top up a phone then get rid of the battery and SIM card? Why the fuck would you do that?'

I was puzzled. So was Emily. She put the bag down and stood up. Walked to the sink and looked out of the window. 'Want another coffee?' she asked.

Chapter 37 - Enlightenment

Emily and I had chatted on for another half hour or so, going around in circles and then I'd gone back to the cottage. I went to bed that night and did my normal thing. Just before going to sleep I mentally listed all the anomalies and mulled them over before drifting off.

The next morning, when I woke up, my head was clear and I felt like I was sitting on top of a block of flats, legs dangling over the edge, the whole town laid out below me. I started to list everything we knew.

We knew that his bank card was missing. We knew that he last used it on 29th July, therefore, between that date and the date of his death, whatever date that was, he either lost it, had it stolen, gave it away, or disposed of it outside the house. Without the card, he would be unable to access his money or make purchases.

We knew that he died inside his home and that his front door was securely locked and that keys were required to lock that door. Yet those keys were not found. Therefore, he either lost the keys, had them stolen, gave them away, or threw them out of the window. Without the keys he couldn't get out of his home.

We knew that he had a new mobile phone and that he'd topped it up with the last purchase made with his bank card. The phone has been found — minus its battery and SIM card. I didn't find a charger for this phone, or any other phone, so, apparently, he rendered his phone useless, yet preserved it in a clear plastic zip-lock freezer bag.

We know that the very last transaction he made with his bank card, was to withdraw £200 in cash on the 29th July, and that during that month he withdrew £1700 in cash…and yet I didn't find any cash in the flat, not even a single coin. I found that strange. I know that cash can be spent and given away but, everything you buy doesn't add up to nice round amounts, there is always loose change. Always.

We know that he was addicted to alcohol, strong lager, cheap wine and spirits. There were no 'live' cans of beer, nothing except empty wine and vodka bottles. There were no fluids, not even water, absolutely nothing to drink in that flat unless your tipple was thick, syrupy, foul piss.

We know that he was addicted to tobacco. That he rolled his own. Like our father used to do. And we know, from his shopping list notebooks, that he bought rolling tobacco, papers, filters and lighters in packs of five. I did not find, apart from empty and discarded tobacco pouches and cigarette lighters, any usable smoking materials. Nothing.

We know that he was in the habit…another habit…of carrying a small rucksack when he went out. And we know that the only thing found in it, by the police, was an old cheque book and a letter from the Inland Revenue, both items now in our possession.

We know that he had a current driving licence, but didn't find one.

And we *think,* or rather, *I* think, that he would have had a wallet, based solely on the fact that a wallet is so useful and that, when I knew my brother, he always used one. But none had been found.

The only conclusions I could draw from this information was that, in the final weeks of my brother's life, he withdrew shitloads of cash and spent every single penny of it, bought his usual booze and drank every single drop of it, bought his usual smoking materials and used every shred of tobacco, every cigarette paper, every filter and exhausted every little gas lighter, topped up a new mobile phone, presumably so that he could use it but then got rid of the things that make it work, got rid of his bank card and driving licence, locked himself in the house then made his keys disappear, turned his TV on, lay down the wrong way around in his Skara Brae bed, covered himself with 5 feet of rubbish, then died.

So, just how fucking feasible is that?

Chapter 38 - The Man on the Ledge

I'd been working in Dan's place for nearly two weeks now. The smell couldn't be gotten rid of without removing virtually everything. The whole floor had been covered in enough refuse to fill three eight-ton skips. Rats and mice had run riot in the place, entering from the drains, when he allowed the toilet to dry out and wherever else mice and rats come from. They'd chewed and scratched holes in just about everything, floors, walls, and furniture. It was like a giant theme park for them, free fast-food thrown in.

Mice are omnivorous, and eating through cables or cable insulation is something they do all the time, causing countless fires and, when they get right through the insulation, their own immediate death. I'd seen it hundreds of times in my job. I'm not absolutely certain why they do all this chewing because, surely, they don't actually eat it, as in swallow and digest? I seem to recall that they chew stuff up a lot because rodent teeth don't stop growing, so it helps keep their teeth in shape. I also seem to recall, now that I'm thinking about rodents and their teeth, that when me and Dan bred Golden Hamsters, one of them had teeth that grew through its lower lip, pinning its mouth shut. Let me tell you, I can think of a few humans I'd wish that on. We had to take the hamster to the vets where, I assume, the vet cut its teeth or something, and told us to put old cotton bobbins in the cage for it to chew on, which we did and we never had the problem of the teeth again. Mind you, mum was a bit mystified that some of her cottons were found haphazardly wound around folded up pieces of cardboard. Now that I'm thinking of cotton bobbins — cooking on gas here now — I seem to recall that he'd suggested cotton bobbins because of the wood they were made from, cotton bobbin wood, from the cotton bobbin tree, because of the way it shredded when chewed, rather than splintered like a softwood would. Not easy to say that, *softwood would.* Bit like that actor fella, Edward Woodward, he was in Callan on the telly. We used to love that, me, and our Dan. He was sort of a private detective, I think. Not our Dan, Callan. Edward Woodward. He was in that film as well, the one where he was a police sergeant and had to go to a remote Hebridean island and ended up getting sacrificed in a burning wicker effigy in the shape of a man. Now, what was that film called. Yeah, I remember, The Wicker Man.

So, mice and rats…they'd made holes in floors and walls and had chewed through cabling, eaten my brother and generally made an absolute mess of the place. Or, to put it another way, they had generally made an absolute mess of the absolute mess of the place.

When Dan's body had rotted, especially in the upper torso and head area, the *fluid* this had created, had actually rotted the flooring, you know, that cheap tongue and grooved chipboard flooring in use these days. Rotted right through in a piece about the size of a male chest and head. Turned the chipboard to slimy mush. Quite interesting to see but not very nice to deal with.

On top of that, the refuse he stored, in places, over five feet deep, had created its own moisture and as a result, large areas of plasterboard had become damp and done what plasterboard does when it gets wet, turned into porridge encapsulated in soggy paper.

All of the flooring and plasterboard were stripped out and replaced, together with all the skirtings, door frames and doors. All the kitchen and bathroom fittings, everything, all skipped.

Now, two weeks after starting, all the new floors and walls were in place. All the new woodwork and doors, electrical sockets, and switches, rewired where necessary, were in. A new bathroom suite with walk-in shower, in and working, new basic kitchen fitted and the new boiler and radiators were in and commissioned, courtesy of Billy no mates, one of my mates. The place was looking good and smelling normal. All it needed now was a good hoovering and a lick or two of paint. Et Voila! Whatever that means. I know I live in France but, I'm not very good with the strangenesses of the language yet. Not sure I'd ever be, to be truthful...not the same as the being honest thing.

I was absolutely tired out, or knackered. I ordered a pizza for delivery and opened a bottle of beer. Halfway through the bottle my pizza arrived and I ate it. Didn't take too long. I debated having a second bottle of beer, a rarity for me and promptly fell asleep, mid debate, in my super comfortable deck chair.

And I dreamed. Or nightmared. Nightmare is probably a better description. An old dream come nightmare that I'd been having since I was a kid.

Have you ever had a dream that is, quite simply, real…not a disjointed thing like you normally have, or normally remember but one that is something that, when you wake up from it, it's something you *believe* has happened and you *don't* believe that it was a dream, even when you know it was. It stays with you for ages, days sometimes. Sometimes it stays with you your whole life from the first time you had it. As this particular dream has done with me. It frightens you and has a real and genuine impact on your mind and it's very hard, if not impossible to shake.

This dream of mine is a double dream, a dream within a dream. You've probably had one yourself. You feel as if you've been conned. You wake up and start to decipher your dream only to find you're still dreaming. I mean, which arsehole invented that? You're safe now, Oh! No! You're not. What's that all about?

My childhood dream is set in the bedroom I shared with my brother at our home in Halewood, South Liverpool. It was a three bedroomed council house within spitting distance of the then Ford factory. The huge mushroom shaped water tower of the factory loomed above the rooftops. The council estates of Halewood, there were three of them, were all built in the 60's, and, as part of the inner-city clearances we were shunted out into the *countryside* of South Liverpool, as we saw it, having been brought up in the grey and brick-red docklands of North Liverpool. We lived in the Boddington Road of the Boddington Road estate and our house was number nine.

Our front door had a concrete 'ledge' over it, presumably to keep the sun or, more likely, the rain off the doorway. Our bedroom window, mine and Dan's, could be reached from that ledge and, us being lads and therefore born to climb and be adventurous, or stupid, it became our 'job' to conquer the ledge by getting onto it from below and once conquered, to then go the extra mile, or four feet, and climb into our room through the window.

There were three different stages to this task. Three different medals you could earn. The window consisted of quite a large side-hung panel that opened, easily big enough for a man to get through, and a narrow transom window at the top, purely for ventilation purposes but, if necessary, a boy could get through it.

So, medal number one, we'll call it, bronze, was to get onto the ledge. Silver was earned by climbing up through the already opened side-hung window. And Gold was earned by climbing up onto the windowsill, where only the transom was open, reaching down inside to flip the handle on the side window, pushing it open and then clambering through it.

Dan easily climbed up onto the ledge by jumping, catching the edge of the ledge and somehow pulling and swinging himself up, getting a slight toe-hold on a brick joint for leverage. From there, he easily climbed in through the open side window when it came to his Silver medal run.

I couldn't actually reach the edge of the ledge by jumping from ground level and Dan refused to hold me up to get a grip of the edge, because he said it was cheating and I got that, I would have said the same in his shoes. But there was nothing in the rules that said I couldn't stand on something. Dan wouldn't let me stand on him but my mate Tich would. Tich though, as strong as he was, just wasn't steady enough or broad enough to give me a 'solid' base from which to start leaping to get a grip on the edge of the ledge. I like saying that…edge of the ledge. So, I dragged the bin out of its cubbyhole, climbed on it then easily, well, it wasn't really easy but I told Dan that it was, managed to pull and lever myself up, finding it easier once I'd managed to articulate my leg to make use of Dan's toe-hold, which when you were using it yourself, wasn't anywhere near as useful as Dan made it look. He made lots of tough things look dead easy my brother did. That's why he was my hero. My first hero. Actually, he was my second hero because grandad was my first hero. Still is. So anyway, I got myself onto the ledge and got my Bronze medal. Mind you, I scraped the skin off my belly and chest, sliding over the edge of the ledge to get down again, which had to be done because each medal started from the ground. That *was* in the rules that our Dan made up.

I got the Silver medal, just like Dan and when it came to the Gold medal, we both managed that as well, though I struggled a little bit once I was on the window sill because my arm wouldn't reach far enough down to flip the handle of the side window. Dan kept telling me to give up before I fell but I managed to reach it and flip it with the aid of Tich's shoe, which I caught one handed on about the sixth attempt.

So, we were both being a bit smug, me and Dan, and agreeing to not let Tich have a go, mainly because he was a world champion at climbing, when I came up with a new challenge. Let's call it Gold *plus*. You had to do the same task but actually enter the bedroom through the transom. It would mean going in head first, slithering through like an eel and dropping onto my bed, which was under the window. Dan said it couldn't be done but I said it could and Tich said he could do it and did we want him to show us. We ignored Tich and Dan had a go. He was just too big. He could get his head and one shoulder in but that was it. He was convinced it couldn't be done, and tried to stop me having a go, saying that I might break the window. But I wasn't having it…competitive little shit that I was. I clambered up onto the ledge, wincing as my scraped belly touched the concrete, jumped, and got the fingers of my right hand into the transom and pulled myself up, pushing with my left hand on the windowsill until my feet were on the sill. And then I just got my head and shoulders through and kicked and squirmed my way through, dropping onto my bed in absolute triumph. When I looked out of the window, Tich was jumping up and down with his arms in the air, like he'd scored a goal for Everton, but Dan had disappeared. When I went down the stairs, he was making a jam butty in the kitchen. I told him I'd done it, expecting him to be pleased but, he wasn't bothered.

Later, Tich told me that Dan had seen me go through and drop but then immediately gone into the house. As far as I was concerned, it wasn't Dan's fault that he was too big to fit through. He'd have deffo done it with no bother if he'd been my age and size.

Anyway, back to my recurring nightmare…I'm walking home late at night from my girlfriend's house. It was maybe two to three miles along well-lit suburban streets with a couple of busy main roads thrown in. I could have got the bus, the 78, but I had a thing about getting on buses at bus stops. I could get on them at a terminus, when they were empty and still, but I struggled to get on one at a bus stop. Don't ask me why because I don't know. Is it because when you get on, people are already there and scrutinise you as you make your way to a seat, wobbling from side to side if the driver has started moving before you've got there? I don't know, but I don't think so. Is it because sometimes you're faced with making a choice between sitting next to the plump girl with the greasy hair and the 'O' shaped mouth, or the pretty girl in the mini skirt with the mouth shaped mouth and you always go for the plump girl with the greasy hair so she doesn't get to feel rejected because of you? And that, in your mind, you just *know* that everyone knows that you really wanted to sit next to the girl in the mini skirt? I don't know, but I don't think so. Or is it because there is always, *always* a man who looks at you with flat eyes, who probably isn't even noticing you, but in your mind he's looking at you as a predator would, sizing you up, deciding what to do about *you*? I don't think so but, maybe. In any case, I could've got the bus but I didn't and never do.

So, I'm walking along, smoking a cigarette and I walk past a bus stop and as I do, a bus pulls up at it and stops to let a woman off. I looked up at the remaining people on the bus, there were just a handful or so, two women on the raised seats near the back, gabbing and nodding their heads at each other, a man standing talking to the driver, probably about football and an old white-haired man asleep with his head resting on the window. The bus closed its doors with a hiss of compressed air and started to pull away and as it did, I caught a glimpse of a man sitting in the front seat on the top deck, craning his neck to look backwards as though he was looking at the woman who'd just got off but he wasn't, he was looking at me. His eyes were flat and expressionless, his face all hard edges and bony, his hair thinning but long and wispy, swept over with a side part. As the bus accelerated away, he turned even further to keep me in view and then he stood up and disappeared as he made his way down the stairs. I saw him reappear on the lower deck as the bus approached the next stop along. The brake lights came on and I saw the man get off the bus. The doors hissed closed and the bus pulled away but I didn't see the man leave the bus stop.

The concrete bus stop was one I knew well and didn't like at all. Not that I have a list of bus stop likes and dislikes, I don't, but this one was, I dunno, *sinister*, if a bus stop can be called sinister, which I suppose it can because I've just done it. It was the only bus stop of its type that I ever saw. Anywhere. Ever. It was all concrete with a corrugated roof, probably asbestos, but the end of it, facing the oncoming traffic had a slit in it about average adult eye height. Like a letter box but bigger.

The man had definitely not left the bus stop and as I got nearer I got the distinct impression that he was looking out of the slit at me. I couldn't see him but I knew he was there, a foot or two back maybe, staying out of what light was available. I walked past the stop but my senses were heightened. If a mouse had come up behind me, I'd have heard it.

I got about fifty yards past it before turning round to check behind me and there was no sign of the man. I breathed a mental sigh of relief because I'd been sure he was going to follow me. After another half a mile I felt like another cigarette. Probably the nervous tension had used up all my nicotine and I stopped to light it. The wind had been increasing slightly since I left my girlfriend's and I had trouble getting my lighter to stay lit. I turned away from the wind and cupped my hands around the flame and as I did so, I caught movement on the other side of the road, about a hundred yards back. I just knew it was the man off the bus.

I stared in that direction but, if it actually *was* a person I'd seen, they were staying perfectly still in front of the tall dark trees bordering the garden of a house. I stood still, watching the area, smoking my cigarette, feeling quite angry that this man was following me. I stood square on to where I thought he was standing, making myself straight and as tall as I could, challenging him to make himself known. Nothing moved and I was beginning to doubt myself when, quite bizarrely, what looked like a pair of eyes became apparent, set in the darkest part of the gloom of the foliage. I stared at them, trying to work out whether I could actually see them or whether they were just a figment of my imagination. And then they slowly blinked and there was a slight shift in the shadows, black on black, as if someone was squaring up towards me. There was someone there, waiting in the darkness of the trees and they were watching me. Following me.

I flicked my cigarette butt in the direction of the eyes, a tiny flurry of red sparks bright in the night, turned, all square shoulders and straight back, and strode off in the direction of my home.

I resolved to not turn around and look again, to not give him the satisfaction of showing that I was worried, but inside me was a slowly rising compulsion to bolt for home, to sprint that last mile. Instead, I walked with my hands open and hanging down by my sides, ready for action, moving my arms in what I thought was a strong military fashion. I strode out like I was on a route march and generally tried to make myself appear to be someone you didn't want to mess with.

I turned the last corner and there, about 200 yards away, was my house, the living room light on and you could see through the glass at the side of the front door that the kitchen light was on as well. I saw a figure moving between the two rooms, probably my mum making a cup of tea or something. I started to feel safe and that I didn't need to walk like a soldier anymore, I knew that I'd reached sanctuary and I turned around to glare in his direction and give him two fingers. And he was right behind me, his face just inches from mine.

And that was when I woke up with a start and, I think, a grunt.

I lay there, on my back, looking at my ceiling. I was breathing heavily and sweating a bit. I could hear my brother breathing in his bed on the other side of the room. I was amazed at how the dream had been so real, at how I could relive every second of it, seeing the women chatting on the bus and the old man asleep. It was just so incredibly real. And I re-examined the eyes in the shrubbery and they were real, they were there, I could still see them in my mind's eye.

I was scared to go back to sleep but at the same time I was calling myself stupid and childish. It had been a nightmare, that's all…just a nightmare, all in your imagination and let's face it matey, you've got a bloody good imagination now haven't you?

But, what if he really did follow me home from my girlfriends though? I thought. What if he's waiting over on the pub car park for you to come out in the morning? What if…all sorts of things ran through my head, none of them nice.

I laughed at myself and said, *have a look then! Get out of bed and have a look!* Always throwing down a challenge. *See if you can see those scary eyes looking at you! It was a nightmare! Prove it to yourself! Have a look out of the window!*

I laughed at myself, got out from under my covers and knelt up on the bed facing the window. I steeled myself, pulled the curtains apart and he was there, standing on our ledge, just inches away on the other side of the glass, his flat expressionless eyes staring into mine, and a silvery bead of drool running down his chin.

And then I woke up.

And now, sitting, or reclining on my deckchair, in my brother's flat, sitting just three or four feet away from his place of death, I had that same dream, that I'd had dozens of times before, except this time, the white-haired man who was always asleep, wasn't. This time, he woke up and looked at me, his head turning to keep me in sight as the bus moved away. And the white haired man looked familiar. It was my grandad, not my mum's dad, my lovely grandad, this was the father of my father, that grandad.

I woke up with a start and for a few seconds I didn't know where I was. I thought I heard my father's voice say *That's our Joe* but then I became fully awake and realised that I'd had a dream within a dream. I got my stuff together, locked up, got in my car, and drove away.

Chapter 39 - Excerpts from the Diary

Wednesday 19th January 2005

2nyt start 7:33pm 45 x 1 + 45 x 5 + 112.50

No kwiki 2nyt. Phone box Diff. woman. Early afternoon. Got2go, the other phone is going. Early hours took Bertie out and he was annoying me with his jerky pulling every time I try to guide him away from anything. I almost lost it with him and really pulled him along the path and grass near kittys wall onto wills grass near to no. 67. I have pulled him worse, it wasn't that bad, but not that good. He didn't stumble over/fall over, but it must have frightened him. He looks up at me and must wonder at what is going on. I shouted at him in a low controlled voice – no one would have heard me – and told him he was a naughty, naughty boy. He then takes his usual route walking fast to the front door, thinking that he will be safe inside, and he always is. He associates going outside with me pulling him.

Thursday 20th January 2005

2nyt started 8:23pm - 24pm 45 x 1 + 45 x 1, or 45 x 2 + 112.50 x 2

Again late 2nyt Bertie annoys me by his pulling, and near Kellys I lost it and yanked him up and down a few times. It must have frightened him at least a little bit, and I think we carried on to Garys etc. While yanking him I shouted something to him in a muffled voice, I doubt if anyone would have heard me. Went to kwiksave, got there late, about 7.55 pm was locking up bike and security shouted to me several times Hey mate you don't need to do that I am locking up now (or soon). I was pretending not to hear him but he wasn't giving up so I turned around and I got the impression that he was going to stay by door so I thanked him and didn't lock bike up. I went in and quickly got what I needed and was out by 8.02 – 3 pm, bike was still there, security wasn't, but Mr McGee and other male(s) staff were going in and out. Mr McGee said Tra matey. He always lets on to me now cos he recognises me as a regular customer.

Sunday 30th January 2005

2nyt start 7:41pm 45 x 5

2nyt lost it with Bertie for barking at Jack Russell. I shouted at him to shut up and at the same tym I yanked him up and down on his lead several times. He landed with his back legs splayed, and he stayed there, no wimpering, so I don't know if he was hurt, or just uncomfortable or just making his landing a bit more comfortable. It shut him up tho. He is 11 years old, not young, and I should remember that.

Chapter 40 - Decorating

I'd been working all day in the flat. It was coming along very nicely. Nearly finished in fact. New floors, doors, all stud walls re-plasterboarded and skimmed. Everything was looking good. I was on the decorating and nearly finished. I could go home to France soon and my mind was already seeing me down those white lanes around my house, disturbing the butterflies and dragonflies.

So, I'd been painting all day, ceilings, walls, undercoating the woodwork. I was knackered, the cumulative effect of weeks of work taking their toll. I wasn't used to it and, let's face it, I wasn't getting any younger. I was still fit for my age but, y'know…

I finished work and decided a bottle of beer would go down nice. Leffe. Belgian. My favourite. There was no fridge but luckily, I prefer my beer unchilled. I can't taste it properly when it's too cold, so a bottle straight out of the box on the floor in the kitchen is good for me. As usual, that one bottle made me very talkative but with no one to talk to, tiredness took over. So, I slept. In the deckchair.

I was dreaming. In the dream I was looking out of a window into trees. Tall trees, like Christmas trees. Dark underneath them, virtually black. In spite of the black, I caught a sense of movement and a dark figure appeared in the edge of the trees, a faint but discernible highlight giving the figure some shape. The figure was looking my way, looking at me. I couldn't see a face or eyes, but I knew that the figure was looking at me.

I watched the figure and the figure watched me. I beckoned and after a minute or so, the figure moved forward, towards me.

Chapter 41 - Comprehension

I was in the flat. Painting. Not my favourite job but one that was crucial to how all the rest of the job looked. So, it had to be right, had to be good. Luckily, it was something I was reasonably good at and somehow managed to do OK at it by switching off. I often did some of my best musing while I was painting. I'd muse on how good it must be to be a professional footballer, or what it must be like to be rich. I'd muse on how good it would be to not be doing whatever it was I was doing and be doing something else instead. And I'd also muse on all sorts of other shite, but only ever muse-worthy shite.

And today, as I brushed and rollered my way towards job end, I'd been musing on the enlightenment that had occurred whilst thinking about all the strange anomalies and details surrounding the death of my brother.

I remember a teacher of mine at school…Mr Adams. Mr Adams didn't like me but I don't really know why. Mind you, not many of my teachers did seem to like me. A few did, but not many. I wasn't disruptive, I was attentive, I wanted to learn. Having said that, and this is probably something I should apologise to Miss Howarth for, I could easily be construed as being inattentive during RE lessons. Religious Education. It wasn't her fault that she believed in what she was trying to educate me about. But I didn't. I never have done and I never will. Nothing that anyone is ever going to say to me will change that.

And so, in her lesson, I remember that I used to ask questions for which there are, apparently, no answers. How did Jesus feed those multitudes with a few loaves and a couple of fishes? How? How did Moses part the Red Sea with his staff? How did Jesus come back to life? How did God or god make the world and why did he take a day off, was he tired? Why does god allow people to go to war and both claim that he's on their side? Why does he allegedly protect little children but allow the Moors Murderers to exist, why does he allow axe-murderers, rapists and megalomaniacs like Hitler to thrive? It just wasn't good enough to explain all that away with 'god moves in mysterious ways.' I'm sorry, but it just wasn't.

I was envious of people who do believe. But then I'm envious of people who take pleasure in fishing and stamp collecting. I couldn't follow those pastimes but I sometimes wished I could. I sometimes wished that my mind would stop it's churning and let me relax, but then if it did, I wouldn't be me. I really wished, at times, that I did believe in God and heaven and all that, because, how comforting must it be to believe in life after death, that there is a plan and we all fit into it? But, I didn't believe. I couldn't believe. And during the lessons of Miss Howarth, I genuinely wanted answers to my questions but, poor woman, she didn't have any.

Mr Adams used to say that his job was to 'enlighten' us, but that it was our job to comprehend. 'What comes after enlightenment Croft?' he would ask, board duster or piece of chalk in hand, and I would answer 'Comprehension sir.' And he would say 'And do you comprehend Croft?' And I would say 'Yes sir.' And he would say 'Prove it, what do you understand from today's enlightenment?'

If you demonstrated your comprehension he would move on until he found someone who didn't comprehend and then he would throw the piece of chalk or the board duster at that unfortunate child. I always said that if he threw it at me, I would catch it and throw it back at him, so I was always ready for that missile coming my way. But it never did. Until the day it did. I failed to comprehend the *coefficient of linear expansion*. It went in one ear and straight out of the other, bypassing all my Numbskulls, who must have been snoozing, or on a coffee break. The board duster came hurtling my way but almost in slow motion. I was quite athletic at school and in one movement, I stood, caught it in my right hand and threw it straight back at him. He dodged and it battered into the blackboard emitting a huge cloud of chalk dust. He told me to stay behind after class, which I did and he asked me why I'd thrown the duster at him. I explained that if someone threw something at me then I was within my rights to throw something back at them. He looked at me without saying anything for maybe 90 seconds, then told me to bugger off.

Mind you, he got his own back during the Teachers v Pupils football match, when I went up for a header and he came in underneath me, catching my legs and I ended up spinning in mid-air and landing on my back, taking all the wind out of me. When I recovered and got up, he just smiled at me. I still owe him for that.

Having said all that, Mr Adams was right. After my Enlightenment of the past day or two, came Comprehension. The comprehension was quite natural, quite normal. It just arrived. After enlightenment, you either have comprehension or you don't and I did.

Dan had died in his flat and someone had knowledge of that. Someone walked away from that flat and locked the door.

Dan had changed the way he bought his booze. He usually went into the shop himself and had been doing so for years, using his bank card to buy. And then suddenly he wasn't, suddenly he was withdrawing cash instead. Booze was still being bought in the same shop but with cash because *someone else* was buying it, which meant that he was probably incapacitated in some way.

That *someone else* was trusted with his pin number and so could withdraw cash…but couldn't have gone into the shop to use that same card because the proprietor knew my brother.

Who would Dan trust with his pin number? His neighbour, Walter Fitzgibbon? Or his sister, Lydia? Anyone other than his sister would surely, or probably have carried on drawing money out of the account until that account was empty.

Someone else covered Dan up with the rubbish. It wasn't possible for him to do it himself because he didn't have arms that were eight feet long and it wasn't feasible for the rubbish to fall on him to the depth and uniformity that it had done. Who was that someone? Lydia.

Dan was either gravely ill and knew he was going to die or he committed suicide. Let's face it, he'd been committing suicide by stealth for most of his life, which is what a lifetime of boozing and smoking actually is. In my opinion. Either way, he wanted to stay in his flat after death and become a feast for the beasts, something that I truly believe he would have been fascinated with. He took part in his own version of the cycle of life and did it in a pretty unique way.

Dan persuaded his little sister, Lydia, to assist him. Maybe he told her there was a will in her favour, which there wasn't, but there must have been some kind of *lure* to get Lydia to act for him in the way I think she did.

Can I prove anything I'm thinking? No, I can't. But at least what I'm *thinking*, coupled with what I know from the enlightenment, is…what's a good word to use here…*plausible*. Yeah, it's plausible.

If Lydia has been persuaded to do what I think she has, then that will be her burden to carry through the rest of her life, and I had no intention of adding to that burden. I'd get the flat finished, we'd put it on the market, sell it and all move on. C'est la vie. Whatever that means.

Chapter 42 - The Dream Changes

The painting had gone well and we had one of our favourite *little meals.*
One of the things about getting older is that you can't eat *big* meals every
day. We don't eat meat every day, maybe having it two or three times a
week, and mostly chicken when we do have it. Have you ever thought of
how many chickens are eaten in the world every day? Where the fuck do
they all come from? It's staggering how many of them must be raised
each week. And then there's the eggs, chickens that never came out of
their shells, millions or billions of them, eggs that are eaten, beaten,
scrambled, boiled, fried and those that are thrown over roofs. Wow! I'd
forgotten that I used to play the egg and roof game. I don't even know
how it started but start it did. Our house, the one where my father abused
his family, had a front door and a back door directly opposite each other.
And one day, I wondered if I could throw an egg over our roof. The first
couple landed on the roof but once I got the trajectory worked out,
getting one over the roof became easy. I was amazed, whilst searching
the street for where my eggs were landing, to discover that they were
landing on the other side of the street, on the pavement. The next line of
thought was that at certain times of the day, there were quite a few

people walking down into the estate from the bus stop and how funny would it be to land one in amongst them. A week or so later I realised that I was never going to witness this happening because I was in the back garden while my thrown egg was landing in the street and so the race to see it actually land began. It took months of training, months of practice, months of listening to my mum asking everyone if they knew where the eggs were disappearing to. But eventually, I got the alignment of egg, roof, chimney, back garden door, hall door, front door, garden gate, lamp post, bus stop, pedestrians, sprint and look casual upon arrival, to actually witness my egg landing in amongst the people off the bus. It was nowhere near as hilarious as I thought it would be. This fella just looked at it, looked at other people walking past and carried on. But I did hear two fellas arguing in the bookies one Saturday afternoon, when my dad had sent me over to put a bet on for him. One was saying that it was a 'known fact' that birds can lay eggs while they're in flight and the other was saying 'why would dee do da doh?', which is scouse for 'Why would they do that though?' So, the egg over the roof experiment *had* been successful. In some way.

So anyway, me and Pam had one of our favourite *little* meals, poached eggs on toast with onion rings. Sounds terrible I know, but try it. Get a plastic bag, couple of tablespoons of flour, load of salt and pepper, throw the sliced onion rings in and shake them all about until coated, then deep fry and dry, serve with a beautiful soft poached egg on buttered toast. Heaven!

We watched some telly, had a nice warm beer and went to bed. tomorrow it would all end, the painting would be done and we could bugger off back to France, the sunshine, and peace. I went to sleep almost straight away, hardly even finishing one page of my latest book.

I dreamed. The dream within a dream again, but it was different. Again. Mostly the same but slightly different.

I'm still walking along, walking home from my girlfriend's. I'm smoking a cigarette and I walk past a bus stop and as I do, the same bus pulls up and stops to let the same woman off. She walks past me and as she does, her eyes slide over me and there's a slight wrinkling of her nose. The woman is my sister Carla, but she looks too old, haggard, her cheeks shrunken and her lips grey. Long strands of grey hair hang down the sides of her face like old curtains.

There were just a handful or so of people left on the bus, two women on the raised seats near the back, still gabbing and nodding their heads at each other, the man standing talking with the driver, I hoped about football but somehow, I knew they were talking about me.

The old white-haired man who had been asleep all my life until the last time I'd had this dream about a week ago, was no longer asleep, but instead, was upright and alert looking, staring at me, his face expressionless. It was my grandad on my dad's side, a man I barely remembered, hardly knew. The bus closed its doors and, just the same as always, started to pull away and as it did, the man sitting in the front seat on the top deck, had stood and was leaning on the back of his seat, staring at me with his flat eyes. The two women stopped chatting and instead, were looking at me. The one next to the window had black hair and thick rimmed glasses and a heavy face, jowly with a big nose…hard looking. It was my grandma. My father's mother. Again, I hardly knew her and barely remembered anything about her, but it was her. The other woman was leaning forward slightly, to get a view of me. She looked like she could have been nice, her face was triangular and pretty, the mouth nicely shaped and bordered with shiny red lipstick, but where her eyes should be were just dark hollows. She was smiling the smile of someone standing behind a bully, knowing that you are about to get what is coming to you, that you are about to get what you deserve. The woman with hollow eyes was my mother.

Chapter 43 - The Dream Changes Again

Done. Everything was finished. The lot! What a feeling that is. You know you're approaching the end of the job, you know you just have one or two things to do but, when you've done them, you can't quite believe there is nothing else to do. Your mind won't let you believe you've finished and you think you're being tricked.

I checked. Walked all around the flat, which didn't take long. It was done. Finito!

I got the last bottle of warm Leffe from the kitchen, opened it, sat in the deckchair and admired the flat. I mean, I wouldn't want to live in it but nevertheless, it was bright and new smelling and fresh looking. Quite swish if the truth be told. I loved crisp lines, so corners and skirtings had to be perfect and they were. I was pleased.

I thought of how it had looked just weeks before, of how it had smelled. It was hard to envisage it now. Almost impossible. But life moved on. The work was done and I could go home and carry on living my life. It was sad that my brother's life had ended in this room, that he had lived the life he lived in this little flat, locked up, unable to see beyond the shuttered windows of his mind. I wanted life to have been different for him but, it was what it was. Life, his life, had led him, seemingly inexorably, to his death. As mine would lead me to my death, albeit down a different path.

I sat there in my deckchair and remembered him fishing and farting a talc cloud. I thought of the things in my life that I held dear, that helped to make me, me, that he had introduced me to. And I thought of the strange urges that drives a man to spurn his sibling, contradictions and conflicts that were impossible for me to fathom because I never had them.

I started to drift in my mind, the beer on the empty stomach, conspiring to befuddle me and I knew I had to close my eyes for a few minutes, have a power nap. I put the bottle on the floor and allowed my eyes to close. As I was drawn down to the void of sleep, I knew I was going to have the dream within a dream again. I just knew. I could feel it waiting for me and momentarily tried to ward sleep off. But I couldn't. I knew I should stand up and walk about, drink some water, eat something. But I couldn't. I was exhausted. Physically and mentally exhausted. Part of me, that belligerent part of me that refused to be beaten, wanted to get inside the dream and fight. Wanted to dash onto the bus before it left the stop, sprint up the stairs and throw the man with the indifferent eyes down the stairs and chant 'I'm the king of *this* fucking castle, get down there you dirty fuckin rascal!' But I knew I wouldn't. I knew that the dream would take its own course, and that whatever happened was meant to happen, that I had no control over the dream.

I took a deep breath, tried one last time to move and get away from the beckoning dream and then suddenly, seamlessly, I was walking along the road, on the way home from my girlfriend's.

As I approached the bus stop, smoking a cigarette, a bus pulled up and stopped to let a woman off. It was my sister Carla. As she walked past me, her head moved, as if her lifeless eyes were scanning me head to toe and up again, her lower face distorted in what looked like disgust. She stopped momentarily and opened her mouth as if to speak. The smell of shit and rotting offal washed over me and a single word hissed out of the maw, filled with malevolence, and drawn out for maximum effect. *'Cunt.'* I had a strong desire to grab her around the throat and throttle her but I couldn't move from my path. I walked past her but could feel her looking at me.

The two women on the bus were now sitting with the white-haired man with the flat eyes. They were all looking my way. My mother's expression was the one she wore when she lay dead in the hospital, an expression of pain and regret, her lips pressed tightly together. She cocked her head slightly to one side, as if she was saying 'I told you not to do that, now look what you've done…'

The bus doors closed with a hiss of compressed air and the bus started to pull away. The man on the top deck, who was stood, leaning on the back of his seat staring at me, moved and made his way down the stairs, his eyes never leaving me. The man talking to the driver turned and looked at me. It was my father. His jaw muscles were working as though he was chewing something and his piercing blue eyes seemed to be illuminated. He spoke over his shoulder to the driver, never taking his eyes from me, and even though the doors were shut and the bus was moving away, I could hear him clearly, '*That's our Joe*' he said, and the driver briefly turned to look at me and his eyes were red and flickering as if they were on fire. He smiled at me and I could see his white teeth gleaming.

As the bus approached the next stop along, the brake lights came on and I saw the man from the top deck get off. As usual the bus pulled away but the man who got off didn't leave the bus stop.

As I got nearer to the bus stop, I could make out that someone was standing looking out at me through the letter box slit and I knew it was the man from the top deck. I stared at him as I walked past the concrete structure, daring him, wanting him to come out and confront me. I wanted to pulverise him, smash his bony face to a pulp, stamp on him, grind him into the ground. But I had no choice, I had to walk past.

Fifty yards past the bus stop I turned to check that there was no one behind me. There wasn't. I carried on walking for another half a mile and stopped to light a cigarette. I had to cup my hands around the flame from my lighter because of the breeze and as I did so, I caught a movement on the other side of the road, about a hundred yards back. It was him, he was standing in front of some tall dark trees but I could see him, lighter dark on dark, his eyes dimly but clearly showing themselves.

I stood still, my eyes intent on his eyes, calmly smoking my cigarette, feeling angry, murderous, feeling violated, like my mind had been scraped raw and had salt poured onto the wound. I was enraged that this 'person' was stalking me. I stood square on to him, standing as tall and as straight as I could, willing him to come out and face me but I knew he wouldn't.

His eyes slowly blinked and I heard a low, phlegm loaded laugh, then they disappeared.

I stood, square on for another thirty seconds and then I flicked my cigarette butt, end over end in the direction of the trees, a trail of red sparks living then dying in the night, turned and strode off in the direction of my home.

Every other time I'd been trapped in this dream, I'd felt the need to escape, to run for home. To get away from the man that followed me but this time, this time it was different. This time I knew that the dream was playing out for the last time, that this time, I would either die in my sleep, or the man on the ledge would be crushed and never invade my world again.

I turned the last corner and there, 200 yards away, was my house, the living room light on and I could see through the glass at the side of the front door that the kitchen light was on as well. I saw a figure moving between the two rooms, probably my mum making a cup of tea or something, except this time she stopped at the frosted glass, as if she was watching me approach across the pub car park.

I stopped and turned around to glare in the direction of my stalker, to give him two fingers. And he was right behind me.

And that was when I woke up.

I lay there, on my back, looking at the ceiling. I was breathing heavily and sweating a bit. I looked across to my brother's bed but he wasn't there. I was amazed at how the dream had been so real, at how all the usual characters had turned into members of my family. I could relive every second of it, seeing the two women becoming my mum and grandmother, how the sleeping man had become my grandfather. I wondered why I would dream about two people I hardly knew and could barely remember. The human mind and the way it works, marvellous and sometimes scary. The things you could think and the worlds you could envisage, imagine, and invent, all of it, all of them real, as real as anything else in your life. Until, suddenly it wasn't real, suddenly you were back in the *real,* real world and your made up one was put away, like a toy, until the next time.

I was still dreaming. I knew I was. I thought I was. I must have been because I knew I wasn't in my childhood bedroom, I knew I was in my dead brother's flat. Reclining in the deckchair. I knew that. I knew there was no ledge beneath the window, no curtains to draw back. There was just a window looking out onto the car park.

It was all over, the dream was dead and a voice said to me, *prove it, prove it, go on, go and look out of the window.*

I got up and moved towards the window. As I neared the glass, I remembered that there *was* actually a flat roof beneath the window, the little front door porch of the flat beneath Dan's, and a tingle of adrenaline started low down in the pit of my stomach and quickly spread through me, my breathing increased slightly and my eyes came alive and alert to a possible danger.

I got to the window and looked out. There was nothing, just my car in its usual place below. *Check the ledge*, a voice said to me, *check the fucking ledge, make sure!*

I moved right up to the window and put my face on the glass so that I could look down to the ledge. To the flat roof. There was nothing and I grinned to myself and turned back into the room.

The skin on my arms registered a tiny variation in temperature, the hairs standing up and as I realised the front door at the bottom of the stairs must be open, my eyes registered a hooded figure crouched at the top of the stairs, that suddenly rushed across the room at me. The street lights from outside glinted on a huge knife and then I was battered to the floor and there was a weight on top of me. My face was hit hard and I felt a blade slice into my right arm as I tried to defend myself and then there were a flurry of massive blows to me around the chest and abdomen and I could hear inside my head a loud grating noise which I knew was a knife sliding across my bones. A harsh voice, hard and soft at the same time kept saying *Blue eyed cunt! Blue eyed cunt!* over and over at me, keeping time with the grating sound. I could hear and feel an invasive sensation that was red hot and ice cold at the same time and knew that I was being stabbed. I knew that I was dying and that something truly fearful, much more so than the person slashing at me, was approaching me fast and hard from up to my left, rushing like a gigantic train towards me and I tried to wave it away, tried to shout, to tell it to fuck off! but I couldn't, and I heard a voice, the voice of my father say, *That's our Joe, he's coming to be with us.*

A massive crackling noise, like thousands of simultaneous explosions went off inside my head and my scalp erupted as a million hot needles pierced me all at the same time and all thought just stopped and I could see myself, a dark man on top of me and I could feel and see my body being battered and shoved about and then another dark shape entered the fray and suddenly that was it.

Chapter 44 – I'm Sixty Six!

Three years later...

It was my birthday, 23rd September. I was 66. Sixty-six. Six times ten plus six. Me. Sixty Fucking Six. *What was all that about* I thought, how can I be 66? Me? How can I be that old? I mean, I'm still me inside my head, it's just me in here, with all the others, my Numbskulls, my security team, it's just me and them. The same me that fought the German hordes down by the docks in North Liverpool. The same me that was desperate to shoot a little baby bird with a bamboo arrow fired from a bamboo bow made by my grandad, ace armourer. The same me that sat on my grandad's knee, coveting his penknife, and surreptitiously peering down his earhole to catch sight of one of his Numbskulls come to the surface for a smoke or something. It's just me in here. Still finding something important to say about the virtues of raspberry jam, the beauty of a house full of Caramacs. Or Snickers. It's just me.

And then there's my brother Dan. He is now getting on for 70. Dan, my hero for a lot of my life, but no more. He didn't die in his midden. Someone else did. An unnamed man who had followed him home one day from the phone box by the tobacco factory. A man who attempted to rob my brother, fought with him, and died at my brother's hand, probably suffocated say the police who suddenly became interested in the man in the midden. An unnamed body that was buried in my brother's pile of shite and…cultivated on its journey to mummification, the maggots and beetles periodically washed from their rotting feast with bottles of syrupy brown piss, so that Dan, the maggot-meister, could assess what could be assessed. The perfect murder?

Dan now resides in a high security psychiatric hospital somewhere in the Northwest of England. Probably not that far from where I now live, having had enough of France and its cheeses. He will never get out.

Some people, I don't even know who they were because I wasn't really paying attention, tried to explain the why's and wherefores of what happened, but to be honest, *truly* honest, I don't need anyone to explain to me what happened and why. I already know all I need to know.

Dan attacked me with a knife, stabbed me in the lung, liver, buttock, arm, shoulder, even cut through part of my bowel. I lost a lot of blood, but I survived. One of the nurses who helped me rehabilitate, said that I was 'too busy' to die.

Lydia, my sister, is in prison, I don't know which one and I don't care. I'll never see her again. Not intentionally anyway. She was persuaded by Dan, on the promise of money, to help him once he'd killed the stranger and asked her for help. She hid him, fed him, and, thankfully, followed him to the flat the night he came to kill me. It was her that rushed him and saved my life. It was Lydia that already had the ambulance and police en route, even before he entered the property. She saved my life, but I don't care. I would not have been in any danger, but for her, so, she owed me. She was doing no more than righting her own wrongs and the fact that her deed resulted in my life saved was irrelevant to me.

My sister Emily was traumatised by the events surrounding the man in the midden. She is recovering slowly but the fact that her twin sister could act the way she did, has done lasting damage, maybe damage that she will never recover from. I help in any way I can but, at the end of the day, we all have to manage our own world, the world behind our eyes, in the best way we can. We see each other every few weeks or so, and still have that good fat head bond.

Pam and I drank our Earl Grey tea and ate our home-made flap jacks, sitting on the wall of the stone structure on top of Moel Fammau and looked out across the Denbigh countryside. The sun was bright through the thin cloud and the breeze was cool but not too cool. Life couldn't be better.

And that, my friend, is the end of this story.

Chapter 45 - The Final Word

Monday 31st January 2005

2nyt start 7.57pm 45 x 6 + 112.50

9.50am no cars here, 307 gone 306 gone. 11.10am 307 here at no. 20.

After 1 or 2 cans I said to Bertie "Do you want to go out or what? (not?)"

It was said in a very loud voice, and it frightened him, and he did want to

go out, but he was "walling" quite soon to come back in, B4 he had

emptied his bladder. I cud be turning into a monster. I hope not. At least I

am aware of it. Was my dad aware of him turning into a monster?

Chapter 46 – The End

Mortal Monsters

The monsters that invade young dreams

sit pale beside the mortal fiends

who'd, casually, on a whim,

break both your spirit and your limb.

The havoc that such demons wreak

destroys young souls, turns bright minds bleak,

who, seeking solace in addiction,

exacerbate their own affliction.

Junkies, alcoholics, hoarders

all are someone's sons and daughters,

to be cherished and protected – NOT,

insane and bitter, left to rot!

Never can it once be right

to ravage lives and thus ignite

that festering fuse that creeps its path

to such a sorry aftermath.

Elynn Lake

Printed in Great Britain
by Amazon

72459013R00315